Josiah Pike

Sioux Captive and Warrior

by

Terry L. Grosz

Print Edition
© Copyright 2015 Terry L. Grosz (as revised)

Wolfpack Publishing
48 Rock Creek Road
Clinton, Montana 59825

ISBN: 978-1-62918-350-3

This book is dedicated to Bo Oryshchyn, extraordinary teacher of art at Rooney Ranch Elementary School, outdoorsman, exceptional father to his beautiful daughters Sydney and Emma, and dedicated husband to the love of his life and lovely bride Stacy. It is for this Renaissance Man and dear family friend, that this work was happily researched and written.

Chapter One

THE SAGA BEGINS

The thunderous whirring sounds of wings from a covey of over 200 sage grouse exploding in alarm from their nearby roost site across the Platte River, by the prairie's low lying foothills, rent the quiet cool pre-dawn morning air like a thunder-clap. Moments later, the large-bodied grouse with their characteristic whirring wings flew over a small group of circled wagons, prairie schooners, and their still sleeping occupants on the meadow below. The large flock of grouse started landing noisily on the side of a nearby grass-covered hill with a flurry and fluttering of wings and cooing calls.

Fourteen year old Josiah Pike, hearing the grouse noisily rising 'to wing' from their roost site across the river and then passing directly overhead, rolled over in his sleeping blankets under the wagon to see what the disturbance was all about. Looking out from under his family's covered wagon to avoid the morning's heavy dew on his bedding, Josiah observed the abnormally large flock of grouse continuing to land on a close at hand hillside. Josiah grinned in anticipation. Figuring a hungry coyote had alarmed the grouse causing them to flee from their prairie roosting, he hurriedly threw back his canvas covers. Here was a golden opportunity for a change in diet in what he and his other immediate family members had been eating for days on end while traveling on the Oregon Trail. Especially if he could pull a sneak on that massive covey of grouse and bag a mess of the large bodied birds for that day's evening meal.

Kicking the rest of his sleeping blankets aside, the fully clothed Josiah hurriedly pulled on his high-topped leather boots that he had been using as a pillow. Rolling out from under the wagon box, Josiah stretched his large for his age 6'2" 180 pound frame and then quietly, to avoid waking his nearby family members, trotted to the front of their wagon. He carefully looked all around in the pre-dawn light because the wagon train was now deep inside hostile Indian country and he couldn't be too careful. Especially since they had been warned earlier by a detachment of patrolling cavalry to keep a sharp eye out for roving bands of hostile Sioux Indians—Indians, whose lands were now being inundated by the crush of white settlers. Indians who liked nothing better than to ambush and loot smaller wagon trains like those of his family and relatives.

Continuing to look all around, he spotted his uncle Otis. Otis had been designated watch that night, the wagon trains lone guard, tender of the camps cooking fire. Typically, he had become bored with the quiet of the night and had fallen asleep in his chair by the fire. The emigrants in their travels to date, had seen several bunches of Indians at a distance sitting quietly on their horses observing the wagon train's westward progress. But to date none had gotten closer than 3/8ths of a mile from the wagon train before quietly drifting out of sight on the endless prairie as quietly as the gentle track of the ever blowing winds across the perpetually waving tall grasses. Satisfied the coast was clear of his earlier concerns of lurking Indian danger, Josiah turned his attention back to the front of his parent's wagon.

He reached into the front box of their wagon and extracted his father's double-barreled muzzle-loading 12 gage shotgun. Checking to make sure the shotgun was loaded and the caps were still on the nipples, Josiah turned and once again made a mental note of the location of the large flock of sage grouse.

Josiah then realized there was someone else standing by the front of his family's covered wagon in the pre-dawn darkness silently watching him. Sensing danger, Josiah started to raise his shotgun up in defense when he realized the lithe figure standing and quietly watching him from a few feet away was none other than his much-loved Indian mother.

"Mother, you surprised me," quietly exclaimed Josiah in a hushed tone of voice so as not to awaken the others still sleeping nearby.

"I did not intend to," she replied as she glided silently over to her son. Without another word, Josiah's mother wrapped her arms around him and gave him a gentle hug.

He whispered, "Mother, why are you up so early in the morning?"

"I heard a strange noise," she replied. She released him and stepped back with a smile on her face.

Josiah's mother was a full-blooded Osage Indian who

his father had married after he had arrived in Missouri. His father's farm and homestead was located next to one of the Osage Indian's earthen-mounded villages. And over time since he and members of the tribe were both farmers, they came to know and respect one another.

Josiah's father had observed a young Osage woman working in their family garden plot tending their beans and squash. And at that very moment, he had been smitten by her beauty. After a white-man proper and traditional Osage Indian courtship, and two fast horses in trade to the woman's father, Josiah's father had married the beautiful young Indian woman with the shining waist-length braids. Josiah's family now happily included his father, mother, his twelve year-old sister, and himself.

"If you hope to kill any of those grouse for our supper this evening, you had better get moving before they leave the country," his mother softly uttered in her Osage language-laced English. With that, she quietly glided over to the camp's central cooking fire to awaken Uncle Otis and then stoke the coals of the fire in preparation for the morning's meal. In the fast approaching light of dawn, Josiah watched his mother glide away as quietly as a white-tailed deer. As she did, Josiah smiled at her dress. She still wore her traditional Osage Indian type of clothing instead of what frontier women of the period wore. She stubbornly clung to her traditional ways in wearing a deerskin dress with leggings. Her dress, which was her favorite, was heavily decorated and the center piece of her garment had a beaded red spider beautifully sewn into the tanned buckskin leather covering her chest. The dress was her favorite, because the spider was a sacred symbol of knowledge of the Osage Indian Tribe and deeply rooted in historical folklore.

Josiah turned his attention back towards the nearby hills. Taking off at a trot in that direction with thoughts of freshly fried grouse for that evening's family supper, he jumped a nearby sandy spring-seep feeding into the adjacent and shallow flowing Platte River. Then he headed directly downstream for the grouse's landing site on the nearby set of rolling hills. As he continued his trot across the prairie, Josiah waved at his uncle Lemuel and cousin Jordan who were bringing in the group's horses, mules, and oxen from their night-watch duties on the evening's feeding grounds. As was the case, they had been there all night protecting the valuable feeding livestock from being stolen by any Indians that happened to be in the area. Holding up his shotgun and pointing it towards the far hill side, Josiah flapped his arms like a flying bird to indicate what he was after. Then he hurriedly continued on his way, but not before the two men had waved back in the understanding of Josiah's early morning hunting gestures. Particularly since they too had observed the noisy flight of sage grouse landing just a short distance away.

After a fifty yard trot, Josiah slowed his pace because as he figured it, he was now close at hand to the landing site of the flock of grouse. If luck would have it and the grouse acted true to form, they would not have traveled far from that original landing site in such a short period of time. Hence, the need for care and quiet in approaching the general landing site so as to avoid spooking the birds before one got within shotgun range.

Stalking his way carefully through the dense prairie grasses and intermittent patches of sage brush, Josiah stayed alert for the tell-tale 'heads-up-watching-him' signs of discovery by the grouse once they sensed his close at hand presence. Once again, if this covey of birds were true to form as had been the other flocks of sage grouse they would first raise up their heads looking for danger. Once danger was identified, the now alarmed birds would explode into the air and sail off to a safer location a quarter mile or so away. When this covey looked up upon discovering his approach, Josiah hoped to line up several heads with his first shot and then kill another large adult grouse on the rise. If his little plan worked successfully, the family would have fresh fried grouse, thick gravy, and Dutch oven biscuits instead of the usual beans, biscuits, and greasy moldy bacon. And, maybe a homemade pie from dried apples.

Whoa! Up went about twenty heads of sage grouse just scant yards in front of him! With that discovery so close at hand, Josiah froze like a block of ice. Then ever so slowly raising his shotgun up so as to not spook the now intently watching birds and with the thought of lining up as many grouse heads as possible for the first shot, he began slowly applying the pressure on the front trigger of the double barreled shotgun.

HEY-YIII-YEI-YEI-BOOM-BOOM-BOOM-BOOM--BOOM, followed by intensifying yells, more shooting, shouting, and screams, instantly shattered the early morning air behind Josiah! Whirling abruptly towards the horrible sounds emanating from the distant wagon train below from where he stood, the huge flock of sage grouse, observing his abrupt close at hand movement, exploded into the air.

Below him at the wagon train, he saw dozens of Indians and their horses swirling around and then streaming through and into the loosely circled six wagons of his family and kin! Those intruding riders were instantly followed by swarms of other warriors magically materializing up from out of the prairie grasses where they had quietly crawled and were hiding!

Within moments those Indians on foot had smoothly streamed through the openings between the circled wagons like water through a sieve! That brought out even more yelling, screaming, and sounds of desperate fighting from the surprised and quickly awakening wagon train's occupants. Within seconds, the space around the wagons was just a swirl of rising dust into the early morning air, riderless horses, barking dogs, and running and fighting white men being overwhelmed by the sheer numbers of Indians! Josiah saw his uncle and cousin and an explosion of Indians all around them! Indians who had been laying hidden in wait in the tall prairie grasses as they pulled off a perfect ambush.

Both livestock herders were dead before they hit the ground from the deadly hail of bullets! Following that and without a moment's hesitation those savages turned and began racing for the battle scene taking place around the wagon train as well. They, too, disappeared into the swirl of dust, milling horses and fighting men at the wagon train's battle site.

Now faced with the realization that the attacking Indians, not a coyote, had spooked the grouse off their roost site, Josiah began running off the hillside towards the swirling battle below.

Sprinting down the foothills and racing across the spring-seep once again, he dashed to the first wagon in the circle of wagons.

There he was met at the edge of the swirling dust cloud of battle by a brightly-painted Indian with a raised war club and a killing sneer across his blue-painted face. Josiah's blast from the 12 gage fowling piece forever removed that sneer...Jumping over the Indian just killed, Josiah raced for the front of his folk's wagon in an attempt to save his mother, Sarah, and twelve year-old sister, Gemma, both of which who were now struggling and screaming in the clutches of two Indians.

Running around the end of the wagon to aid the women, he ran full tilt into an Indian facing the other way just as he removed the scalp from Josiah's now dead father in one vicious yank! As that Indian turned and raised his father's scalp yelling in exaltation, he was instantly nearly cut in two by Josiah's last blast from the shotgun! Not breaking stride, Josiah ran to the Indian in the act of cutting his mother's throat and brained him with the now empty shotgun before he could do so! In doing so, he shattered the wooden stock of the shotgun. The other Indian holding Josiah's sister turned and faced the stoutly built, strong as a mule, Josiah. The savage threw down the uninjured girl and charged Josiah with an upraised war club, chanting his death song.

Ignoring the danger, Josiah swung his busted shotgun with all his strength. Josiah's blow shattered the warrior's upraised arm holding the war club. Then the continued follow-through of the force of that swing slammed the busted shotgun into the side of the warrior's face!

When the Indian crashed to the ground, Josiah quickly stepped over him and swung the busted shotgun once again smashing the struggling Indian's head open! Dropping the busted shotgun, Josiah turned, bodily grabbed up his sister and threw her into their covered wagon. Then Josiah grabbed an ax from its holder alongside the rear of the wagon box.

Whirling around, he saw his mother lanced through the chest by a mounted Indian. She fell soundlessly to the ground, mortally wounded with a surprised look on her face! Screaming inside and trying to move to her side, Josiah found himself instantly confronted by four other Indians with more gathering to his front and sides as the noise of the wagon train battle began diminishing. Little did Josiah realize at that moment in time, that the battle was almost over. As a matter of fact, everyone in the little wagon train were now dead save Josiah and his now terrified younger sister still cringing in the back of the wagon box!

As Josiah faced off on the four Indians immediately to his front confronting them with his ax held high overhead, he could hear the other excited Indians behind him now begin looting the other wagons. Off to his side, other Indians now sped away from the wagon train battle in order to once again round up the wagon train's valuable livestock before it scattered out along the brushy North Platte River. Tears began flooding down Josiah's face. Then a tall Indian who appeared to be not much older than Josiah with a long scar running across his face, was

12

allowed to move forward through the group of now confronting Indians. It was obvious from their actions that the older Indians were encouraging the younger man on what had turned out to be his first war party excursion, to kill Josiah with his bow and arrow—and in doing so, count his first coup over the hated and trespassing white man. The scar-faced Indian with a vicious leer on his face full of contempt, strung an arrow, drew it back fully on his bow and then, "whoomp!"

The lights mercifully went out on Josiah with the terrified screams of his sister Gemma still ringing loudly in his ears...

Chapter Two

A CAPTIVE OF THE SIOUX

As Josiah re-entered the world of the living around him after being struck from behind in the head during the fight at the wagon train, he became aware of the crashing explosions of pain in his head. Especially every time the horse that was carrying him took a jarring step or hopped over an obstacle. As his spinning-in-pain head began clearing, Josiah became more and more aware of his plight and surroundings. He was now laying belly down over the bare back of a horse. His wrists and ankles had been tightly and painfully bound with a leather thong that had been passed from his tied wrists, under the horse's belly and then tightly wrapped around his ankles on the other side. It was obvious Josiah was going nowhere except where his horse was taking him.

Hot pulses of sticky wet blood pulsed down from his head wound and drained into his left eye. Trying to blink away the flow of blood so he could see better, Josiah finally quit worrying about it. It was now beginning to cake on the side of his head from the heat of the sun and becoming covered with the dust rising up from the horse's hooves on the trail, so he would just have to wash it all off later in order to be able to see out of that eye. That was if his left eye even still functioned and he was left alive to do so. But there was one good thing in that his shooting eye on the right side was still functional, he grimly thought.

If he ever got the chance to use his shooting eye again, it wouldn't be used to aid him in stalking a hapless covey of sage grouse but on a larger, deadlier Indian target...

Raising his head, Josiah tried to look to the left or forward on the column of moving horses and Indians. In doing so, he was met with more explosions of pain from that smashed side of his head as it banged against the horse's moving side. Dropping and letting his head hang for a few moments below the belly of his horse so the most intense part of his head pain would subside, he then chanced a look behind him. Trailing behind his horse were a long string of Indians leading what he assumed had been the wagon train's horse herd. The wagon train's slower moving oxen were nowhere to be seen. It was apparent that they had been left behind by the fast moving Indian war party.

Many of the horses were packed high with spoils from that early morning's raid on the wagon train. Josiah also observed numerous bloody scalps hanging from a number of the Indian's horse's manes or on the lances their riders carried! One scalp in particular hung from an Indian's horse's mane whose hair was dark brown in color and with really long braids. Of the wagon train's women, only one woman had such long, beautifully braided dark hair...Josiah's mother!

Painfully looking upward at the rider on that horse,

Josiah made sure he memorized the face of that particular Indian proudly displaying his mother's scalp. If Josiah ever got the chance, that was one Indian who would rue the day he ever lanced a helpless woman. Then he noticed the great curls of dark smoke rising high into the air above the trees along the Platte River. The Indians after looting the wagon train had set it on fire! It was then that his recent family losses really overwhelmed him emotionally. His immediate family members were all gone, as were all his uncles, aunts and their children. Folks like him who had left their soil-worn-out farms in Missouri for better lands in Oregon. Families that were all related and had banded together for the trip of a lifetime to a better life.

Now he was a prisoner with no apparent escape options and had lost all his immediate family and kin. Those thoughts brought a rush of gut wrenching emotions and a quiet flood of more tears. In fact so many tears fell, they partially washed out the sticky blood in his left eye so he could see somewhat better. Then terrified thoughts of his sister raced through his mind! Where was she? Was she alright or had she also been killed? Had she been raped like all the stories one heard about if one was captured by the Indians? Was one of the scalps hanging off a horse's mane or on an Indian's lance hers?

Raising his head up one more time as well as he could, he looked back at the string of warriors and their loaded pack horses carrying goods pillaged from the wagon train. Nowhere did he see his sister riding a horse or walking alongside as a prisoner...

Raising his head one more time to look forward to see

if his sister was possibly on another horse to his front, he was rewarded with a heavy strike from the butt of a rifle to the side of his head! That blow hit him in the area of his previous head wound and Josiah partially blacked out. But not before realizing the Indian who had struck him on his head with the rifle butt, was none other than the young Indian with the scar running across his face... The same Indian who had been encouraged to shoot him with his bow and arrow just before Josiah had been struck from behind by an unknown assailant and knocked senseless!

If he ever got a chance, that Indian with the scar running across his face would be the second Indian he would kill after killing the one who had lanced his mother. And in doing so, that killing would start with Josiah's bare hands wrapped tightly around the scar faced Indian's throat. That Indian's scalp would eventually hang from Josiah's horse's mane as had that of his beloved mother...

For the rest of that day and into the early evening, Josiah went into and out of consciousness.

Old Chief Smoke was the leader of the Oglala Sioux war party which had struck his family's wagon train. And it was Old Chief Smoke who had struck Josiah in the head from behind right at the end of that deadly battle. He had done so after seeing Josiah fighting more bravely then even many of his best and more experienced warriors! So in order to save a brave younger man from a certain death by the scar-faced Indian brave named "Red Shirt" and his great respect for such bravery by any man, Old Chief Smoke and his war club had prophetically intervened.

But, he had also intervened for another reason. Two

days before the battle of the wagon train, the Great Spirit had visited Old Chief Smoke one evening in his tipi as he slept. And in the vision that ensued, the Great Spirit told Old Chief Smoke that he would soon meet a mighty warrior in a battle involving an attack on a wagon train. Much to the old chief's surprise in that vision, the brave man spoken about by the Great Spirit would be a white man born from a marriage of a white man and an Indian! The Great Spirit went on to advise that the old chief was to save that white man from dying in battle. And in doing so, showed the old chief a vision within a vision on how that white man now saved, would someday become a son to him and eventually make a great and fierce Oglala warrior. A warrior who would become so fierce, that he would someday shoot and wound in battle one of the greatest foes of the great Sioux Nation...

In order to identify this brave white-man-warrior, the vision showed Old Chief Smoke that in addition to the man's fierceness on the field of battle facing great odds, the "white-warrior" in the vision would be identified by his unusual piercing blue eyes. Eyes that had been especially given to that white-warrior by the Great Spirit so he could, having come from the Indian and white world, see more clearly into both worlds as well as many other things in life that most other warriors would fail to see. He would also be identified by his bravery at the upcoming wagon train battle trying to save a younger white woman—a younger white woman, who according to the old chief's vision, would also be made a captive, then go on to marry a great Oglala warrior and chief someday. And in that marriage, would present to "Mother

Earth" many fine sons who would become great men in a white man's world while living in a foreign land. It was then that Old Chief Smoke awoke from his vision in the quiet darkness of his tipi.

Lying there in his sleeping furs alongside his wife of many moons, he wondered why the Great Spirit had chosen and presented him with such an unusual vision. Especially one in which he would be responsible for saving a much-hated white man. But before he could ponder further the words and wisdom of the Great Spirit in the vision, sleep overtook him once again—sleep that he knew he would need in the long trip ahead to the east to see for himself the small number of covered wagons his scouts had observed traveling towards his summer encampment earlier. A wagon train carrying white men and their families, who were trespassing on Old Chief Smoke's favorite buffalo hunting grounds. And by doing so, were scaring away all the buffalo with their noise, shooting, and unfamiliar smells. A wagon train that because of its small size, could be easily overcome by the braves and warriors of his band and would yield many useful white-man items that could be used by his people in the coming months.

Later in the battle at the wagon train along the Platte River as predicted in his earlier vision, Old Chief Smoke observed a young white man fighting bravely and in the process killing four of his warriors single handedly in the fight. Then he had observed that same white man tossing a younger white woman into the back of a wagon to remove her from harm's way. Following those brave actions, the young white man had bravely grabbed an ax and faced off against four of his best armed and fiercest fighters. Remembering the vision and what he had been instructed to do, Old Chief Smoke spurred his horse into that segment of the battle swirling around the brave white man before he could be killed. Riding up with his war club, Old Chief Smoke struck the unsuspecting white man from behind with a disabling blow to the head with his war club. When he did, the white man was spun around from the blow's impact and it was then that Old Chief Smoke saw the brave white man's eyes starting to roll back into his head. But before the white man's eyes had rolled back into his head from the impact of the war club's blow, the old chief noticed the young man had unusually profound piercing blue eyes just as the Great Spirit in the vision had predicted…Eyes that were so unusually blue, that upon seeing them, the one looking upon such eyes, found himself looking even more closely out of wonder and amazement at what he was seeing.

By early evening on that fateful day after the battle, Old Chief Smoke had brought his band of warriors back to their summer buffalo hunting encampment located near the Platte River, a location just fifteen miles west from the destruction site of the Pike wagon train. As he did, Josiah, now somewhat more recovered from his painful head wound and still being tied belly down on the back of a horse, tried to be observant of his surroundings. Observant so if he ever got the chance to escape, he would be better informed as to what he had to do in order to be successful and survive. But there was another unusual reason for his extremely deep interest. Josiah, throughout his young life back on the Missouri farm, had always been intensely curious about the Indians he had run across during his everyday activities. Almost abnormally so, as if his interest had been honed because in part, he was now half Indian himself or maybe because had been an Indian in an 'earlier' lifetime...

Missouri Indians that once surprised or observed from afar could disappear just as silently into the dense deciduous forests as fast as a puff of rifle smoke or the upward flick of a tail from a surprised white-tailed deer. Primitive peoples who lived on the ragged edge of existence as he had come to know it and yet, seemed to happily do so without the intervening hand of the white man. And even under his current unusual set of circumstances, Josiah could feel a strong and strange pulling current of intense curiosity rising deep from within. A curiosity which was now greatly manifesting itself in a mysterious almost physical sort of way. Deeply feeling that highly motivated curiosity, Josiah drank in every aspect of the Indian encampment and its peoples located in the valley just below the string of returning Indians from the raiding party. And did so even from his rather uncomfortable position as a captive of those Indians and while still strapped uncomfortably over the bare back of a horse.

Moving down off a long and hilly ridge line, the string of horses and Indians moved slowly into a sheltered oak and cottonwood studded valley below. On one side of the wooded valley ran a small stream which was being heavily utilized by Indian females, older people and children doing everyday activities. That was until they observed the returning war party and then all the Indians scattered throughout the valley began happily converging towards their returning men. Still looking around through his mainly blood unclouded eye, Josiah noticed that there were about forty-five or so tipis scattered around the trees in the valley in a large, loosely circular pattern. Then he noticed a large horse herd at the west end of the valley being watched over by a small number of young Indian boys on horses.

Moments later, the entire war party was surrounded by laughing and talking Indians of every sex and age. Initially there was much loud rejoicing over the success of the raid on the wagon train. Then it became obvious to Josiah that the jovial mood was rapidly changing to one of quiet shock and in some cases outright sadness. Wearying of trying to keep his head up and looking around at what was occurring, Josiah let his head drop once again alongside the warm flanks of his horse as he rested his cramped neck and shoulder muscles. It was at that moment he became aware of the sounds of the camp's mood changing from loud talking, much happy animation, laughing, and celebration, into one with a number of its members breaking into crying, lamenting, and wailing. Soon tremendous sadness stifled the earlier celebrations and more wailing tainted the air by a number of the women over whose male family members from the war party that had not returned. Soon numerous women and children who discovered they had lost their particular loved ones at the hands of Josiah or other fighting emigrants, visited the captive still tied belly down on his horse.

There was much wailing and crying at Josiah's side as

the parties who had lost their men to him took out their grief in true Oglala fashion on the captive. Then there were even several women who had just lost loved ones in the general wagon train battle, who began cutting their hair short for the period of mourning that was to follow. Those actions were followed with much whipping with leather thongs, sticks and firewood across Josiah's back, head and neck as he helplessly laid there tied to his now getting more spooked by the moment horse for all the high-energy negative activity surrounding him. Additionally, several women who had lost their menfolk on the raid began removing the lower joints on their little fingers with the knives they carried. And in doing so, their wails of pain over self-mutilation and grief loudly collided. Josiah finally passed out when the Indian with the scar running across his face struck his already badly bleeding back, neck, legs, and head numerous times with a sizeable stick of firewood.

Thankfully, Josiah did not feel the abuse his body took after that as he drifted off into the darkness of nothingness...Nor did he see Old Chief Smoke finally putting an end to the cruel torture Josiah was undergoing from personally affected family members and their related clans of the encampment over the loss of their loved ones at the hands of their captive. Still remembering the wisdom passed to him from the Great Spirit in the vision, Old Chief Smoke quickly put an early end to Josiah's physical torture. For it would do no good if the blue-eyed white man became an Oglala warrior later on in life, only to have his value in that role diminished because of being a cripple caused by the beatings he was now receiving.

Josiah found himself once again re-joining the world of the living when he began coming-to the following morning. When he did, he found himself lying in the cooling waters of a small creek. Then all of the sudden he painfully snapped out from the dazed fog he found himself in moments before and was now wide awake! He found himself entirely naked and starting to be scrubbed with hands full of sand from the creek bottom by several older Indian women—and in the process, scrubbed with the coarse sand until he bled from numerous spots throughout his body. Especially from those areas where he had been bloodily abused by the tribe's family members of lost kin from the wagon train fight the day before. To Josiah's way of thinking, the Indian women almost seemed to be trying to scrub off all the traces of him ever being a hated white man.

On the nearby bank stood two stoic-looking warriors holding long spears, who were looking on with little or no expressions or emotions registered on their faces. It was obvious to Josiah that they were there to make sure he did not attempt to escape. Finished with their cleansing actions, the two Indian women then gestured for Josiah to go and sit on a nearby cottonwood log which he did. In doing so, he realized that there wasn't a single spot on his body which didn't hurt from the beatings he had received since his arrival in the Indian encampment. It was then that the two old women approached and dried him off vigorously with hands full of grasses. Following that, his head wound was gently cleaned by one of the women of the crusted blood and accumulated dust picked up while on the trail. Then the other woman present gently applied

24

an evil-smelling oily mix of some kind of rancid animal grease and herbs to the still open head wound. That application hurt like hell but Josiah, hanging onto and exhibiting his inner toughness, said nothing of the treatment's subsequent pain.

However, whatever that concoction had been with its excellent numbing properties allowed for his sore head to quickly begin to feel like it would now stay on his neck and not fall off...He then received the same stinking oily treatment over the rest of his body showing any signs of tribally inflicted wear and tear—wear and tear inflicted upon him with his arrival in the Indian village when certain tribal members whose men Josiah had killed in the battle, took out their forms of revenge as he laid tied helplessly over the back of a horse. Following that "tender care," Josiah was provided with his old clothing, clothing which had been previously washed clean of the caked blood, trail dirt and sweat, then hung on the bank side willows along the creek to dry. As he dressed, he realized he was thirsty as all get-out and could eat a mound of his mother's Dutch oven biscuits. Then the magnitude of his family loss and the significance of his captivity manifested itself once again through his mental and bodily pain.

With those realizations now flooding through his mind, the tears just once again surged from his eyes. At that very emotional moment, a large rock slammed off his back causing the two women treating him to scatter for cover. As the women fled, Josiah instinctively tried to reach behind his shoulder in agony in order to rub the new and just inflicted painful wound. Turning in pain, he saw the young Indian man with a facial scar and three other boys of like age laughing at his painful discomfort. Little did Josiah realize this was just the first of many such treatments he would receive and suffer from that group of older boys in the tribe as a captive. A captive that if he were to fight back over such treatment, would be jumped on by a deluge of boys from the tribe and soundly beaten to ensure Josiah clearly understood his status in the tribe as a hated white man.

It was then that the two Indian guards ran the younger men off and gestured with the point of their spears that Josiah was to begin walking back toward their encampment. As he painfully walked back through the main portion of the encampment, he was deluged with a hail of thrown sticks, rocks, and limb wood tossed by tribal members who had obviously been told of Josiah's killing exploits back at the wagon train fight. Ducking many of the projectiles and fending off the others more accurately thrown with his arms and hands, Josiah was finally directed to a lone, in need of repair, tipi. In front of the tent like structure, he was once again at the point of a spear made to enter into the tipi. Just as he did, Josiah's quick eye for detail noticed that all of the nearby tipis' opening flaps faced in the same easterly geographic direction. He also noticed in his walk through the encampment, that many of the tipis had the lower portions of the hide covering rolled up allowing the day's cooling breezes to enter and ventilate the living quarters from underneath.

Once again, Josiah's deeply intense curiosity and fascination of the Indian culture and way of life was continuing to manifest itself regardless of the set of circumstances he now found himself in. For some unexplained reason other than his part-Indian heritage, Josiah felt a unique kinship with such primitive peoples even though members of this band had recently killed off all his family and kin—unbeknownst to Josiah at that time, a kinship and understanding that would more than grow within him throughout the passage of time...

Josiah's two Indian guards grunted something in their native tongue and gestured with the tips of their spears that he was to enter the old and rundown tipi. Crawling inside, Josiah noticed in the dim light that a buffalo hide was on one side of the floor of the tipi and nothing else of any apparent use was scattered about. Sitting down on the hairy skin and with the knowledge of the two braves still stationed outside his tipi in case he tried to escape, Josiah soon laid down and was fast asleep from the emotional and physical exhaustion of the moment in which he found himself. But at least he was still alive and that was more than he could say for the rest of his immediate family and kin. Little did Josiah realize at that moment in time, the change in mind set he would eventually personally undergo and the resultant trail the Great Spirit or "Wakan Tanka" would soon lead him down...A trail in which Josiah would be presented with numerous deadly crossroads and many hard choices to make—crossroads not of his making, but in many cases he would happily consider taking "The Black Road" over "The Red Road" until the deadly work he felt he had to do was done...

Chapter Three

LIFE AS A CAPTIVE WITH A DEADLY TWIST OF FATE

For the next several months, Josiah learned what it was like to be a captive and essentially a slave of the Oglala people. Josiah quickly discovered he had been delegated as a slave to the work responsibilities and labor levels of the band's women. And since he had shown no immediate inclination in escaping during his earlier months of captivity because he had nowhere to go, instead of having two Indian guards, that number had been reduced to just one. And in doing so, fate had cruelly intervened. As it turned out, the one Indian guard who was now watching over Josiah had been the one who had cowardly lanced and killed his mother back at the wagon train battle! The same Indian who had so proudly displayed Josiah's mother's bloody braided scalp from the mane of his horse on the return trip back the Oglala tribal encampment…

Both men soon realized that a deadly twist of fate for whatever reason, had now intertwined their lives in casting them together on The Black Road, or the path of evil. And in doing so, both men internally realized, for different reasons, that a state of deadly deep hatred existed between the two of them until there could only be one person left standing...With that primal level of understanding greatly manifesting itself between Josiah and his new Indian guard named "Tall Bull" at every turn in the trail, a volcanic level of violence laid quietly just below the surface of both men—a level of violence that far exceeded the serene level of lifestyle so in evidence back at the Indian's main encampment.

Josiah's labors for the various female tribal members started at daylight and went deeply into the evening hours many days without any let up. He was fed only twice a day by different female members whom he was assisting on their various work details. And in doing so, Josiah found that the meals were adequate, especially when it came to the meaty portions allowed. And with that mainstay meat product being predominantly buffalo, Josiah soon grew fairly hearty and hale. Plus, he had now healed up from his earlier torture treatment at the hands of the band's members when he had first arrived as a captive. Tortured because he had been the one white man who had so singlehandedly and brutally killed most of the band's warriors who had died in that battle back at the wagon train. And now in life as a captive, he would continue to draw the dirtiest jobs and worst assignments as was required by the females of all of Old Chief Smoke's band. Especially in the numerous lengthy and heavy wood hauling details he became saddled with on a daily basis.

If he was slow in his efforts or sloppy in detail, the women were quick to render the appropriate level of punishment, a level of punishment that when administered, was to be endured without any outward sign of resistance or showing of discomfort. For to resist would only bring more of the same punishment down around the ears of the captive by everyone else who was near at hand. Throughout any workday, good weather or bad, he was totally delegated to the most menial of tasks involving women's work. Those duties included gathering numerous arm loads of wood for the old and the infirm, fleshing out fly covered and greasy buffalo hides, cutting buffalo meat into thin strips for drying which quickly prevented them from being fly blown, watching and turning the meat on the drying racks day and night, tending the meat smoking fires, skinning out the buffalo on several of the band's subsequent summer hunts, constantly gathering water, gutting and saving the important body parts and useful internal organs from the buffalo after each and every hunt (stomachs used as a form of cooking pot by placing fire heated stones into the meat and water filled stomach instead of using an open roasting fire, producing a meaty broth, horns, bones, tongues, etc.), putting up (about fifteen minutes) and taking down (usually in about three minutes) the tipis of the old and infirm when a move was in the offing, loading the horses and dog's travois with packs when the band moved once they had depleted all the nearby horse feed, moved for reasons of sanitation or were following a close at hand herd of buffalo, smoking hides, later to be used as winter moccasins or leggings, skinning deer brought back to camp, the making of pemmican (dried meat pounded to a dry powder, adding crushed berries, warm melted fat and formed into cakes), the never ending tending of fires, assisting the women tanning hides, picking berries and digging edible or medicinal roots, chopping out the brains from fresh buffalo skulls which were then used in the hide tanning process, cutting horse feed, collecting new and replacement lodge and travois poles, making utensils from antler, bone or horn, and every other kind of task in between and so dictated.

Throughout those first summer months of his intensive learning and into the following months of training after the wagon train battle, all of the above became Josiah's daily routine. But it was a routine in which he reveled. The work was hard but it allowed him to remain active, work out his deepest innermost feelings over the loss of his family, and continuing to develop his physical strength. Plus, he was learning the many ways in which a primitive culture survived on the frontier. Ways which would serve him well, especially if he was able to later successfully escape and evade his captors.

But strangely, those thoughts of escape seemed further and further away from reality as his days in captivity progressed and never seemed to materialize as anything more than fleeting thoughts. Thoughts that basically never materialized, because where would he go? Where could he go for help since he was deep within Indian Territory and frankly, did not know where he was since he had never been in this part of the country before? With those realizations, Josiah decided to try and settle into his new life and see what fortunes or life changes it could bring. And with time and his good work ethic, Josiah's life began to change. Some of the older tribal members that he had so thoughtfully served in their time of need were warming up to Josiah and now beginning to befriend him. Other tribal members, instead of mistreating him, now took their time to show an interest in Josiah as something other than a white man captive. Strangely, Josiah began to think of some of the older tribal members to be almost like family. Almost...

The only other ray of light in his life was that he had discovered his sister, Gemma, was still alive! He had discovered her early one morning bathing in a nearby creek and being closely watched over by an older woman. When he first discovered that Gemma was still alive, his startled eyes locked on her, just as she recognized her brother walking nearby. But neither said anything or showed any outward signs of recognition at that time as Josiah continued on his wood gathering detail and Gemma continued bathing. Josiah did that with the realization that if he showed any sign of recognition, the two of them would be kept even further apart and even possibly beaten for such behavior.

Josiah was occasionally able to be around his sister. If they were careful, they could occasionally talk among themselves in hushed voices. But if they were ever discovered doing so, a beating to both was quickly administered. There was still some concern over the captives and their potential for escape, so, to preclude any such adventures, a beating was administered to act as a reminder and discourage any such communications between the two of them. But the important thing was that Gemma was still alive and appeared to be eating better than even Josiah.

She had been made into a slave to a woman who had

lost her husband in the Pike family wagon train fight. In fact, it had been Josiah who had brained and killed her husband with his empty shotgun...That Indian woman initially never let Gemma forget for a moment that it was her brother that had killed her man and treated her accordingly. But at least Gemma was fed properly so she could work hard for the woman and carry out all her assigned tasks. And in doing so, she looked robust, cared for and beautiful in her adopted Oglala Indian clothing. And, that Indian women's harsh treatment of Gemma didn't last long. Soon the older woman found Gemma's easy ways, outstanding work ethic, ability to learn, and easy manners hard to ignore and quickly came to appreciate her for who she was. Especially since the woman watching over Gemma had lost her only daughter to a prairie rattlesnake bite several years earlier, a young woman who would have been about the same age as Gemma had she lived.

After a number of months, the two women became almost inseparable, like mother and daughter. Additionally, Gemma was a fast learner when it came to making Indian clothing, especially those items for the infirm older women of the tribe. Soon she became a favorite among many tribal members and highly sought out for her clothes making skills, skills she had learned from her own biological mother as a youngster back on their Missouri farm.

Basic skills learned as a white and Indian child, that were now being translated into her newly discovered abilities in her beautiful beadwork and quill decorations. Skills that were now also being quickly learned from her supremely skilled adoptive Indian mother. And accompanying those skills, Gemma began picking up and learning the Oglala language from her adoptive mother as well, a skill which helped her even more at becoming endearingly assimilated into Old Chief Smoke's band as an equal. In fact to Josiah's way of thinking, Gemma, with the loss of her biological family, was basically slowly being assimilated into the tribe and seemed to be happily entering into another loving family situation. And somehow Josiah did not resent the fact that his sister was fast finding her way in her world of happiness once again. Only this time in a vastly different culture. Lastly, Josiah discovered that Gemma talked less and less about her biological family and more and more about her newly-adopted Indian family—a sign of Gemma's transformation from that of a white woman into that of a comfortable woman in a totally Plains Indian culture...

However, in Josiah's man-world of being a slave, it was a rugged place in which to live. Especially with many of the band's knowledge of his fighting abilities gained at the wagon train battle and in light of the warriors he had so violently removed from the bands' population. Being considered a white man, his lowly tribal status accompanied by his deadly reputation acquired in that fight found that Josiah's survival road was far more problematic than that of Gemma's. Many of the younger male members of the band still did not like or trust Josiah. As such, he was worked harder than most and his eats many times were almost purposely kept minimal by design or out of outright spite. Especially if he was working for a clan in which he had taken a fellow clan member's life back at the wagon train battle. Many times when the above situations occurred, Josiah ate whatever he could find, pilfer, beg or acquire through any means possible. And in doing so, he was discovering unknown survival skills that he never knew existed within himself. Survival skills which due to his ever increasing physical presence, found him ways in which to survive because he ate more than any other adult male member in the band.

Regardless of the sometimes skimpy eats provided by some of his still bitter masters and the extremely hard work required, Josiah, without realization, was slowly in the act of total mental, physical, emotional, and even cultural transformation. Transformation from that of a white man to that of an Indian in his manners, ways, deeds, and most of all, his bearing. His now 6'3" two hundred-pound frame, was slowly filling out and up, and he was becoming as tough as the buffalo sinew that he had skillfully learned how to process. All the years of hard labor back on his folks' farm trailing the hind end of a plowing mule, removing hardwood stumps, splitting oak and hickory firewood, and continually removing large rocks from their hardscrabble Missouri farm lands by hand, had left their mark on the genesis of his work ethic and physical framing. It was now apparent that his physical framing leavened in Missouri on a hardscrabble farm from daylight to dark was paying off in his present set of circumstances.

His white man's clothing had long since rotted off his body in tatters and his boots for the most part, lacked adequate sole leather. When that became apparent, several sympathetic tribal elders that he had helped on wood gathering and packing details had made new clothing and moccasins for him to wear as gifts. And with his new clothing, his bearing changed even more. Except for his piercing blue eyes, for all other intents and purposes Josiah now looked at first glance and carried himself just like any other Oglala Indian in Old Chief Smoke's band. Josiah's hair which had always been long, had lengthened even further since his capture and now resembled that of the other braves or warriors in the band. A resemblance even more so, since Josiah had chosen to braid his unruly hair into like that of an Indian, especially when involved in many of his dirtier and sometimes more menial assignments. Additionally, Josiah in true Indian fashion did not sport any facial hair. Being part Osage, those physical manifestations did not appear making him even more like an Oglala than a white man. However, his musculature, intense piercing blue-eyed stare, and his fierce unbending stature coupled with his stoic pride, clearly stood him out from among the rest of his Indian captors.

Coupled with that, his outdoor labors had more than bronzed his skin the same color as his Indian contemporaries. Now in the process of growing into a new role, Josiah showed a keen interest in learning the Oglala dialect of the Sioux language. And that deep interest also extended into learning the universal "talk" of the Plains Indians, namely sign. He did so because he found it necessary for his basic survival when it came to a more or less normal existence and relationship in the foreign culture in which he now found himself. And in doing so, Josiah discovered that many of the tribal members he served were pleased and more than happy to share the language learning process with him.

Surprisingly, Josiah was finding out more and more as the months progressed that he was enjoying the many aspects and challenges of his newfound life. In fact, when it came to reading the weather, tracking, processing of animals, and enjoying the hardest of work around the camp, he was becoming one of Old Chief Smoke's best disciples. Even though many of his labors were not considered the work or worthy of a man but that of a woman, he still found pride in his accomplishments—pride in his many accomplishments which, not surprisingly, were a throwback from his previous life as a white man. And when it came to the other skills necessary in order to survive as a primitive in the west, he never let any facet of his new learning experiences pass his quick eyes or the lightning-fast mental grasp of its uses and values. Little did Josiah realize that the transformation of life that was now manifesting itself from within his very heart and soul would someday allow him to walk The Red Road or the good and decent road of life.

Seeing this unexpected change in Josiah and reading it as a genuine promise of his future, Old Chief Smoke had several tribal elders take Josiah under their guidance and quietly begin teaching him "The Way." Tribal elders who were now old men but full of the spoken history of Old Chief Smoke's band and the Sioux Nation's culture as a whole. At first glance, Josiah looked upon the two tribal elders with suspicion as to why their newfound friendliness and intense interest in dealing with a captive and hated white man. Then once under their quiet and knowledgeable spells, his suspicions softened and then he finally looked forward to many of his evenings in the company of such tribal historians and learned men, men who were once accomplished warriors and now because of the passage of time, hardships and the "wearing" of the seasons on their bodies, had found themselves mellowed into autumn's turning leaves...

Under the spell of such knowledgeable men, Josiah discovered himself mentally breathing into his heart and soul the very essence of those spoken words of wisdom and cultural history now being passed on to him in the quiet of the tribal elders' tipis. In those welcome sessions, he learned to differentiate different bird calls, how to find water on a many times water-less plains environment, how to track wounded animals, learn what the tracks he was looking at were saying, which animals would lead him to or from water (horses going somewhere in single file meant they were going to a water source; feeding in a bunch meant they had already watered), how to read the signs of weather; how to tell from a simple moccasin track what tribe the wearer represented, and much, much more that took place in the primitive world. Teachings that some white men had been privileged to hear before but had not listened to or had taken the time to really understand...

Additionally, Josiah learned that the Sioux Nation was significant in their numbers. That because of their numbers, need for food and because of their historical possession of large horse herds requiring good and ample pasturage, the Sioux out of necessity had sub-divided into smaller, more mobile bands. Those bands were usually made up of unrelated families or many times by clans of people who were related by marriage. As it turned out, Old Chief Smoke's band of Oglala were made up of a mixture of inter-married clans and unrelated families.

Smoke's band was larger than most because of the old chief's excellent reputation as a gifted leader and warrior. Bands that were easy to move when necessary and as a result, could more easily sustain themselves when it came to living off the land. Those bands scattered throughout the Sioux Nation's geographic homelands were assembled usually twice a year by runners from other bands for grand buffalo hunts in the spring and fall. Those bands were also gathered during the early summer months which was a time of plenty and set aside for many celebrations such as the seeking of visions, society elections, and cult performances. All of which were followed by the Sun Dance, which was the climax of the summer ceremonial season. Josiah learned that the entire camp could be on the move in about fifteen to twenty minutes, with the old, infirm, and children riding on the camp's many travois during such travels from encampment to encampment.

The elders spoke of the Great Spirit who had given them the buffalo and it had become a major staple in the diets of all the Plains Indians. Especially so once the Plains Indians had acquired through their acquisition, use and mastery of the horse many moons earlier from the Spanish in the southwest—horses that had diffused onto the Plains around 1700 from the Spanish herds in Texas and New Mexico. The elders further spoke of all the items of life the buffalo offered to the hunters and their families.

They also spoke to Josiah on how the camp site was selected, that the chief and his assistants would select an encampment site based on good grazing, having a good water and wood supply, was protected from the winds, and placed in such a manner that the tribe's enemies would find it hard to locate. They instructed that the tipis were generally pitched in a rough circle in the summer camps when times were plentiful and many times scattered out along the valley's water supply during the winter months when times were harder. But for the most part always arranged in a loose circle.

The elders spoke about the sun which might be the home of God and always moved in a circle. And in doing so, sent light, enlightenment, warmth, and growth to Mother Earth and all her peoples. Because of that, members of the band always placed the openings of each tipi facing to the east for the sun's early morning's rays and the way of enlightenment. Hence the arrangement of the tipis in a circle which represented the universe and eternity.

Josiah learned that feminine chastity was highly prized by the Sioux and a male suitor would offer only the most expensive gifts for a virtuous woman. He also learned that the buffalo had been given to The People as a gift from Wakan Tanka, for its meat, bones (made into tools), hides (fashioned into tipi covers, cases for transportation of household goods, shields, robes) and their skulls for religious activities. Then at the end of the summer festival season, a grand buffalo hunt was organized and carried out to gather in much of the winter's food stocks. This was also a time to gather in roots, berries, tubers and medicinals for the long winter months ahead. Those meat food stocks derived from the buffalo hunts would then be smoked, dried, jerked or made into pemmican for the long winter months ahead and times of scarcity.

The elders also advised that many times the braves would have several wives. That was because of the shortage of men due to fighting with other enemy tribes, getting killed while on buffalo hunts, and deadly accidents of all kinds. By having more than one wife, that allowed the women to have someone to talk with when the men were gone and help with the sharing of the work. Plus with extra wives, children would remain plentiful, but that their children were spaced a few years apart so they could be singularly properly trained in all the skills they would need in order to survive as a warrior. Josiah learned that many times during battle, the warriors would take young captives of the enemy as potential slaves. And that some of those slaves so taken would go on to become tribal members and great warriors for the receiving tribe. On and on went the teaching session as told by the elders for weeks on end after Josiah's menial duties were finished for the day.

Included in those many discussions were stories of great battles with other tribes and the white man, tales of great warriors who counted coup, notable buffalo hunts, great vision quests, exceptional Sun Dances when many tribal members participated and then went on to become great warriors, sacred visions that had been received by some members of the tribe, and other notable adventures the band had been involved with historically. Josiah soon came to understand and appreciate why the old men of the band were the tribal historians and responsible for verbally passing down the spoken history of The People. Simply, they had lived what they had verbally shared with others, plus, they were good storytellers. And now it fell to those elders to pass on the tribal histories to the younger members of the tribe, so those "embers of history" would not go out and be lost in the passages of time.

Josiah found that he had been given so much information regarding the life and times of the Sioux Nation and the Oglala within that nation of peoples that he found it hard to remember everything passed onto him. And in the quiet of his evening moments when his work was done and he was not in the presence of the elders, Josiah began committing to his inner being those living scraps of history, life, and the culture he had thus far been exposed to. Then one day he discovered somewhat to his surprise that many of those teachings learned thus far were being tempered and utilized during his everyday living hours. It was almost as if those teachings had been specifically meant for him to integrate into his soul. Almost as if someone in the tribe had seen in him something else other than that of a captive and a gatherer of wood and water...

As the summer progressed, so did Josiah. He was still not allowed to use any weapons yet and if caught handling or examining them, was severely beaten by anyone near at hand. Additionally, the men of Old Chief Smoke's band never let him near any horses unless they directed him to do some needed chore in that arena. And when that kind of activity was performed, it was under their constant guard throughout. Plus all the young boys guarding the horse herds were instructed that if they ever saw Josiah at or near any horses, they were to alert the adult members of the band. It was obvious the fear of his escape and the simmering lack of trust by some tribal members was still present in the back of their minds. Especially so with members of those clans who had lost relatives or friends at the hand of Josiah during the fight back at the wagon train. But, he was now allowed to jerk meat, trap, and set snares in the winter months.

During those times, Josiah attempted making his own clothing, a chore that he found to be never ending because of the wearing work of his menial duties and his constantly growing body. Even Gemma found time to make clothing for her big brother because of his now larger-than-life and rapidly-changing bodily frame. Josiah now stood 6'4" in moccasins and weighed in at a rock solid two hundred forty pounds! His old tipi had since been replaced with a newer one by a number of the band's older warriors and one day, Old Chief Smoke presented Josiah with his own beautifully decorated sheath, belt, and skinning knife. Josiah was so overcome with the old chief's kindness, that for the longest time, all he did was closely examine the useful gift that had been bequeathed to him. Then turning to the old chief, Josiah, in perfect Oglala dialect, quietly thanked the old man for his generosity and trust...But with many of the chief's band of people outwardly beginning to accept Josiah as one of their own, simmering trouble was looming regardless in the otherwise calm valley inhabited by Old Chief

Smoke's band.

Simmering trouble, especially by one still embarrassed young brave with a scar running across his face named Red Shirt. A brave who had been denied counting coup against Josiah during the earlier battle at the Pike wagon train. An embarrassment, because he had been given the chance to kill the cornered and armed Josiah during that fight but had been slow on the uptake in getting an arrow into the white man. And then Old Chief Smoke had intervened. And when he did, the opportunity of counting an easy coup on a white man had been taken from the young Indian with the facial scar. Then many older warriors of the band never let Red Shirt forget his lost opportunity for counting his first coup, because he had moved as "slowly as a cold mud turtle in the fall." That, plus the fact that many younger members of the tribe his age had already counted coup and in doing so, had ascended in the tribal ranks from that of being just simply a brave to becoming a full-fledged warrior in the eyes of The People.

That was when the beatings started in earnest...The Indian with the scar across his face, now personally known to Josiah as Red Shirt, led a worshiping band of nine other young braves of the same age—braves with the same nasty-tempered inclinations toward all whites who had been flooding across their homelands along the Oregon Trail since 1840. And with the settlers came whiskey, a myriad of diseases, especially venereal disease, settlement on sacred lands, and the gross killing and overall destruction of the buffalo. By 1851, the Fort Laramie Peace Treaty had been signed deeding much land to the various Plains Indian tribes and allowed the U.S. government the right to build roads across those deeded Indian lands. But by 1854, clashes with all the white settlers flooding into and across those deeded Plains lands crowding out the Indians had erupted into open warfare!

Whenever it suited his followers, the still smarting Red Shirt who was not allowed to kill Josiah back at the wagon train fight and who was almost the same size of Josiah, would descend on him in the outback with a vengeance. This was especially true when Josiah was out of sight of the village elders on a work detail, a work detail overshadowed by his personal warrior guard. A guard who harbored a hatred for the man he had been assigned to oversee. And a captive young white man, who harbored a hatred toward his personal guard of the darkest of natures for what he had done to a defenseless woman, namely his mother at the wagon train battle. A guard who when approached by a menacing band of younger men, would just sit back and let nature take its course regarding his young charge.

With ten young men laying the rod to Josiah from all sides, he soon found himself laying in a pool of his own blood many times when the boys had tired of the beatings. And each and every time such beatings occurred, Tall Bull, the killer of Josiah's mother and the one guarding him against escape, just stood by and happily leered at the brutal "festivities." For him, a walk down The Black Road was not uncommon. Tall Bull was considered a braggart, bully, and not a good man within Old Chief Smoke's band. As such, no eligible female within the band would consider marrying any man so tribally marked with such a dark persona, no matter what kind of expensive gifts he was to offer for her hand in marriage.

Tall Bull lived with his aging mother and father. Having such an unenviable reputation, he took out his black feelings over being so tribally marked every time he could on any lesser mortal, especially hapless captives. That went double for Josiah because of the obvious dark feelings and historical knowledge the two men openly harbored about each other. Then once Josiah was somewhat recovered and able to walk after the beating he had just received at the hands of the Red Shirt supporters, Tall Bull would make him finish his work detail. Then Tall Bull would escort the battered Josiah back at the end of the day to his tipi like nothing out of the ordinary had transpired. Little did Tall Bull realize that the volcano of revenge steaming from within Josiah was coming closer and closer to the surface of life and erupting. And when it did...

However, knowing what was coming every time in which such a situation with the young antagonists presented itself, Josiah, cleverly out of self-defense, would target three different boys in the group each time before he was beaten senseless. And in the process, "leave his mark" on their faces and bodies before the horde of younger men would then overwhelm and leave Josiah beaten senseless and lying in a pool of his own blood. Once again, Tall Bull did nothing but laugh at Josiah's beatings as he laid there bleeding. Then one day Tall Bull came up with another way to show his total disdain and hatred for the young captive white man.

On three different occasions after the crowd of Red

Shirt's followers had laid out Josiah on the ground in a bloody mess, Tall Bull walked over to Josiah and stood by his side as he laid there on the ground trying to recover from the recent round of beatings. Then Josiah became aware of a warm and salty burning liquid stream being drizzled over his face and other open wounds on his body! Tall Bull was urinating on Josiah in utter disdain!

Most of that time Josiah was so badly beaten, that he just laid there and took what Tall Bull drained out upon his battered and bloody body. These random beatings followed by the urination treatment went on for over a year. But each time a group beating was in the offing, Josiah would once again target three different boys and make sure their faces showed the full force of battle before he was once again overwhelmed by their sheer numbers, flying fists from every part of the compass, and clubs laid to all parts of his body. However, each time such an event occurred, Josiah was also learning how to defend himself and getting better in the typical rough and tumble Indian style.

Josiah was now as bronzed as any other Indian in the band, was strap steel tough as he was now eating better because a lot of the tribal elders were now caring for him in return for his good work, excellent attitude, and his mastery of the language of the Oglala. But it seemed as more and more of the tribe accepted him as one of their own, the hatred increased within Red Shirt's heart. As a result, the group beatings were coming more and more frequently. And when questioned by other members of the band as to his evident physical damage, Josiah remained Indian-like and stoic in his non-explanations. But within his being, the volcano of revenge was brewing ever more fearsomely…

Then the final blade of grass was blown into the prairie wind with the intemperance of the onset of an early November snow storm. Red Shirt was becoming more and more interested in Gemma! By now, she had grown into a beautiful, lithe, and amply-breasted young woman. Whenever she gracefully walked by, many an amorous young man's head would be turned. But Red Shirt had verbally "marked" her for himself and as a result of that public threat, many of the other younger potential suitors, fearful of Red Shirt's physical wrath upon them, yielded that field of interest to him. From the earlier teachings about the Oglala culture by the village elders, Josiah had learned that a young man of the tribe was not allowed to marry until they had earned the right. In earning the right of courtship and marriage, a young man had to be older, around twenty-five years of age, and to have counted coup. However, if the young man had already counted coup, he could marry if he was younger than twenty-five years of age. Red Shirt was under the age of twenty-five and had not yet counted coup...

Josiah, aware of Red Shirt's carnal interest involving Gemma, caught him alone one day and told him that his younger sister would not be interested in having him as a suitor. With a toss of his head and an arrogant smirk over his self-importance, Red Shirt turned and started to walk away from him as if what Josiah had to say meant nothing to him as a full-fledged brave of the tribe. Particularly since Josiah was nothing more than a captive white man. Then Red Shirt as he had planned all along, whirled about unexpectedly with his drawn knife in hand and slashed the tip of its blade viciously across Josiah's chest! Josiah's buckskin shirt fell away in front as the blood flowed from the shallow cut across his chest from Red Shirt's knife. That was not what Red Shirt had planned. He had planned on opening up Josiah like he would a freshly downed buffalo as many of his kind did in order to get at and eat the animal's warm bloody liver!

Josiah, having learned many of the younger Indian's ways, especially their penchant for trickery when common sense would work just as well, and being quick as a cat himself, was prepared for just such a reaction from Red Shirt relative his warning about Gemma. Lurching backwards quickly from the vicious knife swipe where the tip of the blade just barely slit open the skin across his chest, Josiah grabbed Red Shirt's hand and snapped his knife hand downward and hard across his rapidly raising knee. Red Shirt screamed out in pain and dropped the knife when the force of the rising knee against the downward thrust of Josiah's strong hands painfully damaged the smaller bones in his hand and wrist.

Red Shirt grabbed Josiah by the throat with his other good hand and began choking him with his iron grip. Josiah loosened Red Shirt's death grip on his throat with a hard knee driven deeply into the man's groin and then another knee to his face when he stooped over in pain at the unexpected blow to the man's testicles. That knee to the face snapped Red Shirt's head violently upward and backwards! That was followed with a right cross to Red Shirt's nose from Josiah that would have felled a mule!

In that strike, Josiah exalted inwardly over the fact that Red Shirt's nose busted and flattened out across his face like a piece of floppy warm buffalo fat. Blood instantly spewed forth, smearing a red streak across Red Shirt's face and chest. Red Shirt immediately grabbed his painfully broken nose with both hands in snot-blowing agony. When he did, that allowed Josiah to full force strike Red Shirt with another powerful right cross. The impact of that blow which had the full force and effect of an angry mule's kick, dropped Red Shirt to the ground like he had been shot with a large caliber buffalo gun. Standing over him, Josiah in a stern warning in Oglala, advised Red Shirt that his sister was not available as a potential bride and for him to forget about her or he would kill him the next time they met over such an issue!

Red Shirt said nothing, as the bloody foam spewed from his broken nose and now split lips like that from a lung-shot buffalo. With that, Josiah picked up Red Shirt's beautifully handmade knife and jerked off his belt holding a beautifully beaded knife sheath as well. Holding the belt, he stuck the knife back into its sheath and then taking the entire outfit as his own spoils of the battle, walked away. The inner volcano had spewed forth but Josiah was not yet finished with the overall business at hand.

Walking away satisfied that all the earlier beatings he had taken from Red Shirt and his followers had now been partially avenged, Josiah planned his next move. Especially after Tall Bull just moments later had forcefully intervened between the two men and had stopped Josiah from any further physical damage and humiliation of Red Shirt. And when Tall Bull tried to take back Red Shirt's knife, sheath and belt from Josiah, he found that the piercing blue-eyed stare of the man being confronted was not of this world! With that and the feeling of uneasiness creeping over him over the deadly coldness of that stare, Tall Bull stepped backwards and lowered his spear menacingly toward Josiah. The spear was instantly slapped out of Tall Bull's hands! Reaching down and picking up Tall Bull's spear, Josiah snapped the handle into two pieces with just the strength of his hands! Then the pieces were flung onto the ground at the feet of Tall Bull. With that, Josiah picked up the wood he needed to bring back to an elder in the encampment, shouldered the load, and quietly departed.

The next day, Josiah was asked by one of the band's elders who was partially crippled after being gored by a wounded buffalo, if he could bring him some more firewood. The elder advised Josiah that he needed the wood to keep his tipi warm on the upcoming chilly nights and make his old bones feel better. Josiah liked the old man who had been kind to him in the past and told him the wood would be forth coming that afternoon. Heading over to the river, Josiah began gathering up several arms full of heavy dry driftwood for the old man's fire. Hefting all he could carry onto his right shoulder so he would only have to make one trip, Josiah started back to the band's current encampment. In doing so, Josiah grinned. The band's trust in him had been growing by leaps and bounds, especially as Josiah's command of the Oglala language had been almost mastered. He was now allowed to do some of his chores without the attention of Tall Bull being close at hand.

Staggering up out of the river bottom under a hefty load of firewood, Josiah was surprised to glimpse Red Shirt and four of his closest dedicated band of worshipers out of the corner of his eyes waiting for him at the top of the trail in the brush. He could see that every one of the to-be assailants had a large war club in hand! With a battle plan racing around in his head over what he was now facing, Josiah continued walking up the trail toward the five men pretending like he didn't even see them or recognize the danger because the huge load of wood on his shoulder was blocking his view of the ambush to come. However knowing full well what was next in coming, Josiah's battle plan raced around in his head like that of a mad bumblebee trapped in a tipi. Nearing the first young man blocking his way, one who was a heavy-set man named "Buffalo Horn," Josiah at the last second forcefully threw his entire armload of wood violently into that man's face and onto his head. The man dropped like a pole-axed elk, knocked out as cold as last winter's Moon of the Popping Trees ice storm!

Grabbing a heavy chunky limb from the bundle of just thrown firewood, Josiah ducked a club swinging by violently just over his head and then swung his heavy limb upward with all his might at the next nearest antagonist. A man who was a tall and thinly built Indian named Flight-Of-An-Arrow. *Thunk* went the tree limb alongside the man's lower jaw, dropping him instantly as a result of Josiah's mighty swing, a swing and strike which caught the man by surprise! Recovering and stepping into his next swing, Josiah's blow was knocked off its intended course by the third Indian fighter's incoming impact from Man-Comes-Running's vicious swing of his war club. Fortunately Josiah's swing of his club aimed for that man's, head was deflected downward by the impact of his antagonist's incoming club. Deflected really low! Josiah's now deflected club squarely hit the man mightily in the groin, dropping him to the ground and out of the fight in a heartbeat!

Red Shirt and Flies-Fast, the remaining supporter, totally surprised over Josiah's vicious unanticipated attack, stood frozen for a moment or as long as it takes a white-tailed deer to flick its tail-like flag at the first sign of danger. Then Flies-Fast took off running away from the river side battle like his name denoted...

That left a previously battered Red Shirt to face a thoroughly-maddened Josiah alone. An Indian whose nose was already a swollen mess framed by two blackened eyes and a deeply split upper lip from a like altercation with Josiah from the day before. Black swollen eyes or not, Red Shirt could see the piercing blue-eyed look emanating from a white man, who had grown from a boy of fourteen into a man at a very young age because of his life's circumstances. And now a young man, although a captive of the Oglala Sioux, who when faced with adversity, could arise into a towering and killing rage in just a heartbeat. And now that rage was made even the more deadly because of Josiah's super strength, size, adrenaline dump, quickness, learned ability to fight, and total fearlessness. Those facets of combat were all buttressed with the history learned from many previous such beatings on how to fight dirty. Traits that were not only almost "genetic" but now learned and honed from his many months of captivity, hard work, and developing the understanding of The Way…

Picking up the scattered limb wood for the village elder back at the band's campsite, Josiah hefted the heavy load onto his powerful right shoulder once again now that things had calmed down and began walking up the trail to the village's campsite. Walking behind him a short careful distance away came a totally compromised Tall Bull, who had just arrived late to the fight once again for his guard duties. He had been so amazed at the deadly quickness and ferocity of Josiah's attack on Red Shirt's crowd, that the battle was over before he could finish walking down the trail and intervene on behalf of "the fallen." And now, there was no way he was going to challenge Josiah with all his possible supporting Indian counterparts laying behind him bruised and bloody on the ground of battle. Or as in the case of Flies-Fast, running for his life back to the safety of the encampment. For you see, in addition to his other weaknesses, Josiah had figured out that Tall Bull was also a coward. Or in Josiah's mind, a woman killer, namely that of his mother. And that volcano's eruption that burned hot from within Josiah, was getting dangerously close to the surface once again. All it needed was the right set of circumstances in which for it to occur…

Behind him still lying on the ground laid Buffalo Horn, Man-Comes-Running, Flight-Of-An-Arrow and once again, a really badly and freshly beaten Red Shirt…! Two days later, Old Chief Smoke called all the young followers of Red Shirt to his tipi. With little fanfare and

54

with much in the way of stern warnings and gesturing, Old Chief Smoke made it very clear that as long as he was the tribal leader, such fighting among the young braves must cease. Braves were needed to protect the camp and its followers, provide the food for the members of the tribe, as well as killing the hated trespassing white men and members of warring tribes of the camp's historical enemies. Not each other for any reason. No one offered any word of explanation as to what had happened earlier on the creek bank. The old chief's word was the law. But to Josiah's way of thinking, there was the still pressing matter of Tall Bull with the fires of revenge and hatred that burned hotly within his now more than volcanic and captive revenge-seeking soul...

Chapter Four

WINTER CAMP AND A TIME OF SURPRISES...

Once again the chilling winds from out of the northwest were being felt in the newest little valley into which Old Chief Smoke's village had recently moved for its winter quarters. The horse feed had run out at their previous summer location, they were now nearer to better buffalo hunting grounds, a need existed for better camp sanitation, the new location supplied plentiful sources of close at hand firewood, an icy stream ran clear and plentiful near the campsite, and the oncoming change of the seasons had once again historically dictated the move. Plus, the valley they had just moved into provided for better shelter from the north winds and the deep snows soon to encompass the land in its freezing grip. Lastly, the secluded valley had been previously used for many moons by Old Chief Smoke's band and had never been discovered by any of the tribe's historical tribal enemies located further to the east or south.

Heralding this seasonal change, the ducks, geese, swans, sandhill cranes, and birds of prey were migrating southward overhead in greater numbers every day. The gray and fox squirrels were caching every nut they could find and building even larger nests high atop the trees. The snipe had long since abandoned the muddy seeps from along the stream that ran the full length of their new sheltering valley, having done so before the felt coming freeze-up deprived them of their invertebrate food sources. The sharp-tail grouse, sage grouse, and the prairie chickens were forming up into larger coveys for the protection from predators those greater numbers of watching eyes offered during the lean winter months ahead. And the numerous deer and less numerous herds of elk found in the valley's thickets and sagebrush flats were waxing fat.

Standing on a small ridge above the creek in their new valley cradling an armload of firewood, Josiah observed a large black bear hunting along the creek bottom below for anything of interest that might fill his seemingly always empty stomach. Josiah had to grin. The bear was so fat that he just rolled from side to side as he ambled along searching the waterway for any hoped for food item of interest. Josiah was wishing he had a rifle for if he had, a rolling fat black bear would soon grace many cooking pots in his village. Additionally, the bear's body and organ fat, highly prized by the Oglala, would be a welcome addition to the member's winter food stores. Alas, all he had was an armload of firewood because some members of the band still harbored a deep escape distrust of the young man and had continued voicing their concerns to the chief that Josiah not be armed under any circumstances. Because once armed, he would be enabled in any escape attempt he might mindfully harbor. And several other braves had also complained, like Red Shirt and his band of now fearful followers, especially when it came to issuing Josiah either a firearm or a horse. Fearful since they had administered so many beatings in the past, many now feared armed with a firearm, Josiah might just take revenge on those who had bullied and beaten him so many times before when no one was looking...

Continuing on his way with his heavy load of firewood, Josiah noticed the leaves from the oaks and cottonwoods were falling from their branches in swirling flurries every time the wind moseyed through their new winter home site in the valley. And further towards the western end of their valley, the horse herd happily fed along the grassy stream banks eating the season's last green grass before the winter snows arrived and buried the greenery under an icy blanket of white.

This time, instead of being closely arranged in a circle like in their summer camp, there were thirty or so tipis scattered along the creek for about a mile up and downstream. However, located near Old Chief Smoke's tipi were about fifteen tipis scattered around in a loose circle befitting the thinking and tradition of the Sioux culture. As Josiah had learned from the elders on one of his many visits, once selected, the winter camp was expected to remain occupied until about March or April. After that, a new summer camp would be selected and the cycle of nomadic movement would start all over again. He had also learned that the winter months were the times of relaxation. It was a time of equipment repair, replacing lost or broken arrows, and the manufacturing of new clothing, especially the needed heavier winter replacements. Additionally, the winter months were a time for games, feasts, dancing and visits with other members and clans of the village. Winter time was also when love ruled the camp...In the eyes of the tribal elders and The People, those were the happy days. No more would they be required to move as frequently as they had during the summer months following the roving buffalo herds. No more putting up and taking down of the tipis and loading the travois. Yes, the winter season could be the happy times. Then come late spring, the campsite would once again be moved to accommodate the band's daily living needs. Plus, it would place them closer to historically well-used travel routes by the northern herds of the buffalo in the coming months and away from the much hated, ever increasing numbers of white settlers.

In their most recent move to their winter encampment, Josiah made it a point to assist everyone in need of another set of strong hands and back, especially the old and infirm of the band. He did so because since he had been in the band, except for his travails with Tall Bull and Red Shirt and his followers, he had seen kindness, honesty, charity, and brotherhood among the villagers. He had discovered early on that he liked what he saw and wanted to become a part of that ethos and race of Plains humanity. Hence, he always made himself available to help others in their time of need after he had finished with his other assigned tasks.

Unbeknownst to Josiah, Old Chief Smoke and the tribal elders had been watching his every move among the villagers for some time with extreme interest. After the winter move had been made and the band was more or less settled in, Old Chief Smoke held a pow-wow one evening with a chosen number of the tribal elders. Much smoking of the pipe and discussion took place as the gathering held sessions of a serious nature until late into the evening. Finally the discussions being settled, the gathering broke up and everyone retired to their tipis. That was except for Old Chief Smoke.

Gathering up what he needed in a tanned buffalo robe as so dictated by the meeting of elders, he headed for Josiah's tipi. When he arrived, he quietly announced his presence from outside the tipi and was then met at the entrance by a puzzled-looking Josiah. Holding back the flap to his tipi, Josiah let the chief into his sparsely-equipped living space. Old Chief Smoke sat down stiffly by the fire, laid his buffalo robe off to one side and quietly looked around. Inside Josiah's tipi were his sleeping furs set off to one side, a small fire brightly burned in the ring of rocks in the center of the tipi, and a small pile of personal items Josiah had accumulated over his many months as a captive laid at the foot of his sleeping furs. There was very little of survival value that met the old chief's trained eye. Looking up at Josiah as he continued standing out of respect for the old chief, he was beckoned by the old man to sit so the two of them could talk.

For the longest time, Old Chief Smoke just stared into the small fire as if he was carrying a heavy load on his shoulders and the dancing flames might hold an answer to his still remaining question. Then with a determined move, he untied the tanned buffalo skin laying at his side and began rolling it out onto the floor of the tipi. Once rolled out, Josiah could hardly believe his eyes at what he was seeing in the dim light of his fire. Once again and without a word being spoken, Old Chief Smoke looked into the fire as if once again looking for answers in the dancing flames as to what was weighing heavily on his heart. Weighing heavily because of the decisions previously made by the elders and the serious action he was about to undertake. An action which could have long term consequences in the sacred direction of a man's life, especially if the bad spirits intervened…Turning to Josiah, Old Chief Smoke began quietly speaking. In fact he was speaking so softly, Josiah had to really listen to what the old chief was saying over the crackling sounds his fire was making. What he heard brought tears to his eyes.

"Josiah, many moons ago, my warriors attacked your wagon train and were victorious. We captured two young captives and brought back to our people many things that made a white man's life easier. In turn, those things brought back made my people's lives easier as well. But we lost seven good warriors in that battle and that left their tipis empty, quiet, and lonely."

Then the old chief paused as if collecting the rest of his thoughts. After another long moment, he began speaking once again. "Before that battle, the Great Spirit had visited me and told me many things. One of those things was about a young brave white man that I should save from death during that fight at the wagon train because he would someday make a great Oglala warrior. That I did and you were the one I saved just as the Great Spirit had told me to do. Since that day, you have been a captive in my village and have been closely watched by all. Watched to make sure what the Great Spirit said to me in my vision would come true. My elders have watched you without your knowing so we would know what we were seeing in your actions meant you had a good and true heart. You have served me and my people well during these many moons and have shown to me that you have a good heart. In fact ever since your arrival into my village, you have walked The Red Road or the road of goodness and a meaningful life. As a result of that goodness shown, most of my people have come to accept you as one of their own. So it is with a good heart and a clear vision that my elders and I wish to have you become one of us in deed. I know you are a white man and cannot be made into a true Oglala. But, the elders and I feel you would be welcome to join us if that pleases you in your heart. To show the truth in what we feel, I have brought you gifts that you will need to survive if you care to join us. Not everyone in the band agrees with me and the elders but it is time we test the truthfulness of your heart. So, I have brought you the needed gifts of life if you are to survive with us as a white-Oglala."

Josiah hardly believing his senses at what he was seeing and hearing, found it hard to breathe for fear of breaking the almost magical spell of the moment. With those words said, the old chief reached onto the buffalo hide and removed a beautifully beaded belt, knife sheath, and a knife with an elk antler handle. Holding the knife up into the air, the chief whispered something Josiah could not hear and then quietly presented it to him. Holding the beautiful gift in his hands, Josiah felt the tears of emotion coming to his eyes. Those he tried to blink away before the old chief detected his deepest feelings of the specialness of that moment. Then the old chief removed from the buffalo skin a long wooden handled tomahawk with a steel blade and presented that to Josiah as well. Lastly, the old chief removed a heavily used and somewhat battered Springfield .45-70 trapdoor single shot carbine, one that he had taken earlier from the hands of a dead cavalry trooper in a previous battle. For the longest moment, the old chief held the rifle in his hands as if almost second guessing his next move. Finally settling with his inner concerns relative to giving a firearm to an Oglala captive, the old chief handed the rifle to Josiah as well. Josiah was dumbfounded! Holding that rifle in disbelief, he was further astounded when the old chief also handed him six .45-70 cartridges!

"There are still those in the village who do not trust you with such gifts of life. That is why there are only six cartridges for this rifle. That should be all one needs to kill an elk, deer, bear, bighorn sheep, or buffalo if he is careful in their use. When those are gone, come to my tipi and I will have more for you. If you decide to join our village and further prove yourself and worthiness as a warrior, then there will be even more cartridges. But for now, that is the number of cartridges the elders have agreed upon for me to give to you at this moment in time. Use these gifts wisely my son. Also, you are no longer required to do just women's work. As of now, you are free to assist my village anyway you feel is necessary as any other brave or warrior would do. I would hope that you find a wise way to use your new rifle to help the old and infirm of my village and not to hurt those who have been bad towards you. Maybe as a hunter and supplier of fresh meat to those who no longer are capable of easily procuring their own meat supplies. Lastly, you are now to share a tipi with Running Wolf and his wife of many moons, Two Fists. I can see from the look on your face that you don't understand why you are being moved into another man's tipi or why his wife is named Two Fists. When she was just a child, she, like today, is very small in size. As she grew up the other larger children picked on her many times. Finally she got tired of always being picked on and started fighting back. She, even as little as she is, won many battles with her brave heart and two fists. Because of that, she is now called Two Fists and is loved by the whole village as a good women. She and her husband lost all their children many moons ago to the white man's disease that puts red spots all over one's body and makes them very sick with fever before they die. Since that time, the Great Spirit has failed to present them with more children. Now as you know having brought them firewood many times in the past, they are old and infirm. They need someone to look after them and help them with the remainder of their lives. The elders, Running Wolf, and I, have decided that you will leave your tipi and move in with them. That way you will be able to lead a better life, Two Fists will cook for you, they will have company on the coldest of nights, plus, they will have the protection you and your new rifle can offer. Also, you can help them by procuring fresh meat and firewood so they don't have to rely on others around them so much. As you already know, a man's offer to help with difficult female tasks will be traditionally scorned by not only Two Fists but the rest of the women in the tribe as well. But she is old and her back and arms are no longer strong when it comes to hauling in their needed wood supplies. But I sense since you are from two worlds, that of the white man and now the Oglala, you will be able to convince Two Fists that by you bringing in her wood, you will eat better because of her good cooking." Realizing he had just made a "funny" about the wood hauling issue, the old chief slyly smiled broadly. With those words, the old chief stiffly rose having no more to say and quietly left Josiah's tipi.

For the longest time, Josiah just sat there in wonderment over what had just transpired. Then as if to validate the moment, Josiah rose and removed Red Shirt's knife, belt and sheath from his waist. The ones that he had taken from Red Shirt in an earlier battle. Red Shirt's knife, belt and sheath were then laid off to one side onto Josiah's meager pile of belongings. Something in the back of his mind told him to do so because that beautiful knife, belt and sheath would be needed later to celebrate a great event...The new belt, sheath, and knife just received from Old Chief Smoke were then strapped on and fit his large frame perfectly. It was obvious that whoever had made the belt and beaded it so beautifully had been watching him closely to make sure the belt would fit. Picking up his new knife, Josiah found that it was easily sheathed and rode comfortably on his hip.

Picking up the tomahawk, Josiah found that it fitted his hand comfortably and was very well-balanced. Examining the tomahawk even more closely, it appeared to be very aged and the blade was of a style seldom used by the current tribal members. Little did he realize that the tomahawk had at one time belonged to Old Chief Smoke's grandfather and had been used in many battles. And, its battle life was far from over. In fact, the life giving heritage of that tomahawk was far from being over and would soon come full circle... Laying the old tomahawk back down without giving it another thought, Josiah picked up the .45-70 carbine and enjoyed the weight of its heft, balance, and feel. Then the unexpected happened!

Lifting the trap door mechanism on the single shot rifle to examine the bore, he discovered a live cartridge was still in the chamber! Removing the cartridge, Josiah held it reverently in his fingers. The old chief had limited him to just six cartridges. Yet, here was a seventh! To him, there was a special significance to that extra cartridge. Had the Great Spirit left it there for Josiah to find and realize that it was a special gift or possibly an omen of something yet to come? He did not know. But of one thing he was certain. To his way of thinking, that extra cartridge held a special significance and was to be used under only the most sacred of circumstances. Then Josiah caught himself in his thinking. He had just thought like a Sioux warrior! The earlier teachings from the elders were now manifesting themselves in his very thought processes and they were not foreign or unwelcome to his current way of thinking...

Slowly sitting back down by his fire, Josiah just quietly sat there in contemplation over the events that had just transpired. It was another long moment in time before he arose and placed what he considered his special cartridge taken from the chamber of his new rifle into a small leather pouch. Then by the light of his small fire, Josiah fashioned a leather thong from a piece of tanned hide and then drilled holes with the tip of his knife in the leather pouch to hold the thong. The pouch was then strung around his neck holding his special .45-70 cartridge. One he firmly thought would only be used for something very significant. And having come from a Missouri farm where survival and use of firearms was almost second nature, Josiah knew, based on his ability as a crack rifle shot, that the special bullet whenever used, would find its target even from a short barreled, short ranged military carbine...

Arising early the following morning after Old Chief Smoke's previous evening's visit and revelations, Josiah left his tipi and headed out on foot for that area of the stream where he had previously observed the rolling fat black bear. Arriving on his hilly overlook, as expected, the black bear was nowhere to be seen. Dropping down off the hill and walking over to where he had last seen the big bear, he squatted down to read any sign left behind. Picking up the bear's trail and observing a few scat signs, Josiah carrying his new rifle at the ready, moved quietly through the brush and the end of the season thick elderberry thickets along the stream bifurcating the village's new encampment site. A mile up the long valley, Josiah observed movement and then heard thrashing noises in the heavily fruited elder berry and choke cherry thickets alongside the creek.

Suspecting a heavily feeding bear in the dense bushes, Josiah sneaked closer to the area of disturbance for a closer look. Sneaking as close as he dared to the noises in the brush, he stopped and quietly waited for the wind to shift. He did so because he knew when the wind shifted and the bear winded him, he would more than likely stand up for a better look at what had caused this new smell. And in doing so, would expose himself. Then Josiah would have a better chance at cleanly taking the animal. When the wind finally shifted, Josiah heard a loud WOOOF, followed by the immediate presence of a large black bear standing up in the dense thicket with a mess of small limbs, leaves and ripe elderberry clusters hanging from his jaws. BOOM, went his new rifle and due to its heavy recoil causing the short barrel of the rifle to rise, the black bear's head instantly disappeared from Josiah's view. But the elderberry thicket's bushes in which the bear had been feeding were now being violently thrashed around. Soon the noises and violent shaking of the berry bushes slowed, then stopped.

Removing the spent cartridge from his rifle, Josiah re-inserted another live round into the chamber in case the bear was not dead and would require a second shot. With that, Josiah snapped the single shot locking mechanism shut over the new cartridge and fully cocked the hammer. The empty previously fired casing was then placed into a small leather pouch Josiah carried at his waist. He figured in order to procure more ammunition from Old Chief Smoke, he had better have proof that the live cartridges had been used. However, another live cartridge was not needed. The great bear was dead. Walking into the berry bushes cautiously with his rifle still at the ready in case a foul tempered grizzly bear was feeding nearby as well,

Josiah discovered that his black bear had been shot cleanly through the head and was no more. Josiah then thanked the Great Spirit for providing such a fat bear in a ritual he had learned from the elders to be performed upon the killing of an animal. With that ritual completed, the hard work began.

Dressing out the bear, Josiah discovered what he had observed the first time he had seen the bear while standing on a hillside with an armload of firewood. The bear was rolling fat and it was all Josiah could to do in gutting out the animal and rolling it over so its now open intestinal cavity could begin cooling the carcass out. But before he did, he removed as much fat as possible from around the intestines and placed a mound of that valuable fatty material back into the bear's open cavity. With his now slippery handled knife from all the bear fat, Josiah removed a rear ham and in the process took care not to damage the valuable hide. Setting the skinned out ham off to one side, Josiah laid his buckskin shirt over the open cavity to aid in keeping the magpies and few remaining flies in the area from finding and eating or fouling up any portion of his treasure. Hefting the bear's huge hind quarter onto his now bare right shoulder, Josiah headed back to the encampment located several miles distant.

Walking into the encampment, Josiah soon had gathered a crowd of excited little children around him looking on in awe at the great bear's huge ham casually slung over his shoulder. Stopping at his sister Gemma's tipi, Josiah hailed its two occupants from within. When the tipi's owner emerged, a woman known as Two Fawns stood before him. Seeing Josiah standing there with the huge bear ham resting easily on his shoulder, her eyes showed great surprise. Following her from the tipi was Josiah's little sister, Gemma. When Gemma emerged from the tipi, she got a big smile on her face seeing her big brother standing there with the huge chunk of fresh bear meat on his shoulder.

"I have killed a great bear up at the head of the valley. Two Fawns, would you and my sister like to have some and share some of this meat with the other members of your clan? Because if so, there will be more than enough meat to go around for all if you are interested," said Josiah proudly.

Two Fawns walked over to Josiah and poked at the bear's flesh to see just how fresh or tough the meat was. Surprised at the flesh being so fat-covered and not from an old, lean bear, plus excited over what that gift would offer in future great meals, she happily accepted Josiah's offer. With that, Josiah carried the heavy hind quarter over to where Two Fawns wanted it laid so she could begin preparation of the meat. However, Two Fawns said nothing in the way of thanks to Josiah because she was still in mourning over the loss of her husband, Two Fawns' husband being the same man Josiah had brained with his shotgun at the earlier Pike wagon train fight...Realizing the mourning period was not yet over because of Two Fawns' still shortened hair and he being the reason for it, Josiah respected her uncomfortable state of mind over his closeness. In that moment of extreme awkwardness, Josiah nodded at his sister and then quietly walked away. As he walked away, a broad grin formed on Josiah's face. That was his first act of thanks to the old

70

chief and the elders for believing in him and allowing him to partially slip the bonds of being a captive. For now he was able to walk as an equal as a provider for the old, infirm and the unfortunate in the village. The rest would come in time...

Walking back through the encampment accompanied once again by a pack of excited little children, Josiah stopped in front of Running Wolf's tipi, which was set off to one side from the circle of the others around the old chief's tipi. Running Wolf had deliberately set his tipi outside the normal circle of tipis because he had discovered a little spot near a grove of trees and an adjacent wind-blocking hill. Both natural features which to Running Wolf's way of thinking, offered even more shelter from the harsh Prairie winter weather. That plus Two Fists because of her small size, was always cold. And by setting his tipi out of the direct winter winds, Running Wolf found it easier to keep his wife warmer. Little did Josiah realize how fortuitous was the placement of Running Wolf's tipi and what miracle that off to one side placement would play in coming events...

After announcing his presence, the tipi flap opened and out walked the aging Running Wolf. Running Wolf had at one time been a great Oglala warrior and was still one of the village's best horsemen. However, the years had not been kind to him. Though his heart still burned fiercely like that of a warrior's, his body was wracked with pain from numerous horse wrecks, being mauled by a wounded grizzly bear when he was younger for testily shooting an arrow into the great bears rump, and numerous fights over the years with the enemies of the

Oglala.

"Good morning Running Wolf. I have killed a large black bear at the head of the valley. I have no horse to bring the bear back to your tipi. Would you help me with the loan of a gentle pack horse who could pack out a bear without too much of a problem once it smells the odor of the bear and its smell of death?"

"Josiah, you know Old Chief Smoke will not let me loan you a horse as of yet. But I will come with you and bring a horse to help you pack out the bear."

"If you could do that, there would be much bear meat and fat for you and Two Fists, with much more to share with many of the tribe's members if you wish," said Josiah with a big grin. It was then that the flap to the tipi was flung back and out walked a diminutive Two Fists, Running Wolf's wife. Without a word, Two Fists walked straight into Josiah's arms in a surprising embrace and said not a word. But to Josiah, Two Fists' embrace was a small touch of Heaven. Her hug was genuine and it had been a long time since another human being had given him such a hug.

The last time he could remember was the evening before and the morning after, before the fatal fight with the Indians at the wagon train. That was when Josiah's mother had walked by him as he was getting ready for bed. Then as if an afterthought had been provided to her from a divine entity, Josiah's mother stopped, walked back, and gave him a big hug. Then come the next morning, Josiah's mother had silently surprised him with her quiet presence when he had retrieved his dad's shotgun in order to hunt some sage grouse. During that surprise meeting in the pre-dawn darkness, his mother had also given her larger than life for a fourteen year-old man a warm hug as well. In Josiah's mind, now that he thought back on those events, they were prophetic and the last hugs he had received prior to those just given him by Two Fists...

Running Wolf, stoic as a stone but happy in his heart over his wife's outward show of emotion, acceptance, and reaction to their new guest, said to Josiah with a big grin, "We had better get going before the sun gets any higher. We wouldn't want another animal to find our bear or the 'little people,' the yellow jackets, to beat us to the best parts. Particularly if the little people get there first since winter is coming and they are trying hard to store in their winter provisions as well. If they do, it will be difficult taking the bear away from them without getting stung and bitten many times in the process." (Authors Note: Yellow jackets can both bite and sting at the same time! As a 16 year old logger trying to earn enough money to pay for my college, I learned that "biting and stinging" lesson many times over, especially when working as a "powder monkey." A powder monkey is one who uses explosives when blowing stumps or in road building used by any logging operation. And a quick lesson learned as a young powder monkey was that yellow jackets hated the smell of the nitroglycerin in the sticks of dynamite being carried by such workers. Hence learning about the biting and stinging all at the same time ability of the little people as they hunted down and attacked the one carrying such items strongly smelling of nitroglycerin. The same result is in the wind for anyone who disturbs their nest or their

73

feeding activities.)

Finally releasing his grizzly bear-like hug on Two Fists, Josiah said, "Mother, we must be going. Like Running Wolf said, we do not want any other animal to find our bear before we do." Then it dawned on Josiah over his choice of words. The word "Mother" had rolled off his lips like a comfortable everyday event. He now found himself surprised but highly pleased over his choice of words and the strange feelings from within himself that warm moment between the two of them had engendered.

The rest of that day was spent by Josiah and Running Wolf returning to and packing out the huge black bear. They had a little trouble loading such a large and strongly-smelling dead animal onto the pack horse that Running Wolf had supplied. For all intents and purposes, the horse must have figured the men were loading a horse-eating predator onto the back of that nervous critter. After much prancing around and some bucking trying to throw off the smelly beast from its back, plus Running Wolf having to place his buckskin shirt over the horse's head to calm it down, the bear was finally loaded onto the back of the worried animal. Once done, then began the long and slow walk back to their encampment.

Upon arrival, a large crowd gathered and soon a group of women led by Two Fists had dismembered the entire bear. In the happy process, Two Fists saved its skin to eventually be tanned and turned over to a holy man because a bear pelt was sacred and used extensively by medicine men. However, she saved the claws in order to make a bear claw necklace for Running Wolf. With that, she distributed much of its meat to other members of the

74

village. In doing so, many of the members came by later and thanked Josiah for sharing his much appreciated kill. Their job done, Josiah and Running Wolf headed for the nearby creek where they could wash and clean up. As Josiah was soon to discover from Running Wolf, bathing was a twice daily ritual practiced by many Indians of the Sioux Nation. He had earlier observed many Indians bathing but never thought any more about it. He had just never thought about cleanliness being so important to the Indians. In order to put into practice what had been preached by Running Wolf, Josiah soon found himself washing in the creek every morning and evening thereafter. Even during the winter months, Josiah, like many other members of his village, bathed twice daily. Thinking back on his once a week bathing on the farm in Missouri and the same, if they were lucky once on the road to Oregon, Josiah just shook his head. The daily baths left him always feeling refreshed and smelling better than a close at hand bull buffalo after he had been in an old, many times used mud wallow. Once again, Josiah just shook his head over the unclean ways practiced by the almighty whites. With such moments of thinking, slowly, ever so slowly, Josiah was turning the cultural pages from that of being a white man to that of becoming an Indian...

Finished with their bathing, Running Wolf and Josiah headed for the young white man's old tipi. There Running Wolf's horse was loaded with Josiah's meager belongings and the structure was dismantled and laid off to one side for anyone else in need to use. Then the two men returned to Running Wolf's tipi. Once there, those belongings were unloaded into Running Wolf's tipi and Josiah was home...

Later that evening after gathering up a mess of firewood for the fire and on his way home, Josiah was teased by several nearby warriors over his wood gathering detail, a detail normally performed by a woman. The teasing stopped as Josiah turned, and then just gave the warriors a cold, piercing blue-eyed knowing stare, followed with his characteristic, good-natured grin. Following that good-natured run-in with some of his warrior buddies, Josiah re-shouldered his load of firewood and went about his business. No words were spoken further between the two entities, as an unfazed Josiah continued on his way. To Josiah's way of thinking, it was beneficial being raised within two different cultures such as that of a white man and now that of an Oglala. To him, there was no stigma attached in doing hard menial work. In fact, he found wood hauling a lot better chore than staring at the hind end of a mule pulling a plow all day long back in Missouri...Josiah had quickly come to realize that the elders had helped in raising the young of the village when they were younger men and women, and now it was time for those young so cared for earlier to help with the elders in their old age. With that kind of a growing mind set, it was becoming more and more apparent that the teachings of the elders had not only been heard but were now being committed to Josiah's soul and in his daily practice with the everyday issues of life...

Pausing outside Running Wolf's tipi flap, Josiah hesitated for just a moment over the newness of his situation. Then he re-adjusted his load of firewood into his massive arms, ducked his head and entered. The warmth of the tipi comforted his senses as he placed the stack of firewood off to one side of the fire circle for Two Fists to use. Then the wondrous smell of fresh bear meat, cornmeal and wild onions merrily cooking away in a large cast iron pot, with a liberal helping of fresh bear fat mixed therein, graced his senses. That cooking food sure smelled better than anything he had cooked by himself since his capture and subsequent isolation in his old tipi, he thought with a smile.

For the rest of that late fall and into the early winter months before the heavy snows arrived and when they weren't hunting buffalo, Josiah willingly became a major deer and elk hunter for the village's old and infirm. Once again, his inner being reminded him that the old and infirm had raised the children in their younger days and now it was time for the younger ones to return the favor. Plus, Josiah loved the silence and seclusion of being a lone hunter. He also loved the serenity of the prairie's wilderness beauty. And in that wilderness beauty, Josiah pitted his growing skills against the game being hunted, the one shot kills, and the wonderful moments he experienced in sharing his bounty with the other members of the encampment.

Soon Josiah's presence was a welcome sight to everyone, with the exceptions of the murderous Tall Bull and the still often embarrassed and arrogant Red Shirt. The latter was a man who remained in an almost constant state of angry and emotional embarrassment for not having counted coup as of yet even at his age. Even all of Red Shirt's followers had now swung over to having friendly relations and wide respect for Josiah in his new found home and tribal responsibilities. But being the hunter he was with rapidly developing survival instincts, Josiah recognized the evil feelings and bad intentions in Tall Bull and Red Shirt. And as such, Josiah always kept a sharpened eye-out on all of their activities, especially those activities dealing with and about his hated presence by the two men.

Lying in his sleeping furs early one morning during the first snowfall of the season, Josiah reveled in the furry warmth of his bed and snuggled in among its layers even more deeply. Then his eyes shot wide open! Listening, he could distinctly hear the faint sounds of many people quietly walking in the freshly fallen snow around Running Wolf's tipi—a tipi that had been pitched outside the normal circle of tipis in the center part of the winter encampment near a wind breaking embankment! Not a word was being spoken by "The Mystery Walkers." But, the unmistakable sounds of many Mystery People faintly sneaking in the immediate vicinity of Running Wolf's tipi were plainly heard by a now very alert Josiah. And at that time of the morning, members of the tribal encampment would not have been up and about in such numbers and moving about so quietly! Josiah's developing wilderness and survival instincts told him something was in the wind and it spelled danger! And in the mysterious strangers' quiet approach, they had not even alerted the camp's always barking dogs, a fact which told Josiah the strangers now in and among the village had to be other Indians. But who?

Josiah quietly rolled his sleeping furs off to one side, slipped on his winter moccasins, reached over and picked up his knife belt. Quietly rising so as not to awaken the others, he fastened it around his waist. Then once again, he quietly so as not to arouse his new found family from their sleep, picked up his rifle and silently slipped over to the flap covering the entrance to their tipi. Carefully peeping out through a small crack between the flap and the outside tipi cover in the pre-dawn light, Josiah spotted about thirty-five heavily-armed Indians quietly spreading throughout the center of the encampment in a crouched over sneaking position with their rifles at the ready! As the Mystery Indians sneaked through the encampment, they headed directly toward Old Chief Smoke's tipi, a tipi that was marked by an outside staff of eagle feathers firmly planted in the ground and fluttering quietly in the soft morning's breeze. A feathered staff signifying that the village's chief resided therein. Josiah did not recognize a single person in the early morning's feeble light but his instincts told him that an enemy of the Oglala had discovered their winter encampment. Not only had they been discovered, but the center of the camp was about to be overrun by a hostile group of raiders in a deadly early morning's winter raid! A raid being executed before the snows had gotten too deep to conduct any such deadly surprise activities! Josiah's heart raced as he realized he had to do something and quickly, or members of his tribe were soon to be overrun and killed in their own tipis as they slept!

Quietly slipping over to and placing his hand gently over Running Wolf's mouth as he slept, the surprised old man awoke with a start. Josiah pointed to his own lips for silence and then to the entrance of their tipi with the tip of his rifle barrel. After the old man had settled down from the surprise of being awakened in such a manner, he acknowledged Josiah's meaning with the pointed rifle barrel with a nod of his head. With that unusual act, Running Wolf was instantly alert. Then he quietly slipped out from his sleeping furs so as not to awaken his wife, reached over near the inside liner of his tipi, and grabbed his nearby Winchester rifle. Following that, he quietly sneaked over to the closed tipi entrance flap and looked out through a small opening so as not to show any sign of discovery to those raiders now flooding into the sacred circle of the camp's tipis. For just a moment, Running Wolf examined the sneaking warriors and then turned to Josiah with eyes showing great alarm!

"Pawnees!" he whispered into the ear of Josiah. "Enemy of the Sioux!" he continued, as he quietly cocked the hammer back on his lever action rifle by laying it against the side of his buckskin shirt to deaden the metallic 'click' of the hammer going back to full cock.

With those words, Josiah quietly but with the same urgency, slipped his tomahawk into his belt and placed five cold .45-70 cartridges into his mouth for instant retrieval and rapid reloading into his single shot rifle once the shooting started. Knowing he had his sixth and live round in his rifle's chamber, Josiah held his rifle against his buckskin shirt to deaden the sound and silently pulled its hammer back to full cock as well. Looking over at Running Wolf, Josiah told him in sign language to remain at the entrance of the tipi and fight from there. That way, he could provide cover and not be such an inviting target once the bullets started flying about. Then without a further word, Josiah quietly moved the tipi flap aside ever so slightly to see if any other Pawnees were still entering the camp from behind Running Wolf's tipi. None were in evidence, only those Pawnees who had since passed Running Wolf's outlying tipi.

It was apparent the main body of enemy warriors were heading for the center of the encampment positioned in a clump around Old Chief Smoke's tipi. From there, they could do the most damage once their deadly pre-dawn trap was sprung. Quietly slipping out from Running Wolf's tipi, Josiah quietly slipped in behind the Pawnee raiding party, sneaking in a crouched over position like he was one of their own. As he did, he found his mind's senses speeding up like it had when he had first realized his parent's wagon train was under Indian attack many months earlier! But now under the urgency of the moment just like back at his old wagon train during its fatal battle, his fighting and protective instincts were beginning to roar forth like a charging bull buffalo in rut!

Quietly sneaking up to the last Pawnee in line in the raiding party in the pre-dawn light, Josiah breathed in deeply, took the butt of his carbine, reared back, and with his full strength, smashed its stock forward into the back of that unsuspecting warrior's head! Crushing the man's skull, the blow felled him instantly! When the foreign crumping sound of that action was heard by the quietly sneaking raiders nearest Josiah, followed by the moaning groan of the dying man just struck, instant pandemonium reigned! THEY HAD BEEN DISCOVERED! The next closest Indian in the line of attackers spun around upon hearing the rifle butt's crunching sound on soft tissue and bone of the man behind him. He did so only to suffer Josiah's rifle butt being violently smashed into and deeply crushing the bones in his face and the frontal portion of his skull!

That man dropped into the soft bed of snow at his feet and moved no more as well. By then there was much yelling, shooting, awakened women screaming, and more shooting. One of those shooting was Josiah. He had since lined up two close-at-hand overlapping surprised Pawnees and fired his rifle into them from less than eight feet away.

The heavy lead .45-70 slug smashed through both men's torsos like an arrow through the side of an unsuspecting, small bodied deer. Both men dropped like a hawk in a stoop upon feeling the bullets' impact, as Josiah immediately dropped to his knees to reload and present a smaller target in the face of the now returning 'hailstorm' of bullets. When he did, a heretofore unseen Pawnee near Josiah rushed upon him with an upraised tomahawk, only to be felled with a shot from Running Wolf's rifle being fired from the tipi.

Now that everyone was wide awake and responding to the deadly menace at hand, the air was full of the sounds of metal bees as hot lead was flying everywhere! Quickly reloading, Josiah gut shot a Pawnee brave just feet away as he attempted to tomahawk the kneeling surprise-from-behind shooter. Then a bullet tore through the side of Josiah's buckskin shirt, leaving a bloody ten-inch long gash along his side! Fortunately, no ribs were broken when the bullet grazed by Josiah's side. But had that bullet been just an inch closer to his center of mass...Josiah, feeling the burning pain, winced and then continued reloading his rifle in the emotion, adrenaline dump, and desperation of the moment. That was when Running Wolf, seeing Josiah grazed by a bullet, left the security of the tipi, ran over and knelt protectively down at Josiah's side.

The old man then quickly shot another Pawnee as he tried to lance a still kneeling and reloading Josiah. From his kneeling position, Josiah fired as fast as he could with his single shot rifle into the now confused, bunched up and milling Pawnee war party. In doing so, the straight shooting Josiah, dropping other close at hand Pawnees with every bullet fired. Then Josiah was out of cartridges having expended his six allotted shells!

It was then that he saw a part of the battle taking place around Old Chief Smoke's tipi. The old chief and Tall Bull were fighting off five tomahawk swinging Pawnees all at once! Then the unthinkable happened! Tall Bull, sensing he was about to be overwhelmed and injured or killed, took off running away from the fight! And in doing so, left the old chief to face his five adversaries by himself! Josiah instantly saw red at such an act of cowardice!

Jumping to his feet and jerking the leather pouch in the same frenzied motion from around his neck, he jerked out and loaded the Great Spirit's special cartridge it carried into his now empty rifle. By now, the entire area was swirling with fighting Oglala and Pawnees locked in a desperate and deadly battle. As for Old Chief Smoke, he was swinging his tomahawk for all he was worth trying to keep his five assailants at bay, and losing ground in the process! Josiah took off running largely untouched through the melee of fighting men towards Old Chief Smoke. However, a large Pawnee warrior at the last moment leapt in front of Josiah part way through his rescue run. When he did, it was only to mortally 'eat' the stock of Josiah's rifle coming at him at a high rate of speed! Then Old Chief Smoke was knocked to the ground by a glancing blow to the side of his head with the flat side of a poorly swung tomahawk by a nearby Pawnee!

Arriving at the old chief's side the very next instant, Josiah swung his rifle high overhead and crashed it down onto the back of the head of a huge Pawnee warrior who was reaching over and about to tomahawk the downed chief. That Indian was dead before he fell and toppled over onto the top of the old chief! Then Josiah's "Great Spirit shot" rang out and the next Pawnee closest to the old chief with a poised-to-kill lance, was knocked asunder from the close in impact of the hard hitting .45-70 slug ripping and tearing through the vitals of his body! The remaining three braves sensing the danger the closeness Josiah represented, turned to face their new threat. In doing so, a small skinny warrior of the group was instantly brained by Josiah's now empty rifle violently swung in the emotion of the moment.

At that point in time, Josiah was in a towering killing rage like he had been at the battle of the Pike wagon train trying to defend his mother and sister...Letting go of his rifle which now had its stock sunken deeply into the side of the Pawnee's crushed skull, Josiah ripped out his tomahawk from his belt. Swinging it for all it was worth at a now quickly ducking Pawnee warrior to his front,

84

Josiah's tomahawk handle broke off as its blade was buried deeply almost out of sight into the heavy bone of that warrior's shoulder! That tomahawked Pawnee's scream rent the chill morning air in a high pitched shrieking-intensity that was heard even over the rest of the bedlam and noise of battle. Josiah's follow-up knife thrust to the tomahawked man's throat punctuated the man's scream and silenced his agony forever!

The last of the original five confronting Pawnees by Old Chief Smoke chose to flee, only to have the old chief from his position lying on the ground, sink his tomahawk deeply into the last assailant's left foot. Josiah's long-bladed knife soon took out the worry of that Pawnee over the pain he was now feeling, having the old chief's tomahawk painfully stuck deeply into the top bones of his foot...

Then a stream of Oglala warriors whose tipis were strung out along the creek further away, upon hearing the sounds of battle at the main encampment, began arriving into camp in deciding numbers. Soon the raiding Pawnee war party was outnumbered by the fierce fighting Oglala. And then there were none of the enemy left standing! And those Pawnee previously wounded and lying on the ground were quickly and violently dispatched...

Once the Pawnee raiding party was wiped out to a man and the danger was past, Josiah saw the skulking Tall Bull quietly trying to rejoin the fighters from the edge of the encampment like he had been there all along. Without a word, Josiah placed that ugly memory into the depths of his soul of a cowardly Tall Bull running away from the heat of the battle, especially when the old chief needed him the most. He figured someday, given the chance and the right opportunity, he would kill Tall Bull. Tall Bull the coward and the one who had fatally lanced his mother in the chest during the battle back at his family's wagon train! And if he did what he was thinking, he would gladly walk The Black Road to accomplish that which needed doing.

Then Josiah's mind cleared of that killing thought as more Oglala warriors arrived from their far-flung campsites up and down their encampment's creek. It was then that the ritual scalping, disfigurations, and amputations of the fallen enemies' appendages began. Josiah did not partake of any such rituals. He knew from his sessions with the elders that the ghost of a warrior who had died in battle and was mutilated would find himself wandering looking for those lost parts forever and not be allowed into The Happy Hunting Grounds.

That aside, Josiah just calmly retrieved his stuck rifle stock from the fallen Pawnee's crushed skull that he had killed earlier in the fight and wiped it off on the man's winter clothing. Following that, he retrieved his tomahawk's steel head stuck in the shoulder bone of another dead raider that he had struck in his frantic attempt to get past other fighters and rescue his imperiled chief. That took some time as he had to use his knife to dig the steel tomahawk head out of the Pawnee's shoulder bone. He figured the tomahawk's head could still be useful when another handle was fashioned into the steel, hence his effort in retrieval. And this time, Josiah would fashion the handle from a stout oak limb in case another like use for the tomahawk was in the offing. It was then that Josiah remembered the tomahawk's heritage. It had been Old Chief Smoke's grandfather's, one that had been used in many battles and upon his death had been passed on to a younger Old Chief Smoke. And now, it had been passed onto Josiah, who had just used it when he had to save Old Chief Smoke! Truly, the heritage of that special tomahawk had now just come full circle...

Then feeling an unexpected hand being laid on his shoulder, Josiah, still full of emotion from the battle, whirled to face Running Wolf. Running Wolf in turn advised Josiah that Old Chief Smoke wanted to speak to him. Josiah, still in the high killing emotion of the moment, walked stiffly over to the old chief. In turn, the old chief laid his hands on Josiah's shoulders like a thankful father would do to a good son for a deed well done. It was then that the old chief, looking into Josiah's eyes, observed just how piercing blue they were in the still lingering emotion of the moment...

"Thank you for helping me," said Old Chief Smoke.

Sliding his hand onto Josiah's arm, Old Chief Smoke then quietly led Josiah to his tipi. Motioning for him to wait outside near the staff full of eagle tail feathers, Old Chief Smoke entered his tipi. Moments later, he reemerged and in his hand was a beautifully beaded military canvas cartridge belt. Around the belt were loops filled with fifty .45-70 cartridges!

Handing the heavy belt to Josiah, the old chief said, "You no more are restricted to just six cartridges. Now you will be treated just like all the rest of my warriors because you have just become one by counting coup in battle with the killing an enemy." With that, Old Chief

Smoke turned and determinedly walked over to Tall Bull who was standing just a few yards away, still looking around to see if anyone had noticed his flight during the heat of battle.

Moments later, Old Chief Smoke sternly confronted Tall Bull. From his gestures and the looks on the coward's face, the old chief had harsh words for a now very humiliated-looking Tall Bull. And now being so publically humiliated, Tall Bull would strike out in any direction just like a wounded snake. Little did Josiah know just how close that "strike" would come and when...

Running Wolf and Josiah returned to his tipi to find Two Fists scared but safe. Outside on the near-at-hand battlefield, hell was having a field day...Much yelling and exaltation was in evidence as the mutilations of the fallen enemy continued and their bodies were stripped clean of any useful winter clothing or other useful items.

Pawnee's firearms were distributed throughout the band to those who did not possess a rifle or a handgun. Along with that went the previous owner's stores of ammunition. Shutting those horrific sounds from out of his still churning mind, Josiah returned to his restful sitting place inside Running Wolf's tipi. There he settled down and tried to come down from the emotional high still coursing throughout his veins. Once again, Josiah along with Running Wolf, felt the grace of heartfelt hugs from Two Fists.

Outside the tipi, the mutilated Pawnee dead were finally being roped together and dragged off by the village's mounted braves. There they were dumped in a deep ravine three-eighths of a mile away from camp. It was from that final resting place that the worst of the mutilations took place. The dead Pawnee were left for the wolves, grizzly and black bear not yet in hibernation, coyotes, and flesh-eating birds to consume. The rest of that wintery day, a celebration was held for the camp's survivors.

Several Oglala warriors had also been killed but the camp soon learned that because of the surprise and savagery of the attack from the rear of the enemy raiders by Josiah, the worst had not happened in the way of casualties.

As it turned out, when Josiah had attacked from the rear, the Pawnee's heads turned in surprise upon hearing his ominous presence in battle. About the time they did, the now alerted Oglala warriors awoke, streamed out from their tipis, and quickly joined the battle. In doing so, the Pawnees had not yet set up the final stage of their ambush designed to kill every Oglala warrior within the circle of tipis just as they emerged in surprise. If that plan had been successfully carried out, many more of Old Chief Smoke's warrior band would have been killed outright! As a result, Josiah's attack had sounded the alarm in time for most of the camp's occupants to not be totally surprised in battle by the hated Pawnee.

In that battle, Josiah had personally and savagely accounted for the deaths of thirteen Pawnees! When Old Chief Smoke heard of the number of dead that Josiah had killed, he just smiled. Now he knew why the Great Spirit had visited him and had the old chief save Josiah from certain death in battle back at the wagon train. Then the old chief remembered there were several more parts to that vision he had received that had yet to come true…

The rest of that afternoon Josiah just rested. Two Fists had cleaned out his shallow but painful side wound, smeared the wound with an evil-smelling concoction and then had stitched it closed so it could heal. Josiah felt he would be more at peace with himself if he just took the rest of the time that day to reflect over the morning's events, settle down his still racing emotions, and thank the Great Spirit for bringing him through the battle alive. However, in the eyes and hearts of the rest of Old Chief Smoke's band, there was one more thing of importance to be remembered. Josiah had counted coup thirteen times in that battle with the Pawnee! In the eyes of many of the band, captive white man or not, Josiah was now considered a great warrior! And as such, many now wanted to be associated with Josiah in any number of ways. That was because in true Oglala fashion, the status of anyone was enhanced when they were associated with such an example of an outstanding warrior.

Awakening with a start the morning after the great battle with the hated Pawnee, Josiah discovered that Running Wolf was not in his sleeping furs. Two Fists was still sleeping but Running Wolf was nowhere to be seen. Josiah hurriedly pulled on his leggings and winter moccasins, grabbed up his knife, ammunition belt, and rifle. Then so as not to arouse and worry Two Fists, he quietly slipped out from the tipi. Looking around in the semi-darkness of the winter morning's white wilderness enveloping the camp, he at first saw nothing. Then he spotted the barely discernable figure of a man returning from the direction of the band's horse herd located at the head of their valley.

Continuing to watch the approaching lone figure, Josiah soon identified that man to be none other than Running Wolf. Minutes later, Running Wolf quietly approached Josiah in the freshly fallen snow trailing a beautiful looking roan stallion. Josiah, having been raised on a farm around many breeds of domestic animals, quickly realized the high-spirited roan had to be a special kind of horse. Especially if Running Wolf, who was recognized as the band's premier horseman, was himself leading such a fine looking specimen of an animal.

Stopping in front of Josiah, Running Wolf said, "What do you think Josiah? Is this the kind of horse that any warrior would love to own?"

Josiah laid his rifle against the side of the tipi and walked over to the spirited animal with a keen examining eye. As he did, the horse carefully looked Josiah over as he approached with suspicion as well. First checking the animal's teeth, then his legs and finally running his hand over the animal's withers, Josiah said, "It is a beautiful horse. Are you going somewhere this morning?"

Running Wolf let his eyes leave Josiah for a moment and standing a little off to one side of the stead, quietly and reverently appeared to be breathing in the horse's innate strength and beauty. Then placing his hand under the horse's jaw, Running Wolf raised its head slightly and breathed two quick breaths into the trusting animal's flared nostrils. Little did Josiah realize that was Running Wolf's way of transferring his power as a warrior into the horse because of what he was doing and about to do. With that almost sacred moment between Running Wolf and the horse, Josiah detected a deep love and attachment between the man and beast that was almost magical if not mystical. Then Running Wolf said, "This was my last buffalo horse." Then after the longest time in the early morning's snowy silence, he continued once again.

"A buffalo horse is a very special gift from the Great Spirit. He is as fast and quick reacting as is an alarmed bull buffalo. When one is hunting buffalo, it can be very dangerous. The buffalo is very unpredictable, especially when being pursued or chased. If a brave or warrior is not careful and well seated upon a buffalo horse, he runs the risk of being unseated, gored or knocked down and trampled under the hooves of the stampeding buffalo."

When Running Wolf uttered those words, Josiah remembered his teachings from the elders. *"A 'brave' is an Indian who has not yet counted coup. A 'warrior' is one who has counted coup."* Then Running Wolf continued his early morning lesson. "If one has such a horse under him who is always alert to the ways of a buffalo, no matter how hard the beast tries to injure the hunter or run away, a buffalo horse will never be fooled by such actions.

"A buffalo horse is very valuable and will always bring the hunter safely home from the hunt. An Oglala hunter with just such a fine horse can ride like the wind with the reins held in his teeth and his rifle or bow and arrow held in both hands. He guides such an animal with just the slightest touch of his knees and the horse, reading the buffalo's temperament and the hunter's senses through the pressure of his knees, will provide for the hunter's success. This horse was my last buffalo horse and is one of the best I have ever ridden or owned. In the right hands, this horse will lead one into battle or on a dangerous buffalo hunt. And in doing so, bring the warrior home to his tipi safely with much glory or meat to show for his effort at the end of the day."

With those words, Running Wolf paused as if trying to find and say his next and right words.

"I am now getting too old and my bones will not allow me to go on any more buffalo hunts. All I have that is left of me is this horse and the memories of a very old man. I am giving this horse to you because you are such a great warrior and need a horse who will carry you safely like the wind across the waving prairie grasses."

With those words, Running Wolf quietly handed the reins to a very surprised Josiah. Then casting his mist-filled eyes downward, Running Wolf left Josiah and his new buffalo horse to get acquainted. It was at that very moment, Josiah realized Running Wolf was admitting to himself that he was no longer useful as a distinguished warrior and was now going to live out the remainder of his days as the Great Spirit so dictated...

Standing there in surprise over what had just occurred with the animal's reins in his hands, Josiah looked over his new horse once again. The horse in turn, as if almost physically feeling the events of the renouncement of a warrior's life now dimmed by the ravages of time, stood trembling in the winter morning's cold looking over his new owner as well.

Then Running Wolf, having quickly and stoically settled with his inner self over now being relegated to that of an old man of questionable worth, exited his tipi in full control of his emotions. With him he carried a well-worn cavalry saddle and bridle. One in which he had personally killed its owner in a previous battle and had claimed the items as a trophy of that feat.

Handing the equipment to Josiah, he said in a matter of fact way, "Two Fists has breakfast ready for us. Unless you want that woman to use a stick on our heads for not heeding her words, I would suggest we go and eat before it gets cold. But first, make sure your new horse is securely tied off so he doesn't wander off back to the horse herd."

With those words of wisdom, Josiah tied off the horse to the McClellan saddle laying on the ground and then the two men entered the tipi for breakfast.

For the rest of that day and into the following week, Josiah and his new buffalo horse spent many wonderful hours and glorious miles reeling by underfoot as they got used to one another. In no time, Josiah realized his new horse was equal to or even better than his father's valuable quarter horse back on their old farm in Missouri. Josiah had decided to name his horse "Wind." He did so because of the physically effortless ride the animal gave its rider plus his ability to move like his name sake. In those "getting to know each other" travels, Josiah quickly learned the horse underneath him was very unusual.

Wind was extremely sure footed, always alert to any movement in his surroundings, very responsive to Josiah's slightest knee pressure on his sides as to which way to turn, highly intelligent, fast as the strike of a prairie rattlesnake when it came to his responsive movement when surprised, and almost miraculously cognizant of where Josiah's center of gravity was while sitting in the saddle at all times...When Josiah shifted his weight in the saddle, Wind moved his center of gravity accordingly so as not to spill Josiah from his saddle, a trait not found except in the very best of horses.

Soon Josiah had trained Wind to come or react to his hand signals or whistle when he was away from the saddle and out on foot. In fact, Wind seemed to almost enjoy the new learning exercises and relationship he was going through as the two 'animals' bonded together. Within a month of daily contact, man and horse were as one as was buffalo meat and wild onions bubbling merrily away in a cast iron pot over an open fire...

"BUFFALO, BUFFALO," yelled an Oglala brave as he sped into camp on his lathered up horse and acting as the village crier. "Buffalo, just a short ride from here. Gather up your rifles and let us go and replenish our meat supplies," he continued. Soon the entire encampment was ablaze with human activity. Men hurried to and from retrieving their horses from the herd, putting on their winter clothing and checking their arms and ammunition.

Having buffalo that close to camp was considered a blessing from The Great Spirit and everyone dreaming of fresh meat made ready just as fast as they could. In the meantime, several members from a warrior society and hunters of renown, began organizing the hunt so a maximum kill could be made. Soon thirty men had assembled for the buffalo hunt as they awaited for their assignments from the hunt's organizers. Moments later, the men had been divided into two groups. One group would confront the buffalo as they fed and kill as many as they could. And in doing so, eventually push the herd into rifle range of the remaining hunters laying in ambush further along the trail of the stampeding herd being pushed their way.

As the two bunches of hunters separated and streamed off to their assigned places, Josiah found himself and his new horse in the group of ambush hunters. Riding to the far head of their valley, those hunters then rode over the nearby line of ridges ringing the open plains and secreted themselves in the many draws draining those rolling foothills. Those hunters tasked with initially pushing the buffalo into those awaiting to ambush the great beasts were now confronting the surprised buffalo. The faint sounds of distant shooting and then the earth rumbling with the sounds of thousands of thundering hooves from the fleeing herd coming their way could now be felt and heard. Minutes later, a brown blanket of steaming from the cold, rumbling, heavily breathing buffalo, could be seen off in the distance coming their way.

The ambush hunters' hearts raced and their steads shuffled their feet nervously about knowing what was coming next. Then it was time to spring the ambush! Out from the gullies where they had been lying in wait streamed a line of horseflesh and humanity. Into the side of the fast moving stream of the shaggy rumbling beasts who were now turning away from the new perceived danger, the hunters rode with an intensity borne on the wings of need. Josiah quickly found himself alongside a cow buffalo and with the reins held in his teeth, shoved the end of his .45-70 carbine just inches away from the side of the great beast to a spot just behind the shoulder and pulled the trigger.

With the roar of his rifle, the buffalo stumbled and then fell, rolling head over heels in a cloud of flying snow and dirt clods. Wind, in order to avoid the falling and flailing dying buffalo, quickly moved off to one side so as not to be hit by the falling beast. Then as if buttressed by a long ago practiced memory, Wind moved up alongside the next running buffalo with its heaving flanks from the long run and Josiah repeated his earlier feat. That time, the buffalo dropped straight away to the ground and with his flying now lifeless feet and legs, almost tripped up Wind. However, Josiah's buffalo horse had been there before and just instinctively reacted and jumped over the flailing legs without hesitation. Still holding the reins in his teeth, Josiah snapped open the trap door mechanism of his single shot rifle, grabbed another live cartridge from his belt, reloaded, snapped the trap door mechanism shut and pulled his hammer to full cock, all in several fluid motions. It was then that he realized Wind had already placed him alongside his next hard running buffalo. An animal whose bulging, white-lined eyes betrayed its abject terror!

Then from his left side another horse and rider slammed hard into the side of Wind, almost knocking Josiah and his horse into the streaming sides of the stampeding buffalo! Fortunately Wind, feeling the weight shifting of a surprised Josiah from the unexpected collision, adjusted his stride accordingly. In doing so, making sure his body was directly under a now knocked-slightly-off-center Josiah. Then Wind, feeling the recovery of Josiah in the saddle and the closeness of the nearest buffalo, slipped off further to the left away from the plunging danger of the herd and directly behind the running horse that had slammed into him. It was then that Josiah realized the horse and rider that had slammed into his blind side was none other than Tall Bull! Josiah then realized the collision was no accident!

Tall Bull had intentionally slammed into the blind side of Wind in a vain attempt to unseat his rider! And in doing so, tossing him fatally under the hooves of the stampeding herd of buffalo! A rider who would be ground to muddy dirt under the flying hooves of the stampeding buffalo in an instant once he dropped onto the ground after being unhorsed!

Regaining his composure, Josiah looked forward at Tall Bull as he tried to flee his failed destructive effort of the much hated captive white man. Tall Bull was looking back at Josiah to see if he had been successful in unhorsing him and realizing he hadn't, now had a look of concern on his face! Josiah realizing what he was facing, quickly checked the status of his fully-cocked his rifle with the intention of killing Tall Bull right then and there! Then the Great Spirit in all his wisdom intervened. Come the next moment in time, fate was in full bloom…

Tall Bull's horse stepped into an unseen prairie dog burrow's entrance and did a complete, violent head roll, as one of his front legs dropped deeply down into the hole and then snapped off at the knee! When Tall Bull's horse rolled, it tossed Tall Bull onto the shoulders of a bull buffalo in the herd of panicked beasts! For a moment, Tall Bull tried hanging onto the long shaggy shoulder hair of the madly fleeing bull buffalo. Then with a scream barely audible over the sounds of thousands of pounding hooves, Tall Bull lost his precarious handhold and disappeared beneath the bobbing stream of shaggy beasts and their thousands of sets of pulverizing hooves…

In the meantime, Wind had now placed Josiah alongside another buffalo. Snapping back from his "red of vengeance" over what Tall Bull had just tried to do to him and quickly realizing his nemesis was no more, Josiah calmly killed another buffalo. And once again, Wind quickly moved away from the flailing hooves and legs of a buffalo doing its head-over-heels death roll. Ten minutes more of killing and the herd was no more. No more because it had moved beyond easy retrieval distance for the villagers and their encampment.

Riding back with several other exalting hunters who had not observed Tall Bull's murderous actions, Josiah recognized the sloping end of a hill where his enemy had taken his final ride on the shoulders of a stampeding bull buffalo. Slowing and then riding Wind over into the brown looking pulverized earthen trail outlining the path the massive herd had taken in the snow, he began his search. All Josiah could find of Tall Bull's horse were bits and pieces. The rest of that animal was no longer as it had been pounded into the wet mud of Mother Earth. Any sign of Tall Bull did not exist since several thousand of the shaggy beasts had run over his body. And in doing so, had pounded it into the very earth on which Wind now stood.

After a long moment of looking for Tall Bull's remains and finding nothing, Josiah smiled. He did not have to walk The Black Road after all...The Great Spirit had chosen to remove Tall Bull and his black heart all by himself. And had done so with the buffalo herd when Tall Bull had shown by his earthly actions, that he was unworthy of continued life. And in doing so, Josiah was thankful. He was going to kill Tall Bull for killing his mother and for what he had done to Josiah the captive over his many previous months of life. But now, all that was behind him. He could now walk The Red Road in his life and not be bothered with thoughts of The Black Road when it came to Tall Bull. However, there was still the matter of an evil Red Shirt and how that matter was to be resolved. Little did Josiah realize that the Great Spirit had already set into motion a series of events that would soon address that issue as well.

That evening back at the winter encampment there was a great celebration over the successful buffalo hunt, especially when streams of dog and horse-drawn travois labored back into camp loaded with mounds of still steaming buffalo meat in the cold winter's air. To aid in the meat processing, almost the entire village had turned out to complete the process and guarantee that all had a goodly portion of their winter stores of meat on hand or at least being prepared. And that stream of meat did not stop arriving until later in the evening. Now there would be an abundance of winter meat stores for the whole tribe to enjoy. And in the process, Josiah made sure the oldest and most infirm of the camp's inhabitants had all they needed of the fresh meat, including Tall Bull's parents who were now without a meat supplier or main provider...

Come dark after Josiah had made sure Running Wolf's and Two Fists' unprepared meat stores were hung high enough up off the ground in the trees so that the camp's always hungry dogs could not get at it, he retired to their tipi for the evening. There as Two Fists moved around the cooking fire preparing the men's supper, Josiah shared with Running Wolf an account of the day's events. Running Wolf was happy over his buffalo horse's performance, especially when Wind had recovered so quickly after being so viciously and deliberately slammed into from the blind side by Tall Bull's horse. Then Running Wolf got intensely quiet as if something was tugging at his soul.

"My Son. You are now responsible for Tall Bull's parents. They are very old and infirm. With their son and main provider gone, they will be forced to ask for help or depend on the generosity of others. That is OK when times are good and food is plentiful. But when times are bad, Tall Bull's parents may have slim times as well. They are now your responsibility and I expect that you will help them as you have us for as long as they live. Now, let us hear no more about what has happened this day. It is now for the most part a moment lost to only the Cloud People knowing what has happened and the Great Spirit. I will see to it that Old Chief Smoke knows what happened to one of his warriors since he will now be missed by his obvious absence. Now we will utter the name of the dead no more. Because to do so, will cause their ghosts to linger in this world and sometimes when they do, they can do evil things to those of us left behind."

Two Fists served a wonderful buffalo stew that evening and they all feasted until they could eat no more. After a good night's rest, the next few days were crowded with hide preparation, smoking of hides, drying of meat, and the making of extra utensils from buffalo horns so Josiah could be more easily accommodated in Running Wolf's tipi come meal time. And when the winter winds howled and the deep snows blanketed the village, much work was done in the repairing of the old and manufacturing of new clothing. When it really got bitter out reducing any visiting between the clans, Josiah quietly worked on the building and shaping of a new oaken handle to replace the broken one on his tomahawk, the one he had snapped off when he had tomahawked the Pawnee warrior in the recent battle. The one that had come full circle in saving the old chief's life...

Chapter Five

SUMMER CAMP, DEATH, A 'NEW FRIEND', 'BIRTH' OF TWO WARRIORS

Come late April of that year, Old Chief Smoke and the elders met. It was at that council that it was decided the winter camp would be moved to their newest summer quarters. Moved because the horse feed was waning, wood hauling trips were now far distant since the close at hand firewood had already been utilized, sanitation was becoming a burning issue, and the village in general was historically ready for a change in location.

On the allotted moving day, the tipis were quickly disassembled, travois for dogs and horses assembled and loaded, and the valuable horse herd was rounded up and brought closer into camp. The little children, old people and the infirm typically rode on top of the travois. The healthy either walked or rode and the braves and warriors rode at the head and sides of the long dusty column for the protection they offered against the unforeseen. There was much talking, laughter, and barking of camp dogs, as Old Chief Smoke's caravan of humanity and horseflesh lined out and moved along toward their new summer encampment.

Earlier, Josiah had personally seen to it that Running

Wolf and Two Fists' travois were loaded and ready to go. He had also assisted Two Fawns and his sister Gemma, as well as Tall Bull's old and infirm parents. He did so for Tall Bull's parents because it was the right thing to do in his eyes and because Running Wolf had earlier so instructed. Since two of the three of those families had no young men around to help, Josiah happily provided his assistance. Some of the band's warriors chided Josiah for doing women's work in preparation for the move but he just grinned. He had and was being raised in two different cultures and where one prevented such menial work, the other culturally allowed it. So, Josiah did as he pleased and the respect for his ethic and industry continued to grow in the eyes of the people in the village.

As it turned out, Old Chief Smoke eventually moved the encampment about forty miles to the east in ten to fifteen-mile daily stages. That way, the camp would be within an easy day's ride of other like camps within the Sioux Nation and come summer, they could easily partake of all the other village inter-tribal dances, visits among friends in different clans, and finally, in the culmination of the summer's celebrations, the Sun Dance. The Sun Dance was a huge celebration in which numerous bands of Sioux would gather at a sacred central meeting place, construct the Sun Dance arena and then the proving of the young braves sacrifice and thanksgiving could be tested to its limits for the good of the whole tribe.

Then tragedy struck right in the heart of the happy times while moving to their summer encampment! Rounding a low, heavily brush covered hill, the close-at-hand caravan surprised a sow grizzly bear and her three cubs feeding on fresh green grass by a spring! The sow instantly charged and attacked the nearest travois and its older rider riding on top. The travois selected for the attack by the enraged sow grizzly defending her cubs just so happened to be Running Wolf's! Before she could move, Two Fists' head was grabbed in the jaws by the enraged mother bear and her tiny body was shaken so violently, that she was dead before she hit the ground!

Running Wolf, upon seeing the charging grizzly bear heading for his travois, rode from his position at the edge of the caravan firing his Winchester wildly into the air. He did so in the hopes of distracting the great bear as it ran towards Two Fists' travois. Running Wolf's attempt was in vain, as the bear slammed undeterred into Two Fists and delivered a killing bite anyway. As the rest of the nearby travelers and their horses scattered in terror, Running Wolf kept at his hard riding charge right at the enraged bear. Then almost as if the Great Spirit had planned the whole tragic event all along, tragedy struck for the second time in a matter of seconds.

Running Wolf's hard charging race across the prairie floor brought about his downfall! His horse stepped into a black-tailed prairie dog burrow, snapped off its leg and head-rolled in a violent explosion of horse, dust and flying rider. Running Wolf, because of the instantaneous headlong crash of his horse, had no time to react by stepping out from his stirrups or steel himself for the impending impact his body was about to take. He hit the ground with such a force of impact that his body was later discovered shattered in many places when he was later attended to. He died an hour later, never regaining consciousness. As for the revered and much feared sow grizzly, after she had proven her point, she was allowed to quickly retreat with her cubs none the worse for wear. The Indians, realizing why the sow had charged so violently, chose not to kill her because of her cubs. To do so under such circumstances while she was in the act of protecting her young, the villagers feared, would bring down the wrath of the Great Spirit for such subsequent killing endeavors.

To those witnessing the fatal charge on Two Fists' and Running Wolf's violent wreck, most considered it a sign that the Great Spirit had spoken. Both now deceased members of the tribe were old and infirm. To the band's way of thinking, that was the Great Spirit's way of allowing Running Wolf and Two Fists to travel to the Happy Hunting grounds together and join the rest of the Cloud People as husband and wife. Josiah riding guard at the rear of the caravan, was hurriedly fetched. Racing to the scene, he soon realized there was nothing he could do. However, he did cradle Running Wolf's broken and bloody body in his arms until it was apparent the old warrior and recently adoptive father, had passed. With tears streaming unashamedly down his face, Josiah lifted the broken body of his adopted father and placed him next to the love of his life, Two Fists. Then walking over to Wind and holding onto the saddle horn, he cried like he had when he had come-to after the fight at his parent's wagon train. Especially after he had realized that he was a captive and that all of his much loved family and the rest of his relatives were now no more...

Old Chief Smoke had his people gently wrap Running

Wolf and Two Fists bodies together in a tanned buffalo skin and placed high up in the forks of a cottonwood tree, the Sioux Nation's sacred tree of life. The items they needed for the next life were removed from the travois and neatly left around the base of the burial tree for their trip into the next world—that was, except for Running Wolf's much loved 1873 Winchester. The old chief gave that rifle to a grieving Josiah as a loving remembrance of his adoptive father. Then the old chief had several of his warriors throw ropes around Running Wolf's now dead riding horse and drag it over to the bottom of the burial tree. He did so because Running Wolf would need a good riding horse in the next world. After the burial of old friends, the village sadly moved on to their new summer encampment site. And in doing so, never spoke of the recent dead ever again. This they did because their belief was that the more one mentioned the dead, the longer they would wander and linger aimlessly in the land between Mother Earth and the Happy Hunting Grounds.

Josiah remained at the site of the burial tree for the rest of that afternoon and throughout the night. He hurt inside so badly that the tears hardly ever stopped flowing. The full of sprit and wise Running Wolf had been like Josiah's loving biological father. And in turn, Josiah had come to love Running Wolf like his own father. As for Two Fists, Josiah remembered the first hug he had with her. A total stranger, but her hug was so meaningful that Josiah found himself flashing back to the days in which his biological mother had lived and loved. Now Josiah had lost two sets of parents and began to doubt the professed love and wisdom the Great Spirit had for his people...

The following morning after quietly sitting under the burial platform in the cottonwood tree all night, Josiah bade his adopted parents good bye, mounted Wind and planned on never looking back on a wonderful life that could have been. Then remembering The Way as previously taught by the tribal elders, Josiah returned to the burial site, dismounted, took his .45-70 carbine, his cartridge belt, extra cartridges, and placed them high up in the cottonwood tree within the burial robe for Running Wolf's use in his next life.

Taking Running Wolf's 1873 Winchester, Josiah placed it into the rifle scabbard on Wind. With that and a hopeful look towards the rising sun in the east, the source of light and understanding, Josiah sprang back into the saddle of Wind. His time of mourning finished, he began following the well-marked trail his village had left as they continued on their journey towards the happiness of their next summer encampment.

When Josiah arrived later at the site of the summer encampment, he discovered Running Wolf's and Two Fists' tipi set up in the village's circle of life with all the other tipis. Dismounting, entering and looking inside, Josiah discovered it was barren of all things except his sleeping furs, a few personal items and a single, heavily beaded leather pouch. Not recognizing the pouch, Josiah walked over and lifted it up for a better look.

In doing so, he discovered it was extremely heavy. Opening up the flap and looking in, he discovered it was almost clear full of the heavy hitting .44-40 cartridges for his new 1873 Winchester! Then he remembered Running

Wolf's story as to how he came to be the big Winchester's owner. In his next to last fight as a warrior, he had killed a cavalry officer who was using the Winchester. He had claimed that man's rifle, saddle, horse and bridle as his. Later as his band of victorious warriors stripped the dead of any useful items, they also raided the Army supply wagon that had been accompanying the small detachment of unfortunate soldiers. Therein Running Wolf had discovered a case of .44-40 cartridges that were for the dead officer's Winchester. Those he had taken as well since he was now the Winchester's new owner.

Standing there in the quiet and semi-dark of his tipi, Josiah realized someone had been aware of that story and had saved the cartridges from being placed at the burial site. As a result of that thoughtful action, Josiah would have many cartridges for his new rifle. Then it dawned on him. The Great Spirit had given him a "special" extra .45-70 cartridge when he had first received his old trap door Springfield carbine of the same caliber.

As it turned out, that 'special' cartridge had been used to save Old Chief Smoke from certain death in the winter battle against the hated Pawnees! Now he had a large leather pouch full of cartridges for his new rifle. Cartridges that would have been hard to get on the frontier for an Indian, unless one ran across another individual who also had one of the new, like-in-caliber, Winchesters. Had the Great Spirit intervened once again with a sign involving that pouch of cartridges?

Little did Josiah realize at that moment in time that a bullet from one of those cartridges would eventually find itself shot clear through the side of one of the Sioux Nation's greatest adversaries in a battle The People had won. A battle that in the long run, The People would ultimately lose...Then his daydreaming ended and the reality of the moment quickly returned. Once again, Josiah found himself alone in his tipi with little in hand other than a few personal items and good memories, along with many questions as to what his future would now bring...

Early the next morning, Josiah left his tipi and headed for the stream near their summer camp. Finding a clear pool, he washed up and dried himself off with hands full of sweet grass growing nearby. Loving the fragrance the sweet grass gave, Josiah dressed and began currying down his horse. Remembering the love Running Wolf had for that horse, Josiah soon found heavy tears unashamedly streaming down his cheeks and staining the front of the buckskin shirt. It was then through heavily misted eyes, that he noticed Old Chief Smoke slowly walking his way. Not wanting to show any sign of weakness, Josiah wiped his tears away with the sleeve of his buckskin shirt. As it turned out, the last shirt Two Fists had lovingly made for him because his previous shirt was so tattered and worn...

When the old chief arrived, he bade Josiah a good morning with a nod of his head and then said, "Josiah, eight of the horses in the village's herd now belong to you. Its previous owner no longer has any use for them, so, they are now yours. I have staked them near your tipi and I suggest that you make your mark on them so others will know that they belong to you."

Josiah could not hardly believe that he now had

valuable horses and then the realization set in. Running Wolf had horses and it now appeared that Old Chief Smoke had decided those horses would now pass on to Josiah. Especially since he had been so loving and caring for his previous adoptive parents. With those words being said, Old Chief Smoke walked back to his tipi in the encampment and disappeared inside without another word being spoken to anyone. Watching the old chief shuffle away, Josiah could sense that something important was on his mind. Something that the old chief found as a heavy burden or a question in life yet unanswered. Little did Josiah realize that the old chief was thinking about the prophetic vision he had received many moons earlier before the fight at the wagon train.

In that vision, everything had come true except for the fact that the man saved, namely Josiah, was to become the old chief's son. And that the white man saved, would go on to become a great Oglala warrior someday. Little did either man realize another part of that vision the old chief had earlier received was about to come true as well. Come true after a selfless act performed by a brave Josiah that would catapult him upward in the eyes of the entire Oglala band and eventually the entire Sioux Nation once the story was retold many times around tipi fires. And as that story was retold, the words that he was a "great warrior" began crossing many people's lips regardless of the fact that he was a captured white man now living with the Oglala!

Returning to his tipi, Josiah observed eight splendid and spirited horses staked nearby. Figuring those were the eight horses the old chief had spoken to him about, Josiah began closely examining them. Every horse was an excellent looking stead. All were healthy as all get out and as fine a piece of horseflesh as he had ever seen. Then remembering Running Wolf's reputation for being the best horseman in the village, he had to smile. Four of the horses were marked with the "US" brand stamped on their right flanks. Those horses had obviously been taken from cavalry troopers in battle or stolen from their horse herds when the troopers weren't looking. The other four horses looked to be officer's horses. Horses which Josiah figured, based on his judgment of the evident lines of their fine breeding, had been previously commercially purchased by those officers. They were obviously not the normally heavy-bodied, stout cavalry horses commonly issued and ridden by the enlisted men. But those four horses were showing the fine lines of good breeding. Plus, those remaining four horses carried normal civilian brands. Then remembering the old chief's words of instruction on marking the horses, Josiah clipped all their manes in an unusual manner that identified his animals from all the others in the herd. Mounting Wind, Josiah trailed the eight horses back to the main horse herd and let them loose to feed, water and frolic.

Returning from the horse herd, Josiah observed a heavy-bodied buck mule deer still in velvet in a stream side thicket. After a short stalk, Josiah shot and killed the same with his new Winchester. Gutting out the animal, he hoisted it over the back of Wind and then the two of them walked back to the village. There he removed the two back straps and then shared half the remaining deer with Two Fawns and his sister. The remaining half of the deer went to Tall Bull's aging parents as he had been instructed to do by Running Wolf when he was still alive.

That evening, he roasted a small portion of the deer meat over his small fire in the tipi since he now had no cooking pots or other implements. No cooking pots or other implements, since they had been left at the base of the burial site of Running Wolf and Two Fists for their trip to the afterlife. Then he retired to his sleeping furs with memories of happier times with Running Wolf and Two Fists dancing in his head. Finally darkness overtook him as he laid there with a heavy heart once again.

Josiah awakened later the following morning to the yelling of the village crier as he ran through the camp. "BUFFALO–BUFFALO! EVERYONE GET UP AND GET READY. BUFFALO JUST OVER THE RISE AT THE NORTH END OF CAMP. BUFFALO–BUFFALO! EVERYONE GET UP!" he yelled. Seconds later, the village looked like someone had turned over a hive of bees! Men were scrambling for their horses, children were rounding up the larger dogs and tying travois poles onto them so they could help in bringing back to camp the meat from the soon to be kills. Women were all doing the same when it came to hooking up their horses to their travois so they could haul even more meat. Within moments from hearing the welcome words of the close-at-hand buffalo, the camp was in full activity—animated celebration of the anticipated moment in time and the fresh meat and welcome durable hides that would follow.

Josiah hurriedly scrambled out from under his sleeping furs, put on his moccasins, strapped on his belt and knife, loaded extra cartridges into a smaller pouch carried on his waist and picked up his Winchester. Out the tipi flap he went dragging his saddle in one hand and the bridle with his coveted Winchester in his other hand. Laying down the rest of his gear and grabbing only his bridle, Josiah ran toward the horse herd whistling loudly his "come here" call for Wind as he ran forward. Moments later, here came Wind towards him at a dead run after hearing the familiar identifying whistle.

The earlier training Josiah had done with Wind was now paying off. While other Indians were still rounding up their favorite hunting horses, Josiah was leading his horse back to his tipi. Once there, Wind was saddled and Josiah loaded his new rifle's tubular magazine full of shells, until the rifle carried fifteen heavy blunt-nosed .44-40 cartridges. Then mounting his horse, Josiah rode to the center of the village where the warrior society hunt organizers were planning out their strategy on how best to ambush the buffalo for the greatest kill. As it turned out, Josiah and Wind were the second ones ready to gather in the center of the village in preparation for the hunt. Sitting quietly on his horse, Old Chief Smoke made a mental note of Josiah arriving first over even his best warriors…

Soon the hunters were divided among two groups. One group would confront the feeding buffalo at the east end of their valley and begin the hunt by shooting and pushing the herd towards the other group of assembled ambush hunters to the west. Hunters who would lay waiting in ambush until the stampeding buffalo were pushed their way. Then when the moment was right, they would emerge from their places of hiding and slam headlong into the side of the fast moving herd. And in doing so, kill as many as they could and in the same fluid motion, attempt to turn the herd back into the original bunch of pursuing hunters for another opportunity for them to kill as many as they could. A clever plan if it worked out but it could be a dangerous one as well. Especially when one considered that the hunters would be confronting panicked animals, some of which weighed up to a ton and stood seven feet at the shoulder! Additionally, Josiah had discovered early on that buffalo go in the direction they want, not necessarily in the direction someone else wants them to go. Plus the memory of what had happened to Tall Bull on an earlier buffalo hunt, was still fresh in the minds of many who had learned the story sometime after the fact...

The hunt organizers took one half of the hunters and quickly headed out. The other bunch of hunters who were going to set up the ambush at the western end of the valley, sped away shortly thereafter. Once again, Josiah found himself in with the bunch of ambush hunters. Racing down along the creek bottoms and up over the nearby rolling hills, the ambush hunters soon set up in their chosen hidden positions in the brushy thickets at the edge of the prairie. Then hiding out of sight, they quietly waited as their horses rested. Off in the distance, shooting could be faintly heard to the east of their positions.

Shortly thereafter, the familiar thundering rumble of a large spooked herd of buffalo on the run could be heard. With that sound of thousands of rumbling hooves getting ever louder, everyone's heart rate went up in anticipation of the action soon to follow. Presently, fresh buffalo meat, hides, warm raw liver eaten from the side of a fallen buffalo on the prairie, and roasted fatty intestines, would grace many hungry stomachs, meat racks, and cooking pots.

The low thundering rumbling vibrations of the now close at hand oncoming stampeding buffalo were soon being transmitted up through the nervous horse's trembling legs and into the seated riders. As those heard rumblings were transmitted into fast moving moments of time, the ambush hunters, like their horses, waited in high anticipation of what was soon to come. AND THEN, THERE THEY WERE! A carpet of rumbling shaggy beasts with their familiar loping gait thundered into view. A view that displayed a rising cloud of dust and a blanket of dark brown movement that stretched about mile wide with no end in sight! Then the horde of great beasts were upon those hunters waiting in ambush!

Into the moving edge of that swirl of passing buffalo streamed a line of horseflesh and quietly determined humanity. Only the Great Spirit could have conjured up such a moving stream of soon-to-be brown mounds of death splashed across the golden grasses of the prairie. Sliding alongside the heaving flanks of a buffalo showing signs of being winded, Wind positioned Josiah for a killing shot. One shot behind the animal's shoulder from his Winchester immediately dropped the buffalo under the feet of those animals that were jammed nose-to-tail and closely following. Instantly, there was an explosion of colliding and crashing to the ground stumbling and falling animals. Those buffalo stumbling to the ground over the downed buffalo to their front just shot by Josiah, were run over by those shaggy beasts streaming up from behind who were too close to turn away from the pileup! Wind expertly moved away from the tremendous pileup of the beasts and quickly moved up alongside another cow to his front.

Josiah, now in concert with the movement of his horse and the rhythm of the hunt, levered in another cartridge and once again dumped another buffalo with one shot. Feeling the bullet's deadly impact, that buffalo spun off to one side, and in the process, almost knocked Wind off his feet with an unintentional falling brush block. But Wind quickly recovered as Josiah levered another heavy stubby .44-40 cartridge into the Winchester's chamber. Josiah's buffalo horse then quickly sprinted up alongside another massive bull buffalo weighing at least a ton and standing over seven feet at the shoulder! However, that buffalo was angry and dangerous over being stampeded and now being approached alongside by a mounted horseman. Instantly, he flipped his head dangerously off to one side and almost gored Josiah's horse! Wind would have been gored, if he hadn't learned from previous buffalo hunting experiences and anticipated such a move.

With his gained buffalo hunting experience during such previous dangerous circumstances, Wind quickly moved out of harm's way! Moving up once more alongside the great beast and this time before the bull could react to the rider's closeness, the Winchester's bullet snuffed out the life of the brave beast. Down it went in a flurry of dust, snot and a spew of blood from its plunging side after being lung shot at such a close range. Not missing a beat, Wind sidestepped the huge downed bull and moved ahead onto the flanks of another buffalo.

This he did just as the herd began to react to the ambush hunters shooting into the fleeing beasts from the western side of the herd.

In reaction to the danger twenty mounted riders presented as they rode closely alongside, the front of the herd began slowly changing its direction of travel away from the perceived danger at hand. Josiah, noticing that herd's directional change, accordingly adjusted his position by reining back on Wind slightly. With that change-in-direction of movement, the herd inadvertently exploded into two groups and then moments later, quickly rejoined into a solid mass once again. However in doing so, that initial quick herd movement enveloped a careless ambush rider to Josiah's front! Within moments, that rider was riding for his life as he tried to maneuver his now terrified horse out from within the plunging herd to the safer ground outside of the panicked buffalo.

That rider desperately tried carefully maneuvering sideways toward the edge of the plunging beasts, as if by instinct, Wind moved forward alongside another close at hand buffalo just behind the trapped rider. At that point in time, the hapless ambush hunter was only one deep within the edge of the buffalo herd and still trying to escape from the danger of being trapped within the panicked masses. As he did, his horse was gored in the belly by a nearby bull and partially flipped skyward!

When that unexpected goring occurred, its rider was unhorsed and found himself flung onto and riding on the heaving back of another large bull buffalo! That rider, in desperation, grabbed the long hair on the beast's shoulders and hung on for dear life, knowing full well if he didn't, he would soon be plunged under the deadly flailing hooves of ten thousand fleeing buffalo…Then the bull being ridden, in full stride, tried bucking off its rider and running all at the same time. Every time the crazed and frightened animal violently bucked, the rider began losing his grip more and more until he began slipping down over the side of the charging beast!

It was then that Josiah, guiding Wind, sped up alongside the bull now running on the outside edge of the stampeding herd still carrying the hapless ambush hunter and without a second thought, leaned over in his saddle and reached out as far as he safely could in the dust-laden air. In doing so, Josiah grabbed the extended left hand of the hapless rider! In that emotion of the moment, Josiah powerfully jerked and hefted the man upwards off the buffalo and onto the back of Wind! Then a right knee touch to Wind's side and his horse quickly moved away from the edge of the hard charging blanket of buffalo. With that maneuver, Wind raced out of harm's way across the prairie away from the edge of the charging herd of buffalo.

Stopping and making sure no other buffalo were coming in his direction, Josiah seeing the way was clear but still in the dust field kicked up by the thousands of buffalo, looked over his shoulder at his just rescued rider. During his exultant look of excitement over having escaped the danger and rescuing one of his own, his grin of recognition turned to a frown! Sitting on the back of Wind was none other than a thoroughly frightened Red Shirt, Josiah's sworn and hated enemy! For the longest moment, both men just looked at each other in disbelief...Then Red Shirt realizing he had been saved by the much hated Josiah, slid off the backside of Wind and just stood there still not believing his eyes as to the identity of his rescuer.

By then, the great herd had pretty much moved away from the two men as had the rest of those tribal members still hunting the great beasts. Still not believing his eyes, Red Shirt finally said through gritted teeth, "Thank you." Then he turned and with the knowledge that his own horse was dead, began walking the several miles back to the summer encampment to get another horse.

With that and experiencing a funny Great Spirit feeling racing throughout his body, Josiah unexpectedly lowered his hand and said, "Here. Grab hold and we can both ride back to the village so you can get another horse."

For the longest time, Red Shirt just stared at the extended hand. Then he reached up, took the extended hand and was hauled back up onto the rump of Wind once again. Together the two men without exchanging a single word, rode the few miles back to their encampment. There Red Shirt once again procured another saddle and bridle, his having been previously ground to bits under the herd of buffalo, along with another horse. Without another word of thanks or any backward glances, Red Shirt returned to the killing field to celebrate along with the other ambush hunters over their successful hunt. Josiah on the other hand, still not believing the recent turn of events, stayed back in camp to act as a guard on the streams of women and children heading to and from the kill site to recover the meat and hides of the buffalo downed and scattered across the expansive prairie.

Later that evening, the camp celebrated the tremendous success of the kill. Over ninety buffalo had been killed! That included about ten animals that had piled up when Josiah shot one animal and the rest had stumbled and fallen over their comrades and in the process, breaking their necks and shoulders. Much buffalo meat had been procured and not a single hunter had been lost. Plus after many tribal members had observed Josiah and Red Shirt who were sworn enemies returning to camp riding the same horse, rumors abounded. There were many glances at both of the young men as the rest of the members went about their duties looking for answers splashed across the two adversaries' faces as to that weird happening. Especially in light of the fact of the men's much known hatred that existed for each other.

Many of the band realized that Red Shirt's favorite buffalo horse was nowhere to be seen. A horse that Red Shirt was so attached to that the two of them were never far apart. But neither man had anything to say about the incident. So much so, that the entire village was just about ready to pop over what had occurred and what was the reason behind such an unusual event. They soon learned that Red Shirt had his horse killed in the hunt but that was about all the information that became public over that seminal event. However, camp gossip still madly reigned over the unusual and telling event.

As the celebration continued over the hunt's success, outside cooking fires abounded, dogs quit barking because they were so full of meat scraps that they could hardly wiggle much less bark, groups laughed and told stories of the hunt, and it was all good. In the process, Josiah saw to it that ample supplies of meat had been hauled over to Two Fawn's and Tall Bull's parents' tipis so they too would have adequate stores of meat on hand for the days ahead.

Then it happened...Several returning hunters from the ambush group rode into camp escorting the last of the meat-loaded travois. As the meat was unloaded and distributed among the villagers, the word of the ambush hunt at the other end of the valley got out. A hunter, one named "Black Wolf," had observed what had happened between Josiah and Red Shirt. He had observed Red Shirt's horse getting trapped when the panicked herd had separated and then once again had quickly rejoined.

The warrior told the story about how Josiah had ridden his horse dangerously close to the edge of the herd near the trapped Red Shirt. He went on to explain that it was then that Red Shirt's horse had been gored and tossed under the hooves of the herd. And when that had happened, Red Shirt had been vaulted high into the air and had landed onto the back of a huge bull buffalo near the edge of the herd. It was then that Josiah continued maneuvering his horse closer to that bull buffalo which at that time was trying to toss Red Shirt off his back. By now, there was hardly a sound coming from the hundred or so people who had gathered around the hunter-story teller. Then the story continued. The warrior told the hushed crowd that Josiah had bravely ridden alongside the trapped hunter, reached out, grabbed Red Shirt's extended hand and had bodily lifted him off the raging buffalo and onto the back of his horse in one fluid motion! Following that dangerous maneuver, Josiah had wisely ridden away from the edge of the herd and escaped being trampled himself. When the storyteller had finished, there was hardly any sound or movement coming from the hushed and amazed crowd over what had happened at the kill site. Then all of the sudden there was much cheering and happy shouting over a brave man's action to save one of his own.

When the storytelling had finished, Red Shirt just stood quietly by at the edge of the crowd saying nothing. Then he was surrounded by a jubilant crowd of people congratulating him on having escaped death to live another day. Still, he had said nothing...Then the crowd began looking for Josiah. He was nowhere to be found. Moments later, he was discovered behind his tipi currying down his tired and hardworking horse. Within moments, the village had left Red Shirt standing by himself and had surrounded the brave Josiah. Once again, much happiness and congratulations were forthcoming and bestowed upon a man who had saved one of their own from certain death under the hooves of a stampeding herd of buffalo.

It was then that Old Chief Smoke standing alone by his tipi, walked over to an also standing by himself, Red Shirt. "Have you nothing to say to the people about being saved by Josiah and the Great Spirit this day?" asked Old Chief Smoke with a knowing twinkle in his eyes. A twinkle in his eyes because he also knew of the bad blood that existed between Red Shirt and Josiah. With that and no following communication, Red Shirt whirled and strode away into the darkness toward his tipi. As he did, he could still hear all the happy noises being made over his old enemy Josiah for his brave deed...

The next day around noon, the town crier went through the village shouting, "There will be an important meeting at Old Chief Smoke's tipi immediately. Hurry, the chief is waiting for all of you to gather." With those words, the village crier continued on throughout the assemblage of tipis making sure everyone had heard his words. Moments later, tribal members began streaming from what they had been doing as they headed over to the chief's tipi. Soon over a hundred village members had gathered expectantly in the center of the village to hear the words from their chief. Standing there in the center of a circle of humanity stood Old Chief Smoke and Red Shirt...Josiah stood at the outside of the ring of humanity quietly waiting just like everyone else. When everyone had assembled, Old Chief Smoke raised his hand for quiet.

When quiet had descended upon the group, he began. "Yesterday, the Great Spirit chose to save one of your own from being trampled to death by the buffalo. He did so by having one of you, in a selfless act of courage, extend a helping hand during a dangerous moment. The one saved stands before you today and wishes to be heard."

With that, Old Chief Smoke stepped back and Red Shirt, dressed up in all his finery, stepped forward. Drawing himself up to his full stature and in a crisp, loud voice meant to be heard by all, Red Shirt said, "Yesterday, the Great Spirit saved me from being trampled by the buffalo. My horse was gored and I was thrown onto the back of a large bull buffalo. When that happened, my heart was scared. So scared that I cried out for the Great Spirit to save me. Then the buffalo I was riding upon began bucking as he ran with the rest of the herd, trying to throw me under his hooves. Once again as my hands began slipping, I cried out for the Great Spirit to save me. Then I saw Josiah riding alongside the herd of buffalo streaming by and around me. Soon, he was alongside me and reached out for my hand. When our hands locked, he lifted me off the buffalo and onto the back of his horse. Look at me! I am no small man. Yet with Josiah's tremendous arm strength, he jerked me off that charging buffalo and saved me! He did so even though he was not my friend. In fact, for several years since he has been a captive of The People, I have hated him. My heart was bad and over those years that he has been one of us, I have walked The Black Road many times. He is a white man and I hated him and all the other whites for what they are doing to our lands. And in doing so, I have mistreated him at every turn in his river of life. Today, all of that changes. The Great Spirit has spoken and lifted the darkness from my eyes so that I now can see the way of The Red Road. I now see that I have wronged a great warrior. Today I stand before all of you and say that my days of darkness and the mistreatment of this person by me is no more. If Josiah will have me as his brother, it would make my heart swell with pride and I would be glad to call him the same!"

With those last words, a surprised murmur went through the crowd like the wind across the tops of the prairie grasses. The People were stunned over Red Shirt's brave admission and humility. Everyone had known of

125

Red Shirt's black heart towards Josiah and none had figured that Red Shirt was ever capable of remorse or would request forgiveness. Then almost as another gust of prairie wind had rippled across the grasses, the realization of the powerful words just spoken finally hit home to all those gathered. Another soft murmur of approval of Red Shirt's brave and humble words surged through the crowd. Then it stopped just as fast as a blizzard could roll across the treeless prairie…Would often tormented Josiah forgive Red Shirt for all his wrongs over those many moons as a captive? With that question hanging over everyone's mind, all eyes quickly turned to Josiah as he stood quietly at the edge of the crowd. No one moved after that for fear of breaking the spell now hanging heavily in the air! Silence reined except for the raucous calling of several distant crows who had just discovered a sleeping great horned owl, their lifelong enemy, high up in a cottonwood tree...

Old Chief Smoke now swung his eyes toward Josiah to see what his reaction to Red Shirt's public words of repentance would be. As he did, bits and pieces of his earlier vision from the Great Spirit about saving a brave white man who would go on to become a great warrior now flashed through his mind.

For the longest moment, Josiah stood by the edge of the crowd as the entire village silently looked on waiting for his reaction to Red Shirt's contrite words. Then without uttering a single word, Josiah turned his back and entered his nearby tipi! A silence as quiet as a field mouse running through the grass blanketed the stunned crowd over the surprising actions by Josiah. After all, Red Shirt had bared his heart over his past wrongs and it now appeared that Josiah had refused the openly public and contrite apology. The stunned crowd did not know what to do and just stood there in stunned silence.

All eyes turned back to Old Chief Smoke as if on cue, looking for him to show The Way. Old Chief Smoke, just as stunned as was the crowd over Josiah's culturally bad manners for turning his back and walking away, was at a loss for words. Then the old chief's eyes swung from the crowd back towards sudden movement by Josiah's tipi in surprise. His intense questioning looks back towards Josiah's tipi caused the entire crowd to read the surprise in his eyes, turn and look in that direction as well.

Walking out from his tipi, Josiah strode with deliberate purpose down through the still stunned crowd toward the much respected chief. Standing alongside the chief was Red Shirt, and both his and the old chief's faces were showing they were equally perplexed as to what was happening. Walking up to the two men with the crowd still in total stunned silence, Josiah stopped and faced Red Shirt. He quietly said, "For many moons you have made my life very difficult. When I was younger, I was beaten many times by you and your friends for what I knew not. Many a night, I laid in my own blood in my tipi after a beating from you and your friends. And the next day, I said nothing to answer all the questioning looks over my battered appearance. But I survived and have come to love this village and all its people. I heard your words today and my heart tells me they were true. I have never had a brother. I would welcome Red Shirt and be honored to have him as my brother. As a token of what my heart feels this day, I am returning the knife, belt, and sheath taken from you when the two of us walked together in darkness."

With those words, Josiah unrolled from a tanned rabbit skin a knife, beaded belt and sheath ornately covered with quill work and extended it towards Red Shirt, one that he had taken from Red Shirt moons before after a vicious fight between the two of them. In fact, a knife that had been used by Red Shirt when he meant to kill Josiah during one of their fights but had only managed to cut open the front of his buckskin shirt and slice a shallow tear across the flesh of his chest...

For the longest moment, Red Shirt just stood there stunned and then his eyes filled with the emotion of the moment. Taking and holding up the beautifully made knife for all to see, he said, "This belonged to my father who is now in the other world. He gave it to me when I became a brave. It had been his father's and grandfather's before him. Then it was given to me with all of its powerful medicine. And in shame, it was later taken away from me by the Great Spirit and Josiah when the two of us were in the darkness of hate. Now I have it back and that makes my heart full and glad. As I stand here today, Josiah, you are my brother and I will give up my life for you if it is ever called for. Now, we will be as one in life and battle together with others, or perish as one in death. But from this moment on, we will be as one as the Great Spirit is my witness."

With those words, both men embraced as only brothers would do after a long separation. With that open demonstration of courage and forgiveness between the

128

two men, the village showed their approval of what had just happened with much embracing and shaking the hands of Josiah and Red Shirt. Old Chief Smoke's heart was also glad for the "birth" of the two brothers, and now he could see many parts of the sacred vision he had received so many moons earlier coming true. However, there were still several parts to the vision that were unfilled and he would shortly remedy one of those...

Chapter Six

THE CHIEF TAKES A SON AND THE MAKING OF A WARRIOR

Early one morning as Josiah was roasting a piece of deer meat over his inside fire, he heard footsteps approaching the front of his tipi. The footsteps stopped in front of the flap of Josiah's tipi and then he heard the unmistakable voice of Old Chief Smoke saying, "Josiah, are you awake?"

Setting his roasting stick with the half-cooked impaled deer meat aside, Josiah exited his tipi. "Yes, I have been awake for some time. What do you want, Chief?"

"I would like you to come to my tipi this evening. The elders and I would like to talk with you," he said with a twinkle in his eyes and a smile on his face.

Josiah nodded in the affirmative and with that, Old Chief Smoke turned and strode back to his tipi with nary another word spoken. Josiah watched the old chief shuffle away and could not help but wonder why the chief and the village elders wanted to talk with him. One of his problems, his deadly old nemesis Tall Bull, had been killed by the stampeding buffalo. And, he was now as close to Red Shirt as he could be to a real brother. So, what could be the issue requiring a meeting with the elders and the chief since he no longer had any problems with anyone in the village. Then he remembered that earlier he had watched the old chief walking away after the time he had announced to Josiah that he was now the owner of eight of Running Wolf's horses. That day, Old Chief Smoke was shuffling along like a tired old man with a heavy burden on his shoulders that would require making a major decision on his part. Then Josiah remembered his uncooked breakfast as well as being reminded of that fact by the growling in his empty stomach. He sure was not eating as well as he had been when Two Fists was cooking for him he thought, as he re-entered his tipi.

That evening after another lackluster meal of flame-roasted venison in his tipi, he put away his roasting stick and exited his tipi. Heading over to Old Chief Smoke's tipi, he heard several vigorously sounding voices speaking from within the chief's tipi as he approached. Those voices seemed to be in a spirited conversation about a topic concerning him! Quietly announcing his presence outside the chief's tipi, Josiah, as was the custom, waited until he was asked in. Walking around a small circle of sitting elders and the chief, Josiah respectfully made ready to sit. But not before the customary greetings to those respected elders and the chief seated around the fire had been made. Then Josiah said nothing more as was the Oglala custom when invited to a council fire and sat down.

After a respectful period of silence, Old Chief Smoke finally spoke. "Josiah, we have been speaking about you. We all have been watching you as you have worked, hunted and interacted with the rest of the people in the village. You have worked hard and have been very respectful to all the village elders and the old as well as the infirm. Those are qualities we feel the Great Spirit has endowed you with. Those are good qualities and all of us feel that since your capture as a young white man, you have developed into a great warrior. But we ask ourselves, how can that be? You are a white man and not of our blood, heritage, culture or, truly understanding of The Way. But, we also feel the good in the silent language of your body, the respect you have shown our culture, and how you have carried yourself proudly these many moons since your capture. And, all of us sense your comfort and interest in trying to learn about the ways of the Oglala. All of those actions tell us you might like to become one with us! And if that would be your will, you should know there are many trials that you must face in order to totally shed your old ways of the white man to become one with us. Those trials I speak of are of the heart, spirit, mind, and body. Many of those trials require sacrifice of yourself in many forms in order to successfully complete your change from that of a white man to one of The People. But upon completion of one of the most important of those trials, namely the vision quest and only after the elders and our holy man has successfully interpreted what you have seen in your visions during such a sacrifice, can you become one of us. If given this opportunity, what does your inner spirit and heart tell you what path you should take?"

For the longest time, Josiah said nothing. To his way of thinking he thought he was already one of the members of Old Chief Smoke's band. He was well aware of some of the rituals other braves had undergone like the sweat and the vision quests, along with the lamenting in order to seek higher powers from the Great Spirit. But of the inner workings of such rituals and their requirements of the person undergoing such trials he knew little or nothing, especially since they were for the most part uniquely personal quests and private moments between one another or the Great Spirit.

But then, Josiah's head began to dizzily swim in remembrance. He had lost his parents to these people, been made a captive and for many months had thought of nothing else but escape or at least revenge for what they had done to his family and relatives. But as life, the "song of time", forgiveness, and enlightenment would have it, he began to adjust to and then openly came to embrace the wonderful way of life lived by his captors. He had proven himself throughout the months of his captivity and as a result, more and more he was granted greater and greater freedoms. Greater freedoms, until he was now running free like the other male members of the band. In fact, he had long since earned the respect of most of the band as well as that of all the elders. To his way of thinking except for his piercing blue eyes, he was already one of them by his actions and looks. His skin was bronzed from his everyday exposure to the sun, he respected the simple and honorable ways of life the band enjoyed, he loved life's everyday challenges and to his

133

way of thinking, life as an Oglala was better than good. Especially since he had now learned to speak the Sioux language and was also proficient in sign language. He found that he was as healthy as a horse from this type of lifestyle, owned a number of valuable horses, and could ride like the best horsemen in the village. His hunting skills and shooting eye were the best in the village and seldom did he go after an animal in which he did not kill it. And following that, had learned of the many joys that came with sharing his wildlife fortunes with less well-off members of the village. In fact lifestyle wise, his sister had all but become a full-fledged member of the band and was highly respected for her easy going attitude, self-sufficiency, and beautiful quill and bead work. So with both he and his sister's happiness, how could he do otherwise or live better than what he was now doing? These people were now his family and he enjoyed this way of life far better than working on a farm plowing behind the hind end of a mule...Yes, he found himself wanting to learn more of The Way and had all along been quietly desirous of becoming a full-fledged member of the band! Especially since he now considered this his way of life.

Turning to Old Chief Smoke, Josiah said, "I would like to become one of The People. What would I have to do in order to become one with your band in your eyes and in the thinking of the elders?"

It was hard for Old Chief Smoke not to smile at Josiah's words. It truly warmed his heart to hear those words coming from the young man that he held in such high respect. The old chief even found that the vision he had been granted earlier, was finally beginning to lift the fog of the heavy burden of prophecy it had placed on his shoulders. A vision from the Great Spirit that he had been quietly carrying all these many moons. That vision's burden, flying in the face of his culture, of saving a white man in battle for the future of his tribe. Then swirling across his mind came another sudden revelation. One that dove-tailed directly into the last part of his vision and needed to be carried out. "Then it is done!" said Old Chief Smoke in finality as all the elders nodded their heads in approval. "You will now become my 'son' as revealed in my vision given to me from the Great Spirit so long ago. As such, I will be the one to teach you The Way. Teach you The Way, so that you can follow those sacred teachings and truly become one of us! And those teachings will start tonight after you have moved in with me and my wife of many moons, Prairie Flower. That way we will be closer and our time will be better spent in the teachings that are to take place."

Upon hearing those words from Old Chief Smoke, Josiah just sat there stunned over the turn of events and how fast they were moving. In fact, it was all he could do to keep his head from spinning off his shoulders over the changes now taking place in his life! He thought the world of Old Chief Smoke and had in fact saved his life during the winter raid by the hated Pawnees. Now as he figured it, Old Chief Smoke was in the process of saving his...

With the decisions now made concerning Josiah's new life, the elders rose and without a word filed out from Old Chief Smoke's tipi. Prairie Flower on the other hand, cleared out a spot in their tipi for Josiah's sleeping furs and then quietly disappeared. Moments later, back she came lugging what few belongings Josiah had. As she did, she couldn't help but think of the great Sioux warrior, Crazy Horse, a warrior she had never met but had only experienced through the many stories told and retold around the fires about the greatness of the man. And in so learning, had come to know and respect the man greatly for his many good deeds. He too had little in the way of personal goods and always shared whatever he had with the members of his tribe. Just like Josiah had been doing for many moons in Old Chief Smoke's band...

That evening, after a meal of stewed buffalo mixed with thick corn meal, edible roots, red pepper flakes, and wild onions, Old Chief Smoke, sitting with Josiah, began teaching him The Way. Sitting down by the fire in respectful silence, the two men looked into the dancing flames as if they expected some sort of sign contained therein to show itself. Then after a long silence like the old chief was in the process of gathering in all of his thoughts, he finally quietly began speaking.

"Josiah, without a vision, even though you have the makings of a great warrior, such a man without one is next to a grasshopper. You will be nothing in our world without a vision. For you see, without a vision to lead you through life, you will have no protection from evil, no source of power in battle, no voice in the council, and no source of wisdom which leads all great warriors. In order to receive these gifts, you must do many things. For you to receive the Great Mystery from the Great Spirit into your life, you must go into solitude, fast, and thirst for two to five days. That means you must go on a vision quest to find such solitude. That vision quest must take you to a dangerous place where wild beasts roam. There you can beg the spirits in all humility to take pity on one's self. Pity, so that you can achieve protection, sources of power, and wisdom throughout the 'all' of your life."

Then the old chief paused as if once again gathering in his thoughts on what he wanted to say next. "Before you can go on such a quest however, you must first undergo a sweat so your body will be cleansed. Then one must purify one's self by rubbing himself dry with sweet grass, sage or pine needles. Following that, one must rub himself with white clay signifying purity. Taking a buffalo robe smeared with white clay which Prairie Flower will provide, you must travel by yourself to a place of seclusion for the lamenting or crying that is to follow as you seek your sacred vision. You must not eat or drink during this period of time and you must ask the Great Spirit to take pity on you. Your vision quest site must be as high as you can reach so you will be closer to the spirits. When you find such a place, make yourself a bed of pine needles or sage, which to The People is a sign of purity. But before you decide on a vision quest site, you must bathe once again and stand in the smoke of burning sage or pine needles for more purification of your spirit." With those words, the old chief went silent as if gathering in more thoughts on what a seeker of a vision must do in order to be successful in this all important quest.

After his long silence, Old Chief Smoke began instructing Josiah once again. "In the sacred place of your vision quest, you, during your lamenting or vision seeking, must pray for the spirits to take pity on you and show you a sign. When praying or crying for a sign during your vision quest, make sure you are holding a branch of sage in your hand. Remember, the vision and token you may receive will be determined by the character of the seeker. So make sure your mind is pure, clear of any bad thoughts, and is full of crying for the spirits to take pity on you. Lastly, if your vision quest is successful and the spirits give you a token or sign of what you seek, that vision will then be interpreted after you return by our holy man, Fast Antelope. And if you have been successful in receiving a vision that will give you strength throughout your life and bring health to not only you but the entire village."

"Now, I have talked long and am growing tired. But, tomorrow we will start with the first part of your vision quest ordeal with a sweat. When that is finished and you have bathed once again, we will paint you with the sacred white clay. Prairie Flower will give you a buffalo robe that has been painted with the sacred white clay and then you must go forth and find the proper location for your vision quest." With those words, Old Chief Smoke rose and headed for his sleeping furs since it was late and the day had been full. Moments later, Josiah did likewise in his new home. However, Josiah found sleep hard to come by. Once again he found his head spinning crazily over all that had been said and the possible life changing events, if he so chose, that had just been laid out before him. Lying there and thinking, he wondered if he would be able to accomplish what the elders and Old Chief Smoke

138

expected of him. Especially since he was a white man and not an Indian. Soon the warmth of his sleeping furs, the day's emotions, and the darkness of night closed in around him...

The following morning, the occupants of Old Chief Smoke's tipi were up at the crack of dawn. Today was a special day and Prairie Flower had prepared a huge breakfast for her two men. In the excitement of the moment, Josiah hardly tasted anything that crossed his lips. But remembering the two to five day fast that was coming, he ate heartily. Outside and along the nearby creek, the elders had already constructed a sweat lodge and had heated the rocks to be used in that ritual. Following breakfast, Old Chief Smoke and Josiah striped everything off except for a loin cloth. The two men then entered the already hot and steamy atmosphere found inside the small and confining space of the sweat lodge. There Old Chief Smoke taught Josiah many prayers that needed to be said to appease and make the spirits happy. He also gave more instructions to Josiah on what else to do during his vision quest. The intense heat and moisture seemed to be draining much from Josiah as he and the old chief sat in the cramped quarters of the sweat lodge deep in discussion. Then more preheated rocks were added in the sweat lodge by the assisting elders and sprinkled with sacred water. The intensity of the heat and humidity rose even higher and then two elders also entered the sweat lodge. All three tribal members now profusely sweated and jointly instructed Josiah on what they felt would be expected of him by the Great Spirit during the vision quest.

After a long sweat with much instruction being given, Josiah and Old Chief Smoke exited the sweat lodge and bathed together in the welcome coolness of the nearby creek. Then Old Chief Smoke dried Josiah off and painted him from head to toe in the sacred white clay. Finished, Josiah gathered up his white clay smeared buffalo robe and taking one long drink of water that had to last him, Josiah without another word, headed for some distant cliffs with which he was familiar. Distant cliffs where he had successfully hunted deer, elk and bighorn sheep, that he figured would also now meet his vision quest site requirements.

A half day's walk across the prairie soon found Josiah climbing toward a massive formation of rocky bluffs, bluffs that he had visualized from his past hunting experiences in the area as a satisfactory location for his vision quest site. For an hour after reaching the base of the rocky bluff, Josiah climbed ever upward. Now he was wishing for a cool drink of water as his throat became parched in the heat of the midday sun and the exertion of the moment he was enduring. But further upward he climbed as Old Chief Smoke had instructed during their time in the sweat lodge. In order for the vision quest to have the best chance for success, Josiah had to reach an area that was so high it would be close to the spirits and physically dangerous to occupy. Soon he found himself on a point of rocks overlooking the broad expanse of the living prairie far below. Flooding his vision were numerous herds of buffalo and elk appearing as dots or as a moving brown carpet in among the yellow-green grasses of the prairie for as far as he could see.

Crawling out further onto the selected point of rocks, Josiah found a small flat spot on the rocky shelf just long and wide enough for one to sit or lay back on. Leaving his sacred buffalo robe, Josiah walked back off the rocky point to a nearby stand of sagebrush. There he collected as many sage bush limbs as he could carry and brought them back to the rocky ledge that was to serve as his vision quest site. Then as instructed by Old Chief Smoke, he made a bed of the sacred sage brush branches and leaves upon which to lay when sleeping. Off in the distance, he observed a spotted eagle soaring in lazy circles and felt the cool breezes from his high place up in the rocks cooling his sweating body. This had to be the right spot for a vision quest. It was high, physically exhausting to get to, rocks would form the base of his uncomfortable bed and from here he could call upon the now close at hand spirits to hear him as he began his sacrifice, thought Josiah.

Laying down his buffalo robe on the small shelf of rock and sagebrush, he sat and let the cool of the area refresh his still sweating body from the exertions of his long climb. Then he saw the spotted eagle stoop and catch what appeared to be a fleeing jackrabbit in the valley's heated shimmering haze laying far below. Following that, it was as quiet as a burial ground for the rest of the afternoon up on his rocky point except for a few cooling breezes wafting by.

When darkness finally overcame the light, Josiah was still sitting rock still and praying for a sign. Finally in exhaustion from his labors of the day, Josiah laid down and tried to sleep. However, the cooling breezes felt earlier in the afternoon had now turned colder and he found himself eventually sitting up and wrapped shivering in the buffalo robe. As it turned out, sleep was not a friend to Josiah that evening. When the sunrise the following morning peeped over the horizon to the east, the direction in which he was facing, it found a cold, numbed, and exhausted Josiah looking worn and haggard. All that day, Josiah's hunger and thirst overrode most of his thoughts. But still he lamented for the spirits above to hear his cry. All of which were to no avail. Maybe because he was part white man, the spirits would elude him, he thought.

Come sundown that second day with the arrival of the long shadows, found Josiah tired, hungry and extremely thirsty. But still he prayed on hoping for a sign so he could leave the mountain, return to his tipi for some rest, food, and drink. Little did he realize those were not the earthly thoughts the Great Spirit was looking for from his desirous supplicant. Darkness drifted in still finding Josiah waiting for a vision, any kind of a vision! But his reward for his vigil was only the flat, uncomfortable, cold stone ledge upon which he was sitting as the evening's chill began seeping deeply into his bones once again. That night, his second on the mountain, he slept naught and dreamed little of anything else but something to eat and drink—so much so that any kind of a vision would have had trouble coming through and into Josiah's food and water troubled mind, body, and sprit...

It seemed like it took forever for the sun to rise on the third hungry and thirsty day, as Josiah waited for its warmth to warm his cold body after another cold restless night. The rest of the third day's morning, Josiah drifted into and out of a restless sleep and dreams. Dreams of home back in Missouri, dreams of the excitement of the trip to a far-away land called Oregon, days of discovery on the Oregon Trail and the many new exciting sights and sounds that travel presented, awaking from sleeping under his dad's wagon to the sounds of several hundred sage grouse sailing over his wagon, stalking the grouse with his shotgun, the fight for life at the wagon site and then, he would awaken with a start! Again in the afternoon on the third day, sleep, hunger and thirst overtook him and he found himself mentally drifting once more back to the wagon train site. There once again, he was on the hillside chasing sage grouse and then the soon to prove deadly attack on his folk's wagon train began below...

Darkness found Josiah sitting on his rocky ledge once again as his third day of his vision quest continued. Once again, the night's cold crept into his bones and true to form, found him quietly praying to the Great Spirit for a token or vision. Not finding any response to his praying reverently, Josiah began praying loudly to the spirits now teasingly whistling around him in the night's chilling breaths of wind. And in doing so, prayed loudly for those spirits to have pity on his long suffering self. Nothing showed itself that evening and once again, Josiah drifted off into another night of listless sleep and cold shivering. Hunger had since left him, but now, he was so thirsty. So much so, that he thought if he had a knife he would let a little blood from his arm and drink it!

Later that night, a prowling grizzly bear discovered an exhausted Josiah in the process of nodding off. When Josiah realized that he was not alone and in danger, it surprised him just how quickly he aroused himself and lobbed enough large rocks from his vision quest site above the critter, that the great bear quickly retreated and left him alone. Then he remembered Old Chief Smoke's words about his choice of a vision quest site. He had to select one which had to have an element of physical danger in order to show his true character to the spirits...Once again, Josiah slept little on the third night of his lonely vigil.

Josiah was so exhausted by the fourth day without food, water and little sleep that he missed the exact moment of that day's sunrise. Awakening and happy to see the rise of the sun for its warmth, he tried to stand, but in doing so, found himself wobbly from hunger, lack of water, and his cramped sitting on the stone cold ledge of rock. Finally getting his legs under him, Josiah once again raised his arms in lament to the Great Spirit and asked him to give him the strength to carry on. Then collapsing back onto his buffalo robe on the flat rock, sleep fitfully finally overtook him on the morning of his fourth day. His head had no more than dropped onto the robe, when he began having visions of himself hiking the hill back by the wagon train stalking the vast covey of sage grouse. Closing in on them, he raised his shotgun at a cluster of grouse heads and fired his shotgun. Nothing happened! The grouse did not fly but kept on eating like nothing had happened. And he had not killed nary a grouse from shooting at them from such a close range! Taking aim once again, he fired. Again, the feeding grouse just ignored the shotgun blast and nary a grouse fell...

With that, Josiah snapped back from the world of

fitful sleep into the fourth day of his vision quest. Then it dawned on him! He had seen sage grouse twice on his third day of the vision quest and now had seen them once again on the morning of the fourth day. Was that his sign? He knew naught but figured he could last one more day and if no vision appeared, he would then return in disappointment to Old Chief Smoke's tipi for some food, water, and quiet rest. After all, he was part white man and maybe white men were not capable of experiencing or successfully performing vision quests.

That evening found Josiah on the fourth day of his vigil, once again shivering under his buffalo robe. His head was now swimming from the lack of food and water and his eyesight was now betraying him, especially when looking at distant objects. But he still had hope as he rose in a wobbly fashion, outstretched his arms and looking skyward once again, asked the spirits to have pity on his soul and give him a sign. Exhausted from that little bit of exertion of standing and raising his arms skyward, he collapsed onto his buffalo robe and slept soundly for the first time in four days.

Once again in that sleep, he was mentally back at the wagon train and hunting that same large covey of grouse. Only this time when he found them, the grouse stood as tall as he did and out of fear, he did not shoot at them. Then he saw the grouse feeding vigorously on the ground, and they were eating smaller Indians who had stolen Old Chief Smoke's horse herd. Then after the grouse had finished eating all the bad Indians, they turned and walked a few yards away and began eating smaller in size cavalry troopers! The cavalry soldiers were shooting their rifles at the sage grouse but their bullets were not hitting or killing the birds! Not one time did the troopers ever kill a sage grouse! Soon the grouse had eaten up all the troopers and then they flew safely away to the far north to a cold appearing land Josiah did not recognize. Then the dream was gone and he was wide awake! Shivering but wide awake! What had he just seen? His mind whirled from the lack of food, water, sleep, and now from what he had just seen in his delirium. That same flock of sage grouse had appeared FOUR times in TWO of his dreams...Then out of exhaustion, he laid back and did not move a muscle until daybreak on his fifth and final day.

Carefully working his way down off the mountain from his vision quest site on wobbly legs, Josiah was happy to be on the flatness of the prairie once again. However, Josiah discovered that his gait was slowed from his lack of food and deep thirst. In fact, he was so thirsty he could not even swallow! About a mile or so later, Josiah came across a ground seep that had been recently visited by a herd of buffalo. The free running water was muddied up and polluted from numerous buffalo droppings but to Josiah, his first taste of water in five days was one of the best he ever had! Then as he arose from laying on his belly drinking from the hoof-pounded spring seep, a disturbed covey of sage grouse walking for that same spring to drink rose from the nearby tall grasses in a noisy clattering of wings as they fled to a nearby densely sage brush covered flat...

Later that afternoon, an exhausted Josiah entered Old Chief Smoke's camp accompanied by numerous bands of excited children happy to see him and barking camp dogs.

Soon more of the villagers had gathered alongside as Josiah slowly continued slow-walking up to the chief's tipi. Hearing the excited voices outside his tipi, Old Chief Smoke emerged and seeing his son slowly arriving, broke out into a big smile. Half collapsing and half standing in a wobbly fashion, Josiah said, "I am home, father." Those words warmed the old chief's heart and surprised Josiah that those words had come from within his heart and rolled over his lips like water flowing in a brook. But no matter, he was home, soon to be fed, and then into his sleeping furs for some much needed sleep. However, that was not to be.

Old Chief Smoke gathered up some new clothing that had been previously fashioned for him by Josiah's sister Gemma and Prairie Flower. Following that, the old chief hustled Josiah over to a small pond in the camp's nearby creek. There Josiah washed off the white clay, dirt and sweat, dried off with sage and sweet grass, then put on his new clothing. He had lost a fair amount of weight on his vision quest but for the most part, the clothing fit. Then it was off to Old Chief Smoke's tipi. There Prairie Flower ran off her husband and the village elders that had anxiously gathered to see if Josiah had experienced a vision. Without another word, Prairie Flower took Josiah into the tipi for something to eat and some peace and quiet. When Old Chief Smoke was finally allowed to return to his tipi that evening, Josiah was still fast asleep and Prairie Flower warned her husband not to awaken him...or else!

The next day the old chief was about ready to pop! He had so many questions that he could hardly stand himself.

Had Josiah received a vision? Would the village elders and the holy man of the village accept any vision received by a white man as one having come directly from the Great Spirit? Was it even possible for a white man to have an Oglala vision? On and on went the questions across his mind until the old chief could hardly stand himself. However, Prairie Flower had said to leave Josiah alone or else and he was listening to those words of fire coming from his much loved and diminutive wife of many moons...

The next morning, Josiah had finally awakened from his deep and exhaustive sleep. Prairie Flower fed him a hearty breakfast of roasted buffalo loin because she knew Josiah was in for a long day. Finally finished with his meal and having polished off a long drink of water, Josiah was ready for the elders and the much respected holy man of the village. It was only then that Prairie Flower abandoned the tipi to go and visit her nearby sister, leaving Josiah to the chief and the elders to discuss the business of the vision quest. Moments later, the tipi was filled with the chief, tribal elders, a holy man named Fast Antelope and Josiah.

Fast Antelope began the vision quest questioning. "Josiah, were you successful in having the spirits visit and if so, what was your vision so we may interpret it to see what it means?"

Josiah leaned back against his back support from his sitting position and slowly said, "I am not sure. But here is what I dreamed on the third and fourth days of my vision quest. On the third morning, I dreamed of being back at my wagon train and a covey of grouse had just

148

flown overhead where I was sleeping under a wagon. I went to hunt them and then awoke. On my third evening, I found myself drifting through the clouds back to my old wagon train before the fight. In that dream, I was hunting a large covey of sage grouse and just about to shoot. Then I awoke. On the fourth morning when sleep finally overtook me, I drifted back through the clouds and once again, I was hunting that same covey of sage grouse. Getting close to the flock, I raised my shotgun, lined up two bird's heads who were looking right at me and shot. When I shot, nothing happened! Not a bird moved as if they didn't see or hear see me shoot. Then I shot again. Once again, not a bird was disturbed or moved. Then I came back from the spirit world and did not dream further that morning. On my fourth day in the evening as I slept, I once again drifted through the clouds back to hunting that same covey of sage grouse. Only this time, they were larger than me! The grouse stood at least thirty feet tall and out of fear, I did not shoot. Then I looked at what the feeding grouse were vigorously eating on the ground. They were eating bad Indians who were smaller in size and were sleeping near a fire in the evening by a large herd of Old Chief Smoke's horses! I did not recognize who they were or where they were from based on their dress. But I knew they were bad Indians who had stolen Old Chief Smoke's horses from his winter encampment! Then after the grouse had eaten all the bad Indians, the grouse walked off a few yards and began vigorously feeding once again. Only that time, they were eating smaller in size cavalry troopers and their horses, dozens of them! The cavalry troopers were shooting at the grouse many times but their bullets were not hitting the birds! Then I awoke once again. I do not know what that means nor do I know if that was a true vision in the eyes of the Oglala. But, that is what I saw in my dreams."

Then Josiah tried to examine Fast Antelope's weathered and sunburned face for any sign or reaction to his visions. It was only then that he could see amazement splashed clear across the holy man's face! Then Josiah looked at the other elders and the old chief's face for their reactions. All of them looked stunned! Then Josiah began to wonder and fear he had somehow said something wrong, especially in light of the fact that the Oglala strongly believed in the power of the vision quest and what the vision meant to the one lamenting. And, he did not want all of the elders and the holy man to think that he had told them a lie. Especially since honesty in telling a story about a vision was of the highest importance in the eyes of the Sioux. And if one lied about what he saw or made up that he had seen a vision and in reality had not, Oglala legend foretold that bad luck would plague that individual for the rest of his life.

For the longest time it was so quiet in the old chief's tipi that the breathing from the old men could be plainly heard. Then Fast Antelope said, "Josiah, you were truly visited by the spirits in your vision! Not only once but four times! That is a sign of strong medicine. What you received in the way of the vision was determined by the goodness of your character. The spirits recognized you were of good character and blessed you with the strongest of visions. The sage grouse, a strong and noble bird of the prairie and sagebrush, is your sign! From now on until the

Great Spirit comes for you, you must carry a token of the sage grouse on your person for strength, protection, and as a source of power and wisdom. You must also paint your horse or war shield with a symbol of your vision in order to help in carrying you through life not only in battle but the good times as well."

Then Fast Antelope paused and with closed eyes, appeared to be almost in a self-induced trance. By then, the energy in the tipi from the elders was so intense that one could even hear the slightest movement of their clothing when they stirred. Suddenly, Fast Antelope's eyes flew open once again and that time he spoke slowly and with much deliberation. "Josiah, your vision tells me many good things. When you first shot at the grouse on the fourth day of your vision, they did not move. They did not fear you or your gun. You fired twice and still the grouse were not afraid. That tells me, you, like the sage grouse, will not be afraid in battle and will ignore the bullets and arrows being shot at you by your enemies because they cannot hit or hurt you!"

With those words from Fast Antelope, it got so quiet in the tipi one could hear a grasshopper rubbing his wings with his legs as he flew through the air some distance away...Then he continued on saying, "Later on the fourth day of your vision, once again you were hunting the grouse. But that time, they were larger in size and bigger than you. That part of the vision tells me that your power is great! That you will be larger than all of the prairie in your wisdom, sacrifices, strength and ability to see into the worlds of the Indian and white man. However, that last part of your vision is troubling. It tells of many battles to come in which you will be involved. It showed that you with your great power, will vanquish bad Indians and be involved in many battles with the white men's horse soldiers. My thoughts of the grouse in your vision eating Indians and cavalry who were shooting at them to no effect, says that will also happen to you in battle. Your vision from the spirits and its great power will lift you above the battle and deflect any bullets or arrows that are shot at you. You must always remember these words and be not afraid when confronted by the bad of our people or the hated white man. Lastly, because of the size of the sage grouse, your wisdom will be greater than that of many others. Learn to respect that wisdom and understand what it means, because it will carry you well in battle as well as the rest of your life. What I have seen here today because of your great vision, is that much good will befall the Sioux Nation for a time. But be aware, the sign of many soldiers shooting at the grouse also speaks of many bad things happening to The People in the coming times...And when that happens, living will be bad for our people. The People will be like the cavalry soldiers being eaten by the grouse in your vision. In the moons to come they will also be eaten themselves..."

With those words out, Fast Antelope leaned back, closed his eyes and became lost in his age and thoughts of what he had just learned from Josiah's vision quest. As for the elders, they were satisfied with what they had heard. Rising in the realization that Fast Antelope was finished with his interpretation, they filed out from Old Chief Smoke's tipi. They did so in order to be alone in their thoughts and examine with their hearts what Fast

Antelope had interpreted and predicted about Josiah. There was a lot to think about seeing that Josiah was a white man in an Oglala culture. Finally, Fast Antelope rose and quietly left the tipi without saying another word. That left Old Chief Smoke and Josiah sitting there in the cool and quiet of the old chief's tipi.

After a few moments of silence, Old Chief Smoke said, "Josiah, when the bands gather this summer in celebration of the Sun Dance, you need to consider going through that ceremony. It is difficult but it is the ultimate proof that a warrior is willing to give thanksgiving and sacrifice himself for the good of the people. Be thinking about that my son because it is not a ceremony to be taken lightly. In fact, you may want to seek another vision to see if that ultimate sacrifice at the Sun Dance is for you. And if that latest vision shows you The Way, then you must follow your heart."

One month later, during another lamenting or crying session to seek another vision on whether he should participate in the coming Sun Dance, Josiah got his wish. In that vision received on the third day of his vision quest, he saw himself clothed in a red waist to ankle length cloth and the rest of his naked body heavily painted. The vision also showed him with leather thongs tied on each end of a holed, V-shaped folded hide which had been hooked to sticks thrust through the skin in his chest. Knotted on the other end of the folded hide was a single leather thong which had been strung out and tied to a center pole in a lodge covered with evergreens. In that vision he also saw himself straining mightily against the deeply imbedded sticks attached to the chest skin while tied to that leather thong attached to the center pole. As he leaned against the main leather thong tied to the V-shaped hide attached to his chest blowing an eagle wing bone whistle, he saw himself walking in a half circle back and forth by a center pole and under his feet were dead and dying cavalry soldiers! He also saw that his face was contorted in great pain and blood ran from his chest and dripped onto the floor of the Sun Dance Lodge. His vision also revealed another scene. Josiah was walking alongside his new brother, Red Shirt, who was undergoing the same sacrifices at the Sun Dance ritual. And under his feet were dead and dying cavalry soldiers as well...

Chapter Seven

THE SUN DANCE

Sitting around a small campfire after a day of successfully hunting deer, Josiah and Red Shirt cooked strips of venison back straps with their cooking sticks. Those cooking sticks being made from green willow gathered from along a nearby stream because they would not burn as readily as would dry sticks when held over an open fire. For the longest time, the two friends just quietly cooked dinner and looked into the dancing flames as if looking for answers to a question hanging in the air and over their souls at that moment in time. A shared heaviness that spoke of adventures to come but from not they knew where...Little did the two of them realize the Great Spirit was preparing them to become great warriors in the mighty Sioux Nation. And in order to do so, was intertwining their lives in their every thought and deed like the close brothers they had become. Those preparations included many perceptions and deep feelings on that which was to come. In short, the two men had become the closest of brothers, thought like brothers, and unbeknownst to them, were being prepared by the Great Spirit for their land of shared adventures, like brothers...

Then Josiah turned from looking into the flames of their campfire saying, "My brother, I have finally made up my mind. I am going to participate in the Sun Dance later this summer. I do not quite know what is involved but Old Chief Smoke says if I am to become a full-fledged warrior of the Oglala, that is something I must do. What are your thoughts about such a matter?"

For a long moment Red Shirt just looked at Josiah as if looking to see if he was really serious about participating in the sacred and grueling Sun Dance ritual. Then Red Shirt realizing Josiah was as serious as a river stone was hard, had a strange look suddenly come over his face, which was immediately followed with a big grin. "Then it is settled. I will also participate in the Sun Dance alongside my new brother and will be there to offer him support if and when he weakens and falters like an old woman under a heavy load of fire wood."

"Falters? Falters? Why you smelly old marmot. I will not falter but will be there to pick you up when you fall to the ground like a head shot buffalo," Josiah quickly responded with his characteristic wide smile. Both men, now the closest of brothers since the Great Spirit had intervened in their once challenging lives, laughed loudly at each other antics. Then in his heart Josiah thought, having a brother like Red Shirt sure has made life a whole lot easier than it had been, especially now that he had a constant companion in everything he did instead of an antagonist like he had in Red Shirt in the days long past. But at the same time he had other thoughts...strange thoughts. In his latest vision, he had witnessed himself undergoing the Sun Dance. He had also witnessed Red

Shirt dancing as well and in both instances, with his head swimming in pain, had seen dead and dying cavalry soldiers lying at both of their feet...Letting his thoughts drift away like the smoke from their campfire, Josiah got back to the really serious business of cooking his evening meal.

The following evening, after Red Shirt and Josiah had returned from their hunting trip, they spent their first moments giving parts of the three deer they had killed to the old, infirm and widows of the band. Then parting company, Josiah retreated to the nearby creek to bathe, followed by a quick trip to Old Chief Smoke's tipi for the warmth it offered. En route, he was greeted by his new mother, Prairie Flower, who was cooking supper over their outside cooking fire. In a way it brought back memories of his mother cooking over an open fire on the Oregon Trail and his anticipation of his favorite Dutch oven biscuits to come, thought Josiah...Then Josiah quickly shook those sad memories of yesteryear from his mind. As taught by the Oglala, it was not good to remember or speak of the dead because in doing so, that caused their ghosts to linger between the two worlds instead of going to the Happy Hunting grounds and happily joining up with the rest of the Cloud People.

As he walked up to Prairie Flower, he handed her a full length of back strap removed from a large doe deer he had shot earlier that morning. That prime piece of meat brought an instant smile from Prairie Flower, as her thoughts turned to the next day's supper and the cooking magic she could do with such a tender piece of venison. Grinning at Prairie Flower's obvious smile of pleasure

157

over the venison treat to come, Josiah gathered up her small frame and gave her one of his grizzly bear-like hugs. In turn, he got a joyfully swung wooden cooking spoon alongside his ear for such a public exhibition of emotion in front of nearby onlookers in the village who were looking on at the two of them as they showed signs of affection for each other.

About then, Old Chief Smoke emerged from his tipi and a big smile spread across his face over his new son's antics with Prairie Flower. He was also pleased that his new son had safely returned from the hunt. "Were you and Red Shirt successful in your hunt?" he asked.

"Yes, father. Red Shirt and I killed three large, fat deer and have since distributed the meat throughout those in the village needing it the most."

"That is, except for this wonderful piece of back strap which we will have for supper tomorrow evening," said Prairie Flower as she held up the long venison back strap slab of meat for the old chief to see.

The old chief smiled and then he could see a very serious look on Josiah's face. "What is the matter, my son?" asked the old chief. "Have you and Red Shirt been having trouble like the two of you did in the past?"

"No father. He is as he said he would be in front of the entire village. He is my brother and I am his. We will walk the Red Road together for as long as the Great Spirit allows us to remain in this world. But I have been thinking of other things. In my latest vision quest after you told me I should dance in the Sun Dance Lodge, I saw things I have never seen before. Things that make me concerned about how I will do when I participate as a dancer. Those thoughts have been riding heavy on my heart because I don't want to fail or cause you or the members of the band to lose face if I am unable to perform as is required. Remember, I am a white man and not of the blood of an Oglala. Therefore, I have questions about myself and my ability to successfully complete the dance. I have also had visions of many dead and dying soldiers at my feet. Unlike the soldiers being eaten by the huge grouse, these men in my vision were at both Red Shirt's and my feet at the Sun Dance circle. I have tried pushing such thoughts from my mind because Fast Antelope has said these things of my vision are of things yet to come but I am finding it harder and harder to do."

"Son, after your latest vision quest about dancing in the Sun Dance, we talked little because I was not sure if that was what you really wanted to do. Now that I see you are certain that you want to dance in the Sun Dance Lodge, I think it is time that we have a talk about the Sun Dance, what it means and what it will require of the participant. Tonight after supper, we will talk. But let us talk no more about dead and dying soldiers. I fear such things will only bring harm to The People. Especially if such killing is to happen in the days to come. The whites are becoming more and more like the grasshoppers in the fall and we are like the lone eagle in the sky. They are the many and we are but the few. Let us hear no more about what you have seen for I fear such visions may come true."

Later after that evening's supper, Josiah and Old Chief Smoke retired to the smaller fire inside their tipi. There the two men sat down and the old chief, after a few long moments gathering up his thoughts, began Josiah's instruction on the background and rituals of the Sun Dance ceremony.

"Son, sometime soon we will be contacted by a member from another band and advised as to where the Sun Dance lodge for this year is to be built. Then the bands of the Sioux Nation from all over will gather at that location and a great encampment will be built. There you will see like at our camp, that the tipis will be arranged in a great circle around the Sun Dance lodge. It will be a grand event and much happiness will be present from all who are gathered. It is customary that everyone wear their best dress, ride their finest horses and bring all their food during such a sacred occasion. They need to do so because there will be much feasting, visiting between friends and clans, gambling, storytelling, and racing of our fastest horses."

With those words and an obvious grin of anticipation over the events soon to come, the old chief paused in his teachings. Josiah, reading on the old chief's face just how solemn the reason for such an occasion, remained stilled out of respect for the moment in time that he was now being privileged to experience. Then the old chief began once again. "Summer is the time for many of our ceremonies and rituals to be performed or carried out. It is the time of much happiness among The People. The Sun Dance is our most important ceremonial event and is ranked above all our other ceremonies of sacrifice and thanksgiving. It is usually performed when all the different bands of the tribe are reassembled following our winter dispersal. The Sun Dance itself is only held when the moon is full because that is when the Creator or Grandfather is shining down his eternal light upon the whole world. When the location for the Sun Dance has been determined, specially qualified people are appointed by a holy man of renown to locate and cut down the center pole or the 'first pole.' Those selected to cut down the center pole to be used in the Sun Dance will be looking for a cottonwood tree with a fork in the top. A cottonwood tree is used because it is considered sacred to the Sioux Nation. Sacred, because the cottonwood tree taught The People from the shape of its leaves, how to make a tipi. Once a tree is selected, it is chopped down, dragged back to camp and placed into the ground at the site chosen for the Sun Dance lodge. Then other poles are cut and placed in an outside circular framework around the center pole. Following that, the roof of the lodge will be built with smaller logs and covered with green tree branches. Finally, the holy men place religious offerings in the fork of the center pole and the finished bundle of offerings is called a Thunder Bird's Nest." Once again, the old chief seemed to run down on his collection of thoughts and paused. Josiah, lost in his thoughts over the amount of cultural information coming his way, remained quiet so as not to disturb the learning essence of the moment.

Moments later after assembling his next set of thoughts, the old chief spoke once again. "The People believe that the dancer's physical suffering at the pole in the center of the Sun Dance Lodge, are taking upon themselves the agony and suffering of The People. This is done because the hardships and the unexpected are a way of life for The People. So when the dancers dance and physically suffer, that is their way of giving thanks and providing proof beyond a doubt of the sincerity of the dancer's gratitude to the Great Spirit for His responses to their pleas for the benefit of all The People." Once again the old chief paused as he prepared to describe the actual ceremony to his new son, a potential dancer.

"If you decide to become a dancer, you will be provided a helper or an assistant. If that dancer is to be you Josiah, I will be your helper. Once again, if you choose to dance, you must fast, drink no water, be purified and painted in a special way by me prior to participating in the Sun Dance. Following that, I will be there to encourage you during the dance and later to cut you down if you have not torn free or cut off the ragged pieces of remaining flesh from your body. Those pieces of flesh will then be placed on the ground around the center pole as an offering to the sun."

It was at that moment that Josiah stopped the old chief asking, "Where is my flesh to come from?"

"If you become a dancer, you will be seated facing east. Then I will have you move your shoulders back and push your chest forward, with your arms hanging loosely down at your sides. I will pinch up your chest skin on one side of your body and run a knife through it. I will then do the same to the other side of your chest. Wooden skewers about four inches long will then be pushed through and under the slits made on the left and right sides of your chest. For each participant, there will be a long leather thong tied to the top of the center pole in the Sun Dance Lodge. A long flat strip of hide will then have a hole cut

162

in its middle and that will be threaded onto the leather thong tied to the center pole. Then a strong knot will be tied at the end of that leather thong so the piece of hide cannot slip off. The hide will then be pulled down the leather thong to the knot and folded into a 'V' shaped piece of skin. Once that flap of skin is folded into a 'V' shape, small holes will be cut on each side of the bottom of the flap of hide. Those holes cut into the bottom of each side of that flap of skin, will then be individually placed over the ends of the skewers stuck under the skin on each side of your chest. Lastly, you will be helped to your feet by me and I will pull you back hard on the leather thong to see if the flaps of skin placed over the skewers in your chest are secure and will hold once you lean back against them. Once in that position, you and the other dancers must lean hard against the pull of the leather thong attached to the center pole and walk back and forth in a half circle in prayer facing the Thunder Bird's Nest. As that is done, you will be blowing a special eagle bone whistle that I will make for you. When you are walking back and forth, you must sag against the leather thong in order to eventually tear the skewers loose from the flesh of your chest! Come sun down if you have not torn the skewers free from your chest, then I will cut you down. Following that, I will cut the loose flaps of skin from off your chest and leave the skin on the ground around the center pole. Those strips of skin will then be prayed over by both of us and then you are free to return to my tipi and have Prairie Flower treat your wounds and give you some water. It is then that your successful sacrifice to the Great Spirit will bring much good to The People and

163

yourself for the seasons of life that follows."

With those finishing words for the evening, the old chief rose and joined his wife in their sleeping furs. Josiah did the same in his sleeping furs but it was hours before he could sleep because of all the information presented that evening by the old chief. Information that he found whirling around and around in his head like a dust devil on the prairie before the fury of a coming thunderstorm rolls over every living thing below.

After breakfast the next morning, Josiah was surprised with a visit from the band's holy man, Fast Antelope. Once invited into the old chief's tipi and sitting down next to Josiah, Fast Antelope unrolled a tanned rabbit skin to reveal a single dried and heavily dry-smoked wing from a sage grouse. "Josiah, I have for you a symbol from my medicine bundle representing your power that was revealed to you during your first vision quest."

With those words, Fast Antelope handed a sage grouse wing that was beautifully beaded on the wing's leather covered humeral bone to Josiah. Taken completely by surprise, Josiah reverently handled the wing and could almost instantaneously feel its powers magically surging through his body. Turning to Fast Antelope, Josiah thanked the holy man for being so thoughtful in providing him with the symbol of his power, especially since he had not yet found the time to acquire a sage grouse symbol of some sort for himself.

"Wear this token in your hair so that your enemies can see the power that flows through you, a power that will take their lives and also so the Great Spirit knows who to protect from the flight of an arrow and the speeding bullet in the dust and confusion of battle," said a very stern faced Fast Antelope. "For to lose this symbol of your power for whatever reason, will bring about the destruction of your life. For you see, this will cause the bad spirits to enter your life, attack and remove you from Mother Earth! Once you lose or remove this symbol of your power, your life is in jeopardy from the bad spirits who will come at you just as fast as the grouse flies when frightened. They will do so because you are a white man living as one of us. Pay heed Josiah. I speak with a straight tongue about the warning I have given you, for I too have had a vision...A vision that the Great Spirit will not allow me to share with anyone. Pay heed, Josiah, to my words of warning! For not to listen will quickly place you among The Cloud People!"

With those ominous words of caution ringing in his ears, Josiah sat there stunned over Fast Antelope's stern warning. It was then that Fast Antelope rose and without another word being spoken, left the old chief's tipi. For many long moments, Josiah sat there fingering the beautifully beaded sage grouse wing, the new found source of his power. Then paying heed to Fast Antelope's final words, Josiah carefully and firmly attached the grouse wing to a braid in his long hair. To make sure of its proper attachment and paying heed to Fast Antelope's stern words of warning, he had Prairie Flower check the knotting to make sure the sacred wing was firmly affixed. Leaning back on his back rest from a sitting position in the quiet of the tipi, Josiah let his mind move freely about over what had just transpired. Josiah had never seen Fast Antelope so serious and agitated in anything previously that he had done as a holy man. It was even more apparent that whatever Fast Antelope had seen in his recent vision, had badly shaken and scared the holy man. And Fast Antelope had a reputation for being a fierce warrior and hardly afraid of anything before he became a holy man. With that realization in mind, Josiah silently vowed never to forget Fast Antelope's words of wisdom and warning. However, like all young men who consider themselves immortal, his mind quickly drifted from the serious to other things...

To his way of thinking, he was just a short step away from becoming a full-fledged Oglala warrior. He had counted coup against the hated Pawnee, had successfully completed several vision quests, and was now preparing to become a dancer at the fabled Sun Dance. And upon completion of the Sun Dance, Old Chief Smoke had advised him that was one time within their culture that a warrior could be given a proper tribal name. However, the old chief had also advised Josiah that the Great Spirit had yet to visit him with a new name for Josiah. Once again with those thoughts of things to come running through his mind, Josiah had already like many other young men, began diminishing Fast Antelope's words of warning because of other more pressing issues flooding his mind...

Two weeks later, Spotted Eagle, a Hunkpapa Sioux warrior from Chief Running Elk's band, rode into Old Chief Smoke's village. In meeting with Old Chief Smoke, Spotted Eagle advised the old chief of the location of the soon to be held Sun Dance. With those words of the pending celebration happily ringing in Old Chief Smoke's ears, Spotted Eagle rode off to advise other nearby bands of Oglala of the coming event and its location.

The very next day found Old Chief Smoke's band on the move further north and east toward the reported location of the soon to be held Sun Dance. This they did because the Sun Dance festivities once started, from the cutting of the first pole to the end of the Sun Dance itself, only lasted about ten days. Then the festivities would end and the tribe would go out on a grand buffalo hunt. Following that, they would once again disband and disperse into more manageable and smaller bands for the harsh winter months lying ahead. Five days of travel found the old chief's band of Oglala, traveling over the last of a series of rolling hills toward the grand encampment arrayed in a long, sparsely wooded valley below.

From upon his horse, Old Chief Smoke smiled his approval of the chosen site. He knew that the Sioux did not like living or gathering in the dark timber because of the chances of being surprised and attacked by their enemies. A sparsely wooded valley suited the tribes needs best because of its openness and yet still readily available supplies of firewood and horse feed. Stopping on the last hill, the old chief took in the view below with great joy. Below him in a grand array, laid an encampment of about one hundred fifty tipis arranged in a huge loose circle around a circular, stand-alone structure with a green tree branch brushed up roof. That circular structure was the Sun Dance Lodge. There were numerous horse herds scattered throughout the great valley, gaily dressed people walked about and the air was filled with the noisy haze of the camp's barking dogs as they greeted two and four legged strangers into their midst. Running the full length of the valley, a slow moving stream was dotted with watering horses, children at play and people bathing or gathering water for the day's meals.

Breathing in deeply the spectacle of life laid out below, the old chief gestured with a wave of his arm for the band to enter the festivities. Moving his band to the northern edge of the grand encampment near a small wooded area with plenty of water, the final camp site was decided upon. Then the work of setting up their encampment began. The horse herd was positioned out in a location where they could be watched and not intermingle with other horse herds in an area where there was plenty of grass and water. Their encampment was placed within the northern edge of the great circle of tipis and soon members from Old Chief Smoke's band were foraging in the area for firewood and water. And in doing so, began happily mingling with other old friends, as well as those members from other like clans. Throughout this flurry of activity, Josiah assisted many of the very old and infirm in setting up their camp sites. Then he strode off into the cottonwood timbered area gathering up arm loads of wood for Prairie Flower and several other older villagers.

Once again, several braves and warriors from other bands who did not personally know the history of Josiah heaped ridicule upon him for doing women's work. Even women from other bands began making unfriendly remarks about a warrior doing women's work. But that harassment soon stopped as warriors from Old Chief Smoke's band put out the word that Josiah was a white man who was also a very fierce warrior, a warrior who lived in "two worlds" and that was just his way of doing things. Then the word got out among those gathered that Josiah was the one who almost single handedly had saved Old Chief Smoke's band from the winter attack by the Pawnees—an attack where he personally had killed thirteen Pawnee warriors by himself and was soon to participate as a dancer in the Sun Dance. After those words had filtered down among those gathered throughout the grand encampment, Josiah found that whatever he did, no more sour looks, demeaning words or questioning eyes followed his sometimes unusual, non-traditional actions.

Then it was time! In preparation for the ritual of the Sun Dance, Old Chief Smoke and two elders prepared a sweat lodge for the beginning of the purification ceremony that was to follow. Following the sweat lodge and bathing ceremonies, Josiah began a fast with no food or water. The next day before daylight, Josiah along with the other soon to be dancers were escorted into a tipi where a renowned priest or "lodge maker" instructed the soon-to-be-dancers on what was expected of them during the ceremony. At the end of that instruction, Old Chief Smoke took Josiah back to his tipi. There in the quiet of his tipi, Old Chief Smoke instructed Josiah that all pledges who entered the sacred Sun Dance Lodge had to not only be purified but painted in a special way by their sponsor. With those words, Old Chief Smoke instructed Josiah to strip down to just his loin cloth. Then Old Chief Smoke tightly wrapped and tied a heavily painted red cloth around his waist so it would not come loose during the duration of the dance.

Looking down, Josiah saw that the cloth was let down until it hung all around from his waist down to his ankles. The old chief who had been through the ritual of the Sun Dance as a young man then began the second part of the dancer's preparation. Old Chief Smoke began painting Josiah bright red from the waist up, and in doing so, advised Josiah that red represented all that was sacred to The People. Following that after the red paint had dried, the old chief painted a black circle around Josiah's face telling him that the circle represented The Spirit. Then Josiah had four vertical black lines painted on his chin, which the old chief advised represented the powers of the four directions. Black stripes were then painted around his wrists, elbows, upper arms, and ankles, which the old chief, now sweating profusely as he performed his duties, advised those stripes represented the bonds of ignorance that tied the dancers to Mother Earth.

When Old Chief Smoke had finished his preparation of Josiah, the two of them quietly walked through the village to the Sun Dance Lodge as other tribal members looked on in respectful silence. As they did, Josiah remembered back to one of his previous vision quests. In the vision from that quest, he had seen himself dressed and painted for the Sun Dance ceremony as he was that very day...Entering the cool quiet of the brushed over Sun Dance Lodge, Josiah saw other pledges being prepared for the final ceremony. Seated two dancers to his right, sat his friend and now brother, Red Shirt. His face was contorted in pain. Then Josiah's eyes went down to Red Shirt's chest area. There protruding from his bloody chest were the two skewers fastened under cuts made in the skin in preparation for what was to come.

It was then that Old Chief Smoke had Josiah sit down on a wooden stool. After Josiah had been seated, the old chief instructed him to face to the east, thrust his shoulders back and let his arms hang loosely at his side. Having done as instructed, Josiah was painfully surprised when the old chief deftly pinched up a large amount of skin and muscle from his left breast with his hand and quickly thrust a knife through the upraised mound of flesh! Wincing in pain and surprise over the rapidity of the old chief's movements, he was breathlessly surprised once again as the process was quickly repeated on his right breast. As Josiah sat there trying hard not to cry out in pain and get his wind of surprise back, he closed his eyes and bit down hard on his teeth. Red Shirt was saying nothing about the pain he was enduring and Josiah sure as the grass was green, was saying nothing of his painful discomfort as well...Then the old chief pulled up the bloody wide strips of skin on each side of Josiah's chest and deftly slid wooden skewers under each of the slits. Not slowing down because of the pain Josiah was feeling as was betrayed by his deeply halting breaths, the old chief continued with the ritual preparations. Reaching up and grabbing the leather thong fastened to the center pole and taking the flap of tanned hide fastened at the thong's end, he slipped both ends of the skewers through the holes previously cut in the lower ends of the hide for such purposes. As he did, he whispered into Josiah's ear that the leather thong to which he was now attached symbolized the sacred rays of light from the "One

Above."

Following those last words, the old chief helped Josiah to his feet and then moved him backwards a few steps until the thong holding the hide attached to the skewers of his chest was taught. Then to Josiah's surprise and pain, Old Chief Smoke pulled him back hard on the thong to make sure the skewers hooked into the hide on the end of the leather thong would hold when the dancer leaned backwards and that the strains on the ends of the skewers were even so that he would not prematurely pull them out. When he did, Josiah saw stars and found it difficult to breathe once again from all the new pain crashing through his body and head. But, he was here of his own accord and just gritted his teeth as he kept his eyes tightly closed. That was when Old Chief Smoke whispered to Josiah for him to open up his eyes and look at the Thunder Bird's nest. And as he did, pray that his sacrifice would be heard by The Spirits and in doing so, bring happiness to the whole tribe.

"Remember Josiah, I say again. Always look at the Thunder Bird's nest as you dance and pray. Otherwise, your sacrifice will not be heard by the Spirits above." Then a small eagle bone whistle was thrust into Josiah's hands from the old chief. Looking down at the whistle, Josiah saw through his pain-hazed eyes that it had been painted with numerous red and yellow dots. On the end of the whistle was attached an eagle plume feather, which would extend outward every time he blew into the sacred whistle. At that time, Josiah noticed that all the other dancers had been helped up and were standing like him, taught against their leather thongs. Then a holy man instructed all the dancers to lean back against the thong, pray and dance in a half circle around the pole.

It was then that Josiah remembered through the haze of his pain what Old Chief Smoke had instructed him about earlier while he was being painted. The old chief had instructed Josiah that he had to always lean back against the thong pulling against the skewers attached to his chest. And that when dancing, he was to lean back, rise up onto his toes and continue blowing the sacred eagle bone whistle until he was able to pull free from the skewers or until he was cut down at the end of the day. Once he had ripped lose from the skewers or he had to be cut down, the loose flaps of skin from his chest would then be cut off and placed at the foot of the center pole. There he and Old Chief Smoke would pray together to the Great Spirit that Josiah's sacrifices had proved beyond a doubt the sincerity of his gratitude to the Great Spirit for His responses to their pleas.

For the next four hours, Josiah strained mightily against the skewers fastened into his chest all to no avail. Josiah was a stoutly built man and his chest muscles were thicker than most because of all the hard work he had been doing. And when Old Chief Smoke had pinched up his skin, because of that extreme musculature running across Josiah's chest, he had taken a substantial amount of muscle tissue along with it! Because of that deeper than usual incision, Josiah was now paying the price for being so stoutly built. By now, the skin and muscle had been pulled hugely outward but the elasticity of the deep tissue incision held him fast to the unyielding thong. The pain was so intense, that Josiah found it hard to lean back, walk on his toes and blow the eagle bone whistle with a "just" heart. But he pushed those thoughts of extreme discomfort from out of his mind, overcoming his pain somewhat and carried on.

Soon several dancers faltered and one even fell to the ground in a swoon. However, the others continued on and so did Red Shirt and Josiah. Then Red Shirt ripped free from his bonds and dropped to the ground in a bloody, exhausted mess. Helped to his feet, he was seated and then his helper took out his sheath knife and cut large pieces of loose flesh hanging from Red Shirt's chest and placed them at the base of the center pole. Then the helper assisted Red Shirt to his feet and the two of them moved to the pole and pile of severed flesh, where they stood quietly in prayer. Finished, Red Shirt was helped from the arena. But not before he gave words of encouragement in passing to Josiah to carry on in good faith. Then Red Shirt was taken back to his helper's tipi for some drinking water and the bloody wounds on his chest to be cared for.

Meanwhile, Josiah continued with his shuffling dance of pain, prayers offered to the Great Spirit, and his many efforts to tear free from the unforgiving skewers still attached to the unyielding flesh attached to the long thong. However, the cuts in Josiah's chest made by Old Chief Smoke had been too deeply made and the musculature beneath the skin still stubbornly held fast, as he continued his shuffling-whistle blowing pace. Another hour passed and Josiah found himself to be the last dancer in the arena who had not yet pulled free. And no matter how hard he pulled, he could not tear lose from the skewers attached to his breast tissue. They were just too deeply imbedded into the musculature of his flesh! By now, he was getting weaker from the fast, loss of blood, constantly burning chest pain, and exertion from the constant unfamiliar shuffling dance-step while pulling against the thong.

Saying his prayers one more time to the Great Spirit, he found his mind was now beginning to play tricks on him. Through his mental haze, he saw his folks standing by their wagon train beckoning to him. He saw his uncle Lemuel and cousin Jordan bringing in the wagon train's livestock from their night feeding grounds. They too were beckoning for him to come and join them as well. And then from on high above the ground like he was floating in the air, he saw himself below as a young man stalking a large covey of sage grouse...Then that vision passed and with surprisingly renewed strength, Josiah gave a violent wrench against the hide holding the skewers inserted deeply into his chest. In doing so, he tore free from the skewers and snapped the leather thong binding him to his earthly bonds in the same motion!

When he ripped free, breaking the main leather thong tied to the central pole in the process, an almost eerie reverent sound swirled around all those multitudes gathered to watch the dancers. A sound like that from a deep cave with the wind softly blowing through it! That was followed then by an eerie abject silence over the symbolism just represented by Josiah breaking free from his bonds of the flesh and the snapping of the sacred leather thong, a silence that was deafening in and of itself. Sitting Bull, a Hunkpapa/Lakota, and the most revered of the holy men in the encampment, rose from his position

175

of respect from within the now totally silent and still shocked crowd. Without any words being spoken, he gracefully moved through the respectfully parting and still stunned audience of onlookers to the Sun Dance arena. Josiah just stood there trembling in pain and exhaustion, as the much respected holy man made an unexpected approach. Now the silence from the onlookers was so profound that one could hear the neighing of a horse from a distant horse herd at the far end of the valley's huge encampment.

Quietly walking up to Josiah, Sitting Bull reached out and placed both of his hands upon the exhausted dancer's shoulders. For the longest time, Sitting Bull just looked deeply into Josiah's piercing blue eyes saying nothing. Josiah, utterly surprised by Sitting Bull's unannounced physical presence, stood as still as he could, quit wobbling, and then looked deeply back into the old holy man's dark eyes. Neither man blinked...By now, the onlookers hardly dared to breathe over the spectacle mystically taking place before their eyes. Then Sitting Bull quietly spoke.

"Blue-eyed white man, the Great Spirit has smiled upon you this day. Not only have you honored Him with your true character in the Sun Dance but also with another symbol of your great powers this day. Never, have I ever seen anyone break the sacred thong from the central pole holding a dancer." With that, Sitting Bull took out his knife and carefully removed the flesh hanging from Josiah's bloody and now showing signs of deep bruising, chest. "Come with me," said Sitting Bull as he gently took Josiah's elbow. With that, they both solemnly walked to the center pole. There Sitting Bull and Josiah prayed to the Great Spirit. Sitting Bull for the Great Spirit to always shine His goodness upon such a warrior and Josiah asking for much goodness for his village. Then Sitting Bull walked over to the foot long piece of busted leather thong laying on the ground, picked it up and returned to a still wobbly and now totally transfixed Josiah. Reaching up, Sitting Bull removed Josiah's sage grouse wing from Josiah's long braid and then removing his sheath knife once again, cut slits into each end of the leather thong. Sitting Bull then tightly attached one end of the thong to the grouse wing-bone and the other end of the thong now holding the sage grouse wing onto Josiah's long braid.

"Wear this always, white man. For the Great Spirit has smiled upon you and will continue to do so as long as you wear the sacred thong and the wing of the grouse together. Today you made big medicine. Your strong medicine and a recent vision I had about a blue-eyed Oglala warrior that I did not understand, but now do, has touched my heart and opened my eyes. And in that vision that I did not earlier understand, I now know it was telling me that someday, the two of us will walk many trails together! Trails that will be both happy in strange lands across a big water where we will walk together but only after a great battle against the enemies of the Sioux Nation. But before we go across the big water, those trails traveled after that great battle, will lead us into the northern lands, where winter lives and a Queen Mother watches over all her people. There we will have but a short peace. Then we will make a trip to a land of misery and a blackness will overcome me personally and the rest of The People...It is with those thoughts in mind and what I have seen this day, that I must say, the Creator has touched my heart and opened my eyes. It is because of those things, with the guidance of the Creator, that I give you your sacred name to be used when among us as one of us! From now on, you will be known to The People across the prairie as the great warrior, Josiah White Buffalo! Josiah White Buffalo, because the white buffalo is sacred, strong, has many great powers, and are rarely found among all the others gathered around him."

With that, Sitting Bull in all his respectful elegance, grace, and bearing, turned and quietly walked out from the Sun Dance Lodge and back to his tipi. It was then that Old Chief Smoke approached and holding a still hazy Josiah's arm, proudly escorted him from the Sun Dance Lodge. Back at Old Chief Smoke's tipi, Prairie Flower fretted over Josiah and his wounds with her favorite medicinals. Sitting for the first time in many hours, the exhausted Josiah felt his strength slowly returning. As he did, he couldn't help but seeing an unusual look on Old Chief Smoke's face. One that he had never seen before...

"Why the strange look in your eyes this day, Father? Did I not do well in your eyes?"

For the longest moment, Old Chief Smoke just looked at Josiah, then said, "Josiah, you brought great honor and strength to yourself and my band, and this is the first time I have seen a white man so honored as Sitting Bull had spoken. I have heard of stories of other great warriors who came from a captive white woman and an Indian man, like Quanah Parker of the Comanche being so honored. But never from a captive white man from a willing Indian mother. As our holy man Fast Antelope has said, your power is great and I am honored to have you as my son." Then Old Chief Smoke got quiet and unusually reserved. Finally, he quietly spoke once again.

"I have been asking for a vision from the Great Spirit for a name in your honor to be bestowed upon you after the Sun Dance as is our custom. For many nights I have not been blessed with any visions. I began to think the Great Spirit was angry at me for something I had done that displeased Him. Now I know why I was never given a naming vision for you. The Great Spirit was waiting for you to show your character, courage and sacrifice in the Sun Dance before He allowed a name for you to be brought forth. Then He honored you even further by having such a great and revered holy man like Sitting Bull being present when you honored the Great Spirit. The Great Spirit chose to have you named by one of our greatest holy men in the Sioux Nation. No greater honor could ever be expected, given or fulfilled. You are truly blessed my son, but just remember. Like Fast Antelope has said, you must remember to always wear you symbol of power and now that Sitting Bull has also tied another sacred symbol to your symbol of power, namely the broken piece of leather thong, you must wear that as well. For to do otherwise will bring the bad spirits down upon you."

Then having said his say, the old chief left the tipi so Josiah could relax and get some rest. However, rest was not forthcoming to the newest warrior in Old Chief Smoke's band. Lying there on his sleeping furs with the terrible burning pain across his chest, Josiah White

Buffalo wondered over Sitting Bull's prophetic words. Sitting Bull had a vision that he could not understand until he had seen Josiah performing the Sun Dance. Then when Josiah had snapped the leather thong attached to his chest, apparently Sitting Bull had seen the goodness and great power in Josiah and in the sage grouse wing. And in doing so, had figured out what his vision that had been sent earlier by the Great Spirit really meant. But to Josiah White Buffalo, most of Sitting Bull's words remained a great mystery. What had he meant about the two of them walking many trails together? What was the thing that he had called "the big water"? What about the great battles taking place and going to a country where the winter sleeps and is watched over by a Queen Mother? And finally, the deep blackness he had spoken about coming over The People? Laying back on his sleeping furs and not finding the answers to any of his questions, Josiah White Buffalo finally found the silence and darkness of a deep but fitful sleep...

And in that deep and fitful sleep, many visions visited Josiah White Buffalo but none answered the questions he held.

Chapter Eight

WINTER CAMP, THE HORSE HERD BATTLE, BUFFALO HUNTERS AND BLUECOATS, THE COMING STORM...

The huge encampment around the Sun Dance Lodge lingered for a few more days as the visiting and feasting continued. Then a grand buffalo hunt was planned and carried out, as all of the bands were running low on fresh meat after all the feasting and celebrating surrounding the Sun Dance ceremonies. Josiah White Buffalo and Red Shirt did not participate in the buffalo hunt because their chest wounds were still draining fluids and the dust and jolting ride on a horse during the hunt would have done nothing for either of them in the way of any healing. After the buffalo hunt, many bands remained at the grand encampment for a few more days drying and smoking the meat and processing the hides for use in the winter months to come. This they did in order to preserve the meat stores and lighten the amount of weight they would soon be transporting to their winter encampments. Then one by one, the bands straggled off to the sites of their chosen winter encampments after saying their many goodbyes to their other friends and clan members.

However, Old Chief Smoke and his elders had met several times seriously discussing where they should make their next winter encampment. They also met with many of the leaders from other bands as to good locations for a northernmost winter's encampment. Discussions they found necessary in the face of the tremendous encroachment of the white man. Especially those of the buffalo hide hunters frequenting Old Chief Smoke's historical summering and wintering grounds to the south. And with all the encroaching white man settlers and buffalo hunters came the U.S. Cavalry to protect them from the many clashes between the various bands of the Lakota and the Northern Cheyenne. Clashes that were occurring almost on a weekly basis, especially with the settlers of the land. Every day, more and more settlers flocked to the new lands, lands that were historically considered sacred and possessed by the Lakota and Northern Cheyenne. Especially the Black Hills, which were considered a sacred burial grounds for many of those of the Sioux Nation. And every day, numerous bands of Lakota and their Northern Cheyenne neighbors found it harder and harder to maintain their historical and nomadic, free living life styles in the face of such encroachment.

Finally, the band's winter encampment decisions were made. Old Chief Smoke and the elders had decided they would move further north than the band had ever lived in years past. That decision for such a radical move had been made because of several concerning factors. The "Iron Horse," whose rails were now laid across their ancestral hunting grounds, were causing many of the buffalo to concentrate further north and south away from the train's main travel route. Plus, because of the overall disturbance the iron rails caused, the local buffalo herds had also changed their historical migration routes so much, that they too were now moving further and further away from Old Chief Smoke's ancestral grounds of occupation. Also with the advent of the iron rails, more and more people were moving into and homesteading the prairie, and in doing so, moved the local buffalo herds even further from their normal feeding and wintering grounds. And without the buffalo, the main source of hides and meat, Old Chief Smoke and the elders discovered they could no longer prosper on their historical southernmost lands. So, the decision had been made to move further north into the high Plains, an area initially proposed to be set aside for the exclusive use by the Sioux Nation under the 1868 Fort Laramie Treaty. And like many other treaties due to the rapid westward expansion of a new nation, one that was predictably soon to be broken.

Come the appointed moving day, members of the band said their goodbyes to their friends and remaining neighboring clans, broke camp and formed up into a protective caravan. Fifteen days of traveling later found Old Chief Smoke's band at the northernmost leading edge of the northern Plains of the Sioux Nation's historical lands of occupation, lands that the Sioux had occupied since being forced out from their ancestral homelands in the eastern woodlands of the current day United States in the early 1700s. Then being chased from there in the present day State of Minnesota, to finally the Plains by the warlike Chippewa Indians, a group of warlike northern Indians who had been supplied firearms by the British in 1745. As a result of possessing such new and superior firepower, they were able to push the Lakota Nation from their original home in the eastern woodlands out onto the Plains in an area that was further south of the Chippewa Nation's now occupied homelands.

Moving into a ten mile long valley heavily dotted with cottonwood and oak trees throughout, Old Chief Smoke raised his arm for the caravan of tired travelers to halt. Surrounded by his advisors, they quietly examined the lands below with a practiced eye. Following the initial look into their new home, the group of elders then rode throughout the valley drinking in its beautiful location and resources. The valley had ample water throughout, wood was plentiful and the prairie grasses was belly deep for their large horse herd. On the northern side of the valley a ring of rolling, tree covered hills were arrayed in such a manner as to block out all but the harshest of the winter winds from the northwest. To the south laid the open plains and on the day the group surveyed their potential winter home, a herd of buffalo contentedly grazed less than a mile distant. With those prophetic symbols of wellbeing provided by the Great Spirit and the surrounding land's overall general lay out, the old chief paused his riders.

"This shall be our new winter home," he quietly stated to his advisors. The advisors to a man, nodded their approval of his words of selection. Then the group rode to a well-watered area that was to be the band's winter home site. With that selection made, a rider was dispatched back to fetch the nearby waiting band. Half an hour later, the barking of dogs and the happy sounds of many people talking and laughing rent the late summer's soft air. With their arrival, the camp set-up began as many of the band staked out their tipis in a loose circle around Old Chief Smoke's soon to be centrally located tipi. As the village set-up continued, the smaller children began happily exploring their new home, as some of the older boys moved their extensive horse herd further west into the upper reaches of the valley for the good grazing it offered. Once the camp was set up, the old chief planted his staff of spotted eagle tail feathers near the front of his tipi and Old Chief Smoke's band of Oglala were at their new home for whatever the winter months and the surrounding resources would bring.

Josiah White Buffalo, still sore but healing up from his Sun Dance wounds and their long ride to their winter encampment site, was more than happy to carefully dismount from Wind. Standing alongside his horse, he hung onto the saddle until the feeling came back into his sore knees from the long horse ride just completed. Then Josiah White Buffalo felt a hand on his shoulder as Red Shirt strode gingerly up to him. He too was still smarting over his Sun Dance wounds saying, "My brother, do you hurt as much as do I after that long horse ride?"

Josiah White Buffalo slowly turned so as not to break loose any of the recent scabbing taking place on his now heavily scarred chest and just grinned. Then turning back to the activity in the circle of tipis around the chief's eagle feather staff now planted firmly into the ground, said, "Red Shirt, is your mother putting your tipi up alongside ours?"

"Yes. What better place to keep track of my weaker brother," Red Shirt replied as he grinned widely over his "funny" just uttered.

"More likely for me to get your 'last part over the creek up and into the saddle' in the morning so we can go hunting," replied Josiah White Buffalo with an equally big grin over his "funny."

The two now close friends unsaddled their mounts and then walked their horses up to the horse herd in order to get the stiffness out from their legs and knee joints after their long ride. Finally arriving, they let their steads go so they could feed and water with the other horses. Following that, the two men walked slowly back to camp visiting like two close brothers who hadn't seen each other for a long period of time were want to do. But as they did, neither man forgot what the excellent deer habitat surrounding their valley appeared to represent in future meat hunting opportunities. Then catching each other looking at the other over their obvious keen interest in the hunting grounds, they both had to laugh. Yes, they were brothers even to thinking alike. Just like the Great Spirit in all His wisdom had dictated...

By then, Prairie Flower had erected their tipi and arranged the family's belongings therein. Josiah White Buffalo then entered and sat patiently as Prairie Flower fussed over him once again applying her medicinals to his still raw and draining chest wounds received from the Sun Dance. Then Josiah White Buffalo quietly slipped into his sleeping furs and fell into a much needed deep and healing sleep.

Later that afternoon, Josiah White Buffalo awoke to

the wonderful smells of Prairie Flower's supper cooking. With that smell hanging aromatically in the air and his belly making hungry noises, Josiah White Buffalo surprised himself on just how fast he could move when supper was served. For the next month, Josiah White Buffalo and Red Shirt stayed mostly around their encampment as they quietly healed up from their recent ordeal at the Sun Dance ceremony.

"BUFFALO, BUFFALO!" yelled the village crier as he raced through the encampment on foot. "BUFFALO AT THE EAST END OF THE VALLEY WATERING BY THE STREAM," he continued.

With those electric words ringing throughout a sleepy camp in the late summer's early afternoon heat, all resting was forgotten as people stirred themselves over hearing such welcome words. Almost immediately, the village was a bee hive of activity. Men raced for their horses, older children placed the travois harnesses on the larger dogs and the women did the same with their pack horses. As that part of the camp prepared for the hunt and harvest to follow, warriors from their various societies gathered by the chief's tipi to lay out the plans for the hunt.

As the men gathered with their horses and weapons, they were once again split up into two groups of hunters. One group would attack the tail end of the buffalo herd still watering and push it up into the head of the Plains near the west side of their encampment. The other group would lay hidden in the creek bottom adjacent the prairie and ambush the thundering herd as it thundered by. Once again, Josiah White Buffalo and Red Shirt found themselves in the ambush group of hunters and they left immediately in order to get well hidden. Meanwhile, the other group raced off to attack the tail end of the watering buffalo herd in order to kill as many as they could. Then they would push the rest of the herd in the direction of the ambush hunters. They did so in the knowledge that any and all kills in either area, would be close to their encampment and easily retrievable before the prairie's quadruped and aerial predators had their way.

Hiding in the dense brush of the confining creek bottom, the ambush hunters busied themselves fending off the hordes of biting deer flies now swarming about them and their horses. Soon their thoughts regarding the hordes of pesky biting deer flies were lost in the living prairie thunder now moving their way. Then a huge dust cloud announced the visual presence of a living brown carpet hurtling in the direction of the ambush hunters. It was then that disaster struck! The herd in its panic and for some other unknown reason, split as it neared the hunters laying hidden and out of sight in wait in the creek bottom. Perhaps the concentrated smells of so many humans hiding in the dense brush being wafted into the herds stampeding leaders borne on a breeze from the northwest provided an early warning to the beasts. But either way, when the herd split, it swarmed along both sides of the creek trapping the twenty ambush hunters hidden therein! Pandemonium reigned! Terrified horses reared tossing off their riders, close at hand charging buffalo blew foams of snot every which way, leaves from smashed bushes flew through the air like so many green snowflakes, heavy clouds of choking dust rent the air from the thousands of pounding hooves, and the panicked firing of numerous rifles split the air like a number of close at hand thunderclaps.

Those buffalo nearest the ambush hunters being hemmed in on all sides by their kin and continuously jammed inward toward the creek bottom, panicked even further over the close at hand shooting. So much so, that smaller streams of buffalo now split off from the splintered main body of animals and poured through the hunters' small party like river otter splitting the water in a quiet beaver pond! And in their continued panic now intensified by the shooting signs of danger, the massive rumbling beasts without regard to their own safety blew through every standing bush and sapling, shattering them into a showering cloud of flying leaves and sticks! The quiet of the well planned ambush had all of the sudden instantly rent the air into one horrendous cacophony of unimaginable sounds!

Josiah White Buffalo saw Red Shirt unhorsed in the first moments of the confusion! Red Shirt then found himself standing alone, firing his rifle as fast as he could at the masses of oncoming streams of buffalo charging down upon him! Within moments, Red Shirt had rapidly killed a number of buffalo, all of which had plowed into the ground and stacked up to his immediate front forming a barrier wall of flesh. But more buffalo continued jumping over their dead comrades as they were constantly being pushed by the force of the panicked herd bringing up the rear. Then Red Shirt ran out of shells as he had shot his Winchester dry!

Standing there defenseless and about to be overwhelmed and trampled by the still oncoming herd,

Red Shirt began singing his death song as he hurriedly tried reloading his rifle. Then all at once, Josiah White Buffalo was by Red Shirt's side! Josiah White Buffalo, with Wind's reins firmly held in his teeth, began quickly shooting with his rifle into the thundering mass of oncoming buffalo. Every time he shot, a buffalo smashed into the growing pile of dead animals already stacking up to his front. And he had a fifteen shot Winchester rifle in his hands making the most of his close-in range shooting...As the dead buffalo deeply piled up in front of the two men, the herd split once again and went around the straight shooting Josiah White Buffalo and the just reloaded Red Shirt.

Both men continued firing as they were now surrounded on three sides with dead or dying buffalo carcasses and the remains of the charging herd! Then it was all over. The herd of buffalo continued thundering out of sight to the west, as the two brothers recently in danger were finally able to relax. But that calming moment and realization that both were still alive had other consequences. Both men, over the danger of the moment and their rapid physical exertions, had busted loose the most recent scabbing on their chests! Now they were painfully leaking blood and lymphatic fluid from the scabbing-over area like they had been shot instead of the buffalo lying dead around them!

Then Red Shirt turned as he finished reloading his rifle for the third time as the remaining herd thundered away in the distance saying, "My brother, once again you have saved my life. Your power is great and the Great Spirit has smiled down upon both of us this day."

Josiah White Buffalo, still coming down from his emotional high of almost being trampled into the dirt by a herd of charging buffalo, reached out with his right hand and placing it on Red Shirt's shoulder said, "That is what brothers are for. That is what they do best..."

Then the two close friends were surrounded with the rest of the previously trapped band of now much relieved ambush hunters. Much hand slapping and embracing among friends ensued over being saved from certain death by the grace from the Great Spirit that day. Then the members of the band saw all the dead buffalo piled up in front and along the sides of the two quick shooting brothers and they marveled. Then a quiet realization swept over the ambush shooters. Had Josiah White Buffalo and Red Shirt not stacked up the buffalo to their front, the herd would have not separated. Instead, it would have slammed down the narrow creek confines destroying all the men and their horses lying in wait! That realization produced a number of quiet and thoughtful moments among the rest of the ambush hunters, as they quietly acknowledged the fact that Josiah White Buffalo and Red Shirt had saved them all from being trampled into the earth with their accurate shooting.

As a group, they had only lost five horses which had initially panicked and run off into the herd of stampeding buffalo. That panic caused all of those horses their lives, as they were immediately gored and trampled to death by the panicked buffalo. But not a trapped hunter had been lost because of the accurate shooting by the two brothers at the point of the stampede. And in doing so, the huge stack of dead buffalo formed a wall of flesh to the men's front, forcing the rest of the herd to split and swing wide around the trapped hunters lying in wait. Later when all their heart rates had finally settled down and they had a chance to look around, the hunters counted fifty-one dead animals. Dead animals around them or scattered across the nearby prairie, that they had collectively killed as they battled for their lives between the two herds of hard charging, close-at-hand buffalo.

Finally acquiescing to the warm sticky lymphatic fluid and blood running down their chests, bellies and onto the front of their legs from the busted loose Sun Dance chest scabbing caused by all their artful dodging exertions during the hunt, Josiah White Buffalo and Red Shirt left the scene. Since Red Shirt's horse had been one of the horses killed in the early moments of panic, he rode back to the village on the back of Wind, Josiah White Buffalo's excellent little buffalo horse. Thank you once again, Running Wolf, thought Josiah quietly to himself as the two brothers rode into their village amidst a crowd of excited children and older, non-hunting members of their band.

While the village celebrated their fortune in fresh buffalo meat and the knowledge that all of their men had returned safely, Josiah White Buffalo and Red Shirt's presence was obvious by their absence. Both men were once again laid up and being tended to by their mothers medicinally trying to salvage their savaged and scabby breasts where the skewers had been attached and later ripped out during the culmination of the Sun Dance ceremony. For once, both men welcomed the smell of rancid bear grease being rubbed into their damaged chests for the relief it brought their freshly savaged tissue.

For the remainder of that month, Josiah White Buffalo and Red Shirt remained about the village as their scabbed over chest areas finally substantially healed. However, both men now proudly wore the examples of a scarified breast as a reminder of the sacred Sun Dance and their sacrifices, sacrifices that had propelled Josiah White Buffalo into the ranks of a warrior and Red Shirt into the ranks of a very highly respected brave—still considered a brave because of his youth and since he had yet to count coup on an enemy as tribal tradition dictated.

Two months later after another successful buffalo hunt in which no one or their horses were lost, the first blasts of winter presented itself in a surprise September snow storm. But the band was ready. Smoking and drying racks had been previously hanging heavy with buffalo meat and the women and young girls had been scraping and tanning numerous buffalo hides from daylight until dark for many days. Additionally, continuous skin liners had been installed around the inside of the tipi poles and filled with the soft grasses of summer for the insulation value it would add to the comfort of those living in a tipi in the northern reaches during the harsh winter months. Life was good and getting better as the band prepared for the rest of the winter snows, howling winds and extreme Northern Plains cold soon to follow.

Deer hunting in the cold of an early October morning, Red Shirt had just downed a massive mule deer buck. As Josiah White Buffalo and Red Shirt struggled to get the huge deer out from a narrow draw into which the animal had fallen into upside-down once shot, they paused and rested. As they did, both men spotted a glint of something shiny a half mile or so away at the edge of a timber line. That flash was just there for an instant and then gone. Both men continued looking in that direction for the longest moment at what had caught their eyes but that quick glint of the sunlight reflecting off a piece of shiny metal was not seen any more.

Then it was back to retrieving their deer from the ravine and loading its heavy front and rear halves with difficulty onto their horses. As the men walked back to their encampment with their one-half a deer over each riding horse, Josiah White Buffalo once again thought he glimpsed a number of horsemen off in a distance slipping behind a set of rolling hills into another dense line of pine trees. Pausing to see what members of their tribe he figured he might see, no further sign was detected. Back at their encampment, the huge deer was shared among four families who were old and infirm or without a man to supply fresh meat supplies. Without a man because he had been lost in a battle, killed in an accident or had died in an unforeseen horse wreck as was commonly the case among Indian tribes. Then it was back to their own families for supper and a quiet evening around the fire in the tipi. Later that evening, Josiah White Buffalo stepped outside his tipi to attend to a call of nature. When he exited the tipi and stood up, a cold wet flake of snow plopped softly down onto his nose. Josiah White Buffalo grinned over the sign of fresh snow for the coming morning, especially since he and Red Shirt had planned another deer hunt the next day and fresh snow would make tracking, silent stalking and getting into a position to shoot much easier.

Early the next morning, Old Chief Smoke's band awoke to about six inches of freshly fallen snow and intense cold. All of which only foretold of even more snow to come, especially if the leaden colored skies overhead and frosty breaths of wind coming from out of the northwest were any indicator. Red Shirt walked to the horse herd and cut out his favorite riding horse as Josiah White Buffalo whistled in Wind. Wind came running and received a handful of oats for his obedience, as well as big hug around his lithe neck. For a moment Josiah White Buffalo was brought back to that fortuitous day when his first Indian adoptive father, Running Wolf, had bequeathed to him his own favorite buffalo horse. That wonderful moment in time had favorably followed Josiah White Buffalo every day since. Josiah White Buffalo then hurriedly curried down Wind and saddled him. Red Shirt arrived shortly thereafter leading his best horse and the two men quickly exchanged expectant glances over their hunt to come.

Both men, dressed in their heaviest winter clothing and carrying their trusty Winchesters, mounted up and headed for their favorite mule deer hunting spot on a long brushy ridge several miles distant, an area known to them as a part of the heavily used mule deer wintering range near their encampment. A type of environment because of its abundance of available winter feed and being mostly wind-blown free of snow for much of the time, which made for excellent deer hunting opportunities. They had no more than arrived at their hunting site, when both men jumped two large bucks bedded down underneath a nearby rocky out cropping. Typical mule deer, both bucks paused to look back at what had spooked them off their deer beds just as they topped the rise they were moving over in which to escape.

BOOM–BOOM went two quick rifle shots and one buck dropped where it was standing. However, the other animal gave a violent kick backwards and continued staggering over the hill. Josiah White Buffalo recognized a mortal hit on his buck because of the animal's exaggerated backwards kick when his bullet had struck the vitals of the animal, just grinned. They had just taken two large buck deer with two shots. With their luck, they would be back at the village in time for breakfast with their animals. Walking up and over the ridge, Josiah White Buffalo found his huge buck laying crumpled up deader than a stone under a dense stand of buck brush. Thanking the Great Spirit for providing such a fat animal, he began dragging the deer back down to where Red Shirt was just starting to gut his deer. Then the two men gutted their deer together and loaded them up onto their horses. Walking their heavily loaded horses back to their encampment, a light snow began falling once again. Realizing they were in for a wet trip if they didn't hurry, they picked up their pace.

Coming down off the last set of hills overlooking the camp off in a distance, Josiah White Buffalo stopped dead in his tracks as did Red Shirt! The huge village horse herd was gone! All of them! Not a single horse remained in their valley! Realizing the entire camp was in jeopardy without their horses, both men quickly led their loaded and now trotting horses down off their foothill and into the still mostly sleeping camp. There the men dropped off their deer and sounded the alarm. With that, other warriors and braves swarmed out from their tipis. Some dressed and some not, but all were looking for the perceived and just announced danger at hand. Soon the word of the stolen horse herd spread throughout the entire camp. The most physically able of the warriors and the band's best runners, now without any mode of transportation, took off on foot to follow the trail of tracks the stolen horse herd had left.

Meanwhile, Josiah White Buffalo and Red Shirt ran into their tipis and filled up their waist pouches with extra .44-40 rifle cartridges. Then running back out from their tipis, Josiah White Buffalo and Red shirt remounted their horses. As he did, Josiah White Buffalo advised Old Chief Smoke who was standing nearby, that Red Shirt and he were going after the horse herd. With that, the two men sprinted out from their camp as fast as their horses could safely carry them without slipping and falling in the freshly fallen snows. Once up at the head end of their valley, Josiah White Buffalo and Red Shirt got off their horses and closely examined the tracks left by the horse herd before the snow covered them up. It was then that they discovered about a dozen sets of tracks of ridden horses herding along the stolen horse herd! Now Josiah White Buffalo remembered the earlier flash of a buckle or something shiny and the brief glimpse of several mounted riders from afar, quietly slipping over a distant set of hills and out of sight. The strange horses herding along their stolen herd, were unshod! The story of the unshod horse's tracks, told the two men the horse herd had just been stolen by other Indians!

Memorizing the direction of travel the horse herd had been driven, Josiah White Buffalo and Red Shirt rather alertly realizing the horse thieves would be carefully watching their back trail for any sign of pursuit, cut off across country for a hopeful intercept. For the first ten miles, the horse thieves pushed the stolen horse herd hard as was evidenced by their tracks. They did so in the hopes of outrunning any Oglala foot pursuit initiated after the realization that their entire horse herd had been stolen. Then when they figured they were free and clear of any close at hand foot pursuit, the horse thieves slowed the speed of their escape. However, miles behind, Josiah White Buffalo and Red Shirt never slowed theirs...

The next morning, Chief Many Hats Peltier, a young Chippewa Indian sub-chief from the Turtle Mountain Band of Chippewa, took note of his surroundings. Peltier, a Chippewa who was now ranging far south of his historical tribal territory, allowed the cold members of the raiding party to stop and build a small warming fire. However, Chief Many Hats Peltier, knowing the fighting qualities of his hated enemy the Sioux, kept a sharp eye on their back trail. He knew better than to stop for long periods of time because the Sioux, once the herd was discovered stolen, would be hot on the trail of the horse thieves with a vengeance. And for the young chief on his first horse stealing foray, he knew that pausing to long to rest, could bring instant death to the men of his raiding party if they were discovered by the herd's owners.

Soon the men were warming themselves as they breakfasted on buffalo jerky. They had been in the saddle for many hours and riding horses in the winter was a cold bone chilling endeavor. But for the moment, they were enjoying the warmth of their fire and the fullness of the moment as successful horse thieves against their hated enemy the Sioux. Then it was back into their saddles and on to pushing the now rested stolen horses and their own mounts further to the north. Once again on horse, Chief Many Hats Peltier kept pushing his men and the stolen horse herd further north toward their own tribal region in the region of current day northeastern North Dakota. He did so knowing they were not safe until they were comfortably back within the external boundaries of the fierce Chippewa Nation. And that freedom and protection from what now had to be a hotly pursuing danger, was still many cold miles further to the north.

Several hours later, Red Shirt pushed his fingers into the warm coals of the horse thieves' now dead campfire. "They are still several hours ahead of us and from the footprints around this fire in the snow, there are eleven men in the party," he grimly announced to Josiah White Buffalo. Leaping back onto his horse, the two men began once again pushing their horses hard on another intercept course to cut off and catch the horse thieves before they got back into their own tribal territory and the safety it offered. And by now, Josiah White Buffalo and Red Shirt realized their horse thieves had to be from the hated Chippewa Nation lying just to their north, since their escape travels had not deviated from heading for that geographic point the entire time.

Come dark, Chief Many Hats Peltier drew his men up short in the heavy timber along a fast freezing stream and lit down. Both he and his men figured they were now more than far enough ahead of any men pursuing them on foot. With that in mind, they could camp and rest for the night. Then after a hard next day, they would be safely back on their own tribe's home range. Soon his men had a fire going, with parts of a freshly killed deer merrily roasting away. Chief Many Hats Peltier had allowed one of his men, using the silence of his bow and arrow, to stalk and kill a deer along the way for their coming supper. And to his way of thinking, that had been a wise decision. They had stolen a complete herd of about one hundred fifty of their hated enemy's horses, were now more than likely far away from any foot pursuit, had a warming fire going for his tired men and now, parts of a freshly killed deer staked out and roasting over their campfire. His was a happy raiding party, even though it was getting colder and colder as they went further to the north into the teeth of another oncoming winter snow storm moving down from the northwest. But to his credit, the young war chief did not drop his guard. He still needed to satisfy his inner concerns of the possibility of danger bred into him by his forefathers. Mounting his horse, he back tracked their previous escape route until he came to a high set of hills overlooking their darkened hoof prints back trail outlined in the moonlit snowy whiteness below. Sitting there quietly on his horse as the cold and darkness enveloped him, he saw no signs of pursuit. Satisfied, he reversed his ride and rode back to his camp, which was identified off in a distance by a small flicker of light emitted through the trees coming from his group's small cooking fire.

However, two other narrowed sets of eyes watched

the lone rider checking his back trail just before he turned and rode off towards the faint spot of light in the timber. For those two sets of watching eyes, there would be no warmth of a fire that evening or freshly roasted venison for their supper. They feasted on the rising anger over those who had dared to steal a tribe's entire horse herd, a horse herd that meant life or death to the village of Old Chief Smoke's Oglala...

Later that night as new falling snows continued silently blanketing the landscape, a lone Chippewa, now dusted with that freshly falling snow, sat on his horse cold and alone. He had been selected by their chief to watch over the horse herd through the night and that he was now doing. But he did so with the knowledge that his belly was now full of freshly roasted venison and his horse was comfortably resting under him. As the Great Spirit looked down upon the tranquil scene, He saw the whirling glint of a blade and the true flight of a thrown tomahawk striking that lone Chippewa sentinel in the neck just below the skull! That killing blow unhorsed him without the man making a sound other than a soft "crump" when he landed in the freshly falling snow!

Josiah White Buffalo moved silently to the man who was quivering his last and removed his tomahawk from the man's spine. This time his solid oaken handle had not snapped off in the heat of battle like his previous tomahawk handle had in the earlier fight with the Pawnee...Wiping off the blood of his tomahawk on the dead man's outer coat, Josiah White Buffalo tied the dead man's horse to a nearby tree. Then two dark and silent figures moved quietly towards the faint light emitted by the dying embers of a nearby fire at the edge of a line of timber. Moments later, both men were quietly standing off to the same side of the sleeping horse thieves looking over at each other in the fire's feeble light. Then they quietly turned so as to face the sleeping horse thieves and as they did, they quietly cocked the hammers back on their Winchesters against the sides of their winter coats for the quiet that action would bring.

"YI-YI-YI!" yelled Red Shirt to awaken the hated horse thieves so they could see who they had stolen the horses from! Instantly ten horse thieves sprang sleepily from their sleeping furs, only to hear and see the muzzle flashes from two rapidly firing, close at hand, Winchesters. Heavy lead slugs from those rapidly firing Winchesters tore into the soft flesh, intestines and hard bone of the surprised raiders as they tried to rally from a fitful, cold sleep, only to meet a world of hot lead. Chief Many Hats Peltier however, instead of standing up in the line of fire like a novice on his first raiding party, rolled frantically off to one side into the darkness, rose and sprinted for where he had earlier tied his horse. Unfortunately for him, his valuable horse was not there! That valuable horse, having been untied earlier and quietly spirited away by Red Shirt out of the line of rifle fire that was soon to come, was now tied elsewhere. Chief Many Hats Peltier, realizing his fate depended on his speed and survival skills, sped off into the darkness of night on foot into the safety the denser timber offered. However, that was not to be for the rest of his young raiding party because of the rapidly firing and deadly aimed Winchesters still hammering away...

Then disaster struck! Josiah's White Buffalo's Winchester had a just fired cartridge expand greatly in the chamber of his rifle! In doing so, the rifle's extractor tore free from the rim of the now stuck cartridge when he tried to hurriedly eject the spent round in the heat of emotion! With a stuck case jammed in the chamber of his rifle, that meant Josiah White Buffalo could not reload another live round into the barrel of his rifle. Realizing what had just happened, Josiah White Buffalo whipped out his sheath knife and using its point, quickly pried out the spent cartridge. In those few exciting seconds of time, one of the horse thieves stumbled over to Josiah White Buffalo with an up raised tomahawk to strike a death blow. That was not to be as Red Shirt's next shot tore through the side of that man's face, killing him instantly and saving Josiah White Buffalo's life! Soon all the horse thieves laid dead or were drawing their final breaths. Red Shirt then quickly started after the sole fleeing survivor, Chief Many Hats Peltier, only to be stopped by the sage words of his brother.

"Let him go my brother. That way, he can warn off any future horse thieves from his tribe never to come into our encampment or home territory ever again." Red Shirt slid to a stop over Josiah White Buffalo's wise words. Returning to the campfire, the dead were then mutilated so their ghosts would wander in a world far away from the Happy Hunting Grounds and the rest of the Cloud People.

That evening, Josiah White Buffalo did not shy away from scalping and mutilating the dead as others had done when the battle with the Pawnee was over many moons earlier. A time when he was still a white man captive and not an Oglala/Lakota warrior. That evening, along with his brother, Red Shirt, they mutilated the hated Chippewa horse thieves so their ghosts would wander forever in the in-between world...

When the two men had finished their grisly task, Josiah reached out and took Red Shirt's elbow. Looking him in the eyes in the dimming light of the dying enemy's campfire, Josiah said, "Thank you my brother for saving my life when my rifle jammed."

Red Shirt looked back at Josiah White Buffalo with a big grin saying, "That is what brothers do...Now I feel better that I have also saved your life, since you have saved mine twice."

Noontime the following day, Josiah White Buffalo and Red Shirt pushing the stolen horse herd along their previous back trail, met the rest of their band of pursuers who were still chasing the horse thieves on foot because their riding mounts had also been taken in the original raid. There was much happiness when the two cold but happy groups met. That happiness became even more animated, when the men on foot now realized they had horses to ride. That included eleven new horses once belonging to the hated horse thieves from the now identified Chippewa Nation and their own mounts from their previously stolen horse herd as well. Plus from Josiah White Buffalo and Red Shirt's horse's manes hung ten fresh but now frozen scalps...

The only scalp missing was that of Chief Many Hats Peltier, the young Chippewa chief who had led the ill-fated raiding party. A warrior who had escaped in the heat of the battle and was still walking "the long walk of shame" back to his nation's tribal lands. A long walk of shame because he had lost the entire stolen horse herd, had his own favorite riding horse captured by the hated Sioux, and all ten of the young men killed on their first raid who had formed the body of his raiding party! As was the tradition of such a proud and fierce tribe of warriors, Chief Many Hats Peltier was never again allowed by the tribal elders to lead a raiding party because of the disaster he had suffered. Years later when his tribe had been relegated to a reservation, Chief Many Hats Peltier went to work for the U.S. Government as a hunter and a cook for a U. S. Army Cavalry unit stationed on his reservation in the Turtle Mountains of the Dakota Territory. (Author's Note: Many years later, a male prodigy of Chief Many Hats went on to an outstanding career working for the Department of the Interior's U.S. Fish and Wildlife Service as a Wildlife Inspector stationed at the U.S. Customs Port of Entry at Dunseith, North Dakota. Wildlife Inspector Scott Peltier did not turn out to be a horse thief in his later life, but, he did "steal" his wife Shelly's heart in later years...)

Two days later, the horse herd and the men from Old Chief Smoke's band rode back into the valley to their encampment. There was much rejoicing over the return of the horses, the fact that none of their tribal members had been killed, and in the numbers of scalps and enemy horses that had been taken. Old Chief Smoke's heart swelled with pride when Josiah White Buffalo stepped off his horse into the arms of Prairie Flower and lifted her clear off the ground in a genuine hug of love and happiness. A show of public affection usually not seen by the band's members among their own kind. But, Josiah White Buffalo was from another world and the old chief and his people had come to understand and appreciate such open signs of affection by the young man.

Two nights later after a meeting of the tribal elders and the heads of several warrior societies, Old Chief Smoke called Red Shirt and Josiah White Buffalo to his tipi. There, because of several earlier natural deaths in the tribal leadership, especially war sub-chiefs, Red Shirt and Josiah White Buffalo were asked if they would like to assume those vacated responsibilities. Both young men, now fully fledged warriors of the tribe, stood there in the presence of the old chief and their elders in shock over the unanticipated honors they had just been offered.

Then Josiah White Buffalo spoke first since Red Shirt just stood there like a stone, stunned in light of the happenings, saying, "I am honored that you feel I am worthy of such a high position of leadership. However, I am still a white man and I do not feel as such that I should lead warriors of the Great Sioux Nation into battle. They should be led by one of their own blood. I wish to remain as a warrior and serve my people from that position of trust." With Josiah White Buffalo's ringing statement, one could tell from all gathered there that evening that those assembled were in a state of shock. Being offered a high position of responsibility and leadership within the tribe and to turn it down was unheard of...But, that kind of a response and associated humility from Josiah White Buffalo was not totally unexpected by the elders who knew him as a great warrior.

Then a still surprised Old Chief Smoke turned to Red Shirt, now a full-fledged warrior because he had counted coup against the Chippewa horse thieves saying, "Red Shirt, you have also been honored with a position as a war sub-chief. What does your heart tell you your answer should be to the Tribal Council this evening?"

For the longest time, not a word was said. Then Josiah White Buffalo spoke up once again saying, "I am very happy that Red Shirt has been so honored. He is of a good heart and is a true warrior in battle. I would follow him anywhere he chose to lead."

Red Shirt just looked at Josiah White Buffalo and had heard his words of support. Turning towards the old chief, Red Shirt said, "I would be honored to be counted among the other sub-chiefs as a war chief."

"Then it is done," said Old Chief Smoke. "Tomorrow we will celebrate the return of our two fierce warriors and the making of a new war chief." With those words, all the Tribal Council members nodded approvingly.

One week later after Red Shirt had been welcomed into the Great Bear warrior society as a new sub-chief, Josiah White Buffalo and his brother were once again hunting deer at their favorite location. Just as they dismounted to put a stalk on a nice mule deer buck, they heard the booming sound of a heavy rifle being fired far out on the prairie to their south. Remounting their horses and forgetting the fat mule deer for a moment, the two men curiously rode over the ridge so they could see who was doing the shooting, especially since the two men had risen before daylight and no one else had been awake in their village who was also going hunting. Stopping on top of the rise of the ridge, the two men observed two open wagons heaped high with buffalo hides and one covered wagon quietly sitting about a quarter mile distant out on the prairie. Then off to their west near a small herd of buffalo, the two men spotted a lone dismounted rider using a pair of shooting sticks who was firing into that herd of buffalo.

From where the two men sat, they could see about a dozen dark spots already laying on the snow near the dismounted man doing the shooting. The words "buffalo hunters" sped through the men's minds! And they were shooting buffalo on Old Chief Smoke's hunting grounds just for their hides and wasting all the valuable meat! Little did the two brothers realize that in a faraway land called Germany, a tannery operator had earlier discovered a way to make a fine grade of leather from buffalo hides. Before all was said and done, over ten thousand buffalo hunters would swarm all over the Plains, disgracefully shooting both the northern and southern herds of buffalo down from their many millions, to just a pathetic handful of animals by 1885!

About then, the small herd of buffalo finally spooked over the sounds of the shooting and smelling the blood from their dead brethren. With that natural instinct taking over, they soon rumbled off out of rifle range from the lone shooter who had failed to shoot the animals into a "stand." Seeing that, the lone shooter rose from his sitting shooting position, gathered up his shooting sticks, and waved his hat for the three wagons and their skinners to come to his location. Once there, they could skin out the buffalo and then move on to the next herd of unfortunates.

Chief Red Shirt immediately said, "Josiah White Buffalo, they do not belong here killing our buffalo. Let us ride closer for a better look and maybe if they see us riding their way, they will leave and go back to where they came from."

Josiah White Buffalo nodded his support for such action and the two men slowly rode down off the foothills toward the buffalo hunters so their actions wouldn't be misinterpreted as coming from hostile Indians. Walking their horses off the hillside, the two men continued walking their horses across the prairie towards the lone buffalo hunter and the approaching wagons figuring they would ask the hunters to leave. It was then that the two men got the surprise of their young lives! ZIPPPP–BOOM, went the sounds of a nearby speeding rifle bullet, followed by the rifle's loud report in the cold winter's air!

Josiah White Buffalo and Chief Red Shirt, surprised over that kind of response to their obvious peaceful presence, immediately stopped their horses in their tracks. As they did, they heard once again the ZIPPPP–BOOM of the heavy buffalo rifle being fired in their direction! That time, the report of the rifle being fired was preceded by a solid sounding "thud," as Chief Red Shirt's horse folded and dropped dead onto the frozen ground without making a sound! Chief Red Shirt, surprised over the killing result of that hostile action, quickly rolled over his collapsing horse's head and sprung back to his feet running with his rifle in hand. At that same instant, Josiah White Buffalo abruptly reined his horse hard to an abrupt turn. Then another zipping sound of a close-at-hand bullet followed by the booming report of a heavy rifle rent the cold winter morning air once again! That time, Josiah White Buffalo reached down and grabbing Chief Red Shirt's outstretched hand, jerked him onto the back of Wind. With that, they fled for the covering brush the nearby hillside offered. Their flight was followed by the zipping sound of another to close at hand rifle bullet speeding past them and throwing up snow to the front of their now racing horse! It was obvious the buffalo hunters were there to stay...

Reaching the brush covered hillside, Josiah White Buffalo did not quit spurring Wind until they were over the first small hill and out of sight and range of the long shooting buffalo hunter's rifle. Stopping once they were over the hill and out of sight of the "searching" rifle bullets, Chief Red Shirt slid off from Wind's back.

"That was my best buffalo horse!" he shouted out in anger through a contorted face. "That shooter will pay for what he did to my horse," he continued shouting in a tone of voice that foretold of the doom to come to the shooter out on the prairie! That was if Chief Red Shirt ever got his way and had his chance...

Then Josiah White Buffalo and Chief Red Shirt made their ways back to the lip of their covering hill on foot, laid down on its backside, and watched the buffalo hunters with narrowing sets of eyes. Soon the trailing three wagons reached the site of the shooter and then the skinners began the grisly business of stripping off the hides and leaving the rest of the buffalo carcass to rot or be eaten by the flesh eaters of the air and land. Those skinners quickly stripped the hides off the dead animals, threw them onto the piles of hides already in the two open wagons meant for hide hauling and then the contingent moved off looking for more unfortunates with the lone shooter riding far to the front of the group.

By late afternoon, not having come across any more buffalo that were within range of the long shooting hunter and his rifle, the wagons headed up into a small draw out from the wind near a nearby ridge of rolling hills and set up their camp. There they hobbled the wagon's horses and mules so they could feed without wandering far from the camp and a central fire was built on the lee side of the wagons parked in a defensive half circle along the hillside. Soon the men began cooking their supper and warming themselves. As they did, another man laid out their bed rolls on the cold hard ground by their now roaring, typical white man's huge campfire. One that could be seen from miles away...

Josiah White Buffalo and Chief Red Shirt now having blood in their eyes over having been shot at, the killing of Chief Red Shirt's best buffalo horse, and the shameless, wasteful killing of the buffalo, slowly tailed the hunters from their trailing position. And in doing so, only the ever present magpies and ravens knew the two men were anywhere nearby in country...Once darkness descended, Josiah White Buffalo and Chief Red Shirt stealthily approached the buffalo hunter's campsite on foot and then paused out of sight in the cold night air. A typical slight winter breeze wafting in from the northwest picked up and with those covering sounds, Josiah White Buffalo and Chief Red Shirt were able to silently sneak even closer up to the very edge of the light of the men's campfire, all the while using the semi-circled wagons as a sight shield. The two open wagons were already piled high with hundreds of frozen buffalo hides and the hunters were now loudly celebrating their day's fortunes. That celebration was soon 'fortified' with several bottles of whiskey being passed around among the group as they gathered more closely around the warming campfire. Soon the air was filled with much happy animation over the day's buffalo shooting successes. As they did, Josiah White Buffalo slipped in closer behind one wagon out of sight and Chief Red Shirt the other. There they waited until the well-armed men had settled in for the night in their bedrolls arrayed closely around their campfire for the warmth it offered. Little did the men realize the "eternal heat" that bedding arrangement would soon generate...

As the buffalo hunter's campfire burned lower and their snoring became heavier after having laced themselves heavily with drink, hell came riding in on a black horse. Josiah White Buffalo and Chief Red Shirt quietly crept in ever closer to the sleeping men. The buffalo hunters had left one man sitting by the campfire on a wooden crate to keep the campfire going, attempt to keep warm, and provide guard duty. But sleep came easily after a while for that man now fortified with much whiskey and food under his belt and as a result, there he now sat on his wooden crate snoring loudly. Snoring loudly, unawares of the forces of hell riding into camp on a black horse. Stalking silently into the hunter's camp after Josiah White Buffalo and Chief Red Shirt figured the six men were fast asleep, they positioned themselves off to one side to stay out of each other's line of fire. But close enough at hand to the six sleeping men to do what they came to do from a very close range. Very close!

Chief Red Shirt, standing over the one who had shot his favorite buffalo horse out from under him, took the toe of his moccasin and jabbed that sleeping man in his side. All the man did was grunt as the whiskey imbibed earlier, kept his survival senses dulled. It was the last drink he ever took, as Chief Red Shirt shot the sleeping man in the head from a distance of two feet away! With the booming sound of a rifle being fired in among the buffalo hunters midst, instantly all the other men flew out from their bed rolls and went for their close at hand rifles or pistols. They only did so to be quickly cut down where they knelt or stood by the two fast firing Winchesters being wielded by Josiah White Buffalo and Chief Red Shirt! As for the camp's guard sitting on the wooden crate by the side of the fire, Josiah saw to it that he died in a sitting position! And the impact from the bullet he had received from such a close range, blew him frontally off his wooden box and into their campfire's burning coals. Shortly thereafter, the burning stink of a human being and his singing greasy hair, could be smelled in the cold night air...Satisfied with the results of their deadly work, Josiah White Buffalo and Chief Red Shirt scalped and mutilated the five buffalo hunters. The sixth buffalo hunter did not need mutilation. The now re-kindled and blazing campfire into which he had been blown was seeing to that...

Awakening later in the morning after a good night's sleep at the dead buffalo hunters camp, Josiah White Buffalo and Chief Red Shirt feasted on fresh buffalo steak for breakfast. Fresh buffalo steak the hunters had carried along with them in one of their wagons from an earlier

213

kill. And did so over a new cleaner smelling, without a dead man slowing roasting in it, located upwind, campfire. After breakfast, the two men rifled the covered wagon's contents, taking what food stuffs, boxes of ammunition, and spare firearms they could find. The rest they left because everything smelled so strongly sour in the buffalo hunter's filthy supply wagon! And to the Indians who always managed to stay very clean even during the winter months, associating with anything that smelled so badly in the buffalo hunters' camp was left behind.

Even the long haired scalps from the unclean men were tied onto one of the recently retrieved from the feeding grounds pack horses, so they could freeze and air dry off by themselves...In the looting of the wagons, Chief Red Shirt discovered the rifle that had killed his horse from such a long distance. It was a .45-70 Sharps single shot, heavy octagonal long barreled buffalo rifle with double set triggers. He made sure that rifle was seized as did Josiah White Buffalo on another like-in-caliber Sharps rifle he discovered while looting the goods in the rear of the covered supply wagon. One that had been brought along as a reserve rifle in case the first one malfunctioned or was damaged in a horse wreck. Also, there were two cases of ammunition that fit the calibers of those two rifles in the wagon. That "find" was gratefully taken and packed onto one of the buffalo hunter's horses as well. Gratefully taken because ammunition for one's rifle made by the white man which had been stolen or taken in battle, was always hard to come by in The People's world.

Having taken all they could pack on the buffalo hunters' horse herd of eleven horses, Josiah White Buffalo and Chief Red Shirt sitting on his new horse, looked the buffalo hunter's camp over one more time before they prepared to head back to Old Chief Smoke's camp. In addition to all the goods the two men had taken, they both now sported a pair of revolvers each around their waists that they had taken off the dead men. Satisfied with all the packing of the buffalo hunter's horses and with Chief Red Shirt astride the main buffalo hunter's spirited horse, they prepared to leave. But not before Josiah White Buffalo torched all the wagons as a warning to all other buffalo hunters to stay away from their land. As for the buffalo hunters' bodies, they were stripped, mutilated, and left where they fell for the flesh eating animals and birds to feast upon. Then their stinking filthy clothing was burned in the remaining campfire occupied by the still slowly cooking "camp guard." They were later to learn that the typical Indian destruction of a white man's wagon train was a big mistake. A big mistake whose blackness would soon overtake the two of them...! A mistake that would soon lead to even more killing.

The rest of that day was spent slowly riding back to Old Chief Smoke's encampment with their heavily loaded pack string carrying all the dead buffalo hunter's looted goods. But in doing so in order to avoid having anyone following them like other buffalo hunters or the cavalry, they rode for over a mile in the tracks of a buffalo herd moving in their needed direction of travel. When they did, anyone trying to follow those who had killed the buffalo hunters, would be totally stymied by the pulverized ground and the thousands of covering buffalo tracks. When they arrived back at their encampment later in the afternoon, they were met by many worried relatives and friends because the two of them had not returned earlier from their usual one day hunting trip. Soon the word spread around the camp of the killing of the hated white buffalo hunters. That was when Josiah White Buffalo and Chief Red Shirt were happily forced to tell and retell their stories many times for all in attendance.

Finally as was the custom for successful hunters, Chief Red Shirt, in his new capacity as a sub-chief, distributed those looted items he and Josiah White Buffalo had seized at the buffalo hunter's ill-fated camp site. Especially coveted were the many firearms that were distributed to those who had no or inferior firearms. Especially well received by the women of the tribe were the cast iron cooking pots, bags of salt, sacks of dried red pepper flakes, flour, tins of honey, cornmeal, and a dozen jars full of what turned out to be pickled crab apples. Old Chief Smoke and many of the elders smiled that evening over their choice of a generous Chief Red Shirt as a sub-chief. Following those sharing events, both men retired to their tipis for some much needed sleep. That was after eating a grand supper prepared by the women of their families, who were thankful for their safe return and for the gifts that had been taken from the hated buffalo hunters and distributed among the many members of the band.

A week later found Josiah White Buffalo and Chief Red Shirt hunting mule deer in their winter migration concentration areas once again. Spotting two large separate bunches of feeding deer, the two men split up and began making their separate stalks on their quarry. Josiah had to walk about two hundred yards to get to his chosen herd of deer but the six inches of fresh powder snow made his walking quietly easy. Keeping the wind to his face, he began his final stalk on the herd of quietly feeding deer. He then heard Chief Red Shirt's Winchester fire one shot off in the distance. From the sounds of the impacting bullet, Chief Red Shirt has a deer down, Josiah White Buffalo thought with a smile. And since they were trying to get enough fresh deer meat for at least four older families back at camp, Josiah continued his stalk with purpose.

Then, *pop-pop---pop* went the faraway sounds of someone firing a pistol! Josiah White Buffalo knew Chief Red Shirt now carried a set of pistols taken from the ill-fated buffalo hunters they had killed earlier. But from the sounds of it to Josiah White Buffalo's trained ear, that shooting came from two different sounding pistols! Breaking off his stalk and fearing the worst, Josiah White Buffalo took off running for Wind who was tied up in the brush some one hundred yards distant. Arriving somewhat winded, Josiah White Buffalo swung effortlessly into his saddle, leaned over Wind's neck and untied him from the bush. Racing along the backside of the hill, Josiah White Buffalo rode to where he figured Chief Red Shirt would be located on the opposite side of the ridge. Jumping off Wind, he ran to just below the crest of the hill and then began crawling towards the rim so he could see and not be seen. For some strange reason, he feared something bad was in the works and both he and Chief Red Shirt would soon be in the middle of it if the Great Spirit had His way.

Peeping over the rim of the hillside, Josiah White Buffalo's worst fears were realized! Josiah White Buffalo saw six U.S. Cavalry soldiers surrounding Chief Red Shirt! Four of the troopers were on the ground and had their pistols drawn and pointed at Chief Red Shirt! One officer and a trooper remained seated on their horses closely standing by Chief Red Shirt. That single horsed trooper was holding the reins of the four dismounted trooper's horses and the officer appeared to be talking in a much animated fashion to the now recently disarmed Chief Red Shirt. Looking closely, Josiah White Buffalo could see Chief Red Shirts rifle and pistols laying in the snow to his front. It was apparent the troopers had surprised, caught and then disarmed Chief Red Shirt when he was gutting his deer. Now it appeared he was roughly and with much animation, being talked to by the officer seated on his horse. Then it happened! Jerking his short barreled, .45-70 carbine from its scabbard, the officer reached over the neck of his horse and knocked Chief Red Shirt to the ground with the butt of the weapon! Chief Red Shirt jumped right back up after being knocked to the ground, but from his vantage point, Josiah White Buffalo could see a red patch of blood forming on Chief Red Shirts temple and begin running down the side of his face. Still the officer kept gesturing wildly with an accusing finger at Chief Red Shirt. Chief Red Shirt just stood his ground and glowered right back at the officer, as the blood from his head wound now flowed profusely down the side of his face, neck and onto his outer winter clothing!

Having seen enough, Josiah White Buffalo crawled backwards below the lip of the rim of the hill and once out of sight of the troopers on the other side, stood up and sprinted for his horse. Removing the heavy barreled Sharps buffalo rifle from its scabbard, the one and same he had taken previously from the buffalo hunter's supply wagon, he grabbed a small leather pouch of its shells tied onto his saddle horn. Then leaving his short ranged Winchester in its scabbard, raced back to just below the rim of the hilltop. Flopping down heavily on his belly once again, he crawled the last few yards to the top. Slowly poking the rifle barrel over the rim of the hill ahead of him and laying on his side, he levered back the action of the big .45-70 Sharps, slid a heavy cartridge into its chamber and quietly closed its action. Then taking a small handful of shells from his pouch, he laid them alongside where they were positioned for quick and easy retrieval. Pulling the hammer full back on the big Sharps, he lined up his sights on the cavalry officer still threatening a very stoic and furiously bleeding from his head wound, Chief Red Shirt. Letting his racing heart still itself for a moment with a deeply and long-held breath, Josiah White Buffalo took deadly aim, pulled the set trigger and then slowly pulled the second trigger on his rifle!

BOOM went the sound of the big Sharps in the cold winter air! Josiah White buffalo could not have shot any better if he had tried. The big .45-70 slug tore through the upper chest of the officer threatening Chief Red Shirt with his pistol. And as fate would have it, that heavy, now deformed lead slug, continued racing right on through the first man and into the side of the trooper sitting alongside him! The one who was holding the horse's reins for the other four soldiers on the ground who were still covering Chief Red Shirt with their pistols! The big slug fired from such a short distance away, unhorsed and killed both men with its one bullet! When that happened, 'the bad spirits came in riding a black horse' once again. Instantly, the surprised four horses being held by the trooper just shot out of his saddle, exploded in four different panicked directions! The four troopers standing on the ground previously watching Chief Red Shirt, instantly broke with the realization that they were deep in Indian country and without their fast disappearing horses, had no hope of survival. All four men broke and ran after their horses as if by instinct brought on by an even deeper fear. Then death came riding in on a 'black horse' once again. Chief Red Shirt grabbed up one of his pistols from the ground and shot two of the close at hand scrambling men as they broke away to retrieve their spooked horses. A loud BOOMING from the hillside, saw another trooper plunge violently forward with his arms flailing about wildly, as the big, pure lead, .45-70 slug broke the man's spine and blew out his heart, killing him instantly! The remaining trooper, seeing all his brethren being shot all to hell, and realizing he couldn't catch his still fleeing horse, took off running across the snow covered Prairie in panicked desperation for the cover a nearby stand of trees offered. He got another twenty yards in his flight for freedom, when the big Sharps BOOMED from the hillside once again! He was later discovered by more of his kind, face down in the snow with a blue-black thumb sized hole in his back and a fist sized hole in the front of his chest, where the massive and now badly deformed soft lead bullet had explosively exited!

While Chief Red Shirt scalped and mutilated the dead troopers, Josiah White Buffalo rounded up all the cavalry detachment's still spooked and badly scattered valuable horses. When Josiah White Buffalo finally returned to the bloody killing ground, Chief Red Shirt had cut off a piece of the officer's shirt and had wrapped it around his still bleeding head wound. By that time, Chief Red Shirt had also stripped off all the soldiers winter clothing down to their shorts and had piled it up so it could be loaded onto the horses for return to their encampment and use by the other warriors if they so desired. Especially since many of the band's warriors, as a form of taunting and intimidation, enjoyed the wearing of dead soldiers clothing when confronting other live soldiers in battle. Little did Josiah White Buffalo and Chief Red Shirt realize just how soon said clothing would be in use by its recipients.

"Thank you once again my brother for saving my life. That cavalry officer intended to shoot me until you changed his mind with a well-placed shot," said a smiling Chief Red Shirt. "They had been out on a patrol looking for the missing buffalo hunters and found the burned remains of their camp and mutilated bodies. And on their way back to Fort Sully, they heard me shoot a deer and came to investigate. I did not hear them approaching in the snow as I began gutting out my deer and they caught me with my back turned towards them intent on removing the animal's insides. Getting me in their sights, I had no choice but to surrender. That is when the officer accused me and all other Indians of killing and looting the buffalo hunter's camp. That was when you came in my brother, just as that officer prepared to shoot me in revenge for killing the buffalo hunters. So, once again, I owe you my life," said a smiling Chief Red Shirt.

"That is what brothers are for," said a smiling Josiah White Buffalo.

Sensing that more snow was in the offing by later that afternoon, the two men did not bother in hiding the tracks of theirs or their now trailing cavalry horses as they headed back to their encampment. They did so with the soldier's horses carrying mounds of good winter clothing, a collection of firearms and their related ammunition. Ammunition and weapons the men of their village could readily use. Half way back to camp, Josiah White Buffalo's ability to read weather patterns came true. A heavy wet snow began blanketing the area and the last mile to their camp, found the two men riding almost in a blinding blizzard.

Josiah White Buffalo surmised thankfully as they plodded along under a load of wet and heavy snow, that no one would ever be able to figure out what had happened to the small cavalry detachment now. Figure out what had happened, because the heavy winter snows would more than cover the bodies that Josiah White Buffalo and Chief Red Shirt had dragged off into the nearest ravine. And come springtime, the scavengers of the air and land would make short work of the bodies once the snows had melted. And if that detachment of soldiers had a Happy Hunting Grounds to go to, that would not now be the case. That was because Chief Red Shirt had scalped and mutilated to a man all the troopers. Being mutilated meant their ghosts would now wander the earth looking for their lost parts and not bother other whole good people in the Happy Hunting Grounds according to their Sioux Indian culture.

Back at their encampment, Old Chief Smoke, upon hearing the men's stories, met them with joy as well as concern. Joy in that both men had safely returned with more spoils for tribal members and sorrow in that the "Bluecoats" were traveling so close to his camp. Other of his band's warriors had observed several groups of soldiers moving about nearby and had hidden themselves from their searching eyes. He found hope though in that the dead soldiers Chief Red Shirt and Josiah White Buffalo had killed, had been left stripped of most of their clothing making them fair game for all the flesh eaters from the land and air. That and the fact that a wet and sloppy late spring blizzard had prophetically covered his men's tracks leading from the kill site directly to his encampment. He also figured what evidence his men had left back at the soldiers kill site, the prairie wolves and coyotes would soon clean up or scatter to the four winds.

Once again, Chief Red Shirt and Josiah White Buffalo distributed the items they had removed from the dead troopers. With those looted weapons, now every brave and warrior in Old Chief Smoke's band had a decent firearm and ammunition As for the used cavalry uniforms and heavy winter gear worn by the troopers, it disappeared among the rank and file of the band's warrior members just as silently as the snowflakes that were falling upon their still undiscovered winter encampment...

That evening, a tired but happy Josiah White Buffalo returned to Old Chief Smoke's tipi to meet a busy Prairie Flower happily preparing supper. It was then, that Josiah White Buffalo realized he was starving. Both he and Chief Red Shirt had not eaten that morning figuring they would be back in camp in time for breakfast. It was now 13 hours since they had left camp and to Josiah White Buffalo's way of thinking, supper couldn't come any too soon. That evening, the three of them in Old Chief Smoke's tipi feasted on Dutch oven biscuits, thick buffalo stew, made even thicker with some of the buffalo hunter's corn meal, all topped off with a jar of pickled crab apples taken from the hunter's looted camp...

During that supper meal, Josiah White Buffalo noticed that Old Chief Smoke was once again unusually quiet and thoughtful. Josiah White Buffalo had seen this behavior many times before and knew the old chief was heavy in thought over something pretty serious. And to Josiah White Buffalo's way of thinking, the old chief's concerns had to rest with all the different tribal warriors entering their encampment now almost on a daily basis. Warriors bringing news of the many battles the other bands were having with the white miners in the Black Hills, many of the settlers throughout Indian lands, and the U.S. Cavalry. Especially the U.S. Cavalry who were trying to defend the settlers, miners, railroad men, and buffalo hunters from the hostile Indians. Additionally, the herds of buffalo, as a result of the above human disturbances, were once again thinning in numbers and moving away from such human activity, making hunting them more difficult for the band. Especially since the Indians were so dependent and in need of the herds of buffalo, if they were to continue their nomadic ways of life.

"Care to share your thoughts with your son?" asked Josiah White Buffalo.

For the longest time, Old Chief Smoke just stared into the fire. Then sitting back against his back rest, said, "Son, I fear for our people and our way of life. As you well know, the whites are flooding into our country like red ants on a disturbed nest mound. They are taking over our lands and killing off all our buffalo or running the herds off their historical feeding and wintering grounds. And when we try to stop them, the Bluecoats come after and punish us like little children. The Iron Horse has crossed our land and now I fear it will bring even more white settlers onto our lands all looking for a place to live. And with the Iron Horse has come many buffalo hunters.

Buffalo hunters who use the Iron Horse to carry their buffalo hides back to the east where the white man lives in even greater numbers. When the hunters shoot the buffalo, they are then left to rot where they fall and our children and the very old go hungry. And now, warriors from other tribes are telling us that the Great White Father in Washington is mad at us. His people had many of us sign the "talking paper" paper at Fort Laramie in 1868 that said a great land would be set aside for us. The talking paper said that no white man shall be allowed to live upon such promised lands, only the Indians. That paper also said that we could live on that land in peace undisturbed by all white men, as "long as the grass was green and the sky was blue." But according to many camp riders bringing us the word from the Sans Arcs, Miniconjou, Brule, Hunkpapa, and from the other bands of the Oglala, that is not true. In 1874, a 'soldier-chief' called Custer, took over 1,000 men into the Black Hills, a land called "Paha Sapa" by the Sioux. A land that is sacred to the Lakota. He did so in order to find a place to build a fort so The People and our lands could be protected by the Bluecoats from the whites. But that soldier-chief called Custer discovered gold in the Paha Sapa. And since that day, those sacred lands have been overrun with hundreds of white men who take the gold metal from the ground that makes the white man crazy in the head. In fact, a Hunkpapa rider has just brought news that a new town called "Deadwood" has sprung up in Paha Sapa as a place for the white miners to live. Now the Great White Father wants to buy back from us those lands he gave to us earlier at Fort Laramie so he can give them back to the white people flooding over those lands. We do not want to sell those lands but our chiefs are told we must sell these sacred lands and then be moved onto smaller lands called "reservations." There the Great White Father tells us we must learn to live like a white man. According to a recent Brule crier, the Great White Father has ordered that if we don't go peacefully to these places called reservations, we will all be forcibly rounded up and made to live there anyway. And if there are those who still do not go, they will be called "bad Indians," and hunted down like dogs and shot!"

Then Old Chief Smoke paused as if to think over what

he had said and prepared to provide his son with more information that he may not want to hear. "Son, since the time of the soldier-chief Custer in the Paha Sapa, some bands of the Sioux Nation have been on the war path with those whites who ventured onto our sacred lands. Many whites have been killed, including many of the Bluecoats who came to save them, as well as numbers of the Lakota. Some tribal members have already been forced onto these places called reservations and the word from those people are ringed with much unhappiness, misery, the white man's sickness, and starvation. More and more bands are now joining the fight against the whites and much killing is taking place all over our lands. I fear it soon will be our turn to join in this war. If we don't, it will be like Sitting Bull has said, "If the white man takes my country, where can I go?" I am like Sitting Bull, This is my land and the lands of my ancestors. If we lose these lands of our forefathers, where can we go where we can live like we have since the Great Spirit gave us these lands and the buffalo so long ago?"

Once again, the old chief paused as if the gravity of the present and oncoming situation flashed across his eyes and rattled menacingly through his knowing soul. A graveness that seemed to weigh even more heavily on his shoulders then it ever had up to that moment in time. So much so, that his shoulders stooped even more than normally. Then he continued. "This trouble has begun creeping towards us like a grasshopper in the fall cold and many of my war chiefs are now saying we too must get involved in saving our land from the white man before he has swallowed it up and The People for all time. Word from our scouts in the field is that the Northern Cheyenne, our friends, were told to move onto a reservation during the last moon. The Northern Cheyenne, like the Sioux, are a proud people. They refused. Our scouts have now reported that the Bluecoat Cavalry in the hundreds, set out to force those Northern Cheyenne living along the Powder River, to move onto a reservation. Since the Cheyenne refused to go to these places called a reservation, a soldier-chief called "Reynolds" attacked their encampment eight days ago. It was a surprise attack and many men, women and children were killed before the Cheyenne drove off the Bluecoats. Then the survivors of the tribe, having lost many of their horses and most of their winter supplies of buffalo meat, fled to seek refuge with Crazy Horse and his people. When they fled, the Bluecoats shot all their horses left behind and burned their tipis along with most of their winter food. And because of that, the Northern Cheyenne have joined forces with the Sioux to battle the Bluecoats to get our lands back."

Once again, the gravity of the situation seemed to almost overcome the old chief as he paused and just shook his head in despair. "These last few days you and others may have noticed many riders from other bands coming into my camp with the latest news of battle for me and the elders. From all the many tribe's scouts has come information telling of a large movement of the Bluecoats towards our people. Scouts from the great Sioux Nation, the Northern Cheyenne and a smaller number of our brothers from the Northern Arapaho Nation, have reported many things. Things that are not good. The Northern Cheyenne scouts have reported that there is a force of Bluecoats getting ready to travel once the grass greens up from Fort Fetterman moving north. They say the soldier-chief "Crook" will be leading about 1,000 men northward along the Bozeman Trail. The Northern Arapaho scouts reported that a soldier-chief named "Gibbon" is getting ready to lead a force of about 400 Bluecoats from the west along the Yellowstone River and will be coming this way about the same time. The Lakota scouts report that a soldier-chief named "Custer" will soon be coming from the east from Fort Lincoln this way. That man called 'Custer' will be leading a force of over 600 Bluecoats of the 7th Cavalry. It now looks as if the Great White Father in Washington is sending his armies our way from the south, west and the east all at the same time! And, The People are in the middle...It looks to me and many others, that the aim of the Great White Father in Washington is to push all of us onto reservations so the white man can have all of our lands and leave us with nothing but dead grass and buffalo chips. I will be meeting with the elders shortly in a Council of War and see what they have to say. I fear we too must soon join the Brule, Sans Arcs, Hunkpapa, Two Kettles, Miniconjou, Sihasapa, Santee, the rest of the Oglala, the Northern Cheyenne, and some of the Northern Arapaho in order to defeat the white man and take all of our lands back. Then we can chase or kill off all the other white men settlers and get our lands and herds of buffalo back as it was in the beginning. It is with those words that I leave you so I can meet with the warrior societies and elders to see what are their thoughts. Please say nothing more of what I speak to the rest of the village until it is time to do so. I do not want them to be scared. Later I will tell my people of the great battles to come and to prepare for more empty tipis if all of this comes to pass..."

With those words, the old chief rose and exited the tipi in order to confer with some of his war chiefs and the elders. Josiah noticed that the old man did not appear he had to duck much when he exited his tipi because of the weight of the known natural world now being carried on his shoulders...

Chapter Nine

THE BEGINNING OF THE END
FOR "THE PEOPLE"

Returning from an early morning elk hunt after Josiah White Buffalo's talk with Old Chief Smoke on the upcoming Council of War, Chief Red Shirt, only a sub-chief and not privy to the ongoing talks of war with the senior leaders, looked over at his brother, "My brother, I have a very special request to make of you. I know how much you love your sister, Gemma. Ever since I saw her, I too have loved her as much as you do. I would like to start seeing her and would like to make her my wife. What do you say to my words?"

Josiah White Buffalo caught completely off guard with those words, just looked over at Chief Red Shirt with his piercing blue and now intently searching eyes. "Have you been quietly seeing Gemma and what does she say?" he asked.

"Remembering your earlier words to me when we were not brothers about seeing Gemma, I have mostly honored your concerns. But lately, Two Fawns, Gemma's adopted mother, tells me Gemma would like to get to know me better now that we are brothers and no longer walking The Black Road like two bull buffalo in rut."

"Then if it is her will to get to know you better and since we are now brothers, I release you from my earlier harsh words of warning about seeing her and only ask that you respect her wishes and treat her well. And if she wishes of her own free will to become your wife, then I will also honor those wishes," said a still surprised Josiah White Buffalo. Surprised, since riding all the way back with an elk on the trailing pack horses and thinking of nothing but fresh elk meat for breakfast cooked by Prairie Flower, he had ridden blissfully along enjoying the morning air. Then being confronted and surprised with Chief Red Shirt's words of wanting to have his beloved sister as his wife, Josiah White Buffalo now found his daydreams of an elk meat breakfast getting fuzzy with the proposed moment at hand...But then thinking it over, he relaxed and grinned as only a big brother can do. His sister was as strong willed as was he. If those were her wishes then so be it, he finally thought with a happy grin.

"Then it is settled. When we get back to our village, I would like to go to Two Fawn's tipi and spend some time with Gemma," said Chief Red Shirt quietly, aware of the huge surprise he had just happily dropped on the stout shoulders of his new brother and now, best friend.

With the surprise of the morning, even over the great running and killing shot Josiah White Buffalo had earlier made on a grand seven point bull elk, he sat on Wind with a huge smile on his face. Now Gemma would have a choice to make and if all went well, be able to get on with her life in and among the other members of the village as a "spoken-for woman." And, she could do worse than marrying a great and growing in stature sub-chief like Red Shirt. Yes, this morning had the makings of a good one, thought Josiah White Buffalo. That was until he had shared most of the elk with other less well-off members of the band and was told that Old Chief Smoke was seriously looking for him.

Entering the old chief's tipi after giving Prairie Flower a back strap from his recently killed elk, the darkness of the tipi left him adjusting his eyes to the reduced light. Then he saw the old chief sitting by the back side of the small inside fire. It was then that his eyes went squarely to the old chief's face. It now looked old before its time and haggard from his lack of sleep. Prairie Flower had said nothing to him about the old chief being sick or distraught but it was clear from the looks on the old man's face that something was wrong. BAD WRONG!

"Sit down my son, we must talk." Josiah White Buffalo quietly did as he was told. "Last night the Council of War decided we must split up the village's fighting men. Half must prepare to go off and join our brothers and fight the whites. The other half of the braves and warriors must stay to hunt and protect the village. It now appears from all our scouts that the Great White Father in Washington is preparing for war against all his children of the prairie. I just heard that six moons ago, the Great White Father had ordered all Indians to go to the reservations or be considered bad Indians. Since many of the bands do not understand much of what the whites tell us, we did not obey the Great White Father over his words of warning. Now he is angry at us. So angry, that he is now making war against any Indians who are not on the reservations. And if he wants war, he shall have it because we are not afraid. We as a nation must fight for our ways of life. Otherwise, we will all die for lack of freedom, disease, starvation, and a broken heart. Especially if we are to be herded onto and made to live on those hated reservations."

For a few long moments, Josiah White Buffalo just sat there looking at the tired and worried face of his adopted father. "Will you be going off with the warriors and braves or staying, Father?" he asked.

"I will be staying to lead what is left of our band that remains. The fighting is for the young people and not the very old like me. Besides, if we are forced to leave this area of our home, I must be here to lead my people," quietly replied the old chief.

"Then with your permission, Father, I would like to be one of those selected from our band to go off and fight the whites," quietly spoke Josiah White Buffalo. Then listening to what he had just said, Josiah White Buffalo realized his many meetings earlier with the elders about the traditions and the culture of the Lakota had not been wasted. He was now a full blooded warrior of the proud Oglala/Lakota and would fight to protect his home. Do so, even if it meant he should die in battle. After all, he still had the strong medicine in his sage grouse wing and the busted Sun Dance thong attached to his braid. And like in his vision, the bullets from the troopers would not be able to kill him. But also like in his earlier vision, the sage grouse ate the troopers as they fired at the birds and he would do the same as well. With his strong medicine, he too would kill as many troopers as it took in order to protect his home and his way of life.

As the Great Spirit looked down upon Old Chief Smoke's tipi, He could see a young white man with piercing blue eyes. A young white man who had been captured in his early life and one who was now shortly, as He had predicted, about to become a great warrior for the mighty Sioux Nation...

For the next few weeks, Old Chief Smoke's village was a bee hive of activity. First a great buffalo hunt was undertaken with many buffalo being slain. Then once hauled back to camp, great activity surrounded the cutting and drying of the meat and the processing of their hides. With that work finished, the warriors and braves now released from caring about adequate food supplies for the village, began making preparation for battle. Many sweats were taken and several of the younger braves who had yet to receive a vision, went off on a vision quest. Fifteen days later, a party of thirty-five warriors and braves sat on their horses in front of Old Chief Smoke's tipi in an obvious heightened state of emotion. Their hearts were true, they had said their goodbyes, their families were now cared for as a result of the more than successful buffalo hunt, and they were now in full battle dress. Each warrior and brave also had one additional horse he was taking along to pack his things and act as a second riding horse in case his main horse came up lame or was lost in battle.

At the front of the group of mounted warriors and braves sat Josiah White Buffalo on his horse, Wind. On one side of his horse rode a Winchester 1873, caliber .44-40 in one scabbard and in a scabbard on the other side, rode a Sharps heavy long barreled, .45-70 rifle. On both hips comfortably sat two .44 caliber Colt pistols. In a leather pouch on each side of the saddle horn rode a bag full of cartridges for each rifle. On his pack horse along with his extra clothing items, rode three more leather pouches loaded with rifle cartridges for his two different rifle calibers and another one full of pistol cartridges. In his long braid attached on his right side, rode a sage grouse wing attached to a short leather thong. Painted on the neck of his horse was that of a fully extended grouse wing trailing a short leather thong. On Josiah White Buffalo's war shield, one made from the tough shoulder hide from that of an old bull buffalo, was a darkened sage grouse wing painted on a red background. His knife and tomahawk rode on his crowded waist. On his red painted face, he had four dark blue vertical stripes painted on his lower chin. Along both thighs were painted streaks of lightning in blue paint. The only thing that differentiated him from a true, native born Oglala/Lakota warrior, was his set of deadly serious, piercing blue eyes.

Sitting alongside Josiah White Buffalo was his Indian brother. Chief Red Shirt had on his battle shirt of red in color calico. He too was armed with a Winchester rifle and wore two Colt .44 caliber pistols on his hips. His horse was painted in sacred colors just like Josiah White Buffalo's had been and his body paint signifying his warrior status was proudly worn as well.

Sitting around Chief Red Shirt and Josiah White Buffalo were thirty-three other just as fiercely painted and well prepared braves and warriors. All wore a sullen and serious look over what was to come and quietly to a man, each wondered how they would do in the heat of the battle to come with the hated white man's soldiers.

Then out emerged Old Chief Smoke from his tipi dressed in his finest battle dress. A supreme quiet reigned around the mounted fighters and the village on lookers grew intensely quiet as this moment in time so dictated. Even the war horses the men rode, seemed to sense the seriousness of the moment and were stilled in their movements and sound.

Quietly standing there, the old chief's heart swelled with pride at the magnificence of the fighters sitting horsed before him. And at the same time, he was filled with the sadness of the moment. Sadness because he realized having been a warrior in like circumstances in his younger years that many now sitting before him would not return...Then he quietly spoke.

"I am not happy that all of you have to fight for what is rightfully ours. Our ancestors are also sad that what they fought for so many moons ago, all of you must now fight for once again. The Great Spirit has armed all of you with The Way and may He follow each and every one of you into battle with His hands wrapped around you. When in battle, show no mercy because your foes will treat you the same way. Scouts have reported that our enemy's the Crow are being led by Chief Plenty Coups, the Shoshones are led by Chief Washakie, along with numerous half-breed scouts and they will be assisting the Bluecoats as they move north from Fort Fetterman. Be careful for they are bad Indians and the Bluecoat chief is using them to track and hunt us down. If our enemies are successful in battle, all of those of us not killed in battle, will be rounded up and moved onto the reservations like the Great White Father in Washington has ordered. And if you kill any bad Indians in battle, make sure they never can join our Cloud People because of what you have done to their earthly physical presence. Make them pay for being bad Indians. As for the whites, make sure you kill so many of them that they can never again make trouble for our nations. This is our land! Make sure we can keep it or die trying..." With those words, Old Chief Smoke turned and strode back into his tipi and spoke no more of such sad things to the young fighting men of his band.

Lead war chief, White Elk, seeing his chief had spoken, turned his horse to the southwest and made for the location selected for all the bands in which to gather. There they would be led by the holy man Sitting Bull and war chiefs Crazy Horse, Left Hand, Rain-in-the-Face, Chief Gall, Brave Buffalo, Joseph White Bull, Crow King, Lame Deer, Hollow Horn Bear, Two Moons, Black Elk, Lame White Man, Little Wolf, Stands-In-Timber and numerous other lesser but highly experienced war chiefs as well.

Two days of hard riding found White Elk's band of Oglala/Lakota slowly moving into a huge camp of Sioux, Northern Cheyenne and a smaller number of Northern Arapaho. The smoky encampment's tipi-layout stretched for several miles up and down Ash Creek and included men, women, children and many horse herds. The din of activity took White Elk's band used to the quiet of Old Chief Smoke's encampment by surprise. Never had the warriors from Old Chief Smoke's band seen so many braves and warriors in one location. Josiah White Buffalo estimated the grand encampment composed of members from the three Indian nations, numbering around fifteen hundred to two thousand braves and warriors alone! As for the women and children, Josiah White Buffalo estimated there were at least six thousand of them in the camp! Their horse herds blanketed the valley almost like the buffalo of old on the prairie. And the smoke from so many buffalo-chip fueled cooking fires, hazed the sky above the entire valley along Ash Creek like the fires set in the fall on the prairie by the Indians to burn off the old grasses and make way for the green grass of the following spring.

Continuing their trek, White Elk led his little band of Oglala/Lakota braves and warriors into the center of the huge encampment. Shortly thereafter, they located Sitting Bull's tipi. Upon hearing their arrival in front of his tipi, they were met by Sitting Bull and Crazy-Horse. The two men were obviously happy to see more warriors and braves arriving. Then Sitting Bull spied Josiah White Buffalo quietly sitting on his horse. Walking over, he reached up to Josiah White Buffalo's extended hand and personally welcomed him with the words, "It is good to see such a warrior with his strong medicine in our camp. There soon will be great battles fought and many will die. But you my friend with the sacred grouse wing and leather Sun Dance thong, will be victorious in whatever you do. Remember my earlier vision at the Sun Dance in which you participated. I told you that my vision showed the two of us walking down many trails together. This is just one of those trails. Let it be a trail blessed by the Great Spirit." Then Sitting Bull and Crazy Horse held a conversation with White Elk about the battles and strategy to come. Turning, Sitting Bull said, "Now go, set up your camp and rest. For shortly, that great battle I speak of will be joined and we will need many rested braves and warriors for us to be successful."

With those words from such a revered holy man, an emotional ripple went through the assembled fighters like the wind across the tops of the prairie grasses just before a summer thunderstorm. It was at that very moment, that Josiah White Buffalo felt such a strong sense of emotion rippling throughout his body that it left him shaking. Then a flash of his earlier vision of the sage grouse eating many soldiers who were uselessly firing their rifles at the birds, rippled through his senses as well. It was at that very moment, that Josiah White Buffalo realized he would fight fiercely in battle and would not be dishonored or harmed.

With those words being spoken by Sitting Bull, both he and Crazy Horse reentered the holy man's tipi without another spoken word. White Elk then led his little band of thirty-five fighters into an unoccupied stand of cottonwoods along Ash Creek and there they made camp. Later that afternoon, a rider stormed into camp and hurriedly dismounted by Sitting Bull's tipi. Soon the entire camp was abuzz with word of an impending battle between the camp's fighters and a long column of approaching U.S. Cavalry. Within moments after the rider's arrival, many chiefs began streaming into a circle of tipis around Sitting Bull's tipi which was identified by its huge staff of spotted eagle tail feathers quietly fluttering in the afternoon breezes. Word soon filtered through the hundreds of gathered braves and warriors, that Crazy Horse had sent word to the soldier-chief called "Crook" that his column of soldiers were not to cross the Tongue River. (Authors Note: Near present day Sheridan, Wyoming.) According to the scouts watching General Crook's long column of over 1,000 men, they had stopped just below the Tongue River and had set up camp. With the arrival of that word, Crazy Horse figured the General had heard his words of warning and that was why he did not cross the river. Several days later however, other scouts reported to Crazy Horse that the soldiers appeared to be waiting for their Indian allies led by Chief Plenty Coups of the Crow and Chief Washakie of the Shoshoni. As it turned out, both chiefs were from tribes that were sworn enemies of the Sioux. And those bands of Indians were now close to entering the soldier-chief's camp.

Then quiet reined until later that afternoon. Riders once again entered the Indian's encampment and went straight-away to Crazy Horse's tipi. There they advised that the soldiers were making ready to cross the Tongue River. With that information, Crazy Horse set his battle plan into motion. Alerting all the chiefs as to his plan, the fighters made ready. In the middle of the night, Crazy Horse set his plan into motion. Taking about one thousand Indian fighters, they rode all night towards Rosebud Creek. Stopping around daylight, Crazy Horse had his fighters rest their horses for the battle that was soon to come.

As was later reported by the scouts, soldier-chief Crook had left his supply wagons, teamsters, and civilians behind and had mounted his infantry on their mules around three in the morning. Taking around one thousand cavalry and his now mule-mounted Infantry, Crook began moving toward Rosebud Creek. It was in that location that Crook figured the reported huge hostile Indian encampment of Sitting Bull and Crazy Horse were located. Little did he realize the actual Indian encampment was located further away on Ash Creek. A site which lay to the west of Rosebud Creek. As Crook's column moved northward along the south fork of Rosebud Creek, he stopped and rested his men and animals around 8:30 in the morning. It was then that Crazy Horse led his fighters into a full-fledged attack! Crook expected the Indian fighters to hit and then run off like they did in so many previous battles. In that flawed thinking, he got surprised. The Indians hotly engaged Crooks men in a pitched and hard fought battle, holding their ground instead of moving away after the first few shots had been fired. Then the order of battle, as in the case of many pitched battles fought on the frontier, got confused.

Soon the two battling forces were scattered across the terrain in small groups over a front stretching in excess of three miles in length! The fighting had devolved into numerous disconnected actions, with numerous charges and counter charges by the soldiers and Crazy Horse's forces. But as the soldiers were soon to realize, they were fighting the finest light cavalry in the world. And in doing so, the soldiers were unable to surround, trap or destroy any large numbers of Indian fighters swirling around them.

As the battle was fully joined, White Elk led his

contingent of Old Chief Smoke's fighters towards a smaller detachment of soldiers from his attacking position on the high ground. Circling the isolated group of soldiers and separating them from any immediate reinforcement, the Indians in true fighting style, exposed little of themselves. In true Plains warrior fashion, the Indians hung onto their horses with one arm wrapped around the animal's neck and one leg hung over the back of their hard charging mounts. Hanging down over the side of their horses and out of sight in such a manner, the Indians would fire from under the horse's neck at their intended targets. In doing so, they exposed little of themselves and the soldiers had yet to learn not to shoot at the difficult human targets the riders presented but shoot to kill their horses. For without a horse, the finest light cavalry in the world was nothing more than a slow moving foot soldier.

Staying together, Chief Red Shirt and Josiah White Buffalo dodged and darted in and among the scattered bunches of soldiers, shooting from under their horse's necks. Not seeing any soldiers falling from their poorly aimed and yet concentrated fire from their Winchesters while shooting from under the moving, jostling necks of their horses, Josiah White Buffalo suddenly left the fight. When he did, he waved at Chief Red Shirt to follow. The two men rode over to a small rocky knoll and quickly dismounted in order to present a smaller target. Josiah White Buffalo placed his Winchester back in its scabbard, grabbed his Sharps buffalo rifle from the other scabbard, then ran to the lee side of the knoll for the slight cover it offered. Laying the heavy barreled rifle along the edge of the hill's rim, he jacked open the action and inserted a

.45-70 cartridge into the chamber.

"Watch behind me so we don't get flanked by the soldiers," he yelled at Chief Red Shirt. Below Josiah White Buffalo on the next ridge line over near Kolmarr Creek, was a closely grouped detachment of exposed dismounted cavalry. By now, several groups of Indians had also recognized that cavalry detachments exposed and dangerous position. Not only were they were a long ways from the main body of troops but were out in the open with no place to run or hide. Recognizing that, a large group of Lakota and Northern Cheyenne broke off their futile, long range shooting battle with Crook and his small detachment holding the high ground to the west.

Wheeling their horses, that group of fighters then thundered down Kolmarr Valley towards the isolated small detachment of dismounted troopers. As the hard riding Indians charged ever closer, they began to lay down a heavy and concentrated fire upon the hapless troopers. With such an onslaught coming their way, the soldiers began to panic and a few tried running to their horses in order to flee. Then one soldier in the group stood up and began calming down and directing his men to regroup, concentrate their fire, and continue the fight. Seeing that soldier calming his men and reacting to his orders, Josiah White Buffalo figured him to be a soldier-chief of some renown. Lining up his sights on the brave, standing exposed out in the open, soldier, Josiah White Buffalo fired. With that long range shot, Josiah White Buffalo saw the standing soldier grab his side and spin over sideways and drop onto the ground. (Authors Note: Captain Guy V. Henry was the officer shot.)

With the soldier-chief's fall, it became obvious that the rest of the soldiers in his group, fearing the long range accurate shooting of Josiah White Buffalo from the high ground and the hoard of Indians charging down upon them along Kolmarr Creek, began panicking and breaking ranks once again. Quickly reloading, Josiah White Buffalo shot another trooper who had just reached his horse in an effort to escape. The impact of the pure lead .45-70 slug tearing through his back slammed him into the side of his horse, who then panicked. Rearing back on the reins, the horse broke free from his handler and sprinted off into the oncoming hard charging approaching group of Indians. There he was quickly captured by a gleeful warrior, who then rode off trailing his prize. Then the attacking horde of Indians heading for the small group of isolated troopers, suddenly broke off their charge and overwhelmed another smaller nearby group of exposed soldiers. Killing all those soldiers, the Indians then began scalping the dead and stripping them of their weapons and ammunition. Rounding up the dead soldiers horses, the Indians fled the scene as more mounted troopers charged their position from the north side of the battle.

Then Chief Red Shirt shouted a warning, "Josiah White Buffalo, more shooters from the next hill over are lining up on top and shooting our way!" Those words of warning had no more than escaped Chief Red Shirt's lips, when the ground exploded next to Josiah White Buffalo in a puff of flying dirt and stinging rock chips! 'CHE-POW' went a million rock fragments from the near miss right next to Josiah White Buffalo. A shot that had come from what was a long range shooting Infantry trooper.

One who was using a long barreled rifle instead of the standard short barreled, shorter shooting range, 1873 Trapdoor .45-70 carbine cavalry troopers were issued and used.

"Josiah White Buffalo, we must leave this position. The soldiers with their long rifles have sighted in on us and are now shooting in our direction from on high," screamed a dismounted and concerned Chief Red Shirt.

'CHE-WHEW', went another close at hand ricocheting bullet. Only this time with unforeseen consequences. The flying rock chips exploded all over Josiah White Buffalo's almost naked and now heavily sweating body. When it did, it left many bloody rock-tears in his skin! Another flying rock chip from that same bullet sailed even higher, clipping off the leather Sun Dance thong on the grouse wing that had been attached to Josiah White Buffalo's long braid! With that, the grouse wing fluttered to the ground unnoticed in the heat of the battle...

'CHE-WHEW', went another bullet as it ricocheted across the rocky slope upon which Josiah White Buffalo rested with his Sharps rifle. Once again, rocky slivers tore into the flesh of Josiah White Buffalo, only this time, all along his right leg. Realizing he was now dangerously exposed to the soldier's fire with their long range rifles, Josiah White Buffalo stood up to run to a more covered position. WHANG! Went a bullet into the side plate of his Sharps rifle, knocking Josiah White Buffalo head over heels and for a moment, senseless as he laid without moving on the rocky hillside!

"Josiah! Josiah!," yelled Chief Red Shirt as he

released their horse's reins and levered another round into his rifle to shoot at a close at hand, hard charging, horse mounted cavalry soldier coming their way. BOOM, went Chief Red Shirt's rifle and the cavalry trooper spun out of the saddle, landing face first on the rocky knoll, dead before he hit the ground!

Josiah White Buffalo staggered to his feet and by sheer survival instinct and muscle memory, tried to open the action on his single shot Sharps rifle in order to eject the spent round and load in another live cartridge. It was jammed and would not move because that last bullet had struck the side plate with such force that it smashed the inside mechanisms together, rendering the rifle useless..."CHE-WHEW" went another close at hand bullet as it neatly clipped off Josiah White Buffalo's remaining long braid at the base of his skull! It was then that Josiah White Buffalo realized something was dead-awful wrong! The bullets were coming so close to his body that he could hear the angry 'zipping' sounds they made as they closely passed. And twice, he could feel the wind of the closely passing bullets against his sweating skin! Then seeing one long braid lying on the ground at his feet, he quickly reached up to feel his other braid. It was then in his still dazed state of mind, that he discovered the braid holding his symbol of power had also neatly been clipped off halfway up by another close bullet! And now his symbol of power, the sacred grouse wing which protected him from all harm, was gone!

'CHE-PEW!' went another close at hand bullet and this time, it found its mark. Josiah White Buffalo spun around from his standing out in the open position as that

247

bullet ripped across the skin of his back! The explosive impact of the bullet's near killing shot, spun him around and flung him to the ground! For the longest time, Josiah White Buffalo could not get his breath from the bullet's brushing action but could hear Chief Red Shirt yelling at him in a faraway distant voice. Then he found himself being cradled in his brother's arms.

"Josiah! Josiah, are you alright? Say something! You are bleeding everywhere! Where are you hit?" screamed a frantic Chief Red Shirt!

Then off in a distance, Josiah White Buffalo heard Chief Red Shirt say, "Oh No! Where is your symbol of power? Your grouse wing and the sacred leather thong from the Sun Dance that Sitting Bull had attached to your braid is gone! What happened to it?"

'CHE-WHEW' went another to close for comfort ricocheting bullet as it impacted on their rocky knoll. That time, both men were splattered with a mess of splintered flying rock chips. Exploding rock chips which blasted into their skins and having the very real effect of painting them red with their own blood on the side of their bodies exposed to the long range rifles of the now accurately shooting dismounted Infantry.

By then, Josiah White Buffalo had somewhat recovered from the near killing shot across his now burning back. It was then that he began realizing through his still fogged brain, that something was dead wrong! According to his visions and the spirit world, this being shot was not supposed to happen. The troopers had shot at the sage grouse in his vision and had not been able to hit or kill any of them. Then the grouse had eaten the troopers. Reaching up, he realized through his still foggy mind, that one braid of his hair had been shot clean off at the base of his skull and the other blown off half way up! And with that, his symbol of power had been shot away! Then Josiah White Buffalo heard the stern warnings coming from a faraway distant voice of Fast Antelope the Oglala/Lakota holy man saying, "Never let your symbol of power given to you by the Great Spirit leave the presence of your body. If you do, bad spirits will come at you because you are a white man trying to be an Indian in their world. Lose your power and you will quickly die."

Realizing the truth in the holy man's words, buttressed among the now numerous zipping bullets being fired by the soldiers with their long range .45-70 long-barreled rifles, Josiah White Buffalo scrambled back to his original shooting position. There he discovered his half a braid with the grouse wing still attached to the fallen lock of hair. Quickly picking up the hair with the wing still attached, Josiah White Buffalo then walked over to Wind and retrieved his Winchester from its scabbard. This he calmly did, as more bullets now whistled around him but now, all flying harmlessly away from his person...As he did, he tossed his ruined Sharps buffalo rifle into the brush. (Author's Note: That Sharps rifle was discovered in 1954 by an arrowhead hunter named Vincent Toni from Maryland who was walking over the old battlefield. A smashed .45-70 slug was still flattened out and imbedded into the big rifle's mangled metal side plate. Had that bullet gone two inches higher or lower, it would have killed the rifle's holder...)

Then Chief Red Shirt and Josiah White Buffalo

dropped down behind their protective knoll and out of the direct line of fire from the Infantry troopers' long-barreled rifles. From there, the two men continued raining fire downhill upon the still exposed, dismounted cavalry detachment below them. Rifle fire that was so accurate, that the group of trapped soldiers finally retreated back to the safety of a hill to their rear being held by General Crook and many of his headquarters staff. As those soldiers retreated under the protection of Crook's long range shooting of the Infantry's long barreled rifles, Chief Red Shirt and Josiah White Buffalo redirected their joint fire onto a group of hard charging Crow Indians coming their way. Their fire from their fifteen shot Winchesters was so lethal, that the Crow Indian's horse charge was broken up and then stopped with a number of their dead strung out along the ground when they were unhorsed. Sensing the futility of charging straight into the accurate and withering fire coming from Josiah White Buffalo and Chief Red Shirt's combined rifle fire, they too also retreated back towards the protection of Crook's high ground position and their many protective shooters as fast as their horses could carry them. And in doing so, went back with eight of their horses being riderless...

At 2:30 P.M., the Indians broke off their side of the battle and left the field. Crook realizing he had escaped with most of his somewhat shot up contingent of troops, retreated back down the trail from whence he came. On his way back, Crook picked up his pack train and civilians and continued retreating back to Goose Creek. (Author's Note: Near present day Sheridan, Wyoming.) There Crook waited seven weeks for reinforcements and played no further role in the major Indian battles that were to follow in the month ahead. A mistake of caution that was to prove to be very costly for the U.S. Army involved in another coming historic battle further to the north...

After that battle and General Crook had retreated, Crazy Horse had his fighters return and make rock piles around the recent battlefield denoting different Indian positions throughout the battle. He also had the encampment's young boys walk the battlefield with buffalo skins pouches picking up the unexpended soldier's ammunition dropped or stacked alongside their original positions for their ready use on their side of the battle lines. Crazy Horse, having been in many battles previously with the troopers, especially during the earlier Red Cloud Indian War, realized that many of the soldiers during the heat of battle would stack extra cartridges alongside where they knelt. That way if the battle got heated, they would have numerous cartridges laying close at hand at their fingertips for the quick reloading of their single shot rifles. And in doing so, not have to fuss with digging them out from their one hundred round canvas cartridge belts hanging around their waists. And then if they were forced away from that location or had to move to a more advantageous shooting position, many times in the heat of battle the soldiers would forget those live cartridges previously stacked alongside their last shooting position.

Realizing the Indian's always pressing needs for the white man's ammunition since many of them were shooting the same caliber weapons, Crazy Horse had sent the young boys out to scrounge up any and all cartridges left behind on the battlefield. In doing so, the young men picked up and filled two large buffalo hides containing hundreds of rounds of unexpended .45-70 rifle ammunition! Ammunition that would play a deadly role in another major battle yet to come. One that would take place three weeks later, and whose results would rock the United States Government, her peoples, and the U.S. Army to its very command core...And in doing so, begin closing the final chapter on the Northern Plains Indians and their nomadic way of life. A life unspoiled and loved until the coming and expansion into the west of the European Man and his culture.

Returning to their encampment after the rather confused battle, Josiah White Buffalo and Chief Red Shirt headed for the creek and bathed, in order to remove the sweat and blood of battle. Both men bore the scars of battle by having chosen a rocky knoll from which to fight. And in doing so, having to feel the wrath of many flying rock chips from nearby bullet strikes fired at them in anger. But there soon would be more of the same...That evening around the quiet of their campsite, Josiah White Buffalo undid his hair and re-braided what was left into one central braid. Then taking a long piece of tough buffalo sinew, re-tied his symbol of power onto that single braid. He would never again be so careless and not heed the wise words from Fast Antelope about keeping his symbol of power firmly attached to his person even in the heat of battle. Well...

The losses to the Indian fighters in the previous day's battle at the Rosebud had been light. Only about thirty Indians had been killed and about seventy were wounded.

The numbers of dead and wounded for the U.S. Army had been about the same. But, the southernmost prong of the three hated U.S. Cavalry contingents converging towards the Indians had been successfully blunted and turned back. For that victory, many prayers of thanks were made to the Great Spirit. And now, new war plans were in the offing relative the other two oncoming prongs of the U.S. Army's still advancing columns. A military operation designed to round up many of the Plains Indians and move them onto reservations. And in doing so, allow the encroaching white race to settle those lands so seized under the flag of battle and in direct violation of the Fort Laramie Treaty of 1868. Under the advice of Sitting Bull, the entire encampment would soon be moved further to the north into the Montana Territory. That way, he figured they would be further away from the pursuing 'horse soldiers' and could once again, pursue their freedom and culture as they had since the beginning of time. Sitting Bull decided they would make their next camp in the valley of the Little Greasy Grass. The white men called that same body of water flowing through the valley of the Indian's next encampment, the Little Bighorn River...

The next morning after the Battle at Rosebud Creek, more factions of Indians kept arriving into the grand encampment. Most had fled their historical places of summer residence due to the increased cavalry patrols rounding up non-reservation stragglers and herding them like cattle onto the now much hated reservations. Herding them to such places, because the U.S. government as of January of that year, had decreed that all Indians not on the reservations would be declared hostile and hunted down by the white man's armies. That way, once the Indians had been removed to the reservations because they would not accept payment for previously deeded treaty lands under the 1868 Fort Laramie Treaty, the white miners and settlers could move onto those tribal lands as they wished without fear of being killed and having their livestock run off by marauding or hostile Indians.

Josiah White Buffalo and especially Chief Red Shirt, were surprised and pleased to see Old Chief Smoke's band of Oglala/Lakota arriving at their encampment in the early afternoon. They too, like other bands of Indians, had fled their summer home grounds due to the increased searching cavalry patrol activity. Chief Red Shirt was happy beyond belief, as was Gemma, to see each other once again. Now that the young couple were once again united, Josiah White Buffalo could just look on at the antics of two people in love with a smile during such troubled times. He smiled even more broadly the following day when Chief Red Shirt took Gemma for his wife. Old Chief Smoke was the officiant to that newest tribal marriage. He had both parties cut a small piece of skin off one of their thumbs, then had their two thumbs tied together. Old Chief Smoke then declared they were now one, just as their blood was now one. Finally, he commanded that the two were to live as "one flesh' ever after. From that day forward until fate intervened, Chief Red Shirt occupied Two Fawns tipi where Gemma lived as the man of the lodge, protector and main provider.

One week later, Sitting Bull had the very large Indian encampment moved almost due north as they headed for the Montana Territory. Seven-sleeps later, the camp's contingent arrived at the valley of the Little Greasy Grass. There the large Indian encampment was spread out along the Little Greasy Grass River for several miles. Once established and the vast horse herds were positioned within selected grazing areas, a great buffalo hunt was carried out. Taking several hundred men, Crazy Horse led the hunters to a large herd of buffalo. After a successful hunt in which over three hundred buffalo were killed, the camp's women and children arrived on the kill site. For the next two days, those buffalo were butchered out and a continuous stream of travois and happy people led to and from the huge Indian encampment. When finished with that detail, the happy times began as everyone celebrated the bounty the Great Spirit had just provided for The People. Over the next two weeks, the meat from the buffalo hunt was processed, friends and families visited each other, marriages were held, and many of the clans celebrated the wonder of their lives quietly among themselves once again.

During those happy times, it was decided by the many chiefs assembled in camp that a sacred Sun Dance should be held. Within days, a site had been chosen, a sacred cottonwood tree with a forked top had been cut down and erected as "The First Pole." Shortly thereafter, the Sun Dance Lodge was completed and a number of the braves made ready to participate. Then a surprise manifested itself among all those gathered. Sitting Bull would also participate as one of the dancers! Come the chosen day after all the preparations had been made on and for the dancers, the much celebrated Sun Dance began. All day the dancers danced, prayed and blew their eagle bone whistles so the Great Spirit could witness their good character and bear witness to the individual dancer's sacrifices for the benefit of The People. One by one, the dancers tore free from the wooden skewers anchored into each dancer's chests. Finally, only one dancer remained. It was Sitting Bull! The old but hearty chief continued dancing through the night and into the following day. After 36 hours of continuous dancing, lamenting and praying, he finally pulled his chest free from the wooden skewers!

Afterwards, word quickly spread that Sitting Bull, the holy man, had experienced a prophetic vision during the Sun Dance. In that vision, Sitting Bull had seen "soldiers falling into their camp like grasshoppers from the sky." Sitting Bull then prophesied that a battle with the soldiers would soon be fought and a great victory would be won by the Indians. But Sitting Bull also advised that the vision carried a warning. After that great battle had been fought and won, the victorious Indians were not to touch anything left on the battlefield. They were advised to leave everything as it fell and not take anything from the battlefield in the way of the soldier's property. For if they did, a great calamity would befall all of their people...With those words of victory still ringing in their ears from such a much revered holy man, The People were overjoyed. Especially since with the passing of every day, more and more bands of Indians were streaming into their camp. And in doing so, swelled the camp's numbers to over seven thousand men, women and children. A number that included about fifteen hundred to two thousand braves and warriors ready to do battle! (Author's Note: Historians are unable to accurately estimate the numbers of fighting men that were in the Indian's camp with the existing historical records on hand.)

Then early one morning, a scout rode into camp advising that a column of about six hundred soldiers were between Rosebud Creek and the Little Bighorn River valleys! The scouts had been observing that columns progress for the last five days and had now brought the warnings of impending danger into the camp and Sitting Bull's tipi. Shortly thereafter, a grand war council of the war chiefs from the Sioux and Northern Cheyenne Nations were quickly held.

That war council was still in session when scouts once again brought in word of the soldier-columns advance coming from the southeast of their encampment. That scout reported that the hated horse soldiers, were now just four miles away from their encampment and closing fast! With that urgent news threading its way through the camp, the council of war ended and the braves and warriors began making their preparations for the upcoming battle. And in doing so, gathered in their war horses, painted their sacred symbols on them and then painted themselves for the impending battle to come.

Then alarm swept through the camp! A cloud of dust was seen at the southeastern end of the strung out along the river's encampment. Then running and panicked women and children swept into the center of the camp yelling that the horse soldiers were at the southeastern end of their camp and shooting at them! Not yet fully prepared

257

for battle, many of the braves and warriors still mounted their horses and sped off in the direction of the sounds of gunfire and dust raising high into the air over the scene of battle in order to fight with the hated cavalry.

Pandemonium reined! Surprised fighters continued streaming out from the encampment in a disorganized fashion both on foot and on horseback. Those warriors were soon confronted with a skirmish line of dismounted cavalry pouring forth deadly volleys of fire at the oncoming Indians trying to defend their encampment. A soldier-chief named Reno had ridden into the far southeastern end of the encampment and attacked the unprepared Indians. However fierce fire from the ever growing numbers of gathering Indian fighters forced him to dismount his soldiers and form a skirmish line. And in doing so, his soldier's horses had been led back into the nearby timber along the river for their safety. Then the increasingly accurate and concentrated rifle fire from the heavily armed attacking Indians forced the soldiers to panic. That was when the soldiers in the skirmish line were forced to break ranks under the unexpected heavy onslaught of Indian fighters. Especially since so many of the soldiers were killed as they stood or knelt in their original hastily formed skirmish line. That plus many of those freshly recruited young soldiers, had yet to experience or participate in any form of pitched battle with the Indians. And on that day, "the blood of the Indians ran hot…" It was at that point that Chief Red Shirt, followed by a number of Old Chief Smoke's fighters, streamed into battle and flanked the soldiers skirmish line. Josiah White Buffalo riding alongside Chief

Red Shirt, thundered his horse right into the dense timber at the river's edge and into the panicked soldier horse-handlers. (Author's Note: In battle, standard military practice of the day was for the cavalry to have one so designated horse- handler grab the reins from four of the other soldiers' horses whose riders were in the process of forming a skirmish line. Then the horse-handler was to remove the horses from harm's way. Once the battle was over, that horse-handler returned the horses to their rightful owners.)

The first panicked soldier Josiah White Buffalo encountered, he killed with one swipe of his tomahawk to the back of the panicked man's head as he tried to ride away from the quickly becoming lop-sided battle. His new tomahawk's oaken handle did not break that time...As the rest of the hard charging Indian fighters smashed into the brush in the timber and through the remaining hastily thrown up skirmish line, the now dismounted soldier horse-handlers broke ranks, let go of their horses and tried to ride off on their own mounts and escape the horde of attackers. As a result of that panic, a rout quickly ensued! As panicked soldiers tried running away from the thundering group of Indian horseflesh and humanity, the close at hand killing was deadly and intense. For the most part, the soldiers dropped their single shot rifles after firing only a few shots and then fled into the timber, as they headed for the safety of nearby high ground on an adjacent hilltop. Josiah White Buffalo killed several more of the crowded together soldiers trying to escape by running over and killing them with Wind's thundering hooves and impacting body!

Then Josiah White Buffalo drew his pistol and killed six more close at hand panicked soldiers trying to flee the Indian's attacking forces. And in doing so, just rode alongside the panicked and fleeing soldiers and head shot every one of them.

Stopping to reload his pistol, he saw that Chief Red Shirt was doing the same and soon about 1/3 of the troopers they had initially encountered, now laid dead or dying along the hastily formed skirmish line or in the dense brush of the adjacent riverside timber! Those who were later discovered dying or badly wounded, were swiftly lanced or shot full of arrows as they laid on the ground or tried crawling away to safety. Those Indians who did not have firearms, disregarding Sitting Bull's earlier words of warning about leaving the spoils of battle where it laid, dismounted and scavenged such weapons from the dead troopers along with their ammunition belts. Horses from those already dead and wounded troopers, were quickly rounded up as prizes once the return fire from the disorganized soldiers had subsided.

Moments later, the surviving troopers in the timber reached the adjacent hilltop above the tree line, dug in, and began making it hot for any attacking Indian fighters charging up at them from below. This they were able to do because the trapped dismounted cavalry troopers now had the shooting advantage by holding the high ground above their attackers. That plus they now had erected barricades of dead soldiers and their dispatched horses in front of their shooting positions which provided additional protection from the hordes of attacking Indians moving against them from below the slopes and the hail of bullets that followed. Then another soldier-chief named "Benteen" with his troopers, joined the trapped Reno and that increased their defensive firepower against their Indian attackers.

Sensing the futility of attacking fortified and now re-staffed positions on the high ground, the Indian fighters quietly slipped back into the brushy timber below and rode hell for leather for their camp. For now, there was another even more dangerous threat. When the alarm of the approaching troopers had been sounded, Sitting Bull organized a contingent of braves and warriors to move all the women and children away from the scene of battle. Crazy Horse on the other hand, continued organizing another contingent of fighters to attack a second approaching cavalry column heading down a long draw from the adjacent rolling foothills directly threatening the center of the Indian's encampment! Chief Red Shirt led the 30 or so remaining fighters freshly gathered up from the battle with the first group of dismounted cavalry back into camp. He had assumed leadership after seeing their original war chief, White Elk, killed by one of the troopers that had formed Reno's original skirmish line. From horseback, Chief Red Shirt could see the dust cloud from a column of mounted cavalry racing down a long draw in the foothills directly towards the center of their camp! However, that column was now being challenged by a contingent of Indian fighters led by Chief Gall and Lame Deer. From his position, Chief Red Shirt could see that the large group of Indians now attacking the second column of approaching cavalry, had blunted the trooper's advance into the village center. And in doing so, had turned that danger away from the village and had them now retreating in disorder back onto the hillside and high ground from whence they had come.

With that, Crazy Horse paused. Seeing those soldier's retreating and realizing that the camp was safe, Crazy Horse raised his hand for Chief Red Shirt's group of oncoming fighters to join him. Then whirling his horse, he headed west, closely followed now by about 100 quickly gathered fighters. In that group rode Chief Crow King, Two Moons, Sitting Bull's nephew Joseph White Bull, Lame White Man, Chief Red Shirt, Joseph White Buffalo and Chief Rain-in-the-Face. That group was also followed by many more late arriving fighters. Racing his group west for a short distance, then turning north and keeping the sounds of battle to his immediate east, Crazy Horse raced up a nearby ravine in the rolling hills adjacent their camp. Once at the north end of the noise of battle, Crazy Horse turned his group of fighters back east until he was directly behind and positioned just north of the terrible noise of the ongoing battle. Once in that position and still behind the rolling hills and out of sight from the soldiers on the nearby other side of the hill, he turned his group of Indian fighters south. In a full charge, they stormed over the last hilltop and down into the scene of the battle below. (Author's Note: That hill was later named "Last Stand Hill" where Custer and a small contingent of his men fought to their last.)

Josiah White Buffalo riding alongside Crazy Horse was amazed at what laid below him when they broke over the hill's rim. Dust was rising high into the air, horrible noises of dying horses, men screaming, much shooting

262

and yelling by the attacking Indians rent the air. Greeting his eyes were dead cavalry horses dotting the hillside on which he now rode, dead soldiers were sprawled out everywhere lying in grotesque positions of death, small groups of four and five living soldiers dotted throughout in disorganized skirmish lines that were slowly being overrun or shot down by the attacking Indians. Underfoot of his now stumbling horse were more dead and dying soldiers lying scattered about in the tall grasses and scattered clumps of sage brush! Off to the southeast, were dozens of Indian fighters kneeling on a nearby hillside pouring deadly repeating rifle fire into the remaining troopers just below Crazy Horse's charging group. It was obvious from the volume of fire coming from that group of Indians to the southeast and their repeating rifles, that its bullets were causing total disorganization and confusion from within the ranks of the now desperately fighting soldiers. On top of that, such deadly fire seemed to be having a tremendous effect on any of the trooper's officers trying to effect an organized firing position. Then looking into the 'face' of the center of battle and directly below the top of the hill, stood, laid or knelt a group of about forty soldiers firing at the Indians off to their east and south. Those soldiers never saw or heard Crazy Horse's mounted warriors bearing down upon them from the north until they were almost within their midst and starting to already stream through the soldier's now highly disorganized battle line!

Josiah White Buffalo saw a man dressed in buckskins (Custer) standing near a soldier still valiantly holding the fluttering flag by its staff. By now the thundering herd of attacking Indian horsemen were within the outside ranks of the soldiers' feeble line of defense! Finally hearing the oncoming horse mounted Indians and then seeing the impending danger they represented, the man in buckskins turned and with his pistol, hurriedly shot into that group of Indians bearing down upon his soldiers! With that shot, Wind dropped like a stone! The man in buckskins had made a lucky shot and had hit Wind dead center in the forehead, killing him instantly! When Wind unexpectedly dropped, he tossed Josiah White Buffalo head over heels. Slamming onto the ground on his belly but remaining unhurt, Josiah White Buffalo leapt to his feet and quickly fired at the man wearing buckskins who had just shot his horse. When Josiah White Buffalo shot in the high emotion of the moment, he did not notice that he had a slight problem. His rifle's front sight had been smashed off dead center and there was a slight bend in the end of its barrel which had struck a rock in his violent impact with the ground...As a result, his shot at the man in buckskins had not gone into the aimed place on his chest but had gone high into his left side. Spinning from the impact of Josiah White Buffalo's errant but not immediately lethal bullet, the man in buckskins grabbed his now bleeding side and wobbling from the impact of his wound, raised his pistol to shoot Josiah White Buffalo from just a few feet away. It was then that the man in buckskins was shot a second time by a close at hand and hard charging Joseph White Bull. (Author's Note: Joseph White Bull, Sitting Bull's nephew, is credited by most historians as the Indian who killed Custer with that last rifle shot.) The man in buckskins with the dish-water blond, closely cropped hair, dropped where he stood from that lethal strike and moved no more. Just as the Great Spirit had predicted many moons earlier in a vision, Josiah White Buffalo would wound one of the most hated enemies of the Sioux Nation, namely soldier-chief George A. Custer in battle...

With Custer killed, Josiah White Buffalo realizing he was carrying a badly damaged rifle, dropped it, drew his tomahawk and ran to a man who was standing behind his dead horse trying to clear a spent cartridge from the chamber of his rifle. One head swipe of Josiah White Buffalo's tomahawk and the man dropped like a stone. Then Chief Rain-in-the-Face thundered past Josiah White Buffalo on his horse and slammed into the soldier holding the flag in the center of the group of soldiers. During that moment, the chief was acting all crazy like as he raced his horse towards the soon to be unfortunate flag bearer. Seeing the Indian antagonist bearing down on him, the flag bearer shot Chief Rain-in-the-Face's horse out from under him. Landing running, Chief Rain-in-the-Face smashed in the head of the flag bearer with his war club, dropping him instantly. Then Rain-in-the-Face moved throughout the center of the remaining bunched up troopers swinging his war club for all his worth. He was acting so crazy, that several troopers broke and ran away from him, only to be cut down by rifle fire from other nearby Indians. Then a close at hand sergeant quickly grabbed up the flag and holding it in the crotch of his elbow, stood defiantly in the midst of the dust and noise of that horrific battle. As he did, he hurriedly tried all the while to reload his pistol. Then that man spotting Josiah

White Buffalo running at him in a full charge with his upraised tomahawk.

Instinctively, the soldier lowered the tip of the flag staff and tried to use it as a spear. Knocking the tip of the flag staff aside, Josiah White Buffalo smashed in the man's forehead with his tomahawk, killing him instantly! Another soldier laying on the ground and shooting over the carcass of his dead horse, saw Josiah White Buffalo struggling to remove his deeply stuck tomahawk from the skull in the now dead regimental flag holder's forehead. Jumping to his feet, he swung the barrel of his rifle towards Josiah White Buffalo and pulled the trigger. BOOM! But in his nervous excitement, the soldier missed from just a few feet away! Just like Josiah White Buffalo's vision had said it would happen when the soldiers shot at the sage grouse. Their bullets would have no effect.

Finally jerking his bloody tomahawk out from the dead second flag holder's skull, Josiah White Buffalo lunged at the soldier who was now using his knife trying to pry the now stuck freshly fired shell casing from the chamber of his rifle. Josiah White Buffalo dropped him with one lethal swing of his tomahawk to the man's head! Then nearby Chief Rain-in-the-Face spotted soldier-chief Tom Custer at the lower part of the trooper's battle group. Racing over the remaining live and many dead soldiers, the chief yelled something Josiah White Buffalo could not hear over the noise of the battle, as he lunged at the man. Tom, in the process of reloading his pistol, did not see the charging, almost out of his mind, chief until it was too late. That was Tom's last moment in history as Chief

Rain-in-the-Face shot and killed him from two feet away! Then the chief calmly walked away from the battle at hand and headed towards the village to get another horse...(Author's Note: In 1874, Tom Custer had humiliated Chief Rain-in-the-Face in front of his peers. The chief later boasted he would cut out Tom's heart in revenge. On June the 25th at the battle of the Little Bighorn, he had his revenge.)

It was at that very moment that the bulk of Crazy Horse's contingent of fighters overwhelmed the remaining few living soldiers on the Last Stand Hill. When they did, several of the remaining panicked soldiers dropped their weapons and tried to flee. They were immediately cut down by rifle fire or were run over by on rushing Indian's horses! It was then that Josiah White Buffalo observed two soldiers, fearful of what was to come, putting their pistols to their heads and pulling the triggers! Then it was over except for the dust to settle and the killing of the wounded! The wounded soldiers were promptly dispatched and soon, realizing the danger was over, the entire encampment of Indians from the village below swarmed all over the close at hand battlefield stripping the soldiers of their clothing, mutilating them in many grisly ways and removing the dead men's firearms and ammunition. Any uninjured horses belonging to the soldiers after the battle, were quickly rounded up and seized as prizes from the hard fought battle. In all, the battle with Custer's main contingent of soldiers was over in about one hour...And within that horrific hour of battle, over two hundred soldiers laid dead! (Author's Note: The number of Indian dead remains a mystery to this very day according to most historians. Their guesstimates run from around thirty to one hundred because it was many Indian's way not to keep an accurate count of their dead. Plus, there was some concern among certain Indians who were there and took part in that historic battle, that if they divulged the numbers of Indians killed and they were small in number, vengeful whites may still try to extract additional revenge for what had happened.)

Remembering Sitting Bulls cautionary words about not taking anything from the main battlefield, Joseph White Buffalo personally refrained from any such actions. With tears of emotion in his eyes, he removed his saddle and bridle from his great little buffalo horse after the battle was over. Then he sadly walked downhill back to camp and saddled his spare horse. For there was still a battle to be fought in the foothills to the east where the soldier-chiefs Reno and Benteen remained trapped. And now, they were dug in on the high ground and had barricaded themselves with their just shot horse's carcasses, boxes of ammunition, wooden crates of hardtack, and the bodies from their dead comrades in order to give the survivors cover by presenting little or no targets to the still firing Indians now surrounding them from all sides.

Finding and joining Chief Red Shirt's contingent of remaining fighters, the two of them harassed the trapped troopers on the foothill with their long range shooting for the rest of that day. Come nightfall, the Indians withdrew back to their camp. There a great celebration was held, even amongst the wailing and death chants by those women who had lost their men in battle. However early the next day, the outlying scouts brought the encampment word of another oncoming column of cavalry coming their way from the west. Sitting Bull ordered the camp to disassemble and the entire camp scattered to various destinations as they headed south. This they did primarily because there was not enough food for all the camp's inhabitants and there was limited horse feed for such a large gathering of their herds. Besides, the four hundred or so oncoming cavalry would have been quickly swept aside by the one thousand-plus warriors in camp had they foolishly attacked such a large force of Indians. When they did disband, many chiefs realizing their nomadic ways of life had now more than likely ended with their previous one-sided battle, quietly slipped back onto the reservations to avoid any further destructive clashes with the anticipated and soon to be arrival of the now very aroused hordes of cavalry.

However come the month of July, a large contingent of Sioux and Northern Cheyenne once again got together for one last Sun Dance. Sitting Bull, Chief Spotted Eagle and Old Chief Smoke's bands were also gathered into this group who had so far escaped the hands of the far reaching cavalry patrols now feverishly combing the prairie. At the end of the Sun Dance ceremonies, many of those remaining Indians, realizing their old ways were now forever gone because the soldiers would be coming for them in increasing numbers and because their major food source of buffalo were fast disappearing, began quietly slipping back in great numbers onto the reservations as well. This they did in the hopes the government promised food supplies there on the reservations would be more plentiful than what they now had. That left about six hundred remaining hostile Indians roaming the Plains as they had done for so many eons. That small group was soon confronted with the word from their scouts that soldier chiefs Crook and Terry were now hot on their trail.

With that in mind, it was then that Sitting Bull ordered his people to disband from the larger group of remaining at-large Indians. This they did because it was so difficult to keep such a large group of people fed and provide enough grazing for their extensive horse herds. Plus a group that size made for a larger target for the hotly pursuing and searching cavalry units. Then Sitting Bull headed further west in Montana and then later to northwestern South Dakota to an area he favored because it was so remote and still had buffalo. That last redoubt was in the general area of Crow Butte. (Author's Note: Located in far northwestern South Dakota.) 'Ten Sleeps' later, Sitting Bull and his band had arrived in the Crow Butte area after managing a buffalo hunt in Montana. But not before picking up about another one hundred still at large family groups of Indians along the way who were also fleeing the Indian hunting parties of the U.S. cavalry. Sitting Bull's encampment now numbered about 350 braves, warriors and their families.

Throughout the rest of that summer of 1876, Sitting Bull and his band members continued hunting buffalo. And in doing so, Sitting Bull's braves and warriors did everything to avoid the cavalry's numerous patrols. But as Sitting Bull had advised, the Crow Butte area was very isolated and off the many beaten paths the cavalry traveled, so for the moment, they were safe. However, the wished for herds of buffalo were no longer in the area and those that were, were in very reduced numbers. The white buffalo hunters had previously discovered the herds in that area and their heavy buffalo guns had taken their toll. Then in the fall of 1876, Sitting Bull's remote location was discovered. However instead of attacking, soldier-chief "Nelson A. Miles" requested a meeting with the great chief. In that meeting, the soldier-chief tried to get Sitting Bull to surrender and move to a reservation. Sitting Bull did not trust the word of the soldier-chief and refused. Then the long running fight continued with soldier-chief Miles pushing hard for Sitting Bull and his entire band's capture.

Soon each day with ever dwindling ammunition supplies, Josiah White Buffalo and Chief Red Shirt hunted for deer and the remaining few buffalo to help keep all the hungry mouths back at camp fed. Every morning, warrior societies organized hunting parties which were sent forth to all points of the compass on meat gathering details. As it turned out come the winter of 1876-77, terrible blizzards blanketed the area. When those weather forces occurred, it made hunting almost impossible and finding horse feed even more difficult under the ever deepening blankets of snow and bone chilling cold. Plus during the winter months, pursuing soldiers purposely occupied the few remaining main buffalo winter hunting grounds. And where the Indians and soldiers crossed paths, the Bluecoat's howitzers kept the Indians at bay in any clashes in which they fought. Many nights, The People went to bed hungry and cold.

Come the welcome spring time when the prairie grasses became abundant, the horse herds waxed fat once again. However, the buffalo were now almost non-existent and the heavily hunted deer and elk were further than a day's ride distant. Further than a day's ride distant because all the close in animals had already been harvested in order to feed everyone back at camp. Come that spring, another problem now arose. Sitting Bull's camp was dwindling in numbers as other starving and tired of fighting members took down their tipis and headed for the dreaded reservations. Now Sitting Bull's camp had dwindled down to just about 150 souls. Then the final blow in living the old and revered life style was cast upon the waters. General Crook, upon receiving word of Sitting Bull's encampment location in the Crow Butte area, moved into this remote land and set up a permanent camp for a detachment of cavalry just 50 miles from the old chief's winter home site!

In April of 1877, a council was held at Beaver Creek by the few remaining, still on the run, Sans Arcs, Hunkpapa, Oglala and Miniconjous. There Sitting Bull, Spotted Eagle and Old Chief Smoke wanted to continue the fight and not dignify any kind of surrender. However, most of the remaining chiefs favored doing what was best for their people, namely stop the fighting and move onto the hated and feared reservations. With that decided, the camp split further into those bands who wanted to surrender and those who would now attempt to reach safety in nearby Canada. By May of 1877, Sitting Bull decided he had no choice but to flee into Canada. His was a choice and that option was offered to members of his band and numerous other remaining Indians in his camp who had not yet decided to move onto the reservations. Sitting Bull did so because his freedom and the honor of the family unit in practicing their culture meant so much to him. In short, Sitting Bull never compromised his principals.

Old Chief Smoke's band of Oglala/Lakota were among those who also chose to flee into Canada in exile along with Sitting Bull. Did so, in order to be under the White Queen Grandmother instead of the Great White Father who was still punishing all his children. With Old Chief Smoke went Josiah White Buffalo, Chief Red Shirt and his new bride, Gemma along with a host of others not wanting to live on the hated reservation in the United States. As Sitting Bull prepared for his trek into Canada, Crazy Horse and his followers finally surrendered at Fort Robinson. (Author's Note: Fort Robinson is located in northwestern Nebraska. It is a well-cared for historic site and well worth visiting.) Shortly thereafter, Crazy Horse was bayoneted in the back by soldiers as they tried to imprison him in a small cell and he fought back. He died shortly thereafter and was buried in the hills above Fort Robinson. (Author's Note: The location of Crazy Horse's grave is unknown. Historians have yet to authenticate any know picture of the great warrior as well.) The Great Sioux War was officially ended on May 7th, 1877, when General Miles defeated the last remaining band of Miniconjou/Lakota not housed on any reservation.

Chapter Ten

EXILE IN CANADA, TRAPPER TOM AND THE STANDING ROCK INDIAN AGENCY IN THE DAKOTA TERRITORY

That final morning while Sitting Bull's encampment prepared to begin their trek to Canada, one last meeting was held by all the chiefs. There Sitting Bull told everyone where he wanted to go in Canada. It was an area where he had hunted buffalo when he was a young man and had loved the game rich area. Plus, the land was similar to their homeland in the Dakota Territory and more importantly, safe from the fearful U.S. Cavalry. With those encouraging words and trusting in their leader, several other chief's agreed to follow while the remainder of the leaders decided they would finally give up. After that meeting, the warrior societies decided there would be a large contingent of scouts flung out far and wide ahead of the escaping caravan. This they planned on doing in order to provide an early warning system relative to discovery by approaching U.S. soldiers and in doing so, give their fighters time to prepare for battle if they were detected. It was also determined in that meeting, that Sitting Bull's, Spotted Eagle's, and Old Chief Smoke's bands would travel in their own groups within the lengthy caravan. And in doing so, each band's group of out riders would be close at hand in the eventuality of any serious problems developing during the trek. Daylight on the early May day of 1877, saw the long trek to Canada begin. A trek that would hopefully lead to a continuation of their culture, freedom, and way of life as they once knew it.

Old Chief Smoke had designated that Josiah White Buffalo and Chief Red Shirt would not only ride protection for the slow moving band of his fleeing Indians but to also hunt and kill any deer, elk or buffalo they ran across along the way. This they were to do in order to provide meat for the old and infirm members of the tribe who had no male means of support as providers. They were also assigned to such duty because they were among his best hunters and shooters, plus, they still had sufficient ammunition in ready supply for their rifles. Ammunition that had been picked up at the Battle of the Little Bighorn by other Indians and shared with the two men. That plus the addition of a new Henry rifle Josiah White Buffalo had taken off a dead Crow scout on the morning Reno's soldiers had attacked the southeastern end of their great encampment. A new rifle because his old Winchester had a smashed front sight and upon further examination, also had a bent barrel as a result of Josiah White Buffalo's horrific horse wreck in the heat of battle on Last Stand Hill (hence Josiah's wounding shot into the side of Custer instead of into his chest where the rifle had been aimed...). This the two men did and every day they managed to bring in several deer or an occasional elk. Along the way on that trip, several of the old and infirm members of Old

Chief Smoke's band died from the rigors of travel and were buried accordingly. Then no one spoke further of the dead in true Oglala/Lakota fashion. As the rigorous travel continued northward and the cold late spring rains and wet snows fell upon the stressed fleeing travelers, further burials of the old and infirm from other bands began dotting the landscape along their way of travel. And, the cold spring rains and wet snows continued taking their toll of the other semi-starved people as they struggled on their trek to their hoped for new home in Canada.

One morning before daylight, Josiah White Buffalo advised Old Chief Smoke that he and Chief Red Shirt would go out again on another hunt along the head of the anticipated travel route of the fleeing caravan. With a knowing twinkle in his eyes, Old Chief Smoke smiled at his son's eagerness to serve and then advised it sure would be nice if he had a mule deer or elk back strap for supper that evening. Josiah White Buffalo had to grin back at his adopted father. The old chief was never one to beat around the bush, he told himself, so, he had better be successful if that was something the much respected old man had requested of his now much loved adopted son.

Riding ahead of the soon to be afternoon location of the fleeing caravan of Indians, Chief Red Shirt and Josiah White Buffalo paused on their hunting trip right at daylight. From there position at first light, the two men surveyed the likely looking deer hunting areas around them from their position at the top of a long line of rolling hills. Then Josiah White Buffalo froze in his tracks! He had just detected the faint smell of burning firewood...Quickly advising Chief Red Shirt of the same, the two brothers dropped below the ridge line from their exposed positions and out of sight. Dismounting and scrambling back up to the ridge top, Josiah White Buffalo followed by Chief Red Shirt, laid down and peeped over their back trail to see if they had been observed. Nothing of interest greeted their eyes. But there it was again! A wisp of wood smoke was faintly detected in the cool stillness of the morning air by both men. Then down below them about one hundred yards away, they heard a horse whinny. Scrambling back down from the ridge top, the two men grabbed the reins of their horses and pinched off their animal's noses so they couldn't whinny back, then led them further downhill into a thick stand of brush in the pines. Tied off, the two men then scrambled back up to the lee side of the ridge top and by keeping out of sight, sneaked up closer to the approximate location on the opposite side of their ridge in which they had heard the mystery horse whinny earlier.

"Had to be other Indians," thought Josiah White Buffalo. "Otherwise if it were white men in the area, they would have stupidly built a big fire which would have alerted every Indian in the country for miles around."

Sneaking back up to the next hill top, both men laid down and peeped over the ridge top once again in the direction they had last heard the mystery horse whinny. Careful they had to be because the horse that they had heard whinny, had either heard their own horses hooves clicking along on the rocks on the rim of the hillside or had smelled the men or their horses. If that had been the case and there were Indian owners located somewhere nearby, they would now be alerted! Looking hard for the

277

next few moments, no action or movement of any kind was seen or heard from far below in the line of trees at the base of the hill they now occupied. Looking along the line of hills, Josiah White Buffalo observed a densely brushed ravine leading into the area from which they had heard the horse previously whinny. Ducking back down behind the rim of the ridge line, both he and Chief Red Shirt trotted along the backside of the set of hills. Once directly opposite the deep brushy ravine, both men quietly slipped over the ridge top and into the dense cover the ravine offered. Then quietly sneaking down the brushy draw, the two men moved carefully ever downward. Then there was the wood smoke smell again! Only stronger now! The smell of wood smoke was that from a smoldering pine pitch wood fire. Moving even slower now because if there were horses nearby, they might sound the alarm or move around nervously and whinny again once they had detected the two sneaking men. And if there were Indians nearby, upon hearing such unusual movement or noises from their nervous horses, they would quickly be on high alert and all chances of surprise would be lost. Slowing their stalking movements for the extra quiet it offered, both men now moved without making a rustle based on their culturally learned ways. As they did, the smell of 'old smoke' became stronger and more pungent from the burning pitchy pine wood that had been used in building the campfire earlier.

Slowly emerging from the now scant cover the brush line offered, Josiah White Buffalo and Chief Red Shirt spotted a remuda of 13 horses tied onto a long rope tie. Every horse in that remuda was now quietly looking at the two slowly emerging and stalking men with rifles in hand. That time they did not whinny seeing the visitors were Indians. Belonging to Indians and seeing Indians slowly approaching was not that unusual, hence their quiet attention. Off to one side of the horses, were packs of what appeared to be white man's supplies. At first glance, there were sacks of flour, tins of crackers, two crates of hard boiled eggs that had been pickled in glass jars, three wooden cases marked, 'US-Cartridges-.45-70', bed rolls, McClellan saddles, axes, coils of soft cotton lead rope, and numerous other items. Swinging their eyes back to the business at hand, both men spotted six Indians covered with blankets sleeping under a dense thicket of pine trees. Then both men froze. Crow! The sleeping men from their dress, appeared to be the long time hated enemy of the Sioux! The same people who had helped Soldier-Chief Crook at the Battle of the Rosebud with Chief Plenty-Coups as their leader! The same tribe of Indians who had foolishly charged Josiah White Buffalo and Chief Red Shirt in that battle and had been turned away by the fierce fire from their two rapidly firing Winchesters…

Both men by instinct and learned culture, quickly rested their lever action rifles against their buckskin shirts and silently cocked their guns in such a manner as to deaden any foreign sounding metallic 'clicking' noises which would have been out of place in the wilderness. Then looking over at each other, the two brothers began silently sneaking up on the sleeping men. As they did, they noticed several half empty bottles of white man's whiskey laying alongside two of the sleepers! That was why the sleeping men had not heard their horse's whinny, thought Josiah White Buffalo. Walking up to the end of the sleeping men's feet with their rifles at the ready, Chief Red Shirt kicked one sleeping man's foot. That man, still feeling the deadening effect of too much alcohol, only grunted and moved his foot away from being jabbed. It was then that Josiah White Buffalo's Henry rifle and Chief Red Shirt's Winchester roared forth...

For the next hour, Josiah White Buffalo and Chief Red Shirt packed five of the dead men's horses with canned oysters, three cases of rifle ammunition, tins of crackers, tins of apricot jam, boxes of raisins, cloth bags of hard candy, several crates containing pickled hard boiled eggs in glass canning jars, surplus bedrolls and the like. It was apparent to the two men doing the loading of the white man's goods, that the Crows had ambushed a military supply wagon and had taken all they could pack after they had killed off its teamsters. It was also obvious that the Crow were far east of their usual hunting grounds and into the territory of the Sioux. Either way, the six now scalped Crow's ghosts were wandering the in-between-world looking for their missing parts...Two unopened cases of 'Grizzly Bear Whiskey' bottled in Deadwood, South Dakota, were left as they were discovered. Both Chief Red Shirt and Josiah White Buffalo knew of the liquids harmful effects and wanted no part of what it did to their people. (Author's Note: Those two cases of whiskey still in their wooden, now somewhat worse for wear crates, were discovered by long time sheep herder Jose Garza in 1963. Opening up one of the bottles, he pronounced it to be fit as a fiddle to his assistant sheep

280

herder and then they wildly indulged themselves. Garza's boss later discovered the two herders sleeping off a two day drunk under the same sets of trees in which the Crows had slumbered their last many years earlier. Word has it from old ranchers in the area, was that Garza and his partner in crime were fired on the spot! Fired because in their drunken stupor, they had neglected their sheep and the coyotes had ruthlessly gotten into them and what they hadn't killed, they had scattered to the four winds.)

Later that morning, Old Chief Smoke's outlying scouts spotted two Indian men coming their way leading a string of 13 horses. Riding out to investigate, the outriders soon realized the two men were from their own band. Then even more excitement followed over the riches packed on five of the 13 horses. Forty minutes later, the moving caravan of escaping Indians stopped for a break alongside the two triumphant warriors. Then Josiah White Buffalo and Chief Red Shirt had to tell all assembled the story on what had happened. Following that, Chief Red Shirt in his capacity as a sub-chief, distributed all the goods and valuable ammunition to all assembled. However, since Josiah White Buffalo had not brought any venison home for the old chief's supper that day, he saw to it that Old Chief Smoke and his wife Prairie Flower feasted royally on white man's food. That evening, they feasted on canned oysters, apricot jam, crackers and then the old chief finished the repast off with a cigar from a box of rich smelling cigars that had been discovered in the supplies. It turned out to be a meal fit for a king. However, all the next day, Old Chief Smoke and Josiah White Buffalo had to use the bushes many times to rid

281

themselves of the rich white man's food...Rich foods that their semi-starved systems were not accustomed to when it came to normal digestion.

Twenty sleeps later and miles above the U.S.–Canada Border, Sitting Bull, Spotted Eagle, and Old Chief Smoke stopped their long caravan of fleeing Indians near Pinto Horse Butte in current day Saskatchewan. By then, Sitting Bull's refugees had swelled to over 1,000 people and 135 tipis. Those additional gathered up refugees, who like Sitting Bull's encampment, were fleeing northward to avoid the cavalry patrols from the United States. But in getting there, there was a small problem. The entire caravan of Native Americans escaping from the United States, were now being quietly dogged by unknown outlying riders. Riders who were not showing any outward signs of aggression but were just quietly pacing themselves along the same route of travel as were the Indians. Finally tired and exhausted, Sitting Bull ordered that their camp be set up in an area possessing good water supplies, much available firewood and plenty of horse feed in the Wood Mountain area. Then the camp's leadership noticed that six white riders were slowly approaching their camp in a way that was not menacing. As Josiah White Buffalo helped several families of the old and infirm set up their tipis, he noticed the white men who had been dogging the caravan for days, were now setting up their own campsite at the edge of Sitting Bull's encampment and in plain view...

Later that afternoon, Josiah White Buffalo who spoke the best English in camp, was invited to a council meeting between Sitting Bull, Spotted Eagle, Old Chief Smoke and a lone mystery white man. A lone white man who had sent word to their camp by one of his scouts that he wanted to speak to all of their leaders. Josiah White Buffalo was invited in order that Sitting Bull could be assured that the white man would be speaking in a "straight tongue." Later in the afternoon, Sitting Bull's chiefs and a "white man chief" sent by the Queen Mother of Canada, met in council. That 'white man chief' was a 'Redcoat' or a member of the Royal Canadian Mounted Police. A man who was named Major James M. Walsh. Josiah White Buffalo and the three chief's in his camp were impressed with the bravery of the lone white man. Bravery because Sitting Bull did not trust the whites and had not let one into his camp for many years and most white men knew that. Yet this man had ridden into their camp and was not afraid. And, the Sioux highly respected bravery. After the pipe of peace had been smoked, Walsh got right down to the business at hand. He informed the chief's that Canada could be a home to all peoples provided they obeyed the Queen Mother's rules. Continuing, Walsh advised that Canada's laws protected everyone; that Canada would punish anyone who violated those laws; that Sitting Bull's band now had sanctuary in Canada; there would be no stealing of horses from other whites or Canada's First People (Indians) because if they did and were caught doing so, they would lose their granted asylum and finally, there would be no raiding across the border into the United States. Finishing, Walsh asked if Sitting Bull and the other chiefs in his band agreed to those terms. Sitting Bull, after discussing those terms in Lakota with the other chiefs, agreed to Walsh's request. As he did, Josiah White Buffalo was impressed with Walsh. He spoke with a straight tongue and in a strange sort of way. A way that Josiah White Buffalo interpreted that the man from Canada would be a good friend to the displaced Sioux. Those feelings he spoke of two Sitting Bull when the chief looked at Josiah White Buffalo as if asking for his input on what had just transpired after the white man from Canada had left the council.

Then Sitting Bull asked Walsh for ammunition for their guns. He continued that they had used most of it up while hunting for food or for protection from "bad white men." And now that they were protected by the Queen Mother, they would use it to hunt buffalo and any other game. This Walsh agreed to, providing they would give their word and not use that ammunition on raids back across the border into the United States. Walsh also advised that there were still many buffalo between nearby Cypress Hills and Wood Mountain. And that the First People, namely the Cree Indians from Canada living in that area, would be hunting the buffalo as well. And if the Sioux discovered the Cree hunting the buffalo, they were not to be interfered with. With that and the council finished, Walsh rose and advised that his Royal Canadian Mounted Police would be camped nearby at all times to ensure that Sitting Bull's people would not be disturbed. Then the chiefs who had been listening to the words being spoken at the council, rose and left for their warrior societies and individual band members so they could be informed of what had been said as well.

That evening as Old Chief Smoke and Josiah White

Buffalo sat around the fire in their tipi, Prairie Flower cooked their supper. She did not cook at the outside cooking fire that evening because of the clouds of mosquitoes that formed around everyone when they did...After supper, Josiah White Buffalo turned to his father saying, "Father, will you tell me about Sitting Bull. He is so revered that even I have a hard time approaching and talking with him out of respect. But I detect that in addition to being a much revered holy man, he is also a great man with a lot of reasons for such greatness. Will you share with me what you know about our holy man so that I might learn more about The Way within the Lakota Nation and its holy men?"

For the longest time, Old Chief Smoke said nothing. He just leaned against his backrest with his eyes closed and smoked another one of the cigars that Josiah White Buffalo had taken from the Crow, several 'sleeps' earlier. Then he slowly opened his eyes, rolled his cigar over to the side of his mouth and with a look of pure joy over being able to smoke real tobacco, began. "Son, you are right. Sitting Bull is a very great man. I will now begin with what I know to be true and also with some of the stories told around the campfires of the man of which you ask. Sitting Bull was born many moons ago and was given the name of "Tatanka-Yotonka" or Sitting Bull by his father, Jumping Bull. (Author's Note: Some historians refer to Sitting Bull's father as one being named "Returns-Again.") That is a Lakota name that describes a buffalo sitting on its haunches. He was given that name after he had fought a number of warriors from a Crow clan as a young man and showed much bravery.

That bravery in battle surprised everyone because at first, Sitting Bull did not show any warrior talents. He was always quiet and did most everything in a slow manner. In fact for a while, he was given the name "Slow" because of his lack of talent and foresight. But, his father always did suspect that someday he would be a great man. In fact, Sitting Bull killed his first buffalo as a boy when he was just ten years old." Then the old chief, discovering that his cigar had gone out with all his talking, took a small stick from the fire with a live ember on the end and re-lit his cigar. Sitting back once against his backrest, he closed his eyes and drew deeply on his cigar enjoying the richness of being able to smoke real tobacco and not just the dried and crushed bark from red willow bushes mixed with smaller amounts of real but hard to acquire tobacco. After a few moments of pleasuring his cigar, Old Chief Smoke began once again.

"As Sitting Bull got older, he began coming into his own as a warrior and a leader of his people. He was a lot like you my son in that he had great respect for all life around him and had dedicated much of what he did for the benefit of others. Soon those qualities were recognized and Sitting Bull was chosen as a leader in the "Strong Heart Warrior Society." After that, he really found his way as a leader and great warrior. In 1863, he first took up arms against the government of the Great White Father. Sitting Bull did that because the Great White Father did nothing to stop the whites from swarming all over our sacred lands like grasshoppers in the fall. In 1864, Sitting Bull as a warrior chief, took up arms once again and fought the Bluecoats at the battle of

Killdeer Mountain. There he counted coups many times and even brought out from battle a wounded friend under a hail of Bluecoat bullets. In 1865, after a flood had almost washed away Fort Rice, he led an attack on that outpost that killed many soldiers and ran off with most of their horses. (Author's Note: Fort Rice was located near present day Bismarck, North Dakota. Legend has it that during the above flood, Libby Custer, wife of George A. Custer of Little Bighorn fame, was tied to a field cannon to avoid being washed away.) In 1868, his skills as a leader and fierce warrior, led him to become Chief of the Lakota Nation. (Author's Note: Some historians refute this claim. They feel that there were many bands of Lakota and within those many bands, there were many chiefs.) And in 1874, when the white miners and settlers began moving into the Black Hills, Sitting Bull declared war against all whites. This was because he would not compromise his freedoms and culture over the many wrongs the white people were inflicting upon The People and their sacred ancestral lands. Sitting Bull is a very stubborn man. He will never bow down to the white man, change his traditional religion or his ways. It was about then in his life that he began having many visions about his people, events in the future, the mystery of things in life about to happen, and their traditional culture.

Soon he drifted away from being a warrior to that of being a holy man. He did so, because the Great Spirit came to him in so many visions that he found he could not be a warrior and a holy man as one in the same. And in one of those visions, the Great Spirit said He would talk to The People through Sitting Bull. Sitting Bull still did fight in some battles like in Chief Red Cloud's war to close the Bozeman Trail but like in the battle at the Little Greasy Grass, he served his people as its holy man and was not a warrior in that battle. And ever since the great victory at the Little Greasy Grass, he has led his people away from the white man and his way of life. He did so, so The People could continue living in our own true culture. And now we are living in Canada where the whites in the United States, who are as numerous as grass hoppers, cannot bother us. Over his lifetime, Sitting Bull being such a great man, has given of himself in other ways as well. He is a very poor man because he has given so much to others who are less fortunate. What he does in this area is a lot of what Crazy Horse did. He has also taken many wives who are very close to him because that is the way of the Lakota. Especially when other men are killed in battle or by accident, which leaves many lonely women and hungry children. Four Robes was his first wife and since then has taken in three others who had lost their men. His second wife is named Snow-On- Her and she is also very faithful to him. Then he has taken two others most recently. One is named Seen-by-her-Nation and the other is known as Scarlet Women. But all are very dedicated and kindly to him as is he to them. So, you are right. Sitting Bull is a great man and much revered by his people for his visions, the giving of himself, and for always seeking of our freedoms. And you my son, have been greatly touched by this great man. Ever since he met you at the Sun Dance and fastened that broken leather thong onto your symbol of power in the sage grouse wing, you have been blessed. As Sitting Bull and Fast Antelope have said, you are blessed with your symbol of power and will go on to become an even greater warrior in the Lakota Nation than you are now. Also if you remember during the Sun Dance, Sitting Bull spoke of things to come that even I do not understand. But one of those things was that the two of you will walk many trails together in the years to come. In those words, I suspect that you will become like a son to him as you have become to me. And in doing so, will continue to walk many trails with him as that son and protector. Just remember to follow your heart and visions in the paths you chose to follow in this matter. But I also fear that there remains many dangerous trails to be crossed in Sitting Bull's world and I sense you will be involved in crossing those same trails as well because of your closeness to him. I also sense that there is no way the white man can ever let such a powerful chief like Sitting Bull keep his freedom." Then once again the old chief's cigar had gone out. So with that, he once again took an ember from the fire, re-lit his cigar, leaned back against his backrest and was lost in his thoughts, the rich taste of real tobacco for a change and the welcome haze of sweet smelling cigar smoke in his tipi for the rest of the evening...

The next morning after his long talk with Old Chief Smoke, Josiah White Buffalo met with Chief Red Shirt and made ready for another hunting trip. As it turned out, Josiah White Buffalo had sneaked out from his parent's tipi so they could sleep. However as he exited the tipi's flap, he heard a great horned owl posted high up in a nearby spruce tree hoot three times. Looking skyward,

Josiah White Buffalo could just make out the faint outline of the great aerial predator sitting on an exposed limb. Josiah White Buffalo had to grin. The Lakota people believed that if one heard the hooting of such an owl, a death was eminent. As a young man in Missouri, he had shot them out from his farm's nearest trees because they used to swoop down and kill his mother's valuable chickens just before the chickens went to their protective roosts at dusk. No one died after hearing them hoot in Missouri except for the owls themselves. That was if young Josiah ever got a bead on their dang ole chicken-killin' hides...

Later that morning, Josiah White Buffalo and Chief Red Shirt set out for a nearby marshy area that was surrounded by several shallow lakes. The two men had heard of an animal called a 'moose' that neither had ever seen in their young lives, much less killed. That would be their quarry for the day. From that afternoon until dark, the two men hunted the watered areas in vain looking for this fabled animal of tall tales that was darker than an elk and many times larger than a deer. That evening not having seen any of their chosen quarry, the men camped in the spruce timber above a nearby marshy lake. For dinner they supped on buffalo jerky and then retired early to their sleeping blankets around their campfire since they had already experienced a long day afield.

The following morning, they arose early and began their hunt once again for the elusive animal called a moose. Around the lake shore and in the adjacent marshes, the air was filled with the early morning's rising mists. Various bird calls rent the cool morning air and on a nearby lake, a northern loon's unique and haunting call welcomed the two hunters to 'his' day. As they silently rode through the sparse timber line along the water's edge, Chief Red Shirt spotted a large, dark in color, deer-like animal, standing up to its belly in the water feeding in a nearby marsh. The animal was surrounded by marsh's plants and was quietly feeding by ducking its head under water and then coming up with mouthfuls of dripping vegetation. Dismounting, Chief Red Shirt led the way with Josiah White Buffalo following close behind, as the two men began stalking the large animal. In fact as the men got closer, the animal in the marsh seemed to be growing bigger and BIGGER...Standing along one side of a spruce tree and using it to steady his rifle, Chief Red Shirt drew a tight bead on the large animal. BOOM went Chief Red Shirt's .38-40 Winchester rifle and SMACK went the sound of a bullet hitting the great animal in the side just behind the shoulder. Without a moment's hesitation, the huge animal stopped eating and started storming across the marsh, running wildly in panic in the direction in which it had been headed, directly toward the two partially hidden men. BOOM-BOOM went both of their rifles in tandem and with that, the moose stumbled, turned and then staggered back into the marsh for the supposed safety it offered away from the flying bullets. However by then it was too late. The effects of being hit with three heavy rifle bullets was too much for the animal's system, as it staggered and then finally dropped into the marsh with a gigantic SPLOOOSH! However, to the two novice hunters therein laid a problem. They had their moose alright but it was located thirty yards away from the nearest shoreline and in fairly deep water!

Once the two figured the animal was dead, they walked shoreward and standing at the edge of the marsh in a haze of mosquitoes, realized they had made a BIG mistake. They had just shot a huge animal and now it laid out in the marsh in over three feet of water. Josiah White Buffalo looked over at Chief Red Shirt with a big grin on his face saying, "You shot it my brother. Now you go out and get it." It was then the futility of the moment struck the two brothers. How were the two of them going to get such a huge animal out from the marsh? Then, how were they to get it back to their village since all they had brought along were their two riding horses...When they used to hunt deer back in the United States, they just took their riding horses and carried any such animals taken on the back of their mounts. Now they had an animal down in the marsh that was the size of their horses!

Shaking his head in resignation, Chief Red Shirt stripped down to nothing and began wading out into the belly deep water toward the dead animal. As he did, Josiah White Buffalo laughed at Chief Red Shirts discomfort walking naked in the cold water and the deep clinging mud from the marsh bottom. Reaching the dead moose, Chief Red Shirt grabbed a rear leg and tried pulling the animal shoreward. The animal did not move one inch! Trying again, Chief Red Shirt was equally as successful as he had been the first time...Turning towards his laughing brother, Chief Red Shirt beckoned for some help.

Moments later, the marsh contained one dead moose and two naked Indian men, who figuratively resembled the northern loons at the end of the lake for what they were attempting to do...With both men now pulling and tugging at the dead and now grounded on the marsh bottom moose's carcass, it moved nary a wit. As the two rather stout men struggled trying to get the moose carcass ashore, they finally realized their efforts were to no avail. That was when both men realized that shooting an animal as large as a moose in a marsh was really not a very wise idea...Wading ashore in a cloud of mosquitoes, Josiah White Buffalo retrieved his knife and then waded back out in the icy cold water to the moose's carcass. There with great difficulty, the two men gutted out the huge animal so it would be lighter and easier to drag ashore. Once the animal had been gutted, both men grabbed a hind leg and tried pulling the still well anchored to the marsh's bottom, moose. Once again, they were as lucky in that effort as was the dead moose's chances of coming back to life. Standing there belly deep in the getting colder by the minute water and deep mud, Chief Red Shirt said, "We best quarter this animal so we can get it out from this marsh before we both freeze to death or are eaten alive by all these clouds of mosquitoes."

Then all at once Josiah White Buffalo looked down in alarm at his naked self in the riled up muddy water. He was looking at thousands of 'worm-like wiggly things' swimming towards him in the water! Then in abject disbelief, he noticed hundreds of other like critters that had already attached themselves onto his bare skin! Gross ugly wiggly things that he had never seen or experienced before in his life. Lifting one leg out of the water and the muddy ooze, he was shocked to see that he was absolutely covered with hundreds of the worm-like creatures (leeches)! And that included covering all his private parts! There were so many of the worm-like things attached to his body that he looked like he had the fur of a bear all attached to all parts of his body that was below the water line of the marsh in which he stood!

"Brother, we have to get out of this water! Look at your legs and waist. They are covered with hundreds of dark brown worm like things!" he screeched in alarm.

Looking down at his naked self covered with hundreds of leeches for the first time, Chief Red Shirt literally exploded out of the water and began lunging for the shore in the waist deep water splashing water every which way. He hadn't taken two steps, when he observed a lone white man dressed in buckskins sitting by their piles of clothing and their rifles! And in his arms he cradled a rifle of his own! Stopping in mid panicked flight from the specter of hundreds of leeches now feasting on his body, Chief Red Shirt quietly uttered, "Josiah…"

Josiah White Buffalo, after having slipped in the muddy ooze of the marsh bottom and fallen butt first into the cold water, was in the process of lunging back up out from the waters. It was then he heard Chief Red Shirt's worried sounding warning in his brother's softly uttered words of concern. It was then that he also looked shoreward in the direction of Chief Red Shirt's intense gaze. There sitting on the bank, he also observed a rather stout looking unknown individual, sitting right alongside their two piles of clothing and cradling a rifle!

"I take it you two be some of my new Indian neighbors to the south from the United States. Do any of you speak English?" asked a smiling Tom Moore.

"We both do," said Josiah White Buffalo, wishing all the while he was just a little closer to his own rifle than was a perfect stranger in a strange land. Especially, when he found himself wearing nothing but his God given grin and a 'blanket' of wiggling worm like things attached all over his naked and still exposed parts...

"Well, well, I be hog tied and roasted on a spit. My name is Tom Moore. But folks around here call me "Trapper Tom." I own a pretty good sized spread down the ways below this here marsh, where I raise horses and cattle in the spring and summer and trap fur bearers for a living during the fall and winter months. Needing some fresh meat and hankering for a goodly chunk of moose steak, I was out hunting myself this morning as well. But, I damn sure did not plan on running into the two of you swimming with all those blood sucking leeches in the marsh like you was either brave as all get out or just damn foolish fellas. You lads may want to exit that marsh for some high ground unless you want to have all your blood sucked dry by a passel of them damn leeches. Plus, I'd say you boys be in a bit of another quandary. That there moose needs to be here on shore and you two, unless you plan on letting them leeches drain you dry, belong up here on shore as well. I'd recommend that the two of you wade ashore and get yourselves proper. And, I'd start pulling them blood sucking leeches off yourn hide unless you want to look funny from all them red bite marks on your carcasses when in bed with one of your squaws."

With that, Trapper Tom stood up and gestured for Chief Red Shirt and Josiah White Buffalo to come ashore.

When he did, that was when the fun began. Both men hustled themselves out of the water and began pulling off with difficulty the numerous blood sucking leeches attached to their bodies. Then it got really funny, as each afflicted man had to pick the other's leeches off from behind each other's hind ends where neither man could see or reach...Plus, some of those leeches stuck in and around the men's private parts, had anchored themselves rather well and had to be burned off with embers from a small fire that Tom had quickly built for just such an occasion and "celebration of Mother Nature in all its full bloom..."

As Josiah White Buffalo and Chief Red Shirt picked off and gagged over their leech removal details, Trapper Tom kept adding his two cents worth of frontier humor to such a rather unusual event taking place in front of God, all the forest critters and anybody else who would want to take a gander...

"Like I said earlier, I live down below this here marsh about a kilometer away and run a few head of cattle and horses when I can keep away the dang Grizzly bears, wolves and bull moose. Especially when the bull moose is in rut and looking over my mares confined inside a corral. I was moose hunting earlier this morning as well in order to help fill up my larder and cache house for when the snows get to deep to piddle around in. In fact, the very moose I was hunting, you two chaps ran across her afore I could get here. But, that is alright. I know where there are others and will visit those places later on. Say, how do you boys figure you will get this here moose out from the water and home afore he spoils or the black bears find and eat him right out from under your very noses? 'Cause them dang black bears can smell food a mile away and do so in a stiff wind blowing from the opposite direction. And, we have a passel of them damn meat eatin' black and grizzly bears scattered around here come every turn in the trail."

Josiah White Buffalo, picking some of the last blood filled leeches off Chief Red Shirt's bare hind end said, "I guess we will cut the darn thing up and cart the pieces home on our riding horses. We just did not figure on how big a moose really was never having seen one before. But once we get him back to our village, there are a lot of older folks who will really appreciate having so much meat to count on."

"Hells fire, Boys. I brought my two pack animals along with me this morning to pack out any moose I got. We can use them to pack your meat back to your village just as well. That would be the neighborly thing to do and I don't mind. Say, is that the same village where the famous cavalry killing Sitting Bull lives that I have heard so much about from our local Constables? If so, I sure would like to meet such a fella and famous warrior. But, first things first. If one of you still naked boys will grab the rope off my horse and then tie it to the rear legs of that there moose, I can have my horses drag him ashore. But if you do, make sure that you are high steppin'. Otherwise them damn leeches who didn't grab you the first go-around, will grab ahold of your softer parts on their next turn-in-the-barrel and then you will be back to pickin' them off like a couple of chickens in the pen pecking at June bugs," he said with an infectious, enjoying the hell out of himself and the situation he found himself in, grin.

He sure did have a point on how to get the moose out from the lake and he sure seemed like a new friend," thought Josiah White Buffalo, as he uncoiled Trapper Tom's rope from his saddle horn. With that, he hustled back out into the marsh and tied off the moose's rear legs. Then remembering Trapper Tom's words of warning about the hordes of swimming leeches, Josiah White Buffalo made certain that if any leeches attached to his body they better have wings. Better have wings, because he was now flying through the water as he headed shoreward... Moments later, Trapper Tom's two stout pack horses had dragged the moose from the marsh's waters and up onto the shoreline. After Josiah White Buffalo and Chief Red Shirt had finally finished picking all the leeches off their bodies they could find and had dressed, the butchering work began. Soon the moose had been skinned out and its quarters tied on the pack saddles of Trapper Tom's two hell for stout pack horses. With that chore accomplished, the three men began a slow journey back to the village. As they rode, Trapper Tom, lonesome for any kind of human company since he lived alone, kept up a verbal chattering like an aroused Douglas squirrel eye-balling another one of his kind high up in the first squirrel's winter cache tree. Josiah White Buffalo just had to grin. His second personal meeting of a white person from Canada had gone rather well as had his first. The man had been more than friendly, even though he did not know either Chief Red Shirt or Josiah White Buffalo. But, that seemed to make no matter even though they were from a nearby, basically foreign Indian tribe. Then he had volunteered his pack animals in order to help them out from a self-inflicted jam. Josiah White Buffalo thought to himself, "If this white man ever needed any help, he would see to it that he got it." Little did he realize just how soon that clarion call for help would be so desperately sounded and needed...

Once in sight of the village, the children upon seeing a strange, armed white man with Josiah White Buffalo and Chief Red Shirt, took off running as they feared the worst. Running and yelling as they ran for home, brought forth a half dozen armed warriors flooding from their tipis after hearing all the children's excited cries. Then seeing that Josiah White Buffalo and Chief Red Shirt were still armed, the responding villagers relaxed. But as the three men more closely approached their camp, something appeared out-of-place to Josiah White Buffalo and Chief Red Shirt! The size of their village had at least doubled since they had left on their moose hunt! And now, there were several thousand more people moving throughout the grand encampment which had now extended in length almost another mile along the small river on which they had originally started! Then Josiah White Buffalo spotted his father coming towards him and spurred his horse on to meet him.

"Father, where did all these new people come from?" asked an amazed Josiah White Buffalo, as his eyes continued scanning the huge encampment in disbelief. A village that had now at least doubled in overall size and their newest arrivals had a horse herd that was immense in size and scattered throughout the encampment in which they currently inhabited!

"Josiah White Buffalo, I have bad news. Your friend Crazy Horse surrendered to the horse soldiers at Fort Robinson a moon ago. (Author's Note: Fort Robinson is located near current day Crawford, Nebraska.) At first, both he and his people were welcomed. Then the soldiers discovered that he was the great warrior Crazy Horse, the one who had helped in wiping out soldier-chief Custer's men at the battle of The Little Greasy Grass. Armed with that information, Crazy Horse was arrested. Then the soldiers tried to put him in a small cell and he resisted. As he resisted being placed in such a small jail cell, one of the soldiers bayoneted him in the back. I am told he lingered for a few hours in great pain and then finally died. That upset his people so much, that they planned on leaving the Fort Robinson area just as soon as they could. This they did many nights later during a great rainstorm which helped cover their escape and hide their back trail. Ever since then, they have been on the run towards our encampment. I am told that some of our people who went to the reservation from our original band who did not want to go to Canada, told them where Sitting Bull wanted to go in this country. And now, they are here. As near as I can tell, Crazy Horse's people number more than two hundred lodges. With our numbers, that means there are now about eight hundred lodges and maybe five thousand warriors, braves, women and children in camp! Most of our new people are very poor and hungry. Their tipis are in need of repair and their horses having been driven so hard, are showing lots of rib bones. I need to meet with Chief Red Shirt and see if his warrior society will quickly organize a buffalo hunt so we will have enough meat for all the new people and hides for new tipi coverings before the snows arrive."

About then, Chief Red Shirt and Trapper Tom rode up with their heavily moose laden pack animals. Josiah White Buffalo introduced his father to Trapper Tom and he could tell from the looks on his father's face that he immediately liked the affable Canadian. Soon, the two older men were jabbering away like long lost brothers. Then Old Chief Smoke saw the huge moose on the pack animals. Walking over to look at the animal, Josiah White Buffalo could tell from the look on his face that he was really pleased. The moose was rolling fat and would make many fine meals for the arriving bands older members who lacked male providers of their own. Soon Old Chief Smoke had provided direction to Josiah White Buffalo and Chief Red Shirt as to which tribal members needed fresh meat the most. Old Chief Smoke also made sure that Chief Sitting Bull received a full back strap for his tipi's many mouths, including his four wives! Then he informed Chief Red Shirt of the same information he had given Josiah White Buffalo relative to Crazy Horse's demise and the obvious fact of the now enlarged camp with its many needs. Leaving Josiah White Buffalo and Trapper Tom to distribute the moose meat, Chief Red Shirt hurried over to the chief of his warrior society in order to suggest a buffalo hunt as soon as possible.

After the moose meat had been quickly distributed, Trapper Tom excused himself so he could get back to his ranch and milk his two cows. But not before Old Chief Smoke had introduced the kindly Canadian to Chief Sitting Bull. Both men had a long chat and Sitting Bull told Tom that anytime he needed any kind of help from his warriors or wanted to visit the encampment, he would be more than welcome since he was now considered a friend of The People.

Returning to his tipi that afternoon, Josiah White Buffalo made sure a portion of the moose hind quarter was given to Prairie Flower so she could fix her husband a dinner of moose meat, his first. After supper that evening, Josiah White Buffalo looked up Chief Red Shirt and was informed that scouts had been sent out by his warrior society looking for the nearest herd of buffalo. Once found, a hunt would be planned immediately. Now that there were many thousands of hungry mouths to feed, there would be need for many more buffalo hunts in the future. With that information, Josiah White Buffalo returned to his tipi, cleaned his rifle, packed his cartridge pouch with extra ammunition and set an edge to his skinning and gutting knives. Especially since the coarseness of buffalo hair when gutting such an animal, had a rather dulling effect on even the sharpest of knives. Then into his sleeping furs he went since he already had such a long and adventurous day. But not before picking off several more now engorged leeches discovered back in crevasses on his body previously searched, that had evaded his searching eyes earlier in the day around the shore of that damn leech filled marsh...

By daylight the following morning, the entire encampment was ablaze with excited activity. A small herd of buffalo had been sighted and a big hunt was being planned. Within an hour, over 300 braves and warriors had assembled and were being assigned their places for the buffalo hunt to be. Josiah White Buffalo and Chief Red Shirt, as always, rode together as the brothers they were. Then as the horseflesh and humanity streamed out from the large encampment, the women and younger Indian males made ready their travois to haul the kill back to the encampment. For once the hunt was over, the race would be on to retrieve their meat from off the prairies before it spoiled or the always hungry land and aerial predators beat everyone to the many carcasses scattered around the kill site.

Sitting on their horses looking at a small herd of about five thousand buffalo in the distance, the men grinned. Soon they would be eating warm liver fresh from the side of a freshly killed buffalo and viewing a carcass dotted plain with the spoils of their successful hunt. Riding slowly off the rolling hills and laid over the necks of their horses looking like a herd of wild horses in order to not spook off the buffalo, the hunters slowly moved toward the small herd. Then just before the unwary buffalo discovered the horses were being ridden by Indians and were not just a herd of wild horses, the hunters sat up in their saddles and charged into the herd. Within moments, the herd was rumbling off in the direction the hunters wanted. For below the rumbling herd about a half a mile distant, waited another one hundred hunters in ambush. And when the surprised herd turned away from those ambush hunters, they would be heading into another cleverly laid trap where the additional hunters now laid in waiting.

Riding up alongside the now thundering herd, Josiah White Buffalo shot his first animal behind the shoulder.

That animal stumbled but did not fall. Josiah White Buffalo had earlier realized the rifle he now was using was shooting a low velocity bullet from a .44 rimfire cartridge. It was no way near as hard hitting as had been his .44-40. But since the Battle of the Little Greasy Grass, that rifle had been destroyed and now he was using one with a lower velocity bullet and less hitting power. But just the same, a close in shot into the plunging side of a running buffalo would be eventually a death warrant for the great beast as it bled out internally. Realizing that first buffalo would soon die from its wounds, he moved forward to the next running buffalo. His current horse was not quite as good as had been his original buffalo horse, Wind, but he was getting experienced and learning fast. Down went his next buffalo and Josiah White Buffalo moved on to the side of the next animal. With his horse's reins being held firmly in his teeth, he levered in another cartridge and shot the hard running animal. Josiah White Buffalo killed ten buffalo in such a manner until the herd was then ambushed by the other hunters laying ahead in wait. As the herd veered away from Josiah White Buffalo and the rest of the hunters into the waiting ambush, he rode off to one side and reloaded his Henry rifle. By now the air was full of dust, the sounds of shooting was coming from everywhere as the buffalo herd was now running in a huge circle surrounded by three hundred shooters and soon the grassy plain was thickly dotted with expiring and dead buffalo. It was a grand sight to see and to once again experience the thrill, danger and freedom of a buffalo hunt all wrapped up into one exhilarating experience. An experience that had been enjoyed and practiced by their kind for eons on the prairies of North America. Sensing the history of what he was seeing, quickly brought forth a smile to Josiah White Buffalo's face. Yes, the trip to Canada as one's new home had been a good one... at least for this first year.

Quietly sitting on his horse and feeling its heaving sides through his legs, Josiah White Buffalo reached up to make sure his symbol of power still remained firmly attached to his braid. It was. Then for some reason his mind swung back to the time many years before when he had been hunting sage grouse and his wagon train had been attacked. He quickly pushed those thoughts of what could have been and the names and faces of the dead from his mind. Just as he did, Chief Red Shirt who had been riding behind Josiah White Buffalo pulled up alongside saying, "Are you hungry my brother?"

"If you are thinking what I am, let's go," said Josiah White buffalo kicking his horse deeply in the flanks. Both brothers sped across the prairie like the wind across the tops of the grasses just before a thunderstorm, as they raced for the nearest dead cow buffalo. Once there, a deep thrust from Chief Red Shirt's gutting knife opened up the buffalo's side. Reaching into the cavity, Chief Red Shirt pulled with difficulty the still warm liver over to the slit made into the buffalo's side. Then another deft cut with his knife and an entire lobe of warm, still quivering and bloody liver laid in his hands. Josiah White Buffalo took out his gutting knife and cut off a large chunk of the liver being held out for him by Chief Red Shirt and began eating the warm organ meat with relish. Chief Red Shirt, taking the remaining part of the liver's lobe, bit into the

305

soft organ meat with gusto as well. So much so, that soon his entire chin and the front of his buckskin shirt was smeared red with the dripping blood from his sloppy but happy eating habits. Then Josiah White Buffalo broke out laughing.

"What is so funny, my Brother?" asked Chief Red Shirt.

"Your face looks like your hind end did after we had pulled all those bloody leeches off after our moose hunt," grinned a pleased with himself over his 'funny' and the picture he had just painted of his brother during an earlier unhappy episode in his life...

With a bloody grin, Chief Red Shirt thrust his hands once again into the buffalo's side, cut off and extracted another large chunk of liver. Josiah White Buffalo took his knife and deftly sliced off another large chunk of the bloody organ meat and then the two brothers shared a quiet and wonderful moment in time. A moment in time that had been going on for over a thousand years by others like themselves, under like circumstances, only in hallowed lands further to the south. Little did either man realize such happy times were soon coming to an end, even in Canada...

The rest of that day was spent in gutting, skinning and quartering out the morning's kill. In total, the three hundred warriors had killed over seven hundred buffalo! For the next three days, a steady stream of Indian women and children followed by their horses and larger camp dogs pulling travois, hauled the sustenance of their lives happily back to camp. By the third day, some of the dead buffalo still remaining ungutted out on the Plains, were getting a little ripe but the harvest was not wasted and eventually gleaned totally from the killing fields. Now the entire village could process the meat and their smoking racks hung heavy with Nature's bounty. As the numerous smoking fires hazed their valley's air, women toiled daily in the staking out and scrapping of the hides. Other buffalo hides were smoked and made ready for tipi covers and outer winter wear. Nothing went to waste. Intestines were utilized, shoulder bones were cleaned and made into future digging implements, sinew was removed and split out for future clothing repairs, bones were cracked and the rich marrow extracted, some skulls were saved for future ceremonial purposes, brain cases on many of the skulls were chopped open and the gray matter removed for future tanning of hides, and on went the life sustaining industry of The People. And what offal had been discarded, the camp's always hungry dogs saw to it that the ever present black-billed magpies, crows, and ravens went hungry during those days of plenty.

The second day after the buffalo hunt, found Josiah White Buffalo and Chief Red Shirt trailing a heavily loaded pack horse. The two brothers were riding towards the head of the valley above where they had killed their first moose. On their pack horse rested two hindquarters of a recently killed buffalo. The two brothers figured they would take the meat to Trapper Tom for helping them with their first killed, problem moose. Not exactly sure of the location of Tom's ranch, the two brothers crisscrossed back and forth over the large area described by Tom as his ranch. In doing so, they worked their ways towards the head of the expansive valley and signs of his home site.

Finally seeing smoke lazily curling up from a stone chimney in a large log cabin backed up by a hay barn in a faraway distance, the brothers headed their animals in that direction.

As they drew closer, they noticed several sets of large corrals adjacent Tom's cabin holding about 40 head of horses, several smaller out buildings and an outhouse. Walking from the still distant cabin, the two brothers observed the lone figure of a man exiting the main cabin and walking over to what was the outhouse set off to one side of the main buildings. Still too far to identify or hail the man, the two men continued slowly on since their packhorse was very heavily loaded. As they got closer to the cabin, Josiah White Buffalo finally noticed six saddled horses tied up alongside the horse rack adjacent Tom's front porch. However, no one was in sight. Getting ready to hail the homestead so they wouldn't be mistaken for 'bad' Indians, Josiah White Buffalo stopped. Something was not right! Tom should have seen the both of them approaching by now, come out from his cabin, and waved them in. Something just didn't look right. About then, the outhouse door flew open and a man stepped out and began firing on the two Indians sitting on their horses! Then the entire front of the cabin erupted with five other individuals streaming out from the cabin door, who were now firing wildly at Josiah White Buffalo and Chief Red Shirt! That was when their pack animal groaned and dropped to the ground, a victim of a bullet meant for one of the two men. With bullets zipping by and snapping the air around their heads in the process, the two men spurred their horses for the adjacent stand of timber for the cover it offered. But neither man made the cover that finger of spruce trees offered...Both men had their horses shot out from under them before they had traveled thirty yards! Fortunately, both men were able to step off their falling mounts in stride and run for cover as more bullets zinged overhead clipping off tree branches above their heads in the process...

Sprinting into a thicket of spruce trees, the two men quickly looked back from their positions in cover at Tom's cabin. Four of the men who had been shooting at them from the front porch, were now quickly mounting their horses and starting out towards where Josiah White Buffalo and Chief Red Shirt had disappeared into the timber. Seeing that and then running for denser cover, both men scampered through the brush looking for denser stands of protective trees. Then Josiah White Buffalo stopped dead in his tracks! He had enough of being shot at! Nobody shot at him without him shooting back in return! Running and hiding in the lower branches of a nearby spruce tree, he turned and watched their near at hand back trail. Moments later, four horsemen hammered into the timber from where they had last seen Josiah White Buffalo and Chief Red Shirt tumble from their dying horses. Figuring the Indians had been hit, the four horsemen thundered into the thicket of trees, ducking the low-hanging branches as they charged into the forest's dim light.

BOOM went Josiah White Buffalo's rifle as he shot the first horseman directly in the face from a distance of no more than 40 feet! The impact of the bullet at such a close range, blew off the backside of the man's head in a giant spew of red which was blown all over the three following horsemen...The second man into the thicket, unable to turn away from the rifle fire coming at them from the front, fared no better. Brushing away flying branches from the first rider plunging ahead of him, he felt little as Josiah White Buffalo's bullet struck him at the base of his neck from twelve feet away! The last two riders realizing they had stormed into a deadly hornet's nest of an ambush, reined back hard on their mounts. Reined back on their mounts and stopping in a slew of flying dirt just in time to have Chief Red Shirt's two fast rifle shots clear both men from their saddles. Those two men were also dead before they hit the ground in a spew of flying dirt, forest duff, and dead spruce needles...

Then as if on cue, both Josiah White Buffalo and Chief Red Shirt took off running for Tom's cabin using a covering finger of timber and the brush along a meandering creek as cover. Shortly thereafter, both still emotionally charged men who were extremely pissed over being shot at, had slipped in behind the close at hand outhouse unseen and had then dropped to the ground. From there, they could hear the sounds of worried men's voices inside Tom's nearby cabin.

"Do you see any of our chaps? They should have been back here by now," said a low voice.

"Naw. But don't worry about them four brothers. They is meaner than a stepped on snake and I expects them to come wandering out with them red skins scalps hanging from their belts. Just give them a few more minutes," said a higher pitched voice whose tone and tenor betrayed a trace of a very worried talker as well...Then there was a long bout of silence from within Tom's cabin.

After another fifteen minutes had gone by, the voices in the cabin started up once again. "I say we leave these damn horses we came to steal and get the hell out of here. Them other boys ain't a-comin' back," said the low voiced one.

"Maybe not, but we came here fer them horses. With all them wars going on in Europe, they will bring a pretty price once we gets them to a Mountie paymaster and sell the damn things," said the man with the higher pitched voice.

Then more silence followed. Finally a muffled voice said, "I say we make a run fer it before them damn natives come and take our scalps."

"I agree but I say we first shove this damn rancher out the door to draw their fire and then we can mount up and skedaddle," said the man with the higher pitched voice.

"Let's do it and be done with it," said the man with the lower voice.

Then Josiah White Buffalo and Chief Red Shirt heard a lot of shuffling noises of boots moving across a wooden floor inside the cabin. Then through one of the cabin's windows they saw their friend Tom who was all tied up, being shoved forward towards the front door. Behind him using Tom as a shield, were two heavily bearded men shoving him along. Shoving Tom out the front door of the cabin in a burst of energy, the two men raced off the porch, leapt into their horses saddled out front and died where they sat! Josiah White Buffalo took out one of the men and Chief Red Shirt shot the other. Both men were dead before they could properly "sit in the saddle and slip their boots into their stirrups."

"Tom. Are you alright?" yelled Josiah White Buffalo from behind the cover of the outhouse.

"Well, I'd rather be moose hunting with you two leech infested chaps then standing around here with these here two scoundrels," he yelled back from his tied up position where he laid face down on the front porch.

With those words of assurance that their friend was alright, Josiah White Buffalo and Chief Red Shirt moved out from behind the outhouse and cautiously walked over to the front porch. Seeing the danger had passed, both men relaxed. There Tom was untied and released as Chief Red Shirt said, "I am glad all this is over. I was getting sick and tired of smelling all those awful bad smells coming from that outhouse we were hiding behind. What do you eat for a living anyway, Tom? Those damn leeches?" asked Chief Red Shirt with a now relaxed and teasing grin meant for his friend.

Then there was laughter all around as all the men began coming down from their emotional highs over the dangers now passed. "Tom, what the hell was this all about?" asked Josiah White Buffalo, as he levered out his empty cartridge and then jacked another live round into his rifle, followed by his releasing the rifle's hammer down to its safe, half-cocked position.

"Them boys must have heard I had forty good horses and were coming to steal them. With so many wars going on around in the Empire, South Africa, and India, the word is out here in Canada that the Queen of England is paying top dollar for good riding horses for her army's to ride and drag their artillery around. I guess these lads figured I was an easy mark being so isolated and all with a goodly herd of valuable horseflesh and decided to come a-callin'," he replied with his usual good natured grin.

"Well, there are four dead ones down there in that finger of timber below your place and these two here. What do you want done with them?" asked Josiah White Buffalo like he was offering someone a live striped skunk to be disposed of.

"Let's hook a rope around the lot and just drag them over to that there firewood pile at the far edge of the timber and leave them. That area has always been bear country because that is where I drag all my sick and dying animal carcasses for them critters to eat. The bears will make short work of their remains and the birds will finish off what they leave," advised Tom like he was talking about hauling off another dead horse or something just as useless to his way of thinking.

"Say Tom, we were bringing you two hind quarters of fresh buffalo meat as our way of telling you thanks for the help and use of your pack horse. You know, when my foolish brother shot that moose way out in that leech infested marsh and we had no way to get the animal back to our camp," said Josiah White Buffalo with a huge grin now that the serious 'varmint-killing' was over. "But those devils shot and killed our pack horse with a bullet meant for my brother and me as well as our riding horses. Think you could lend us one of your pack horses? If you could, we can bring up that buffalo meat so you can begin processing it before it spoils or gets fly blown laying out

313

there in the hot sun near our dead horse?" he continued.

"Sure can. Grab that big Bay out there in the corral, he is broke to lead and pack. While you do that, I will go into my barn and get a pack saddle," replied Tom as he headed off.

With that, Chief Red Shirt grabbed a bridle off a nearby corral post and headed for the Bay. In the meantime, Josiah White Buffalo walked back to where their dead horses laid and removed their saddles and bridles. He then hauled those articles out to where their dead pack horse laid for easy retrieval once Chief Red Shirt arrived with another horse. With that chore out of the way, Josiah White Buffalo walked around to each of the four dead men and took their firearms. Those he hauled back out to the dead pack horse as well. But not before picking out a Winchester '73' from the batch of dead men which was of the hard hitting .44-40 caliber that he preferred. One that packed a greater punch and could shoot further and more accurately than his current .44 rimfire Henry.

Then he went back for the dead men's scattered horses. As he ambled through the dense and quiet forest looking for the four men's horses, a quick revelation ran through his memory bank of a previous experience that nearly floored him! That experience being the earlier incident of the great horned owl that had been hooting from the top of a spruce tree back at the Indian's encampment just that morning. The much believed and feared omen of the Lakota that when one hears the hooting of a great horned owl, a death is close at hand or in the wind. Stopping dead in his tracks, Josiah White

314

Buffalo remembered the elder's discussions from years earlier telling him about the great horned owl story of death and what his ominous hoots represented. For a moment, those thoughts of storied Lakota lore flooded through his mind and into his soul. Those thoughts lingered for just a moment, then they were quickly discarded as a myth. After all, he was still a white man and such things did not happen in his world.

With the abolishment of those thoughts, Josiah White Buffalo rounded up the four dead men's riding horses. By that time, Chief Red Shirt was there with the Bay and with the owl warning now banished from Josiah White Buffalo's mind, the men loaded the two heavy skinned out buffalo hind quarters onto the pack saddle and walked the Bay back to Tom's cabin. Along with them went the four horses once belonging to the dead horse stealing outlaws. Arriving, Josiah White Buffalo tied up the outlaw's horses to the horse rack in front of Tom's cabin. Then he walked with the other two men over to Tom's smoke house. There the huge chunks of buffalo meat were offloaded, boned out on a cutting table by the three men, cut into thick strips, and prepared for the soon to follow smoking process . However before all the butchering was done, several large steaks were removed from the huge hams and laid aside for the men's supper that evening. Following that little detail, the three men began the work of dragging the last outlaw's body off to Tom's distant log pile and bone yard. Tom had already dragged one man's carcass over to his log pile located about 40 yards from his cabin and soon Chief Red Shirt had deposited another one there as well. As for the four men in the fingers of trees below the cabin killed earlier by the brothers, the bears dined heavily that evening in their noisy, bone-crunching style and cool privacy of a pristine northern coniferous forest...The next morning, the gray jays feasted as well whenever the ravens would let them near the four "breakfast tables…"

After taking all the dead men's weapons for their own use and for some of those fighters back at the encampment who had inferior or no firearms, Tom had the two brothers take the outlaws six riding horses as well as a way of saying thanks for the lifesaving assist given to him earlier. That evening, Josiah White Buffalo, Chief Red Shirt and Tom Moore feasted on buffalo steak, fresh potatoes from Tom's root cellar and as many Dutch oven biscuits as they could hold. Dutch oven biscuits that had been slathered in honey that Tom had robbed from a nearby bee tree some months earlier. That night, the men could clearly hear the grizzly bears fighting over who would get the 'leg' off one of the dead men now occupying the distant log and bone pile near Tom's cabin...Come the next morning, all that was left of the two horse thieves dumped near the cabin were a large flock of magpies, ravens, and gray jays looking for scraps from the bear's previous evening's feast. As far as the four dead outlaws left in the finger of trees below Tom's cabin, only splotches of blood scattered about, disturbed soil showing much previous activity, and drag marks moving the carcasses off into the darkened timber, bore mute testimony as to what grisly work performed by 'nature's best' had just transpired.

That morning, the two men left a very grateful

Trapper Tom and headed back to their encampment. Both men were now riding new and hell for stout riding horses, a 'gift' from six dead horse thieves. A gift that had only cost the brother's a total of six bullets...Trailing behind the men were four more riding horses taken from the same group of miscreants. Lastly, they also trailed a beautiful Bay pack horse that would be the envy of their camp. A Bay who was another hell for stout horse that could easily carry out a cow moose if properly packed. A 'gift' from their friend Trapper Tom for saving his bacon and his valuable horse herd from the six horse thieves who had 'added themselves to the bears stored fat supplies' in preparation for their long sleep during the cold months of hibernation.

Rounding a turn into their encampment, Josiah White Buffalo noticed a large crowd of people gathered around Old Chief Smoke's tipi. As they got closer, they could hear many women screeching and wailing their death chants! Hearing that, Josiah White Buffalo quickly spurred his horse and hurried into camp. Bailing off his horse at a dead run, he ran for the old chief's tipi, now the center of sorrowful attention. Once inside, he was confronted by Prairie Flower and her sister wailing to the heavens. Looking over at the old chief's sleeping furs, he was startled to see his adoptive father laid out dressed in his finery and stone cold dead! After getting over his shock, he asked Prairie Flower what had happened. She advised that when she had awoken that morning, she found her husband dead and cold to touch! Apparently, he had slipped off to the Cloud People in his sleep! Josiah White Buffalo could not believe his eyes or what he was hearing. Days earlier, both he and the old chief had sat together talking about his future as a warrior in the Lakota Nation. Now, his adoptive father was gone and had taken with him many of Josiah White Buffalo's dreams of growing old together with the death of the one who mattered the most in his unique and sometimes sadly disjointed life...

Old Chief Smoke's body was taken up high on a ridge where he had commented many times earlier that he could always see an eagle sitting up there on a large rocky outcropping. Tribal members did so in order that the old chief could be closer to the Great Spirit. It was near that rocky outcropping that Josiah White Buffalo quietly placed Old Chief Smoke's remains high up in a burial scaffold for his trip into the realm of the rest of the Cloud People. As Josiah White Buffalo stood by his burial site still in shock and tears, he saw a spotted eagle land on a large boulder about thirty yards away. Then the eagle, cognizant of Josiah White Buffalo's nearby presence, just quietly sat there as a living symbol of life after death. A symbol sent by the Great Spirit to honor the old chief. With tears now really streaming down his ash-blackened face of sorrow, Josiah White Buffalo started walking away from this place of sadness. Then once again, his memories from a past experience flooded into the forefront of his thinking. And in doing so, almost physically overrode his extreme moment of sorrow...The great horned owl story recanted earlier by the elders and the living owl he had seen and heard the day both he and Chief Red Shirt had traveled over to Trapper Tom's homestead with the buffalo meat, had now come home to "roost." Bad men had died there that day after Josiah White Buffalo had heard that owl hoot. Then his adoptive father had passed in his sleep a day later after Josiah White Buffalo had previously heard that owl hoot...White man or not, he was now beginning to believe in the ancient Lakota oral legends about the hoot of a great horned owl and the many bad things that happened thereafter...

A week after the passing of Old Chief Smoke, Josiah White Buffalo stirred and then quietly left his tipi in order not to awaken his still grieving adoptive mother, Prairie Flower. He was now the man of the family and as such, was responsible for Prairie Flower's well-being. And, that meant not only protecting her but supplying her with food as well. Walking out into a nearby horse herd and retrieving his newest horse, the one taken from a dead horse thief, Josiah White Buffalo placed the bridle into the animal's mouth. Turning, he began leading the horse back to his tipi where he could be curried and saddled. Walking along and lost in his thoughts, Josiah White Buffalo instantly froze in his tracks! WHO-WHO—WHO-WHO, WHO-WHO---WHO---WHO, went the call of a great horned owl from the same tree Josiah White Buffalo had first heard him roosting in days earlier! Turning quickly, he once again spied the silhouette of a long-eared owl sitting in the same tree he had seen the morning both he and Chief Red Shirt had traveled over to Trapper Toms. The same day they had the shootout with the horse thieves. Then the owl lifted upward with a great pumping motion of his massive wings and silently drifted off into the pre-dawn darkness without making another sound. Josiah White Buffalo continued watching the owl moving through the timber silent as a shadow until it was out of sight. In fact, silent as the approach of the Angel of Death, he thought to himself...

"What's up, my Brother?" interrupted a surprisingly close-at-hand Chief Red Shirt, which brought Josiah White Buffalo back to the world at hand. "Are you ready for another day of adventure in hunting the wily white-tailed deer?" asked his brother. A brother who was totally unaware of what Josiah White Buffalo had just witnessed and heard.

Not wanting to dwell on the earlier "owl matter," Josiah White Buffalo, still under the spell of losing his adoptive Indian father and realizing his new obligations as the man in the family now that Old Chief Smoke had passed said, "I only hope your shooting eye is on this fair day. Otherwise, I will once again embarrass and bring to the forefront your poor abilities as a hunter."

Chief Red Shirt just threw back his head in loud laughter saying, "Today my brother, I will go with you shot for shot."

With that, the two brothers curried their horses, saddled them and mounted up. For most of the day and into the early afternoon hours, the two men explored the lands far to the north of their valley. Throughout the day, they saw few deer in rifle range and even less buffalo. Concerned over the lack of game discovered in the new lands they had been exploring, they decided they would now return and hunt a different set of rolling and timbered hills a short distance from their camp. That way, they could hopefully catch deer feeding in the late afternoon, kill several and be back at their camp by supper time. Turning without another word being spoken, they headed for that set of timbered hills that had previously produced numerous deer for other members of their band. Trailing their Bay pack horse, little did either brother anticipate the rest of their day ahead. That was, other than bringing home a loaded packhorse carrying several fat white-tailed deer for some of the older and more infirm members of their camp. An encampment with its many peoples who always seemed to be short of meat, especially when it came to the very old who could no longer hunt and the numbers of infirm who seemed to be increasing in numbers daily.

Finally arriving at their new-to-be-tried hunting spot, the two men dismounted and tied off their horses. Checking to make sure their rifles were loaded, off the two ventured into the deep chokecherry brush field lining a creek bottom so they could get into the deer-rich, open breaks beyond located on nearby sagebrush flats. As they plowed through the heavily loaded berry bushes, both men off-handedly stripped off handfuls of the bitter-sweet choke cherries and popped them into their mouths. Since neither man had eaten breakfast that morning, the rich cherry meat helped fill their empty bellies. And as they did, they were careful to spit out the hard seeds the cherries contained. And in doing so, both men relished the sour taste the fruit of the berries offered and tolerated the scummy feeling eating such fruit left on their teeth when eaten.

Quietly slipping through the deep brush, absent-mindedly grabbing another handful of the cherries and stepping off a high cut-away creek bank onto a large 'mound of dirt', Josiah White Buffalo was instantly rocketed skyward! He had just stepped onto the back of a huge grizzly bear sleeping in his day bed by accident instead of what he had thought was just a round mound of dirt! When he had stepped onto the brown mound without a second glance downward because he was looking uphill above him for any nearby feeding white-tailed deer, he instantly was tossed skyward as the very surprised bear exploded in alarm underneath his feet! Smashing head first onto the creek's far bank in a pile of river rock when he came down, Josiah White Buffalo laid there stunned. Somewhat aware in the back of his now confused mind, he realized that he had stepped onto a sleeping grizzly in his day bed! But at that moment in his confused mental state, nothing would work in his mind or physical being when it came to fleeing from such a dangerous situation. Off in the far distance, Josiah White Buffalo could hear the heavy booming of a rifle but he was still so groggy from landing on the river rocks with his head that no matter what he tried to do, he discovered his wobbly legs just wouldn't respond.

BOOM-BOOM-BOOM-BOOM, went what had to be Chief Red Shirt's rifle but even his close at hand shooting hardly registered in his foggy mind when it came to Josiah White Buffalo's ability to pin point from where it was coming. Finally his body began to respond from the whack on his head. Using all his energy, fueled with the terror from within relative to the danger at hand, he finally was able to stagger to his feet. He had no more that staggered to his feet when, WHUMP!   Josiah White

Buffalo was instantly slapped nearly senseless once again by a huge swipe of the irate and still surprised grizzly bear with the swing of his massive paw. BOOM-BOOM-BOOM went Chief Red Shirt's rifle sounding like it was still far away, as Josiah White Buffalo's adrenaline now began really kicking in. Trying once again to scramble away from the maddened and now injured grizzly bear from Chief Red Shirts' attempts to place a killing shot into the vitals of the furious animal, he finally found his legs. Staggering to his feet on wobbly legs, he tried to turn and shoot and then realized the bear's swipe of the paw had damaged his shoulder and arm. Now neither worked very well, other than producing a lot of blinding pain every time he attempted to use the damaged limb.

BOOM went another shot into the great bear from a determined Chief Red Shirt but the bear's adrenaline was also up and the bullets hitting its body at this juncture in the battle, were having little effect. Rising once again, Josiah White Buffalo turned, confronted the now standing bear, and was shocked at what he saw. The bear facing him from just a few feet away, stood at least nine feet tall! Its eyes were the color of blood, its mouth was wide open baring its yellow-white fangs, bloody foam was everywhere around its mouth, and as the bear with its outstretched paws roared, Josiah White Buffalo almost vomited breathing in its foul smelling breath! Finally being able to function after hitting his head on the rocks and being hit with a swipe from the great bear's paw, Josiah White Buffalo raised his rifle and painfully began firing. From four feet away, he shot the bear four times quickly in the chest. All that seemed to do was anger the bear even more! Then Chief Red Shirt commenced shooting from behind the bear once again. Feeling the pain from the shots in its back, the bear turned and stood wavering over all the bullets it had already absorbed. But it was still full of fight and started for his latest antagonist. When it did, Chief Red Shirt took a step backward as he jacked another round into his rifle and fell! The bear was on the downed man in an instant and the next thing Josiah White Buffalo saw, was his brother being grabbed by the bear's gaping mouth and tossed limply skyward like a dead rabbit!

At that point, pain or no pain, Josiah White Buffalo saw red! Stepping right up to the bear's now turned back, he pumped four quick shots into the bruins heaving back. That time the bullets fired from two feet away, posted some effect. Upon the impact from Josiah White Buffalo's eighth bullet (his rifle held fifteen rounds) which broke the spine of the bear, the animal dropped onto the ground and still tried biting everything its huge canines could reach. It was then that Josiah White Buffalo stood right next to the bear and emptied his rifle into the bear at such close range that the hair was completely burned off from where the blasts from the bullets entered the beasts heaving back!

With that flurry of quick shooting, Josiah White Buffalo was out of ammunition! Stepping back, he grabbed a handful of cartridges from his belt pouch and out of that handful, only managed to get two live rounds into the rifle's magazine. The rest of the live shells were dropped all over the ground because Josiah White Buffalo was shaking so badly in the emotion of the moment.

Stepping back into the fray, Josiah White Buffalo jacked a shell into the rifle's chamber, shoved the barrel up to the side of the bear's head and fired. With that shot, the bear's head dropped flat out and stirred no more. Then reloading his rifle once more, Josiah White Buffalo hobbled past the bear looking for his brother. There he laid in a crumpled pile ten feet away like a broken pile of sticks!

"Brother, are you alive. Say something to me," yelled Josiah White Buffalo in panic, especially when he saw the amount of blood all over Chief Red Shirt's upper back and shoulder!

"It is about time you got involved," came a voice from under Chief Red Shirt as he laid there face down on the muddy creek bank.

"Where are you hurt?" asked Josiah White Buffalo.

"All over," came Chief Red Shirts muffled voice as he continued spitting out blood and mud from his mouth. Then he tried to roll over but fell back. With that, Josiah White Buffalo laid down his rifle and helped his brother roll over.

"Once again my brother, you have saved my life. But this back and forth between the two of us trying to save the other has got to stop. Otherwise the Great Spirit is going to get tired of all our foolish efforts trying to save one another and will just let us get killed so He won't have to fuss over either of us ever again," he said through a twisted in pain grin as he tried once again to sit up.

It was then that Josiah White Buffalo saw that Chief Red Shirt's shoulder and back had deep and numerous claw marks. Then he saw there were four deep puncture wounds on his shoulder where the bear had grabbed him with his teeth and tossed him high into the air. Helping him over to the creek, Josiah White Buffalo took off his brother's shirt and began washing off the blood and wiping out his wounds. Once finished cleaning him up as best as he could do, he examined his own wounds more carefully. Fortunately, other than a deep cut on his head where he had struck the opposite creek bank and five deep claw marks across his chest and shoulder, he was in pretty good shape considering it was him that had stepped onto a sleeping grizzly bear in his day bed in the first place...

Somewhat later, Josiah White Buffalo had gotten Chief Red Shirt mounted on his own horse. On the nervous but steady Bay pack animal finally rested the two skinned out hind quarters and the front shoulders of the great bear. After all, meat for the village is what the two brothers had come for and regardless the trouble they had in getting it, they were coming home with something. The rest of the bear was left. Left because it had 23 bullet holes throughout and the meat was badly bloodshot from all the wildly shot bullet's impacts. The trip home that day lasted into the early hours of the evening. By the time the two riders arrived back at the village, both men had stiffened up from their wounds received in the fight with the bear and had to be helped off their horses into the waiting arms of other tribal members. But, Josiah White Buffalo still wore the symbol of his power as an Oglala/Lakota warrior and its sacred protection had not allowed him to be killed.

That was when Josiah White Buffalo was advised Prairie Flower had not returned from her earlier wood gathering detail! Other tribal members had gone out looking for her but because of the fall of darkness, had called off their search and had returned. By then, the two brothers were so stiff from their wounds and in such pain, that several other women and Gemma took turns cleaning out their damaged areas. Finished with the cleaning, the women applied medicinals and wrapped those heavily torn areas with cloth previously obtained from the traders.

However the next morning at daylight, Josiah White Buffalo, without his brother Chief Red Shirt because of his now festering deep puncture wounds, sorely mounted his horse and with several other warriors from Red Shirt's warrior society, headed out to find Prairie Flower. Josiah White Buffalo knew where she usually gathered her firewood and headed there first. By mid-morning, they had found Prairie Flower's tracks and had begun following her. That was when her tracks in the dusty soil were discovered being intercepted and followed by the tracks of a great bear! Picking up the pace, a hundred yards later the rescue party discovered where that bear had caught and killed Prairie Flower! All the men found that remained at the grisly scene was part of her pelvis and her head. The bear had eaten all the rest of the diminutive women...

Josiah White Buffalo was beside himself with grief and a sense of tremendous loss over what they had discovered. Now both of his latest set of adoptive parents were gone. A similar situation had presented itself earlier in his life when his first adoptive father, Running Wolf, and his wife, Two Fists, had been killed by a great bear and a horse wreck. Now, he was without parents once again..."Dogging" the great bear's easy to follow tracks, the three men continued their cold tracking of the murderous animal. It was then that Josiah White Buffalo realized the bear's tracks were leading towards the choke cherry thickets in which he and his brother had violently encountered the grizzly bear sleeping in its day bed along the creek the day before... An hour later, the tracks being followed led right to where Chief Red Shirt and Josiah White Buffalo had surprised the great bear sleeping in its day bed! A place where the great bear had been more than likely sleeping off a recent "meal" of "Prairie Flower..."

Painfully stepping off his horse, Josiah White Buffalo walked over to the remains of the grizzly bear Chief Red Shirt and he had battled to the death. Not wanting to see what he figured was about to be discovered, he took his gutting knife and opened up the bear's bloated stomach. Inside were parts of an undigested human and bits and pieces of clothing. Clothing that Josiah White Buffalo recognized as that belonging to Prairie Flower!

Without a word on what he had discovered since it wasn't necessary, Josiah White Buffalo mounted his horse and the three man rescue party rode quietly back to their village. Back at camp, Josiah White Buffalo took back the bear meat from the dead grizzly he had given to others to eat the day before not realizing it was from a bear which had killed and eaten one of their own. Reloading the bear's quarters back on the Bay, Josiah White Buffalo removed it from the village. Once far enough away from the village, he dropped the front and hind quarters upon the ground for the scavengers of the land and air to enjoy. He would not allow the meat to be eaten by other members of his tribe because of Prairie Flower's "taint…" Then he sadly turned his horse for home and an empty tipi. Once again, Josiah had been cast adrift by life's forces of fate. First he had lost his biological parents, then his first set of adoptive parents, Running Wolf and Two Fists, followed by his most recent adoptive parents, Old Chief Smoke and his wife Prairie Flower…Was he ever to be blessed with a whole family or would he be forced to wander forever looking for what he had lost? Would the legend of the hooting great horned owl and its Angel of Death ever leave him alone?

For the next two weeks, Josiah White Buffalo and Chief Red Shirt confined their travels to just slowly walking around the encampment and daily bathing. Their wounds were such, that Gemma not only cared for the men but made sure they avoided any strenuous horse travel or hunting trips. But in doing so, the two men had the opportunity to move around the large camp and meet its many new people. However, such activity began to have a down side. They discovered that many of the young braves who were not yet warriors, were chafing under the quiet controlled rule of the Canadian government. Sitting Bull, in exchange for asylum in Canada, had declared that his braves and warriors would not raid the numerous settlers in the area or any of the free roving bands of Cree Indians. The other condition of their asylum was that Sitting Bull's warriors would not use Canada as a home base from which to conduct raids into the United States. Those restrictions were causing many a young brave who wanted to ascend into the hallowed ranks of that of a mighty warrior by counting coup on an enemy, to chafe mightily.

Soon Josiah White Buffalo and Chief Red Shirt discovered that almost nightly, clans or groups of the camp members were pulling up their tipis and heading back into the United States in order to live on the reservations. This they did because it was harder and harder to find enough buffalo, elk or deer to keep their families fed. And those Indians did so in the hopes that there would be more food on the reservations provided them from the U.S. Government then they were finding there in Canada. As Josiah White Buffalo and Chief Red Shirt were soon to learn, the lack of buffalo was due to all the demands the Sioux and Cree Indians were increasingly making on the smaller herds of fast disappearing animals in Canada. (Author's Note: The buffalo herds in Canada were but minuscule in numbers compared to the approximately 65,000,000 animals found in the northern and southern bison herds in the United States.) That and because the many newly arriving settlers and buffalo hide hunters, were now having deleterious effects on the buffalo's overall numbers as well.

Two weeks after Josiah White Buffalo and Chief Red Shirt's battle with the grizzly, found both men able to withstand the jarring ride of a horse. And a week later, found both men out on a scouting trip to locate more buffalo to augment the band's meat supplies. Winter was fast approaching and with that, their encampment was slowly being reduced in numbers daily as many members trekked south back to their homeland in the U.S. But even with reduced numbers, the remaining tribal members had to set aside a supply of meat to aid in their overall survival throughout the winter.

Pre-dawn one morning found Josiah White Buffalo and Chief Red Shirt riding for the area between Cypress Hills and Wood Mountain. The ever present R.C.M.P. scouts who had been permanently assigned to Sitting Bull's encampment had indicated there were still herds of buffalo in that area. Sitting Bull, realizing that his people were struggling to get enough to eat, had previously ordered Josiah White Buffalo and Chief Red Shirt to scout out that area and bring back any news of a herd of buffalo so his encampment could lay up their winter meat stores. In the meantime, Sitting Bull and Chief Spotted Eagle would go and see R.C.M.P. chief Walsh to see if his government would provide some food for the encampment so they could make it through the coming winter of 1878.

For a week, Josiah White Buffalo and Chief Red Shirt scouted out the Cypress Hills and Wood Mountain areas. Finally, they located about 500 buffalo in a small isolated valley. But, they had also seen numerous Cree scouting parties out and about looking for their winter meat supplies as well. Realizing the importance the small herd of buffalo represented to their own tribe, both men rode day and night back to their village with the news. With the news of the discovery of the small herd of buffalo, the village became a stirred-up bee hive of activity. Braves and warriors made ready with their weapons and buffalo horses, while the women of the tribe began assembling travois and traveling tipis to be used while on the upcoming buffalo hunt.

Two days later, the tribe's scouts had relocated the

small herd of buffalo quietly feeding in their little isolated valley. With that, Chief Red Shirt's warrior society set out the hunt plans and woe to anyone who did not follow the plan. Even the thrill of the hunt was overshadowed by the desperation of the moment if the hunt was unsuccessful. Unsuccessful because the tribe's scouts had discovered a large Cree encampment several miles away and they appeared to be getting ready to hunt the same herd of buffalo as well. Time and killing was of the essence before the Cree arrived because the R.C.M.P. had cautioned Sitting Bull not to interfere with the Canadian Cree Indians hunting operations. But, that was then and this was now. Sitting Bull's people were hungry, needed fresh hides for their tipi covers, were ready for the hunt, and the Crees had yet to arrive. So the hunt was on!

Separating into an initial hunting group and a number of warriors to lay an ambush, the parties headed for their places in the planned line of the hunt. Soon the sounds of shooting and the thundering rumble of thousands of hooves could be heard in the crisp morning air of the hunt. As the herd of buffalo began sounding like they were coming closer to the ambush hunters quietly lying in wait, new shooting could be heard off to one side of the herd of the oncoming buffalo! Realizing something wrong was happening, out the ambush hunters charged into the still oncoming herd of frightened buffalo. It was then that the Lakota realized the surprise shooting was coming from a number of Cree Indians who had ridden into the middle of the panicked herd and had split it into numerous and scattered running bunches. The well planned buffalo hunt had now evolved into a number of smaller disjointed hunts by members from both tribes. As a result of the hunt plans going array, not many buffalo were killed by either tribe. Soon acrimony reined over the killing field as to who had killed which beast. Finally peace reined as each tribe finally settled for half of the kill while the remainder of the herd had rumbled off into the distance and out of sight.

Heading back with less than half the meat needed for the coming winter, the tribal members rode in knowing silence. They knew that there would be much crying of hungry children over the winter months in many tipis over the pain caused by empty stomachs. Upon their return from the buffalo hunt, many more tipis were pulled down as their inhabitants realized life in Canada was becoming impossible and headed south for what life had to offer on the dreaded reservations. In the meantime, Sitting Bull had returned from his meeting with "Mountie Chief Walsh." He had been told that the tribe could expect little or no help from the Canadian Government. (Author's Note: By 1878-79, the remaining Canadian buffalo were also scarce. And to the Canadian Government, Sitting Bull's people who were using Canada as a refuge, were becoming an embarrassment. Hence, their refusal to feed the remaining native refugees from the United States in the belief that it would force them back onto the reservations in the United States.)

The evening after the hunters had returned from their less than successful buffalo hunt, Sitting Bull called a meeting of the elders. They met into the wee hours of the morning before they finished with the business at hand. When they did, many important decisions had been made.

The next day Sitting Bull announced at a tribal gathering that the Canadian Government would no longer help them with food and ammunition supplies. It had been decided by the chief's and elders during the previous evening's meeting that because the Canadians could no longer help his tribal members and the wildlife food stocks were basically depleted, the struggle to maintain their traditional way of life and nomadic freedoms were over! Sitting Bull said, "Starving is no longer an option for my people." Then Sitting Bull announced that their present encampment would be left for another that was closer to the boundary line between Canada and the United States in the hopes there would be more food in the new location for the tribe to harvest.

Then looking around the large crowd of people, Sitting Bull spotted Chief Red Shirt quietly sitting on his horse at the edge of the crowd by his brother. "Chief Red Shirt, would you please come here?" Surprised over Sitting Bull's request, he dismounted his horse and handed the reins to Josiah White Buffalo. Walking down through the respectfully parting crowd being made for a warrior who was now much revered by the tribe, Chief Red Shirt walked up to the old chief. "Chief Red Shirt, the other chiefs and the elders have spoken. Because of your presence in battle and service to all our people, they have decreed that you are now the chief to Old Chief Smoke's band!" Without another word, Sitting Bull handed a staff of eagle tail feathers, a Lakota symbol that represented a chief's status, to Chief Red Shirt. Then he loudly proclaimed, "To Chief Red Shirt. May you bring honor to the staff of your new position of leadership as did Old Chief Smoke during his many years as a leader."

For about ten seconds not a word was heard from the surprised crowd over the event they had just witnessed. Then all at once the villagers loudly murmured their support for Chief Red Shirt and his new position among The People. Floored at what had just happened, Chief Red Shirt did not know what to say. Then a very proud Gemma slipped out from the crowd and into his arms. As she did, she smiled happily up at her man. Back up at the edge of the crowd now happily moving forward in order to congratulate their new chief, Josiah White Buffalo smiled as well. Now his sister would have a very good man and respected tribal leader as her husband, thought Josiah White Buffalo. Little did he realize what was in store for Chief Red Shirt and Gemma as a result of Sitting Bull's recent decision...

The next day the entire camp was in an uproar. Today was a moving day as Sitting Bull had decreed. However, both Josiah White Buffalo and Chief Red Shirt were heading north as fast as their horses would take them. Finally arriving at Trapper Tom's cabin, they found him outside chopping wood. Riding up to their friend they greeted him and told him the news that their tribe was leaving the area. Tom was saddened about the leaving of his two friends but indicated he understood. He realized that if they had nothing to eat, they had to move on so they could take care of their families. Then Tom surprised both of his friends saying, "If you two brothers ever change your minds and decide to come back to my place, I will have a place waiting for you. The Canadian Government has designated me as one of their official raisers of horses for the Canadian and British Government's military in this area. And with that decree, I soon plan on expanding my horse herd and ranch acreage to accomplish such tasks. Come back and work for me and you can live right here on my ranch as my partners in peace and comfort. There will always be a need for my horses be it for the government or the settlers as they come passing through. So, you two think about it and the offer will remain open for as long as I live. Also, I have great news. My rancher friends to the east, the Oltrogge family, have a daughter that I fancy. Her name is Wendy and we have been courting these last couple of months. She is a great gal and if she will have me, I plan on marrying her. That is if I can get her father's permission. They are of good German stock and do not like parting with their kin unless they can be assured that one like me, can make a nice home for Wendy and be a good hardworking husband. So if you boys decide to come back, I will be better able as a provider when it comes to the meals than I have been feeding you. Plus, this little gal is a pistol. I would think she would take to you two as if you were her own sons. So, good news!"

Both Josiah White Buffalo and Chief Red Shirt broke out into big smiles over Trapper Tom's good news. Then Chief Red Shirt responded, "I also have some good news. Last night Sitting Bull and the tribal elders made me the new chief over Old Chief Smoke's band." With that news, Trapper Tom had to vigorously shake Chief Red Shirt's hands and give him a big congratulatory slap on his back. Then realizing they would both be needed back at the now packing village, the two men once again thanked Tom for his friendship. It was then that Tom said, "Follow me boys. Your camp can't travel without fresh meat." With that, Tom hurried over to his cattle corrals followed by the two brothers who had questioning looks on their faces. Opening the corral gate, Tom entered, cut out six hefty steers and herded them out the open gate with the help of the brothers. "Here you two. Take these along with you so your band of folks can have some fresh meat while traveling along the trail. Now git. You two have a lot of work ahead of you, so git. Now just don't forget me or my standing offer on a place in which to live and work if you so decide."

Mounting their horses after one more good bye, the two brothers began herding their six steers back to their camp. Pausing at the end of the big meadow at the far end of Tom's valley, both men turned and waved good bye to their friend. Tom, watching his two friends ride off, sadly waved back. Little did Tom realize those words of offer to his two friends for a place to live and a life on his ranch, would someday make him a very happy grandpa...

For the next 'six sleeps', Sitting Bull's now greatly reduced in size band of people because so many had already left for reservation life in the United States, moved southward towards the boundary between Canada and the United States. All along the way, the assigned R.C.M.P. scouts shadowed the traveling caravan. Finally locating above the United States, just north of the Dakota Territories, the band made their final home in Canada. Within days, emissaries from the United States who had been informed of the band's recent southward movement by the R.C.M.P., had entered Sitting Bull's camp. There they told the people to come to the reservations and if they did, they would be made rich and happy. Within weeks, numerous other tribal members believing the words rolling off the 'forked tongues' of the recent emissaries, stole off and headed south to the reservations in the United States. And in doing so, dwindled Sitting Bull's camp even further in its numbers with many of those remaining being the old and infirm.

Sitting on their horses while out deer hunting miles from their new camp, Chief Red Shirt and Josiah White Buffalo got happily surprised. Below them in an isolated valley near the Missouri River breaks fed four remnant buffalo from the great Prairie herds of yesteryear! And, one of the buffalo was a white one which was considered sacred by the Lakota...Amazed at what they were seeing, the two men just sat there in wonderment. Coming back from their amazement at seeing any buffalo, much less a sacred white one, they checked their rifles. Then the two men leaned way over the necks of their horses so they would present a silhouette like that of a wild horse and not that of a horse ridden by a man. With that ruse, they slowly worked their way downward onto the valley floor below. Using a creek and its dense covering stands of willows, the two men rode slowly towards the four buffalo who were feeding still a distant forty yards out onto the prairie. Figuring that was as close as they could get without spooking the animals, they stopped and quietly re-checked their rifles. Gathering up their emotions and with a nod of the head, the two hunters burst out from the cover of the willows at a dead run. It was a second before the buffalo realized there was danger close at hand. When they did, they immediately bolted for the valley's protective, brush lined Missouri River breaks. The first cow fell to Josiah White Buffalo's shot behind the plunging animal's shoulder. Down that animal went in a cloud of flying dirt and old buffalo chips. Chief Red Shirt's calf buffalo bit the dust in the same manner seconds later. That left an old grizzled bull and the sacred white buffalo running neck and neck. Just as the two men moved their hard running horses up alongside the terrified beasts, the white buffalo quickly lunged sideways with a swipe of his right horn and disemboweled Chief Red Shirt's horse. Red Shirt flew through the air not expecting such a reaction from the fleeing beast and was rolled across the cactus-studded Prairie as his rifle flew another twenty yards through the air.

Upon landing in a cloud of dust, Chief Red Shirt's back and behind was peppered with needles from the many scattered prickly pear cactus in the area. In the meantime, his rifle hit the ground in such a manner, that it busted off its stock. Josiah White Buffalo figuring he would come back for his brother, kept spurring his horse onto an even greater effort before the two buffalo got into the Missouri River breaks and disappeared into the dense brush. Riding up alongside the old bull buffalo, one shot behind its shoulder dropped him like a rock. That left the white buffalo who was still running like the wind. Slowly moving up alongside and cognizant of its previous goring action on Chief Red Shirt's horse, Josiah White Buffalo finally was in the killing position where he wanted to be just off and behind the left flank of the speeding animal. Shoving his rifle ahead of his horse's head, Josiah White

Buffalo all of the sudden became singularly aware of the white of the buffalo's eyes. They were pure red and ringed with the white of fright.

BOOM! His Winchester roared and one of the rarest mistakes of nature staggered but kept running. Levering in another round as he tightened his legs holding the side of his racing horse, Josiah White Buffalo rode alongside his namesake one more time and fired. BOOM! That time the white buffalo staggered and then ploughed headfirst into the dusty bank of the brush line of the breaks. He had almost made his get-away but he had the bad luck to run across his human namesake...Riding slowly around the buffalo and making sure he was dead, Josiah White Buffalo turned his horse around and made for where he had last seen Red Shirt unhorsed. Finally riding up alongside his standing friend, he broke out laughing. Chief Red Shirt, the mighty warrior, was carefully pulling cactus needles out from his tender back and behind. Dismounting, Josiah White Buffalo aided his brother in the sorrowful business of removing numerous cactus needles from one's hide. Then Josiah White Buffalo got to laughing once again.

"What is so funny? I don't find it so funny," said Chief Red Shirt in a grumpy sort of way. Then Josiah White Buffalo said, "Well, I have been here before. Only the last time I was picking leeches off your behind that you could not reach..."

Finishing the ticklish part of his detail, Josiah White Buffalo walked out across the prairie until he found Chief Red Shirt's broken rifle parts. (Author's Note: Cactus needles are barbed on their tips. When pulled out from one's body, they have a tendency to tear out the flesh with the end of their barbs. That makes the removal process painful to say the least...) Bringing those parts back, both men examined the rifle. Instead of a clean square break across the 'wrist' or narrowed portion of the stock, it had splintered diagonally into two pieces. In doing so, it had broken in such a manner that with brass wire wrapped tightly around the break and dampened buffalo hide overlaid on the stock and allowed to shrink-dry, the rifle could be made almost as good as just fresh from the factory. (Author's Note: With the hard use on the western frontier, many an Indian's rifle fell to the same calamity. Being ingenious, many a rifle's stocks were repaired in such a manner. A trip through any good American history museum displaying Native American artifacts, will most always have a rifle or two repaired in the manner described above).

Then the work began. Because they were a good distance away from their village and without pack horses since they had been hunting deer, the two men decided they would gut the animals to prevent spoilage and then return to the village and get some help. There were no two ways about it, four buffalo in their village would go a long way in helping to reduce the hunger in many of its women, children, old, and infirm. Especially since the last of Trapper Tom's generously donated six steers given to the tribe for its trip south, had been totally consumed just two days earlier. Approaching the last buffalo to be gutted, namely the white one, both men noticed it eyes were red, its nose was pink, its hooves had a pinkish hue to them, and the inside of its ears were pink as well.

Josiah White Buffalo had indeed killed a white buffalo, an albino and a very rare freak of nature. Then the special moment in time hit the two men almost simultaneously.

"Josiah," said Chief Red Shirt, "you have killed your namesake! I can never remember any Indian, much less a white man turned Indian, who has been so blessed with such sacred powers and symbols of life as have you. First the sacred grouse wing that has carried you through much danger and now a white buffalo. You and your powers never fail to amaze me. You are truly looked down upon favorably by the Great Spirit." Josiah White Buffalo found that he had no other words to add to Chief Red Shirt's historically pointed comments...

Gutting the white buffalo so it wouldn't spoil, Josiah White Buffalo cut off a lobe of its liver, raised it to the Heavens and offered thanks to the Great Spirit for the unusual bounty. Then he and Chief Red Shirt feasted on steaming hot raw buffalo liver until they could eat no more. (Author's Note: Buffalo liver is rather strong tasting in and of itself. Then dripping bile salts from the gall bladder all over the liver prior to eating like the fur trappers of old used to do, makes the meat almost inedible! To the author's way of thinking, one who has tried buffalo liver both ways, adding the bile salts makes the strong tasting organ meat taste like it is covered with weak battery acid...).

Since Chief Red Shirt's horse had been gored and killed by the white buffalo, it was decided he would ride back to the village on Josiah White Buffalo's stead since a single horse could go faster with just one rider. There the chief would gather up what help was needed and return so the meat could be salvaged and used back in the village. After Chief Red Shirt had left, Josiah White buffalo kept watch over the four very valuable buffalo so the meat eating critters could not eat their fill. Sitting on the side of his white buffalo, Josiah White Buffalo was happily surprised when a covey of sage grouse flew out from the nearby Missouri River breaks and landed in the prairie grasses not forty feet away. Then happily satisfied there was no danger close at hand, they fed off into the prairie eating insects and small succulent leaves from the ground cover. Looking skyward, Josiah White Buffalo thanked the Great Spirit once again for his many blessings.

Come nightfall, Josiah White Buffalo built a large fire center to their buffalo kill to keep away the wolves who had since smelled the blood and gut piles from the dead buffalo. Prairie wolves who had gathered and were now hungrily circling the area looking for a chance at a meal. Additionally, the light from his campfire would help guide back the chief and some of his followers to the little out of the way killing ground. Just before dawn the next morning, Josiah White Buffalo could hear the barking of dogs and the sounds of happy voices coming his way. As they did, the hungry wolves who had been circling the dead buffalo all night, drifted silently off into the pre-dawn darkness like a downy duck feather floating aimlessly in a soft morning breeze.

Standing there by his dead name sake, Josiah White Buffalo welcomed Chief Red Shirt and a group of twenty women bringing travois to haul the meat back to their encampment. Accompanying them were about 30 braves and warriors. Braves and warriors who remembered what the Crees had done to them on their last buffalo hunt further north and were now determined to never have that unfortunate incident ever be repeated. Then everyone had to quietly and out of reverence, gather around the carcass of the sacred white buffalo. Several of the braves and warriors took small handfuls of the animal's hair and secreted it away in their carry-pouches to be made into sacred amulets later on. With the moment over of examining the sacred white buffalo, one that no other members had ever seen in their lives, the next most important thing got underway. Since the tribal members had traveled all night and had not eaten after they left camp, several cooking fires were lit and soon the morning's air smelled heavily of roasting buffalo liver, heart and some of the smaller fatty intestines. Once everyone had eaten their fill, the work began. As the women began dismembering the buffalo and loading their travois, Josiah White Buffalo and Chief Red Shirt carefully finished attending to the remains of the white buffalo. The women had skinned out one-half of the creature, removed all its meat on one side and then rolled the skeleton-half onto its side. Then the upside was skinned out, the precious meat was removed, and loaded on another collection of waiting travois. When the women had finished with the white buffalo, Josiah White Buffalo and Chief Red Shirt took over.

Laying out the hide with the fur side down, the two men had one of the women remove as much flesh as she could that remained on the skin side. When finished, Josiah White Buffalo cut off the white buffalo's head and loaded it onto a travois. The remaining hide was then rolled up and loaded onto the travois carrying the head. Finished, Josiah White Buffalo smiled. He planned on making the white buffalo's head a gift to Fast Antelope, one of the band's holy men. With that, the holy man could make it into a ceremonial object. As for the hide, Josiah White Buffalo decided he would ask his sister, Gemma to prepare and tan the hide so he would always have it with him to be used along with his sleeping furs. That way he would always be surrounded by the sacred white buffalo, his namesake.

By late morning, the skinning, butchering and loading work had been accomplished. Once again, the cooking fires were relit and soon the smell of roasting buffalo small intestines, a favorite for the excellent fatty taste they provided, were being consumed by the yard. Not near any close at hand water source, the intestines were turned inside out, brushed free of the plant matter inside, and then roasted. Any remaining plant matter not burned off in the open fire roasting process and discovered in the cooked intestines during consumption, were quietly removed and discarded. Finally satiated, the happy group began their long trip back to their encampment and their soon to be other happy tribal members over the buffalo meat bounty.

The following morning, the tired and weary group of buffalo hunters and meat transporters finally arrived back at their camp accompanied by a host of barking camp dogs and excited noisy children. Soon villagers had gathered all around for their share of the bounty. But as dictated by their culture, the old and infirm were provided for first. As the bounty was dispensed, Josiah White

Buffalo carrying a partial back strap from the white buffalo, walked over to Sitting Bull's tipi. There stood the elder chief with a smile on his face over the bounty his two favorite hunters and the Great Spirit had provided for his people. Hearing the newest commotion outside their tipi, out poured Sitting Bull's four wives. Soon they had gleefully gathered around Josiah White Buffalo and his large chunk of meat. Handing the meat over to Four-Robes, Josiah White Buffalo soon found himself in the arms of four very excited and all talking at once happy wives! They soon quickly let him go of him as all four wives hustled back into their tipi with their huge chunk of buffalo back strap to begin preparations for their evening meal.

"Chief Sitting Bull, that is the meat from the sacred white buffalo I killed during the hunt. I thought you and your wives might enjoy having some fresh buffalo meat for a change over the deer, bear and few elk Chief Red Shirt and I have been able to bring back into camp," said Josiah White Buffalo.

Sitting Bull smiled and then said, "Josiah White Buffalo, son of a white man, I told you that someday you would become a great Lakota warrior. That is what my vision said and that is what you have become. But remember, we still have many trails to travel and a great water to cross over before the Great Spirit lets us travel with the Cloud People according to that earlier vision. Please plan on having your evening meal with me and my wives this evening." With those words, Sitting Bull still smiling over his people receiving the buffalo meat bounty from two of his greatest hunters, turned and without further words, re-entered his tipi.

Taking that as his cue to leave, Josiah White Buffalo walked over to the travois holding the hide and skull of the white buffalo. There he removed with difficulty the heavy head from the beast and staggered over to the tipi of Fast Antelope, the tribes other holy man. Announcing his presence outside his tipi, Josiah White Buffalo was soon confronted with the holy man. As soon as Fast Antelope saw the great white and shaggy head, his face changed from holding a questioning look as to who was outside his tipi to one of extreme surprise. Then seconds later, his face changed quickly to pleasure.

"Fast Antelope. You were the first to read and explain to me about the power of my sage grouse dream and symbol. Today, I have for you a symbol of my namesake which I killed. I have brought you the head so you might use it in sacred ceremonies." With that, Josiah White Buffalo handed the massive head over to the still very much surprised and now extremely happy holy man.

"Josiah White Buffalo. I have heard about such an animal from my grandfather and my father. Neither of them had ever seen such an animal. But all of them had heard about such an animal in stories told to them down through the years. Now I am privileged to hold such a sacred animal's part in my hands. I do not know what to say. But know when I pray to the Great Spirit, your name will be in those prayers. Thank you for bringing me such a good omen for our people. Especially in our time of great need when our lifestyle, traditions, and very lives are threatened. I do not know why we have such troubles. Perhaps it is because the Great Spirit is mad at His children. I just don't know. But, I will use the skull of this symbol in all of my prayers and I thank you for being such a great warrior and friend." With that, the holy man struggled back into his tipi reverently holding the white buffalo's massive and still bloody head like it was his first new born baby…That head would later be skinned out and the skin tanned so it could be used as a headdress in special ceremonies.

About then, Josiah White Buffalo realized he was exhausted from the long ride and little sleep. Walking over to Old Chief Smoke's tipi in which he now lived, he lifted the flap, entered and laid out on his sleeping furs. Moments later, he was in the land beyond time. The next thing he heard was Four-Robes softly calling out his name from outside his tipi. Rising, Josiah White Buffalo exited his tipi and was confronted by Four-Robes.

"Josiah White Buffalo. It is time for supper with Sitting Bull and all of us. Will you please come," she said, as she turned and walked back to her tipi.

Following, he soon entered a warm tipi smelling of something wonderful. Sitting Bull gestured where he was to sit and soon Josiah White Buffalo was in heaven. In his bowl were freshly dug wild onions, big chunks of fresh buffalo meat, all cooked together in a thick cornmeal mush.

Once the meal was finished, Sitting Bull's four wives made quick work of the cleanup and immediately left the tipi as if their exit had been prearranged. With that, Sitting Bull leaned back on his back rest, lit up a small pipe full of tobacco, inhaled deeply and closed his eyes. For the longest moment, nothing was said. Then the old chief between obviously deeply enjoyable puffs on his pipe said, "Josiah White Buffalo. I have several sons. I have watched you over the past moons and I am happy at what I see. True, you are a white man but your blood is now of that of a Lakota. You have turned into a great hunter, even braver warrior in battle, and a much revered and gentle person to our old and infirm. You are what a father would want for a son. Early on, you were honored by being adopted by the great warrior Running Wolf. When the Great Spirit took him, He gave you to Old Chief Smoke. Once again, the Great Spirit took him up to the Cloud People and now you once again belong to Mother Earth. I would like to change that. You have been in many of my visions and now I now wish to include you personally into my life. I would like to adopt you as one of my sons if you will reward me with such an honor. What do you say to my words which have been spoken with a straight tongue and open heart?"

Josiah White Buffalo just sat there in shock upon hearing those words coming from such a great man. A man who was revered by his people and was totally uncompromising when it came to his culture as well as his freedoms. And, a holy man who had many visions given to him by the Great Spirit so he could serve his people. For the longest time, Josiah White Buffalo was speechless. Previously, he had been adopted into several kind families only to lose them. It had gotten into his mind that he would roam Mother Earth for all time without anyone to love or have him to hold. Now the great Sitting Bull had just asked him to join his family. Once again, he could have a family and someone to love.

Almost afraid to accept because of what had happened to every other family he had been a member of, he found himself sweating in the presence of such a great man and his still hanging question of a new life as a son in a new family...Finally Josiah White Buffalo's hesitation had lasted so long, that the old chief stopped puffing on his pipe and had fixed his questioning eagle like stare on Josiah White Buffalo.

"Yes, I would like to once again have a father and be like a son. Yes, I would like to have a mother once again to fuss and make over me. Yes, I would like to live in a lodge that has a living heart," he quietly replied, realizing what this moment in time and in his unique life this opportunity represented.

"Then it is done," said Sitting Bull. "You will be like my other children and continue to make me and my people proud. In fact as my adopted son, you will not have a mother. You will have four mothers," he said with a chuckle. The rest of that wonderful night was like a whirlwind. The two men talked far into the night. Their talks even continued after the four wives of the great holy man had long since returned and had gone to their sleeping furs. But not before the women had all warmly embraced their newest adoptive son within their family...

Then the old chief said, "Josiah White Buffalo. As you can see, there is hardly any more room left in my tipi with my four wives and all. I would ask that you continue living in your own tipi but in all family events and meals you will come to my tipi and partake. Do you have any problem if we live that way?"

"No," said Josiah White Buffalo. "Since I consider

myself to be a village hunter and provider, that will work out the best for me and what I do. That way I can rise early and not be a disturbance to anyone else wanting to sleep. 'Father', I would prefer it that way. The only thing I would ask of you is that you treat me like any other warrior. That will engender me with the warrior societies and allow me to take my rightful place among the other tribal members."

Once again, the old chief had to smile. In his previous visions where he had dreamed of Josiah White Buffalo, the man had been shown as in a truthful and loving nature to all tribal members. He truly had become a great Oglala/Lakota warrior as the Great Spirit had predicted.

With that, the old chief put out his pipe, rose and extended his arms towards Josiah White Buffalo. Josiah found that the old man's hug was genuine and meaningful. Exiting Sitting Bull's tipi, Josiah White Buffalo did not remember landing a single step over to his tipi sitting outside the sacred circle of tipis. In fact, he remembered little of anything of that walk because of the extreme joy he now felt over the events that had just occurred. Finally, he was once again 'home' and a member of a loving family. He found that 'his feet hardly touched the ground on which he walked' now that he was a member of a real family once again...

The next morning Josiah White Buffalo arose, bathed in the nearby creek and then walked over to Chief Red Shirt's tipi. There he announced his presence and soon had his sister in a warm embrace. An embrace that clearly showed to all looking on of her great love for her big brother. A man who was also now a great and much respected warrior of the Sioux Nation. "Gemma, if I bring you my white buffalo hide will you tan it for me. That way I will be able to use it as a sacred sleeping fur in my bed and always be surrounded by my powerful namesake?"

Gemma smiled and nodded her acceptance of her brother's request. She was known within the band as one of the best makers of clothing and the finest tanner when it came to tanning any kind of animal skin. She found her heart happy over her brother's simple yet important request. Later that afternoon, Josiah White Buffalo dropped off the heavy fresh hide and was rewarded with another hug from his proud sister. Some time later, a beautifully tanned white buffalo skin resided in Josiah White Buffalo's sleeping bundle. An animal skin that had been scraped clean of any animal residue and staked down and thoroughly washed in the riffle of the nearby creek prior to being tanned. A now fully tanned buffalo skin that glistened white in the light of day and was as supple as a freshly tanned rabbit skin. Now Josiah White Buffalo was surrounded every day with the sacred symbol of his power, namely the grouse wing and slept in the safety and comfort of his namesake.

Life in Canada, especially the following winter months, were cold, cruel and many of the villagers went hungry numbers of nights. Josiah White Buffalo and Chief Red Shirt hunted every day no matter the weather in order to provide as much meat as was possible to the village. Especially to the very old, the infirm and those who had many children whose husbands were not very good providers. Many times when they returned to camp, their game was already frozen as it laid across the back of the Bay pack horse and tribal members had to help the half frozen men off their horses and into the warmth of their tipis. (Author's Note: Riding horses in the winter months, no matter the clothing worn, can many times be a very cold proposition. Riding a horse in cold weather while wearing buckskins would not be a warm ride!) And once again and frequently, the numbers of villagers kept reducing as families pulled up stakes and moved further south onto the reservations within the United States. Their reasoning was they felt it was better to venture into the unknown on the reservations than starving in Canada as they were now doing with regularity.

With the arrival of the warmth of spring, life improved. The horse herds eating the new emerging grasses waxed fat. Then there were the wonderful additions of colts to the herds, which were always welcome to what had been once the "finest light cavalry in the world." However, with the arrival of spring, many of the younger braves now chaffed under their chief's previously agreed to travel and raid restrictions in play with the Canadian Government. Then it happened! In the spring of 1879. A raiding party of braves along with a restless Sitting Bull hungry for the life of the old days, on a whim, crossed the border into the United States! There they confronted a contingent of U.S. Cavalry let by soldier-chief Miles. The attack surprised the unprepared soldiers and for a while it looked like Sitting Bull and his raiders would be successful in defeating the hated enemy. Then General Miles turned his quick firing howitzers on the Indians and they fled in 'explosive' panic. That was when Miles chased them back across the Canadian border and then reported the illegal incursion into the United States to the Canadian authorities!

As it turned out, Josiah White Buffalo and Chief Red Shirt had been away on a prior extended hunting trip and were unaware of the last minute plan to cross into the United States on a raid. Both men were shocked over what had happened when they returned with four pack horses loaded with six deer and a large elk and became aware of the news. Especially so, since Sitting Bull's previous peace arrangement with the Canadian Government vowed no raiding into the United States. The other thing that shocked the two hunters was the complete absence of any fresh buffalo sign observed during the entirety of their lengthy hunting travels! By that time, for the most part, all the buffalo were now basically eliminated from Canada. They being victims of over shooting by the numerous starving Canadian and American Indians, crowds of settlers arriving daily onto the buffalo's home range, and the destruction caused by the remaining wasteful hide hunters. And now, the American Indians had a very resentful Canadian Government over their illegal incursion into the United States. A government who were wishing the Indians would leave and return to the U.S. In fact, the one R.C.M.P. supporter named Walsh, had since been transferred 160 miles away to Fort Qu' Appelle because of his leaning sympathies with Sitting Bull's band. And if that wasn't enough of a problem, more and more of Sitting Bull's band were slipping away daily as they headed south for whatever life would bring them on the reservations in the United States.

For the next two years, Sitting Bull's band struggled with starvation on a daily basis due to the lack of game and the tribes need for food. Almost weekly different clans abandoned their dream of being faithful to the resistance and headed south to the reservations set aside for them in the United States. Those who remained were faithful to the tribe's ideals of resistance and to chiefs Sitting Bull, Spotted Eagle, and Red Shirt. But hunger seemed to cross every tipi's threshold at each turn in the trail. Hunters from the village combed the surrounding lands for deer and the few remaining elk and when they were successful, the people rejoiced. Josiah White Buffalo and Chief Red Shirt, being the most dedicated and successful hunters in the tribe, were forced to range far and wide in their hunting travels. When they left camp, it was with their four best pack horses and seldom did they ever return without meat laden horses for the encampment to enjoy. But four wild game loaded pack horses did not an entire village feed...For two years this struggle for food supplies without any aid from the now very alienated Canadian Government continued.

Come the spring of 1881, Sitting Bull's encampment numbered around 200 souls compromised in great part of the very old and the infirm. Getting ready to embark on another hunting trip, Josiah White Buffalo and Chief Red Shirt had their preparations interrupted by a runner. Sitting Bull, the elders and the remaining chiefs were expected immediately for a council meeting of great importance. With that, Chief Red Shirt released his riding and pack horses back into the tribe's horse herd and the

355

planned hunting trip was put on hold. When Josiah White Buffalo entered camp after currying down his horses, he noticed it was abuzz with verbal activity. Something large was at hand and had everyone talking. But for now, all they could do was wait for the important council meeting to end and for any following announcements to be made. Seeing that would take some time, Josiah White Buffalo retired to his tipi. He did so because he and Chief Red Shirt had been on hunting trips twenty of the last twenty days trying to find meat for the village and he was just plain bone tired.

The next thing he heard was Chief Red Shirt's voice calling him from outside his tipi. Rousing himself, Josiah White Buffalo exited his tipi into the day's brightness and was confronted by a grim looking Chief Red Shirt.

"Josiah, the council has decided to surrender to the authorities in the United States! They feel it is better to starve in that land than here in Canada. Sitting Bull figures the struggle to live our traditional way of life has ended because all the buffalo here in Canada have been killed off. And without having any buffalo to sustain our way of life, we will all eventually starve. So, it has been decided the encampment, minus those who wish to remain in Canada, will leave for the United States and surrender to the hated U.S. Army located in Fort Bufford in the Dakota Territories before the next moon ends."

"However, Gemma and I will not surrender and return to the United States to live like dogs on the reservations. We have decided to remain here in Canada as free people and make this country our new home. We are doing so because all of Old Chief Smoke's band wishes to surrender and quit living the way we are. Since they will no longer need a chief because they will be following Chief Sitting Bull onto the reservations, Gemma and I no longer wish to be obligated as members of their band. I am going to return to Trapper Tom's ranch and take him up on his offer of land on his homestead and to work with him in the horse and cattle business. Gemma is with child as I speak. And, I refuse to have my child and any other children born in the United States where their government has continually lied to us, broken every treaty they have signed, and then attacked and killed many of our women and children when we did not do as they said. No! I will live out my life here in Canada as a free man, raise horses, cattle and my children in peace and make a better life here. Hopefully Trapper Tom was speaking with a 'straight tongue' when he offered us a home near him. For if it is to be, then that is where Gemma and I will leave our bones in a burial platform when the Great Spirit calls us to join the other Cloud People." Then having boldly spoken what was in his heart and seeing the incredulous look on Josiah White Buffalo's face, he stopped so his brother could speak.

"My brother, is what you say what Gemma wants? Because if so, than I am happy for my sister. She is all I have from my 'white life' and I would hate to have her hurt in any way. But it sounds like that the two of you have thought this move out and are clear eyed in what you want to do. I think moving up with Trapper Tom is a good move if you want to walk away from your people and start a new life. I feel Tom has spoken the truth about wanting us to come, live, and work with him. But, I am now Sitting Bull's adopted son and must go with my new 'father' to make sure he will be alright and not mistreated. He is getting older now and will need a provider and I intend to stay with him. However, if something happens to him and the Great Spirit carries him off to the Cloud People, then I too may come back to Canada and take Trapper Tom up on his offer of a new life as well. When you and Gemma go to Trapper Tom, I will go with you and make sure his word is true. If it is, I will rest easier and feel better in letting my only sister stay in Canada. You had better be good to her or I will come back and put you back in that marsh where you shot your first moose and won't let you out until those leeches have covered you up like ants on a dead grasshopper," finished Josiah White Buffalo with a big grin. With that, both brothers hugged as close brothers will do and then off they went. Chief Red Shirt to let Gemma know of what he had just told Josiah White Buffalo and Josiah off to be with and support his newly adoptive father in whatever he had chosen to do, no matter the consequences. Consequences like imprisonment, loss of his firearms, horses, and their ability to be free and live the traditional life of "a People of the prairie…"

On July the 7th, 1881, Chief Red Shirt, his wife Gemma heavy with child and Josiah White Buffalo trailing six pack horses with all their family's belongings, ventured north to Trapper Tom's ranch. Their horse string also included the big Bay Tom had given them as a gift. A horse which was now to be returned. There he met them on his front porch when he observed the three of them coming towards his cabin. But, he was now not alone...Standing by his side was a women who the brothers and Gemma soon discovered was the love of Tom's life, his new wife, Wendy. Wendy immediately took to Gemma seeing she was pregnant and soon the two ladies were inside the cabin and talking up a storm (Gemma had never lost her ability to speak English). Meanwhile, the three men were soon in serious conversation about Sitting Bull's desire to return to the United States and surrender. Red Shirt on the other hand, made it clear to Tom that he intended to stay and live in Canada as a free man providing he could make a living. Hearing those welcome words, Tom reiterated his offer to both men and pledged acreage on his ranch for their future home sites and a job in his horse and cattle operations. Operations that now included providing horses and cattle to the Canadian and British Governments for use by their field armies as means of transportation and food. Red Shirt accepted Tom's offer and both he and Tom shook on the deal. "What about you Josiah?" asked Tom hopefully. Josiah White Buffalo let Tom know that he appreciated the offer but he would return and go back to the United States with his newly adoptive father. Disappointed over losing his friend, Tom then let it be known that the offer of a job and land upon which to build a home would 'remain standing' if Josiah White Buffalo so choose to accept. With that, the two brothers hugged aware of the unknowns of life now facing each other. Seeing Gemma standing on Tom's porch with tears in her eyes, Josiah White Buffalo sprang up the steps and gathered his sister in his arms for one more time. Neither had any final words to say to each other because of the emotion of the moment. Releasing his sister, Josiah White Buffalo descended the porch steps and shook Tom's hand in grateful thanks. With that, he swiftly leapt into the saddle of his horse and rode south back to his band. A band whose old and infirm members would soon need and welcome his strong arms and back in aiding them to prepare for the long trip ahead and its many unknowns. As he rode out of sight from Tom's ranch and from what had been his latest little family, he noticed that like back at the wagon train when his mother had been killed, his tears were freely and unabashedly flowing as he felt that same moment of sorrowful emptiness now forming deeply inside...

On July the 10th, 1881, Sitting Bull led his band of about 200 men, women and children towards Fort Bufford in the Dakota Territory. (Author's Note: In current day North Dakota near the confluence of the Yellowstone and Missouri Rivers.) Most adults in Sitting Bull's trailing bands of Oglala/Lakota and Humkpapa/Lakota were the old and infirm who remembered the traditional ways but also realized they would starve to death if they remained in Canada. On July the 19th, 1881, Sitting Bull surrendered to Major David Brotherton, U.S. Army. From there, Sitting Bull and his two bands of Lakota were treated as prisoners and sent to Fort Randall near current day Pickstown, South Dakota. There, they were confined for twenty months as prisoners. True to his word, Josiah White Buffalo accompanied his new adoptive father and four mothers in all their travels, trials and tribulations like the good son he was. He was never to see his Oglala brother Red Shirt and his biological sister ever again due to a surprising event that took place years later in the current State of Nebraska along the Platte River. He never knew that Gemma's firstborn, a son, was named Josiah...And, Trapper Tom and his bride Wendy, happily became little Josiah's grandparents.

Chapter Eleven

BUFFALO BILL CODY, DEATH OF SITTING BULL AND JOSIAH RETURNS TO THE WHITE WORLD

In the late summer of 1883, Sitting Bull and his little band of Hunkpapa and the remnants of Old Chief Smoke's Oglala/Lakota, were relocated from their confinement at Fort Randall in the Dakota Territory to the Standing Rock Agency located in current day northwestern South Dakota. Once there, Sitting Bull's band settled near the Grand River not far from the great chief's birthplace. There they lived in their tipis until the original buffalo hide coverings weathered out and then those coverings were changed to Agency supplied canvas. Quickly discovering canvas not sufficient for long term use in the extreme South Dakota weather as tipi coverings, Sitting Bull had his little band build cabins since the longer lasting buffalo hides for their tipis were now no longer available. There they lived more comfortably within their new enclave of log cabins against the ravages of typical Dakota Territory freezing winters and hot humid summers. And in doing so, began their slow emergence from that of a Prairie nomad into the traditions of the white man's world.

In addition to all their other adjustments, little were any of the band's members aware of a traveling show that had been organized earlier by several western frontiersmen that would soon go worldwide and be seen by thousands of amazed people. A show named "Buffalo Bill's Wild West." A show that marginally depicted to astonished audiences bits and pieces of what the fast disappearing old west was really like. That show would soon touch Sitting Bull in 1885, twenty of his warriors and their families in their action packed programs put on for excited white audiences nationally as well as internationally. And in doing so, allowed a number of Sitting Bull's people a chance to leave the reservation and see parts of humanity and the world that they never could have imagined existed.

In the late summer of 1884 and into the spring of 1885, Josiah White Buffalo remained with Sitting Bull and his clan camped in the Grand River area of South Dakota. As an ever faithful son to the old, yet still revered great chief and holy man, plus his four wives, Josiah White Buffalo served as the family's hunter and main provider. In doing so, he was able to provide foodstuffs and other white man's goods above and beyond the meager stores routinely provided to the Indians from the Standing Rock Agency's warehouses. Times were tough and food supplies promised by the U.S. Government were often meager, sometimes stolen by unscrupulous whites and sold, or were never provided in the promised quantities or in a timely fashion. As a result, Josiah White Buffalo extensively hunted deer and what few elk remained in the area on an almost daily basis. Those meat supplies were then provided to his family and other older and infirm family's within Sitting Bull's enclave who lacked a male provider. Come the depths of winter, Josiah White Buffalo ran a trap line for foxes, coyotes, Prairie wolves, bobcats, bald and golden eagles. The raw bounty he gained from his trapping successes were brought back to Sitting Bull's encampment and then the old chief's wives would skin the animals and beautifully tan their hides. Come spring, Josiah White Buffalo would take the finely tanned furs and valuable eagle feathers to the Agency Trading Post, swap them for ammunition for his rifle, food stuffs needed back at their cabin, and some white men's clothing which was now slowly supplanting the traditional Indian's way of dress.

In the early summer of 1885, Josiah White Buffalo accompanied Sitting Bull to one of the tribe's annual beef allotment activities. There the government would supply beeves on the hoof to the numbers of Indian family's on the Standing Rock Indian Reservation. The bawling and nervous beeves were herded into a large centrally located corral and there the braves and warriors would hold a "cattle shoot." An activity that was reminiscent of what they did to the buffalo in the old days when they had those herd animals confused and milling around in a "stand." As the shooting progressed and the smell of blood hung heavy in the air, the rest of the trapped cattle, alarmed over those smells of death, would panic. Soon they would be racing around within the corral's unyielding structure in terror. By then, those doing the shooting became even more excited and inaccurate in their shot placement. That scene soon evolved into wounded cattle moving around gut shot and with broken legs or shoulders as the frantic shooting continued until none were left standing. Then everyone would quickly hop over the corral, run into the center area of slaughter and claim their meaty "prize." Hardly anything was wasted due to everyone's extreme hunger for meat. Soon all that remained were the paunches of the unfortunate animals scattered about within the corral. Then the rest of the useable parts were hauled off on pack horses or in wagons by the hungry Indians. Within the hour, the smell of many cooking fires and the odors of cooking meat would be hanging heavy over the many clan's various campsites.

However, Josiah White Buffalo took no part in the corralled animal's slaughter. He had been too busy intently counting the herd as it was being herded into the enclosure. Realizing something was amiss, he counted the animals once again as they slowly milled around within the confines of the corral before the shooting started.

"Father, the cattle allotment for this area was for 55 families. I only counted 45 beeves. Where are the other ten animals of the promised allotment?"

"My son. That is the way the white man counts. He promises one thing and many times provides another. In the case of our beef allotment, this area of the reservation is allotted 55 beeves twice a year. I have also noticed that upon every delivery there are always ten beeves missing. I have asked the Indian agent where those beeves that had been promised to us went. He always says that they were lost in the brush along the creeks and rivers when they strayed as they were being herded here from their home ranch. As I said earlier, I too have noticed that ten animals are always missing and presumed lost. Yet my questioning words always seem to be lost in the white man's ears. Those numbers of lost animals are never made up and our people go hungry because of the white man's crooked way. That is just the white man's way," quietly repeated Sitting Bull as he turned to leave the area and oversee his four wives as they butchered and then began smoking and drying their beef allotment for later consumption during the harsh winter months that laid ahead.

But, one man did not just turn and walk away from the obvious "wrong." Josiah White Buffalo watched the three cowboys leading their horses back to the trading post, there job of herding the animals to slaughter now finished. They had been the three who had herded the cattle from a nearby ranch to the reservation after they had been purchased with government funds. Now, they were walking over to the trading post laughing and talking with the U.S. Indian Agent James McLaughlin. Josiah White Buffalo sensing a lingering injustice, discreetly trailed the four men back to the trading post. Once inside the trading post looking like he wanted to purchase something off the shelves, he could hear the four men laughing loudly in McLaughlin's office. Sensing from the tone and tenor of the men's loud talking that something was 'truly dead wrong' in their 'herding' actions, Josiah White Buffalo quietly slipped out the door and trotted back to Sitting Bull's cabin. There he hurriedly saddled his riding horse, grabbed his '73' Winchester, a pouch of shells and quietly left without explanation. Riding over to a nearby hill overlooking the agency trading post, Josiah White Buffalo quietly sat and watched from his hidden position within a brush patch. An hour later, the three cowboys left the backdoor of the trading post, mounted up and ambled off toward the nearby Grand River breaks. Little did the three men realize that a set of piercing blue eyes, unlike those of an Indian, were intently watching their every move. As the men finally disappeared out from sight, Josiah White Buffalo dropped down into the brushy river breaks and was soon on the easy to follow back trail of the cowboy's shod horses.

Two hours later, the three cowboys rode into a small camp hidden in the river's breaks. There by a small campfire sat a single cowboy. Soon the four men were all around the campfire pouring themselves steaming cups of coffee and loudly laughing. It was then that Josiah White Buffalo, now afoot and hidden nearby, observed the four cowboys counting out their share of the money for their herding activities. That money was soon divided and placed into each man's shirt pocket. That was followed by more laughter, especially when a bottle of whiskey was produced from one of the men's saddle bag. Then instead of coffee, whiskey was poured into the men's cups and more loud talking and laughter soon followed.

"Those stupid Indians caint even count. We showed up with our usual ten beeves shy as McLaughlin had ordered, dumped them into the corrals and then got the hell out of the way afore we was shot by them crazy Indians. Afterwards, like always, we met with McLaughlin, got our share of the money from him for making them ten beeves 'disappear', got a good snoot full of his best whiskey, and then got the hell out of there afore we was discovered cavorting with him. Now all's we got to do is push them ten doggies from the Indian's original allotment back over to the McMaster Ranch and leave them as McLaughlin ordered. He has some kind of deal where McMaster pays him for those beeves and then keeps his mouth shut as to where they came from. It is like that old outlaw McMaster gets those government beeves at half price and in doing so, gets to expand his own herd at the government's expense. Either way, we, McMasters and McLaughlin win or the Indians loose. That will teach them bastards to kill off our cavalry soldiers and Custer," said the cowboy who appeared to be the leader of the bunch. With those words, all the men roared with laughter and then began preparing their supper.

Josiah White Buffalo had heard enough. Walking back through the brush to his horse, he mounted up and began his quiet search for the Indian's ten beeves still hidden somewhere along the river's breaks. An hour later, Josiah White Buffalo found the ten beeves in a makeshift rope and stick corral. Making short work of the rope with his knife, he began quietly driving the cattle up over the hilly breaks towards the reservation. Below him soundly sleeping were four cowboys with their snoots full of McLaughlin's good whiskey. Pushing the cows hard across the prairie under a full moon, Josiah White Buffalo made good time. Along the way, he pushed his beeves up into the backside of another herd of free grazing cattle and did so in such a manner, that his ten cattle's hoof prints as well as were his horses, were intermixed with the grazing herd. This he did for about three hours until his little herd's tracks were completely intermixed with the free grazer's herd. Then out the ten cattle went into a nearby small creek as Josiah White Buffalo pushed them hard upstream towards the Indian reservation. In doing so, he figured the streams flowing waters would soon wash away any trace of being traveled from within by a small herd of cattle along with the hoof prints of an unshod Indian pony.

Finally arriving back at the Grand River encampment right at daylight the next day, Josiah White Buffalo aroused Sitting Bull and advised him about what he had discovered and done. The old chief with a twinkle in his eye, quietly rounded up ten of his most trusted braves and had each man take a steer to a clan of the most needy. When he did, he instructed each man to advise the recipients of the beef to butcher it immediately and not say a word to anyone, especially the resident Indian Police. With those ringing words of caution in place, each brave loyal to Sitting Bull and unawares from whence the beeves had come, disappeared to all points of the compass pushing ahead of each of them a single head of beef. Soon, it was like the earth had swallowed up all the animals. But a steady stream of thankful Indians entering Sitting Bull's cabin the next day, spoke quiet volumes of their appreciation for what their great chief and holy man had done for them.

The next day, the reservation's hated Indian Police, suspecting foul play by the Indians, combed the tribal home sites looking for information relative to the "stolen beeves." They discovered nothing in the way of information as to what they sought and dutifully reported the same back to a still steaming mad McLaughlin. From that day forward, the Indians receiving their beef allotments made sure they had several warriors at the gate counting the animals entering the corral and if they were shorted, McLaughlin heard about it. However, a serious problem of consequence arose over the disappearance of those ten beeves. The Indian agent McLaughlin, figured Sitting Bull was somehow behind 'his disappeared beeves', vowed to get even if it took him forever. Regarding that matter of consequence, it took McLaughlin just five years to extract his revenge...

In 1885, a famous national figure arrived on the reservation. It was a man named "Buffalo Bill." Buffalo Bill was a man before his time. He greatly respected the Indians even though he had fought against them during the recent Indian Wars. He also knew that the tribes had not gone to war until they had been misled, lied to or driven into fighting for their sacred lands by unscrupulous whites or the 'treaty breaking' United States Government. Buffalo Bill also knew firsthand the United States Government had done them many wrongs by lying and cheating the Indians on every treaty they had ever signed. And, he publically said so! Being a previous Medal of Honor winner and great showman, the American people out of tremendous respect for such an individual, listened to what he had to say regarding the plight of the Plains Indians.

However on that day in 1885, Buffalo Bill was on a different mission. In 1883 he had started a show called, "Buffalo Bill's Wild West." In that show he tried to depict what the west had been like, especially now in light of the changing and vanishing times of yesteryear within the United States. His mission was to capture an earlier and wonderful time and place of historic events and in doing so, educate his audiences on a truly unique period of time in history that was now fast disappearing. And to his way of thinking, the west wasn't really 'wild' unless it had Indians and neither was his show. Hence Buffalo Bill's trip to the Standing Rock Indian Agency to meet with one of history's most well-known and acclaimed Indian chiefs and holy men, Sitting Bull!

Indian Agent McLaughlin meeting with Buffalo Bill, was all too happy over the showman's proposal of using Sitting Bull and some of his followers as real life props in his show. To McLaughlin's way of thinking, it was better to have a 'trouble maker' off the reservation instead of on it. McLaughlin had his Indian Police escort Buffalo Bill to Sitting Bull's encampment where the two men finally met. There Buffalo Bill informed Sitting Bull of his hoped for plans in including both he and 20 of his warriors plus their families, to accompany him throughout the United States and foreign lands as members of his traveling show. Buffalo Bill advised Sitting Bull on how he planned on having the Indians "fake rob" stage coaches or "attack" wagon trains in the arena, only to have the cavalry or cowboys drive off the attacking Indians and save those being "attacked." He also advised that he would like to have the great Sitting Bull, the man most famous for being involved in the fight with Custer, to ride around the arena one time during the end of each performance so the people could see the great chief. Then

Buffalo Bill instructed Sitting Bull who had remained quiet during the entire meeting, that his people would be well fed, duly compensated and cared for. And that he, Sitting Bull, would be paid fifty dollars a week and his warriors twenty dollars for their weekly performances.

Finally Buffalo Bill ran down from his presentation and then Sitting Bull spoke. "I will have my answer for you in one day." With that, Sitting Bull turned and quietly re-entered his cabin and disappeared.

Walking over to Josiah White Buffalo who had been quietly standing behind the old chief, and Buffalo Bill sensing that man's importance to Sitting Bull asked, "Well, you seem to know him quite well. What do you think his answer will be to becoming a part of my show?"

Josiah White Buffalo, who at 6'4" and towering over Buffalo Bill in stature quietly said, "He will give you his answer tomorrow..." With that, he turned away from the great showman and walked off to curry his horses. Buffalo Bill could hardly stand himself. Here he had made a wonderful offer to a great and well known war chief, only to be quietly told to wait for an answer. A move he had not anticipated. Yet now more than ever, he knew the great chief and his fellow warriors would be a vital addition to his Wild West show. So as instructed by Sitting Bull, he would wait. By the way, what was with the tall and stately Indian he had just met with the piercing blue eyes? That eye color was not natural for a normally dark eyed Indian. Yet that man was an Indian just as sure as frogs didn't have hair, thought Bill...

Throughout the late winter of 1885 and into 1886, Sitting Bull, twenty of his warriors and their families toured the United States and parts of Europe in Buffalo Bill's Wild West Show. There during every show, the Indians would 'attack' wagon trains or stage coaches and then the cavalry or cowboys would safely snatch those being attacked from the jaws of the cruelest of fates. There would be lots of shooting (blanks) into the air in the 'fierce' battles being fought but the cavalry or the cowboys would always win.

During one of those play acting roles was when Josiah White Buffalo met one David Briggs. It was during one of their play-acting roles when the Indians were attacking a wagon train that the cowboys with their guns blazing, attacked and drove off the 'offending' hostiles. As they closed with the Indians as the play-acting had been scripted, David Briggs slammed the shoulder of his horse unexpectedly and with malice into the side of Josiah White Buffalo's horse! Surprised, Josiah White Buffalo's horse lost his footing and at a dead run, slammed headfirst onto the ground! Josiah White Buffalo, feeling his horse starting to fall through his tightly clasped knees along the animal's sides, quickly stepped off running, turned, and out of instinct honed over his many previous real life battles, leveled his rifle menacingly at Briggs!

Briggs, seeing Josiah White Buffalo pointing the rifle at him yelled, "Take that rifle off me you damn savage or I will bust your head!"

Josiah White Buffalo, realizing Briggs had ridden into the side of his horse intentionally in order to shamefully and deliberately unhorse him in front of the breathless audience, gave the cowboy actor a steely look of clear understanding as to what had just occurred and then slowly lowered his rifle. However, Josiah White Buffalo's piercing blue eyes said it all...Briggs swore one more time at Josiah White Buffalo and then rode off with the rest of the cowboys still chasing the fleeing show Indians. With that, Josiah White Buffalo led his horse out from the arena and into the stable area to check his horse for any injuries caused in the crash. Stabling his horse, Josiah White Buffalo examined the animal for any outwardly appearing injuries. It was then that the troop of cowboys from the recent staged act thundered into the basement stable area with their horses. As Josiah White Buffalo continued checking the right shoulder of his horse because the animal had developed a limp, he heard the nearby threatening voice of David Briggs boom once again like that of a bull buffalo in the rut.

"You piece of crap! If you ever point your rifle at me again, I will dismount and whip your ass in front of God and everybody else in the audience watching. That is the trouble with you savages. You don't know your place. By the way, what kind of savage are you anyway. Injuns don't have blue eyes, they have dark eyes. Look at you. You are nothing but the spawn of a savage and a white women they probably raped. And now you are here acting like a real Injun. You are nothing but the spawn of a puke-female and a drugstore Injun. I was an infantry soldier under General Crook at the Battle of the Rosebud and we whipped you bastards right and proper-like. I also helped bury Custer and what was left of his men after they was butchered by you savages at the Battle of the Little Big Horn. So you see, I have no use for any of you or your kind. If I had my way, I would kill every damn

374

one of you son-of-a-bitches instead of 'molly-coddling' your 'thieving hides' and displaying you as a real part of the American West. Hell, you ain't nothing but a bunch of gut-eaters," snarled Briggs through a menacing set of tight lips.

Josiah White Buffalo just calmly tended to his horse as Briggs spouted off saying nothing during the man's tirade. For Josiah White Buffalo knew if he was to say anything to the loud mouth, it would be backed up with the blade of his razor sharp knife...

Then Briggs fortified with a nip from a whiskey flask carried by one of his cowboy cohorts, launched into Josiah White Buffalo once again. As Briggs continued mouthing off, Josiah White Buffalo kept quietly currying his horse, all the while ignoring the mouthy cowboy. By calmly ignoring Briggs and his running mouth, all it did was to set the cowboy's 'juices' into full emotion.

"By God, I am going to git off my horse and teach you insolent cur of a savage a lesson. I will teach you to ignore me and what I have to say. Hold my horse Jim," Briggs said as he handed his reins to a fellow cowboy actor. Stepping off his horse with a rush, Briggs strode over to where Josiah White Buffalo was bent over currying his horse's belly. "Turn around you stinking Injun and look at me when I am talking to you," growled Briggs. Not getting any kind of a reaction to his strident words, Briggs made his next ill-fated move.

When he grabbed Josiah White Buffalo by the back of his shirt, Briggs got the surprise of his life! Josiah White Buffalo whirled around from his currying duties and in a flash, had his knife at Briggs throat before the cowboy could blink!

"Help me," squeaked out Briggs to his cowboy buddies through a set of now terrified eyes rimmed with a large circle of white showing around the edges.

With that, five of his cowboy friends bailed off their horses and ran to the aid of the mouthy and now very much subdued and terrified Briggs. When they did, Josiah White Buffalo was looking over the oncoming group of cowboys wondering which one he would kill next after he had slit the throat of one David Briggs...

"HOLD IT RIGHT THERE!" bellowed Buffalo Bill Cody as he entered the stable area to see if Josiah White Buffalo and his horse were alright after the nasty spill they had taken in the arena. "I ought to let him cut your God damn forsaken throat," shouted Cody as he walked right up to the angry and now surprised group of men. "Do you idiots know who this man is? No? Well, I have taken the trouble to find out about him. He is Josiah White Buffalo and a much respected Oglala/Lakota warrior within the Sioux Nation. Why hell, he has personally killed over twenty horse thieves, Indians, cavalry soldiers, and idiot-stick cowboys like you in his lifetime. Briggs, you are damned lucky I got here when I did. And, that goes double for the rest of you damn cowards as well. This man would have cut up and killed every man-jack one of you before you could have lifted a hand to help your miserable selves! Plus, he is Sitting Bull's adopted son. Your stupid actions could have cost me a prized piece of history in Sitting Bull and audience pleaser in the show if you would have done something stupid to Josiah White Buffalo. I will be damned if I am going to put up with this form of stupidity any further. Put down Briggs and your knife Josiah White Buffalo. As for the rest of you miserable scoundrels, I am tired of your drinking and whoring around at every town in which we play. All of you get your hind ends down to my paymaster and draw up what is owed. Then get your miserable carcasses off the set before I call the authorities and have you forcefully removed. Now git," Cody commanded in a steely tone of voice, one that was not to be disobeyed! After all, the old Indian fighter had been in heated battle before and had killed as well...

Turning to Josiah White Buffalo who had not cracked a single smile during the entire proceedings, Buffalo Bill said, "Josiah White Buffalo, I am sorry for the treatment you have received from some of my previous employees. It won't ever happen again and if it does, they will get the same treatment that Briggs and his gang of five outlaws got. Are you and me square regarding this issue of bad behavior on their part?"

Josiah White Buffalo slowly nodded in the affirmative, just as the crowd above the underground stable burst out in roaring applause over the appearance of Chief Sitting Bull riding around the arena with his magnificent long flowing, double train eagle feather headdress. That brief glimpse into history- past never failed to bring down the house and this audience was no different. That show was over but, Josiah White Buffalo was going to discover that he was not finished with one David Briggs and his gang of five...

After each show, Sitting Bull and Josiah White Buffalo would quietly walk the streets of the cities in which they performed observing the white man's world and his way of life. They saw even greater suffering, poverty, homelessness, and people begging than they ever could have imagined. When confronted with such misery, Josiah White Buffalo could see in the great chief's eyes much amazement and sadness over what he was observing in the white man's world. But he said little other than acknowledging the wasted human lives with a sad shake of his head. Shaking his head in amazement and sadness, because in the Indian tradition and culture, they did not let the old and infirm rot along the way like the white man hide-hunters did a dead buffalo in the hot Prairie sun after they had stripped off its valuable hide...

Then true to his vision when Josiah White Buffalo had undergone the Sun Dance years earlier, Buffalo Bill's traveling Wild West show went to Europe. It was as Sitting Bull had predicted, based on that vision of Josiah White Buffalo during the Sun Dance, "That they would travel many trails together, move to the Queen Mother's country where winters were long, and cross over a "big water" together before the Great Spirit took them up to the Cloud People..."

Finally after traveling many miles by train and ship doing numerous shows in many cities in the United States and Europe, Sitting Bull tired of the travel and human misery he was witnessing in the cities of the white man's world. It became plain that he had decided he had enough of show life and longed for the quiet Prairies of the land of his birth. Leaving his Hunkpapa/Lakota entourage behind at their request so that they could continue in the show making money, Sitting Bull and Josiah White

Buffalo, after just four months in Buffalo Bill's Wild West Show, went back to the Standing Rock Indian Reservation. When he boarded the train back in the United States taking him to the nearest town next to the reservation, Sitting Bull uttered to Josiah White Buffalo, "I would rather die like an Indian than live like a white man." Then he quietly boarded the Iron Horse for his long trip home. By then he had also realized that the white people were like so many grasshoppers on the prairie's blades of grass in the late summer. And that the Indian Nations who had fought so hard to keep their lands were just like those grasshoppers. That is, they were doomed to die and disappear from the land just like the grasshoppers did once the 'white man's winter winds of change' harshly blew...

Back on Standing Rock among his encampment on the Grand River of his people, Sitting Bull once again was home where he belonged. There he rejected Christianity being pushed upon him by the white men and continued to honor his people's traditional way of life. Little did Sitting Bull, his people and Josiah White Buffalo realize there was 'hope and tragedy' on the horizon in 1890 that would once again transform their intertwined destines in a way they never imagined.

In an earlier treaty rendered at Fort Laramie, the Great Sioux Nation had been promised almost of all of current day South Dakota, "as long as the grass was green and the sky was blue." But by February of 1890, the U.S. Government had broken that treaty. The government broke the Great Sioux Nation's South Dakota land mass into five smaller reservations in order to accommodate the hordes of settlers now invading and settling on those once solemnly promised treaty lands. The government's thinking was to grant each Indian 320 acres of land within those smaller reservations and teach those new land owners the white man's way of farming. Onto those newly divided lands the government flooded the reservations with able bodied contract farmers to teach the Indians, ones who had previously led a nomadic life, how to till the soil and reap its benefits. As fate would have it, drought ravaged the lands that first year, crops withered and died, the Indian Agencies cut the rations in half in order to force the Indians to remain as farmers on their own parched lands, and with that, the 'new land owners' began starving.

It was during that period of hard times that a new religion began flooding across the land advocated by a Paiute Indian prophet named Wovoka. As a base for the new religion, Wovoka maintained he had been given a vision by the Great Spirit. In that vision, the Great Spirit had informed Wovoka that he was to initiate a "Ghost Dance" for all the Indian peoples, based on the traditional "Circle Dance." (Author's Note: The traditional Circle Dance symbolized the Sun's Heavenly path across the sky.) And if performed as the Great Spirit had shown in the vision, the Indians could rid the lands of the whites and restore the Native American back to their traditional ways of life.

It was just a matter of time before the hope of this new religion swept across the plains tribes and into the Great Sioux Nation like a wind-driven fire across the dry Prairie grasses. Soon more and more of the people began to hold out hope for this new religion and what it promised. After hearing over a period of months about this new religion, Sitting Bull summoned his friend "Kicking Bird," a Minneconjou/Lakota of renown. Whereupon he asked Kicking Bird to go to Wovoka in the current day State of Nevada and learn all about this new religion. Then Kicking Bird was to return to Sitting Bull's camp and share what he had learned with the Sioux holy man. In the meantime, Josiah White Buffalo listened to the stories of what this new religion promised and quietly dismissed it on its face. He had seen some of the white's big cities as a young man before being captured and knew of the white man's great numbers. And in doing so, realized there was no way any kind of a dance would absent the lands of all the hated whites and return it once again back to The People like in the traditional days of the old. But, Josiah White Buffalo could also see all the starvation and misery around him on the reservation and what The People were going through. And in his mind, it was easy to see why the Indians were holding out such fervent hope that this new religion would be their salvation. But he also had feelings of worry for what this new religious movement might bring down on his friend's heads if it went array or was negatively misinterpreted by the white government agents running the reservations.

Understanding of such things and its possible consequences, Josiah White Buffalo pushed the reality of such Ghost Dance thoughts of salvation from his mind and continued hunting the river's breaks and open Prairies for the elusive white-tailed and mule deer. This he did in order to provide fresh meat for his family and for those other less fortunate living around him in Sitting Bull's encampment. And seldom did a day go by when he was unsuccessful in providing fresh deer meat for Sitting Bull's encampment. However, the Ghost Dance form of hope and salvation, coupled with the inevitable reality of despair, was strongly on its way and would soon reveal itself among The People in a manner in which they never suspected.

Months after Kicking Bird had left to meet and learn about the Ghost Dance, he finally returned in October. On the evening of his return, Josiah White Buffalo was in Sitting Bull's cabin when Kicking Bird walked in unannounced. Kicking Bird tiredly sat down after his long ride and was quietly fed supper. As he ate in silence, surrounding Indians from the encampment realizing he was present and the importance of his return, quietly and respectfully pushed into Sitting Bull's cabin. As they did, a hush fell over the cabin's crush of humanity as they respectfully waited for the great warrior to finish his supper so they could hear what he had discovered in the faraway lands of the Paiute Prophet, Wovoka. When he had finished his supper and finally spoke, one could have heard a mouse squeak among all those assembled waiting in hope for what he had to say about the power of the much vaunted Ghost Dance.

At first Kicking Bird started out slowly and then as his enthusiasm increased, his almost magic words sped over his lips and into the willing ears of those crowded into Sitting Bull's cabin. He advised that he had spent many hours with the Paiute Prophet Wovoka. In those learning sessions, Wovoka had advised that he had stood before

God and had seen all his ancestors enjoying themselves in their favorite pastimes. The Great Spirit then advised Wovoka that each person remaining on Mother Earth must love one another and not fight; live in peace with the whites; must work hard and not lie, and must not engage in the practices of warfare among themselves or with the much hated whites. Then the Great Spirit had advised Wovoka that if those teachings were closely followed, the Indians on the earth would then be united with all their friends and family members in the other world. It was at that moment in time, that Kicking slowly took a proffered cup of water and drank deeply. To Josiah White Buffalo's way of thinking, the long drinking pause was almost for the magical effect it was having on all of those gathered in attendance. In doing so, Kicking Bird seemed to be enjoying being the center of rapt attention and the profound effect his presence and words were having on Sitting Bull's band of desperate and suffering people.

Realizing everyone was hanging onto his every word, Kicking Bird started slowly sharing once again his new found information. He then said, "One must follow those basic teachings and in order for the Ghost Dance to be successful, the dancers have to dance for five days and four successive nights. On the last night, the dancers must dance until dawn on the fifth day. They were to dance the traditional Circle Dance and on the morning of the fifth day after they had finished dancing, everyone was to bathe and then go home. Every six weeks, the dancers must dance and afterwards hold a great feast. If you do that in accordance with my instructions, the traditional Indian way would be renewed and the white society would decline."

Then Kicking Bird spoke the words that were truly magic to the ears of all of those assembled in Sitting Bull's cabin. "If everyone dances as they are supposed to do, the prophecy said that come the next spring when the grass was high, all the Indians who had faithfully danced the Ghost Dance would be lifted up into the sky. There they would remain looking back down onto Mother Earth. Then the earth would be covered with new soil and bury all the white men while the Indians remained safely high up in the sky watching. When the new earth was all laid down, those faithful Indians would be returned back to Mother Earth. After that happened, the soil would be covered with sweet grass, running water and the great herds of buffalo and wild horses would return along with everyone's now happy ancestors!"

Josiah White Buffalo was just as quiet as all the rest of the cabin's visitors that evening when Kicking Bird brought forth those words of hope. Then as if an afterthought while he still had the group's rapt attention, Kicking Bird said, "When the Lakota dance, they must wear specially made Ghost Shirts so they can repel bullets. Also, when we dance and sing the sacred songs, we must ask for the destruction of all the whites." It quickly became apparent to Josiah White Buffalo that when Kicking Bird spoke those new words of instruction, he was adding other ominous words and special dance moves into the more forgiving original teachings he had spoken about just moments earlier! In short, Josiah White Buffalo realized Kicking Bird was adding and mixing his own bitter feelings and more militaristic approaches into the sacred Ghost Dance. (Author's Note: Teachings that would ultimately lead to dire consequences among all the Plains Indians and especially so during a later massacre between Chief Big Foot of the Minneconjou/Lakota and the U.S. Cavalry at the battle of Wounded Knee.)

When Kicking Bird had finished speaking, Sitting Bull remained silent for the longest time as if processing the words of Wovoka. Then he instructed Kicking Bird he was to teach all his people the sacred words, songs, and dances as had been given to him by Wovoka. With his respected words of leadership paving the way, a murmur of excitement went through the assembled cabin full of hopeful Indians like the wind across the prairie tops of grasses just before a thunderstorm. As people streamed out from Sitting Bull's cabin into an even larger gathered crowd standing outside because there was no more room in the cabin, much excited talk swept through the ranks. Especially now with the words of Kicking Bird ringing in amongst the ears of those assembled.

For the next two weeks, Kicking Bird taught the faithful on the Standing Rock Reservation the sacred words, dance moves, and songs of the new Ghost Dance. And during that period of time, the actual Ghost Dance activities and all the whispers that came with it regarding ridding the earth of all the whites, began filtering out and into the ears of the Indian Police and Indian Agent McLaughlin. Soon fear began to build in the government's ranks as the agency authorities personally witnessed the actual Ghost Dance fever sweeping across the different clans on the Indian lands under their control. Soon the fear of what they didn't understand arose and in response to such fear of the unknown, McLaughlin had Kicking Bird and his volatile teachings removed from the Standing Rock Reservation. But now, the Ghost Dance had reached fever pitch by a starving and hopeful people looking for the return of a traditional way of life they had once known and loved. And now McLaughlin's actions relative to the Ghost Dance activities sweeping his reservation, over reacted once again. A runner was sent to the nearest military garrison requesting an additional cavalry detachment be sent to the Standing Rock Reservation post haste. Then McLaughlin, still fearing the Ghost Dance activity going on around him and the powerful influence that Sitting Bull could have on its followers, decided to have him arrested and removed from such inflammatory activities. He figured that with Sitting Bull's leadership gone, the reservation would return to normal and the Ghost Dance activities would disappear into the prairie's forever blowing winds.

On the 15th of December and not waiting for the extra troops he had summoned, McLaughlin struck. He arranged for a 39 man contingent of his Indian police led by Lieutenant Henry Bull Head and four other volunteers to strike Sitting Bull's encampment around 5:30 in the morning. His police were to surround Sitting Bull's cabin to preclude any escape and place him under arrest. Then the great chief would be brought back to the agency headquarters and jailed.

Around 4:30 that fateful December morning, Josiah White Buffalo quietly arose in Sitting Bull's cabin, dressed for the cold weather, grabbed his rifle and exited the cabin. The day before he had discovered a small valley nearby that was wintering a herd of deer. It was to that area he would ride trailing a pack horse that morning to see if he could successfully kill several of those animals because his cabin was running low on meat. Walking over to the horse corral, he selected out a riding horse and saddled it. Then roping another horse to serve as a pack horse in case he was able to kill any deer, it was also bridled and led away from the other horses in the corral. A quick curry job in the winter's darkness and then he saddled and mounted his riding horse. Trailing his pack horse, Josiah White Buffalo rode eastward towards his recently discovered valley being used by a small herd of wintering deer. Letting his horse lead the way on the narrow hillside trail in the darkness, Josiah White Buffalo quietly rode towards his day's destination. (Author's Note: To those who have not ridden horses very much, their eyesight in the darkness discerning any trail walked is very good.) Little did he realize that history and a major change in his life was on its way and would arrive about one hour before daylight back at Sitting Bull's encampment in the form of a contingent of the Indian Police!

Lieutenant Bull Head, Red Tomahawk and the rest of their contingent of arresting Indian police, along with four volunteers, rode over the last set of foothills overlooking Sitting Bull's darkened cabin laying quietly below. Riding slowly and quietly to avoid the rest of the encampment's detection, the men dismounted and silently surrounded Sitting Bull's cabin to preclude any chance of his escape. It was now 5:30 in the morning and pre-dawn light was showing the faint arrival of another day to the east.

Lieutenant Bull Head knocked on the door of Sitting Bull's cabin and soon faint rustling could be heard from within. Moments later, the door was opened by Sitting Bull's wife, Snow-On-Her. Upon seeing the dreaded Indian police gathered at her door so early in the morning and fearing the worst, sent her scampering out the front door onto the snow covered ground and soon she was out of sight. It was then that another wife of Sitting Bull, Four Robes, arose and met the police at the front door.

"Agent McLaughlin wishes to see Sitting Bull. I am here to take the chief to see McLaughlin," advised Lieutenant Bull Head. (Author's Note: Sitting Bull was not told he was to be arrested. He was to be told that Indian Agent McLaughlin just wanted to see him. That was the plan in order to preclude any violence upon the Indian Police by Sitting Bull's near at hand camp supporters. That plan was soon to go 'dead' wrong.)

Without a word being spoken, a candle was lit behind Four Robes by another of Sitting Bull's wives. It was then that Lieutenant Bull Head could see the old chief arising from his sleeping furs, getting dressed and then he came to the front door of his cabin with a questioning look on his face.

"Chief Sitting Bull, I am here to take you to see Agent McLaughlin. He wishes to see you and we have a horse outside for you to ride. Would you please come with us?" said the lieutenant. It was then that Lieutenant Bull Head discovered Snow-On-Her, the wife who had initially fled upon seeing the Indian Police at her front door, had warned the male occupants from several other nearby cabins of the police's ominous presence. Now those supporters of the chief were coming on the run to see what was happening and that could mean danger if those warriors realized the purpose of the Indian Police presence. And now, even more supporters were being aroused from their sleep upon hearing the early morning commotion and were coming as well!

Realizing the more he delayed in getting Sitting Bull 'horsed' and on his way the better, Lieutenant Bull Head grabbed the old chief by his elbow and forcefully escorted him to his now arriving horse being led by a volunteer. Pushing back against being man-handled, the old chief fiercely resisted the lieutenant's hold on his arm. It was at that moment in time that all hell broke loose!

As Sitting Bull fought back against being forcefully 'horsed', Lieutenant Bull Head tried boosting the old chief up into the saddle. BOOM, went Catch-The-Bear's rifle as he shot Lieutenant Bull Head in the side, as he tried to protect his chief from being forcefully taken! The impact of the bullet striking his side slammed Bull Head up against the side of the horse brought to take Sitting Bull to the agency lockup! Bouncing back off the side of the now panicked horse, Lieutenant Bull Head shot Sitting Bull in the chest and then in the head at point blank range with his pistol! Down went the great chief just as more of his supporters arrived from their nearby cabins and joined in the shooting fray. Numerous shots were fired in defense of their chief by a number of his supporters and from the Indian Police defending themselves as well. When it was all over and the smell of burned gunpowder had drifted off into the dawn's early light, sixteen people laid dead! Eight Indian Police following orders from an overwrought McLaughlin and eight Lakota, including Sitting Bull, laid dead in the cold December morning's air. The savior of any more from either side being killed, was the arrival of a small contingent of late arriving cavalry to rescue the Indian Police. But in the end, in addition to all the other stilled hearts, laid the most famous Lakota of them all. The great chief and holy man who only wanted to be left alone so he could ride out his days in the saddle alongside the Great Creator. A great man who now laid bleeding and cooling out in the December snow. A man whose visions had led the great Sioux Nation victoriously in one of the greatest of its battles with the U.S. Seventh Cavalry at the battle of the Little Big Horn and in part, contributed to its ultimate demise as a free people. He was now lost to the ages and the Cloud People... (Author's Note: Sitting Bull was later buried in Fort Yates in current day North Dakota. Years later in 1953, his remains were exhumed by his relatives and he was re-buried near Mobridge, South Dakota, not far from his birth place along the Grand River.)

BOOM-BOOM-BOOM—BOOM-BOOM-BOOM!
Josiah White Buffalo whirled around in his saddle from atop a long ridge and looked back towards Sitting Bull's encampment from where the sounds of furious and intense shooting could be heard. Being that Sitting Bull's encampment laid down in a long draw, the sun's rays had yet to expose the site to view in the pre-dawn darkness. However, Josiah White Buffalo realized a fight was in progress, whirled his horses around and headed them back as fast as he could in the snow and over the frozen terrain. As he got closer to his home site, he could still hear the

sounds of battle and now, even the faint notes of a cavalry bugle in the cold morning's air! All that did was dangerously spur him on to an even faster pace and as is the case when one dangerously pushes a horse under frozen ground conditions, the animal slipped and fell hard onto the frozen ground. In doing so, Josiah White Buffalo was unhorsed and slammed onto the rock hard frozen Dakota ground! That was the last thing he remembered!

When Josiah White Buffalo came to, he could barely see through his still blurred eyes. Moments later after his head had cleared somewhat, he observed his riding horse was standing quietly off to one side with what appeared to be a broken shoulder from the fall onto the frozen rock hard ground. Staggering to his feet and with a decided limp from a damaged hip received in that fall, Josiah White Buffalo hobbled over to his suffering horse and put it out of its misery with a single pistol shot to its head. Removing the saddle and bridle from his dead horse, Josiah White Buffalo saddled his pack horse. Then sorely swinging up onto the back of his now saddled pack horse, he picked his way gingerly back down the ridge line to Sitting Bull's now sunlit encampment. There the whole encampment was a bee hive of frantic activity. Riding into camp, he was met by a host of his warrior friends who told him of the death of his adoptive father at the hands of the Indian Police! And, that they had taken his body with them when they left. Sitting on his horse, Josiah White Buffalo began physically shaking uncontrollably in disbelief over the terrible news. Then he could hear the wailing and shrieking of numerous encampment women lamenting over the loss of their loved ones as well. Now sick to his stomach and alighting down gingerly because of his wrenched hip received in the fall with his horse earlier, Josiah White Buffalo entered the home cabin of his adoptive father and four mothers. The cabin was basically empty and showed the signs of its contents being emptied hurriedly and was now abandoned! Walking outside, he was met by his older friend Pale Wolf and asked what had happened to his "mothers." Pale Wolf advised they had fled Sitting Bull's cabin fearing reprisal on the part of the Agency Indian Agent and had scattered for the homes of their sisters in other clans. This they had done in order to hide from any further persecution just because they were the wives of their now deceased, famous husband.

Then Pale Wolf took Josiah White Buffalo to the spot where his father had been shot and laid on the snow as the very life drained from his tortured soul. There was an immense amount of blood indicative of a bad head wound but little sign of struggle on the iron hard frozen ground. Reaching down, Josiah White Buffalo dipped his fingers into the pool of frozen blood and held them there for a long moment as if through those actions, he could somehow connect and tell his adoptive father good bye. As he did, his warm fingers began melting the frozen blood on the iron hard ground as if the 'one now passed' somehow understood the depths of his son's deep grief and the love that he had held for the one now with the Cloud People. Once again, the forces of fate had abandoned Josiah White Buffalo and deprived him of any family and the warm arms and embrace of a mother. It was as if he was to wander alone like a lost buffalo calf on the prairie until the forces of fate intervened once again, or he too joined the Cloud People...

Without another word and with the hard realization that 'this life' was now over, Josiah White Buffalo walked back into the quiet of the cabin and over to the area of his sleeping furs. There he rolled up his sleeping furs within his namesake white buffalo robe and tied them down in a bed roll ready for travel. Reaching under a hidden crevice by the corner of the cabin behind a missing chink in the logs, his fingers closed over a leather sack full of gold and silver coins. Those he extracted and placed into a pouch tied onto his belt next to his now well-worn sage grouse wing. Grabbing up another nearby pouch of rifle and pistol shells, his bed roll and with another long full look at what had been a vestige of his 'old life', he quietly exited the cabin without a backwards look. Walking over to Sitting Bull's horse corral, Josiah White Buffalo cut out a good riding horse and an extra hell for stout pack horse. Turning, he walked over to his other pack horse still standing where he had been left when he had arrived back at the encampment only to find his life once again off kilter.

Packing one pack horse with a few personal items and his sleeping furs, he saddled another riding horse and leading the two pack horses, Josiah White Buffalo quietly left for the agency trading post. Riding silently with tears of emotion falling from his eyes and freezing on his cheeks in the cold winter air, he once again heard the dreaded omen! Off in a line of trees below Sitting Bull's old cabin, Josiah White Buffalo heard the eerie hooting of a great horned owl. The very sounds that Lakota legend 'spoke' about when death was riding nearby on the wind...Shaking such 'Indian' thoughts from his head, he let his white man's world take over his senses and purpose of direction as he continued riding toward the agency trading post. Arriving shortly thereafter, he entered and began looking around with an obvious focus in his mind as to the new mission at hand. As he did, the white clerk eyed him suspiciously as if Josiah White Buffalo was there looking to steal something. Over the next half an hour, Josiah White Buffalo picked out four long sleeved wool shirts, two pair of the new Levi Straus jeans, socks, a heavy winter coat with a fleece lining and collar, a pair of saddlebags, a sturdy pair of cowboy boots, a heavy leather belt, a wide brimmed hat, two pair of leather gloves, a 3/4 length rain slicker, a coffee pot, a cast iron frying pan, a twelve inch Dutch oven, a couple of knives, a sack of sugar, dried coffee beans, flour, a bag of pinto beans and a pair of panniers in which to carry all the goods he was about to purchase in which for his pack animal to more easily carry.

"You mean to pay for all of that Injun or are you just messin' with me? 'Cause if it is the later, I will toss your miserable blue eyed carcass so far from this store, you won't hit the ground until spring," growled the potbellied clerk with a disgusted and impatient look on his face over his customer's obvious, almost random, shopping actions.

Turning, Josiah White Buffalo gave the clerk a cold look that fairly burned a hole into the counter behind which the clerk was standing. So much so, that the clerk nervously reached under the counter, withdrew a double barreled shotgun, cocked its hammers over both barrels and laid it back on top of the counter for 'all' to see and appreciate its "meaning." That action on the part of the clerk was followed by a "just you try this on for size" look...

Ignoring the clerk's actions, Josiah White Buffalo said nothing as he continued randomly shopping for what he figured he might need in the days to follow. Finally finished with his shopping, Josiah White Buffalo placed all the items on the counter next to the obvious fully cocked '12 gage street howitzer' saying, "How much for the lot?" With those words and actions, he met the cold disbelieving looks of the store clerk over the amount of goods laying on the counter with an equally deadly cold blue-eyed stare.

After five minutes of "ciffering," the store clerk said, "That will $36.73, cash on the barrel head! And I ain't interested in no damn furs or a broken down old nag for trade."

Reaching into his pouch holding the extra money he had earned over several years of trapping, Josiah White Buffalo extracted two twenty dollar gold pieces and quietly laid them on the counter.

"Where the devil did a stinking Injun like you get such money? Did you rob a settler or somethin'?" snapped the clerk through his heavily tobacco stained and crooked teeth.

Leaning over the counter so close to the clerk's face that he could smell the stale whiskey on the man's breath, Josiah White Buffalo said, "I took it off a dead cavalry captain that I killed and scalped at the battle of the Little Big Horn!" Josiah White Buffalo's words were followed with a piercing blue-eyed stare that was so intense that it could have killed a cricket crawling up the wall of an outhouse at twenty feet!

With those words, that intense blue-eyed stare and the rest of his cold and stoic body actions, the clerk got the message. "Yes Sir," he replied as he hurriedly scrambled over to the cash box to make change. When he did, Josiah White Buffalo quietly reached over and removed the two caps off the nipples on the man's shotgun that he had left unattended on the counter. He was able to do so because his pile of recently purchased articles shielded his furtive hand movements when he removed the shotgun's caps, rendering the firearm inert. The caps were then quietly palmed and dropped into an open-topped pickle barrel sitting on the floor next to his right leg adjacent the long counter.

Returning, the clerk gave Josiah White Buffalo his change. Josiah White Buffalo put the remaining coins back into his coin purse and returned it to his carrying pouch tied onto his side. That movement to his coin purse caught the store clerk's eyes once again. Josiah White Buffalo then scooped up a mess of his newly purchased items into one of the panniers and took it outside. There he fastened it onto one side of the pack saddle on a pack horse and then reentered the store for the rest of his goods and the remaining pannier. Loading the rest of his items into the last pannier, he lifted it up off the counter, turned and prepared to leave. As he swung the pannier up onto his shoulder, he found himself facing the muzzle of the double barreled shotgun being held belly high by the whiskey-soaked store clerk with the bad breath and even worse looking tobacco stained teeth!

"Now you piece of shit Injun, lay that pannier down and hand me that pouch of coins where you got them two twenty dollar gold pieces from. Since you took them off a dead cavalry captain, I feel it is only right that I take them from your miserable carcass. And if you don't do as I tell you or you make just one false move, I will cut you in half with this here scattergun. Then, I will let the rest of your foul smelling kind who come in after 'you meet your Maker' this morning to clean up the mess," growled "whiskey breath."

Josiah White Buffalo laid down his full pannier alright. Right alongside the clerk's head with all the speed and might with which he could muster! It just so happened to be the pannier holding, among other items, the heavy twelve inch cast iron Dutch oven...Down went the clerk with a loud CLUMP onto the saw dust covered and tobacco spit stained wooden floor. But not before he had squeezed off one trigger of his double barrel shotgun at point blank range at Josiah White Buffalo's belly! That squeezing of the trigger was followed by a loud CLICK, as the hammer dropped onto the uncapped nipple of the shotgun. A nipple that did not have an ignition cap thanks to Josiah White Buffalo's quick thinking in removing it when the clerk had gone to the cash box to make change earlier in their transaction!

With that, Josiah White Buffalo leaped over the counter with his now drawn knife in hand and grabbing the stunned clerk's greasy long hair, twisted his head back and slit his throat clear to the glistening white vertebrae of his neck! Then Josiah White Buffalo stood up, picked up his pannier off the floor in the process to avoid the tell-tale staining rush of blood streaming all over the floor and vaulted back over the counter. As the blood squirted all over the place from the dying man's last heartbeats, he grabbed his throat and squirmed all over the floor smearing his blood even further amid gurgling and choking sounds. Soon he laid still except for numerous small twitches the body makes as it adjusted to life no more as 'it' had known it.

Reaching behind the counter onto a nearby shelve, Josiah White Buffalo calmly removed six boxes of Winchester .40-82 rifle cartridges from one stack of ammunition and the same number of .44 caliber pistol cartridges for his handgun from another. Throwing those into his pannier, he hoisted it over his shoulder, took the dead man's 12 gage shotgun in his right hand and smashed its exposed hammers and stock over the top of the counter rendering the weapon useless. With that he calmly walked out from the store, placed his pannier over the other side of his pack saddle to balance the load on his pack animal, mounted up, and turned his horses towards the south west. After all, Buffalo Bill had always told him if he ever needed a good job as a ranch hand, head to the small town of North Platte in Nebraska. His "Scouts Rest Ranch" of 4,000 acres laid just to the west of that town and he, Buffalo Bill, could always use another good hand. And once there as a ranch hand, he could earn thirteen dollars a month plus "found."

As he rode off from the agency store in the December morning's cold on the Standing Rock Indian Reservation, Josiah calmly glanced all around him. The cold wintery country side was barren of any other individuals who might have been out and about and recognized him coming from the trading post. Also, there was no sign of the hated Indian police. Realizing he was free and clear of any accusations of foul play, he hurried his horses onto a well-worn trail littered with previous hoof prints and droppings as he headed due south and west. After traveling several miles on the heavily traveled trail to hide the distinction of his horse's tracks, Josiah turned his horses cross country even further southwest as he headed for Buffalo Bill's Scouts Rest Ranch in Nebraska and a new life. After all, since he had now decided to return to the white man's world, he might as well start out as a cowboy. His love for that which was wild and the out of doors had been his life for many years. And in that profound style of living, he wished to continue in his now white world to be. That evening as he rested out under the stars along a frozen stream, he built a typically large and smoky white man's fire. Into that went all his previously worn buckskin clothing that would have marked him as an Indian. That was, all except his leather thong tied to a now well-worn sage grouse wing. That Indian symbol of his power had carried him safely thus far and he figured it would carry him the rest of the way until he was ready to join the Cloud People. Taking his frying pan, he melted a mess of snow over his fire until he had a pan full of water. Then Josiah took his knife and using the reflection of his head off the water in the light of the fire, removed his long braids and most of his remaining long Indian-like hair with his knife. Those many years of growth also went into the fire as did their memories. Finally, he crawled into some of his newly purchased white-man's clothing and in doing so, took the time to look himself over approvingly in the firelight. Lastly, the worn leather thong given to him by Sitting Bull during his earlier Sun Dance activities with the sage grouse wing still attached, was looped through his new pistol belt. Like Fast Antelope had advised, "Wear it well. For to remove it for any length of time as a white man acting as an Indian will bring the wearer nothing but a host of evil spirits." However, now that he was a white man once again, he found that he could not remove and throw away his sacred symbol. It had carried him through many dangerous situations and since it was a part of his previous life, it stayed...

The hot coffee tasted good that evening as did the roasted deer heart from a deer killed earlier in the creek bottom. The rest of the deer would be loaded onto the second pack horse the next morning and in the winter's cold air, would last him for the rest of his trip to a ranch in the white man's world. That night Josiah slept comfortably in his sleeping furs surrounded by his old namesake the heavy white buffalo robe. The prairie wolves and coyotes sang him to sleep that evening under the soft glow of the twinkling stars overhead and the dying light from his campfire. But before he drifted off, he thought back on his happy years as a Lakota and the people he had loved and lost. Then the possibilities of his new life began flooding through his mind and that was the last thing he remembered as the night and all its spirit world revelations, quietly overtook him.

Dawn the next morning, found Josiah Pike and his

pack string still heading due southwest. Days later found Josiah Pike just east of the Town of North Platte, Nebraska, as he traveled westerly along the North Platte River on its northern side.

Skipping the cattle and homesteader's settlement of North Platte because Josiah wasn't totally ready to reintegrate into the white man's society just yet, he kept to the well-traveled Oregon Trail. And being that it was still in the depths of winter, it was not traveled by wagon trains and hordes of people. (Author's Note: Wagon trains traveled the many routes west in the late spring, summer and early fall months. This they did to avoid the deep mud and snows of spring and late winter, plus their need for grass which was needed to 'fuel' their beasts of burden pulling the heavy wagons). Never having been in that part of the country for many years, Josiah missed the turnoff to Buffalo Bill's Scouts Rest Ranch. Finally realizing his mistake, he turned north from his path along the North Platte River, crossed the Oregon Trail and continued into the quiet Prairie hoping to run into a homesteader who could show him the way to Bill's ranch.

Riding through a heavily wooded draw later in the day, Josiah was all of the sudden drawn up short by something he had never seen before. It was an unusual fence running the full length of the draw. Josiah had never seen such a fence in his lifetime and he got off his horse to examine it more closely. It was a four strand wire fence alright but this one had sharp steel barbs woven into the main strands of wire every few inches! As it turned out, it was Josiah's first run in with a new to him type barbed wire fence. It was also a revelation that was to become a factor in making a major turn in Josiah's life, all though he did not know it at that moment in time.

"Ain't never seen such a 'cattle-holding' contraption ever before?" quietly came a voice from the draw's brush line a few yards distant. Josiah's surprise over having another human being so close was totally complete. First the new 'fangled' type of a fence and now the unknown close at hand stranger's voice coming at him from just a few distant yards.

Whirling and going for his pistol in surprise, Josiah heard the quiet voice from behind a dense stand of trees and winter dead brush once again. "Whoa there, Partner. Never meant you no harm. Just a-doin' my job of riding fence for my boss, "Ma Perkins." Who might you be all here out in the middle of nowhere and in the dead of a damn cold Prairie winter?" asked the mystery voice.

With that, a slimly built cowboy with a graying pencil thin mustache rode out from behind a dense stand of dormant choke cherry bushes that were "thicker than fleas on a dog's back." The "surprise cowboy" held his horse's reins in his one hand and his gun hand held high in the air signifying he meant no one any harm. That he did since he did not recognize what kind of a stranger he was dealing with and truly meant him no harm.

"You surprised the hell out of me," said Josiah, still showing signs of complete surprise.

"Didn't mean you no harm. You surprised me as well out here in the damn middle of nowhere in the dead of "Old Man Winter." My name is Oliver. Oliver Barnes. What handle do you go by cowboy?"

Relaxing because of the now approaching cowboy's

402

easy and friendly manner, Josiah replied with his "white man world given name."

"My name is Josiah. Josiah Pike. I missed the turnoff to where I figured was the direction to Buffalo Bill's ranch and was trying to find a homesteader who could provide me better directions than Bill had given me some months back."

"You know old Bill do ya?" asked Oliver as he rode right up to Josiah.

"Sure do. Used to ride in his Wild West show. He always said if I ever needed a job 'cowboyin' to head for his ranch and he would sign me up. I guess I got lost a little," continued Josiah with a sheepish grin on his face.

"You sure did, Partner," said Oliver as he removed his well-used leather glove and stuck out his hand to shake Josiah's. "But hell fire. If you need a job and you ain't stuck on working at Bill's ranch, how about trying out my bosses. It is a 6,000 acre spread just west of Bill's and she just lost her husband, Jim Perkins, to a damn bad horse wreck three weeks ago. "Ma Perkins" is always looking for a good hand or two as am I. Since I am her foreman, she has asked that I keep a sharp eye peeled for any good hands lookin' for work. How about givin' her a try. Especially now since many of her older hands up and rode off after her husband Jim was kilt. They did so because they was a-sayin' they ain't ranchin' or workin' for any female boss because it ain't right. But she is a good boss and a top hand in and of herself. Plus, she pays two dollars a month more than most spreads in these here parts. If you can ride, rope and shoot, how about givin' her a look-see. She keeps a clean bunk house and when she sets a spread for her hands in the evenings and on the weekends at the family table, it is a sight to behold for our sorry eyes," said Oliver with just a lilt of hope in his voice in persuading Josiah to come over to his line of thinking and look his job offer over.

"Well, I am not much of a roper but was raised on a farm and know what hard work is. Been around horses and mules all my life so it can't be all that bad just being a full time cowboy. And no, I am not fixed on working just for Bill. I just would welcome a nice place to work, a good place to eat, a warm place to sleep, and a steady job. Say, what does she pay a month?" asked Josiah as an afterthought.

"She pays fifteen a month if one has his own horse and saddle, two home cooked meals a day in her ranch house when her hands are working close to the headquarters and less than that for grub when out on a drive or on the trail. But, Ma doesn't allow no swearin' or drinkin' around the ranch headquarters unless she is a part of it. That way she keeps her hands from gettin' all liquored up and commence fighting one another. But away from the ranch she says all her boys can 'let her rip'," replied Oliver as he warmed up even more to the younger Josiah.

To Josiah, Oliver appeared to be in his 50's, was of slight build and had pale gray eyes that spoke to those of possibly being a 'great warrior' in his younger days in his white man world. He sat well in his saddle, his choice of horseflesh was splendid and his eyes were always moving taking in all the sights around him. Kind of like an Indian, thought Josiah. Then Josiah noticed faint notches in the wooden handle of Oliver's Colt .45 which was resting easily on his small hips. It was covered with what appeared to be notches deliberately cut into the wooden grips of his pistol!

That was when Oliver caught Josiah's gaze resting on the handle of his .45!

"Those notches were made in my earlier days when I was a U.S. Marshall in the Oklahoma Territory. I was younger then, quicker than greased lightning if given a fair chance and never drew unless the other man made the 'first move to meet his maker.' And, I never kilt anybody who didn't need killin'. Now that I am older and wiser, I just want a quiet place on the range to rest my bones, earn a day's pay for a day's work and rest my head without worry come sundown. I sense in your eyes and demeanor that is kind of like you. I have no regrets and left no bad tales behind me to be told in my absence. But those days of history aside, how about ridin' fence with me these last couple of miles so we can get better acquainted. Then when finished, we can head 'for the barn' and I can introduce you to my lady boss, Ma Perkins and some of her good home cookin'.' What do you say to that suggestion, cowboy?"

For the rest of that day until nightfall, Josiah rode with Oliver and got to begin to know the man. He turned out to be not only a gentleman but a damned good cowboy as Josiah was quickly learning from his actions. Oliver rode as if he were a living part of his horse, his ever moving eyes didn't miss a thing, and he heard many things going on around him before he 'saw what he had heard.' He swung to and from his horse like an Indian, had an easy gait when walking and reflexes like that of a snake in the warm sun. Every time he found a break in the fence, he had it fixed in short order from tools taken from his saddle bags and never wasted a movement or moment in doing so. Soon, both men were visiting easily like close friends would do as they worked the fences for any breaks as they drifted back towards the headquarters ranch. In the process, Josiah shared only his "expanded" version of life as a Missouri farmer, leaving out his portion of life as an Oglala/Lakota captive and warrior. Realizing most white men had fought the Indians in one way or the other with many a man still carrying a grudge, Josiah felt it best not to divulge any of his Indian background and just let those moments in time remain his and his alone. Plus, as was the way of the times, many men did not share their previous lives with anyone else or reflect on past questionable deeds they had performed. That they did figuring they were best left unsaid. However, a part of his background did arise later in the afternoon as Oliver repaired the top strand in the fence that had been broken by an elk that had not leaped high enough when trying to clear this new obstacle and had busted it in the process.

"Say Josiah, why do you wear that old sage grouse wing tied to your belt?" asked Oliver as he twisted the two broken strands of the barb wire fence expertly together with another short piece of wire. "Doesn't that damn thing get in the way when you need to make a quick draw and shoot?" he asked.

"That sage grouse wing was given to me by an old Indian holy man a long time ago as my symbol of strength and protection. I have never had anything bad happen to me as long as I wore it, so, I guess the damn thing works as a matter of fact," he replied quietly without any betraying emotion showing in his voice. In that reply, Josiah made sure his face did not reflect any other information other than that given as well. With that explanation, Oliver had no further questions regarding the odd looking and well-worn grouse wing hanging loosely from Josiah's belt. And to Josiah's way of thinking, that history was now long past and like Lakota tradition, one did not speak of the dead.

That evening, Josiah had the opportunity to meet Ma Perkins over a fried chicken, homemade gravy, mashed potatoes, pickled beets, and sourdough biscuits supper. Ma Perkins was an older women but Josiah noticed that she walked like a women born in the saddle and her bare arms not only showed some muscle but numerous scratches from pitching hay and other hard ranch work. Once again he had to inwardly grin. Being raised as an Indian he had learned many things. One was to always listen to what was being said and more importantly, how it was said. Another trait was to always keep one's eyes moving and "seeing" everything no matter where he was. When he did, it was amazing what he could see and learn from such "seeing." He liked what he saw in Ma Perkins and her other two most recently hired cowboys sitting around the supper table that evening. Liked what he saw in that Ma Perkins seemed to treat everyone sitting around the supper table like it were her own kids in a family setting. And to be quite frank, Josiah had a lot of room in his heart for more of the same when it came to being involved in a family setting or sort of way.

He had been previously introduced that first day to two other new men as they were washing up and combing their hair before coming into the ranch house for supper. The two new men and brothers were known as "Clifton and Thomas Davis." During supper's conversation with the Davis brothers who were new to the prairies and that way of life, they had numerous innocent questions for Josiah and he for them as they tried to get to know one another. Josiah was able to once again tell his story as if he had been a Missouri farmer 'for a long time' and had come west to seek his fortune instead of always looking at a mule's hind end all day behind a plow. Not to mention, always having to walk in fresh mule poop and smelling the methane 'perfume' emitted from that mule's hind end when he was straining while pulling the plow through difficult virgin ground after eating a big meal of fresh green clover. Those words brought lots of hearty laughter from all assembled over Josiah's way of presenting many of his funnier experiences. And just to be on the safe side, Josiah just expanded his life on a Missouri farm to account for his years, ignored his Indian upbringing which may of led to trouble around the supper table because of past animosities with the Indian culture, and let it go at that.

As for the Davis brothers, they were nothing short of a happy horse wreck. Josiah got an eye and ear full as he happily loaded up his plate for the second time on his first home cooked meal in weeks from the talkative brothers. First of all, the Davis brothers were happy as all get out to be working for Ma Perkins because she reminded them of their much loved mother that they had left back in a place they called Northern California. And in that sense of loneliness for their mom, made them more than talkative, which betrayed their easy and gentle style of living life to its fullest. Both brothers were well built and appeared to be just as stout as Josiah's dad's biggest mules back on their Missouri farm. However, they also appeared to be as quick as a cat even though each man weighed in at over two hundred pounds, a weight and size that was considered large for any man of that day.

Both men had started out their careers as apprentices to their equally stout father, a man named Marshall. A man who was considered one of the best blacksmiths and a friend to all who knew him in a place they called the Northern Sacramento Valley of California. Marshall had since passed but not before he had gifted to his sons his excellent work ethic, his joy of life and the great love and respect he held for his wife and their mother, "Sylvia." Both Clifton and Thomas had taken on their father's blacksmith trade and had prospered. Having done so, they then had invested in a paddle wheeler in order to expand their family business. Since the men lived in a small California town named Meridian on the Sacramento River, it was only natural they went into the paddle wheel, farm implement, and grain transportation business. Both men apparently had gifted mechanical abilities and as such, could fix anything mechanical, including an always balky steam engine on their new paddle wheeler. With their new paddle wheeler plying the farm trade up and down the Sacramento River, the boys had once again prospered. So much so, they named their sleek paddle wheeler after their much loved and respected mother,

Sylvia. Soon, their sleek new steam driven paddle wheeler bore the name on its proud bow of their beloved mother, "The Sylvia."

It was then the two boys quit shoveling in huge forkfuls of mashed spuds and gravy as their previously jovial attitude changed slightly. According to the boys, calamity struck soon thereafter. They had traveled upstream to the small river town of Colusa one fine fall day and had taken on a huge load of sacked grain to be transported down river to Sacramento, their state's capitol. Apparently according to Clifton, who liked to be called "Scooby or Skippy," they had mistakenly taken on to much grain for the draft of what their new paddle wheeler drew. Something they should have realized since the river was running low that time of the year. Halfway down the Sacramento River, their new paddle wheeler struck an unseen rock in the river and went to the bottom in about four minutes! Everyone escaped with their lives but the two boys' reputations as river captains suffered. With that single black mark against their names and no one wanting to take a chance shipping their products down river with them if they got another boat, their transportation business lagged. It was then that the Davis brothers decided to move back east and begin their lives anew in that part of the agriculturally-mining-cattle business developing United States. A part of the country that was hugely expanding in its farming and ranching industry now that the Indian menace had all but disappeared. Hence their fortuitous and timely arrival on Ma Perkins ranch and their new employment as blacksmiths and cowboys. Throughout supper that

410

evening, Josiah found himself easily laughing and having such a grand time with his new found friends, that he decided to sign on and become one of Ma Perkins cowboys as well. In turn, Ma Perkins was all too happy to hire on another good hand even if he couldn't rope 'worth sour owl droppings' as Josiah had somewhat 'off color for around the supper table' put it.

To Ma Perkins way of thinking, she was a good judge of horseflesh, breeds of cattle, grazing conditions on the range, and humans. And in that Josiah fellow, she figured she would now have another good cowboy in her midst working her spread. As for Oliver, the old man of the bunch and the outfits natural leader as well as the ranch foreman, along with the Davis brothers, they figured they had a good hand in Josiah and were looking forward to working with him even if he couldn't rope for 'sour owl droppings' and always wore a dumb looking sage grouse wing attached to his belt where ever he went, even to the outhouse...

Later that night after Ma Perkins had hired on Josiah, he lay there awake in his bunk thinking. Amidst the snoring and stale tobacco smells in the bunkhouse he felt a welcome calmness flooding over him. Once again, he felt he just might be considered as 'family' in and among the Ma Perkins ranch and her people. And again, he found it difficult not to think back over his many days as an Oglala/Lakota, his previous adoptive parents, Red Shirt, his sister Gemma, and his many adventures as a Sioux warrior. But that was then and this was now. He wished so hard he could be part of something not always in flux but permanent. Permanent in the closeness of friendships and a future. Amidst the snoring and the cooling of the bunkhouse since the fire in their potbellied stove had long since gone out, Josiah rested comfortably and warmly wrapped up in his old namesake the white buffalo hide. There was just something comforting in that old buffalo hide that evening as the winter's cold closed in and around his exposed face and nose. But the rest of his body and, his heart were once again warm with the thought of being one of "Ma Perkins boys…"

For the next five months of his life, Josiah learned what it meant to be a cowboy working for $15 dollars a month and "found." The men in the bunkhouse were up at the crack of dawn and did not return to wash up for supper until dark. The work was hard and sometimes dangerous but Josiah loved it. He along with the Davis brothers and Oliver were becoming a close knit band of brothers. As a result, Josiah learned to rope, build fence, ride and repair fence, deliver calves, make Dutch oven biscuits around a campfire, herd cattle, brand and ear notch the yearlings, repair wagons, shoe horses and with Clifton's help, learned the fundamentals of being a good blacksmith when it came to properly 'rimming' a wagon wheel or its hubs. As he learned and progressed in the trade, Josiah discovered many of the wonders of living in a white man's world. There were sometimes Saturday nights allowed in the Town of North Platte with all its sordid wonders of humanity. There were holidays celebrated that he had long ago forgotten about after being taken a captive and his white men relationships with the original ranch hands were now as close as he and Red Shirt had been. But more importantly, the other cowboys since hired and now working for Ma Perkins had accepted him as an equal for who he was and highly respected his everyday work ethic. By now, Ma Perkins had managed to hire eight other good hands who could "throw a loop" and a grouchy old bastard named "Cookie," who smelled of sweat, sour tobacco juice and raw onions for the ranch's cook when the hands were out on the range for extended periods of time. As for the "grouchy old bastard" hired as a cook, he could make Dutch oven biscuits and pie crusts that were so light, one had to eat them fast or they would drift off into the air. However, his brand of coffee was so stout that when drinking it, it was like partaking of an angry mule's kick. And more than once when a cowboy was cut up by accident, the cook could sew a 'whip stitch' over any kind of wound that was "smoother than a school marm's thigh…"

Ma Perkins original ranch only had 1,000 out of its 6,000 acres fenced. Since more and more homesteaders were moving into the country and letting their livestock range for all the 'free grazing' they could get, a fence around the ranch's external boundaries soon became a necessity. Initially, Ma Perkins had her cowboy's string up a four strand barb wire fence on the 1,000 acre piece. But, many of her neighbors objected over what they claimed when using a barb wire fence was a cruel way of injuring their free ranging cattle and sheep. But Ma Perkins persisted, finding it was more useful in keeping her beeves on her home range and not having them being 'hit' with a running iron and all of the sudden becoming someone else's "meat on the hoof." Or, her registered stock, after being bred by the running-loose homesteader's mangy stock, causing her quality cows to drop their calves at all times in the worst part of the winter months unexpectedly. And in doing so, causing an unacceptable loss in her herd's annual production through the loss of calves freezing to death born during blizzards. Soon all her neighboring ranchers and settlers called a meeting of all the area homesteaders in order to present their grievances regarding using the new and what they considered cruel barbed wire fences. The local sentiment was they had always been able to free graze on any open lands and now by damned, they were going to continue come hell or high water with their old grazing practices. However at that meeting, Buffalo Bill also advised he was going to fence in his ranch as well because of the rampant outside grazing and the constant mixing of herds and mangy range cattle bloodlines with his blooded livestock. With his support for the new fencing program, that pretty well put out the fire from the outraged nesters over their free grazing and barbed wire concerns. It was about then that most realized the untamed old west was on its way to becoming tamed. From then on, it was a race to get the ranch fenced in and the nesters and their wandering cattle and sheep fenced out.

On one of those occasions when Josiah and Oliver were riding the range in an attempt to keep some of their cows yet unfenced on their own property and not into the nesters gardens or destroying their young orchards, they rode upon an ugly discovery. A cow giving birth to a late calf had been discovered by a predator, killed and partially consumed! All that remained of the newborn calf was part of its afterbirth. Dismounting and without giving it a second thought, Josiah put his earlier learned tracking skills as an Indian to work. Grabbing his new Winchester Model 1886 .40-82 out from its scabbard, he jacked in a cartridge, dropped the hammer to a safe-half cock position and began examining the kill site. It didn't take him long to ascertain who was the cattle killing culprit. The tracks around the kill scene brought back some old 'black' memories...The tracks were from the unmistakable, long- clawed grizzly bear! A huge predator that had been born, breed and fed on the large herds of buffalo that once roamed the Plains. Now that such legendary critters were gone, the grizzly had been forced to feed on the next best thing such as the newly established herds of cattle and sheep that now dotted the Plains. Taking off at a ground eating trot with his Winchester in hand like an Indian, Josiah was closely followed by his friend Oliver riding his horse and leading Josiah's. For about a mile, Josiah tracked the bear in a fast trotting and head down manner watching the cold trail in traditional Indian style without giving it a second thought. Oliver, riding behind the fast moving Josiah, did so in amazement. The last time he had observed such fast tracking techniques being utilized, it had been when he was after a killer in the Indian Territory of Oklahoma and while using an Indian as his guide! He saw little difference in how that guide had tracked the cold trail of the much hunted killer and Josiah performing the same technique on the grizzly bear...That was, running along the cold set of tracks with one's head looking down while moving at a ground eating pace off to one side of the trail to avoid disturbing the original track. And in doing so, only occasionally looking up to see one's direction of travel and if any danger was close at hand.

Rounding a much rubbed smooth bolder left by the glaciers, Josiah dropped into a heavily brush lined gully. (Author's Note: Even on the prairies of today, if one is observant, they may discover large old boulders sticking up out in the middle of nowhere in the prairie soil. Boulders that were left behind when the glaciers melted and receded many thousands of years ago. Closer examination of those large boulders will many times reveal a well-worn deep trail still visible all around the base of that boulder. And, the sides of that boulder will be worn smoother than a new born baby's hind end after a bath from the thousands of buffalo, who over many years of time, historically used it to rub on, loosen and remove old scratchy hair left over from the winter). Shades of the last time he had gone into such a gully only to step upon the back of a sleeping grizzly in his day bed, thought Josiah with a grimace. Slowing his pace, Josiah began quietly walking out the track of the cattle killer instead of moving at his usual ground eating gait. Dropping down into the bottom of the steep gully, Josiah now slowed his pace to that of a silent stalk. On the hillside top of the gully, Oliver staked the horses, grabbed his single shot, .45-70 Springfield Trapdoor rifle and began following Josiah quietly as he could along the rim as he looked into the bottom of the gully at Josiah's progress. In doing so, he was amazed at just how quietly Josiah was stalking the great and many times when aroused or cornered, extremely dangerous species of bear. A species of bear that was fast disappearing from the prairies in the face of the many settlers moving out onto the range and the predator hunters roaming and removing the last remnants of the wolves and grizzly bears that remained.

For the next twenty minutes, Josiah stalked the now fresh tracks of the bear in the soft mud of the small creek that was trickling down the gully in which he now slowly moved with caution. Then there it was! The strong stench of rotting meat, urine and sour feces impregnated mud hanging thickly in the air...Slowing his stalk to where he was almost imperceptive in his movement, Josiah laid his big Winchester against his shirt and quietly cocked the hammer. The next thing he knew was he was looking up into a brush patch at the great bear facing him from above and just a few feet away! Quickly swinging his rifle, Josiah shoved its barrel almost into the chest of the bear and touched it off! BOOM, went the heavy cartridge and instantly Josiah's world exploded! As the roaring and injured bear hurtled himself at Josiah, he fell over backwards but his many years of instinct as an Indian took over and he quickly jacked another shell into the chamber of his rifle as he fell! Then Josiah was completely buried under 850 pounds of a frothing at the mouth and now insane with pain, wounded grizzly!

Up on the gully bank and upon seeing the attacking bear, Oliver swung his rifle toward the maddened animal and snapped off a shot of one of his heavy .45-70 slugs into its back of the thrashing bear. In doing so, he took a chance on injuring Josiah if his bullet went clear through the bear and into his partner who by now laid completely out of sight buried under the enraged bear...But in the end his shot was true. The grizzly was so large that the .45-70 bullet just broke the bear's spine and lodged itself into the chest muscle on the underside. Just as Oliver fired, he heard another somewhat muffled BOOM! That time, Josiah had the presence of mind, although laying under an enraged grizzly bear trying to kill him, to shoot from that somewhat awkward position. With that shot which went under the chin of the bear and out the top side of its head, it groaned, crumpled, and laid quivering and bleeding profusely on top of Josiah!

"Josiah! Josiah! Are you alright? Say something!" screamed Oliver as he scrambled off the side of the gully's wall and down to the battle scene below, stumbling and almost falling head first into the mound of dead bear in the process.

"Oliver. Quit yelling. I am fine except this damn bear is squashing the life out of me with its great weight. Get the damn stinking bleeding son-of-a-bitch off me and hurry afore I expire or drown in his blood," yelled Josiah.

As Oliver tossed his rifle off to one side, reached down and hefted up the bears dripping head, Josiah was able to crawl out from under the dead animal. Scooting his bottom out from under the dead bear with Oliver's lifting help, Josiah took a moment to get his breath back and let his heart rate slow down to that of a normal human being. Finally, he was able to stand. He stood wobbly at first over his near death experience and then quietly thanked the Great Spirit for His help. To Josiah's way of thinking, he may now be a white man but it surely didn't hurt to call on the Great Spirit every once in a while when one was in a tight spot...Then with a quick look, it dawned on him! His Grouse wing! It was gone! Grabbing the bear's head and telling Oliver to help him, the two men managed to get the animal partially rolled over. When they did, Josiah saw his sage grouse wing laying in the soft sand of the gully bottom all smeared with blood. Reaching down, he quickly picked up the grouse wing, cleaned it off as best as he could and quickly reattached it back on his belt where it belonged.

"There," he said to no one in particular, "now that I have my good luck charm back at my side, I once again will be alright."

"Damn, you sure weren't kidding when I asked you earlier about that grouse wing and you told me an Indian holy man had given it to you as a good luck charm. It damned sure worked to my way of thinkin'," said a still amazed Oliver. However, something still hung heavy in the back of his mind. The way Josiah had so expertly cold tracked that grizzly bear across the dry Prairie soil reminded him of his expert Indian tracker back in Oklahoma. The same tracker that he had used to cold track down killers hiding from the white authorities in the Oklahoma Indian Territories. There was no way any white man except maybe an old time Mountain Man, could cold track a critter like Josiah had just done. That was pure and simply an Indian technique. Yet, how could it be? Josiah was a blue-eyed white man? Being an old time law man with great powers of observation, his interest was now more than piqued over what he had just observed. That was something he was going to have to get to the bottom of or hell was a cold place to be in," thought Oliver.

Together the two men skinned out the old boar grizzly. Its hide had not been too badly rubbed and both men figured a good pair of chaps made from the grizzly hide would be a great reminder of an earlier adventure. However, getting the smelly, blood soaked hide back to the ranch house was somewhat problematic. Neither riding horse would initially carry the hide. Finally, Josiah mounted his horse and Oliver gently hefted the hide up onto the lap of Josiah. Then and only then his horse would transport the bloody hide... but just barely!

On the way back to their ranch house to clean up and show everyone what happens to 'those' who chose to eat someone else's beef, Oliver could contain his questions no more. "Josiah, where did you learn to track like an Indian?" Oliver asked as he studied the man's face for any suspect 'physical tells' like he had learned early on to do as a mostly solitary lawman.

For the longest time, Josiah said nothing in response to Oliver's intruding question. It was then that he realized there was no way he could forever keep his secret in the white man's world of being a captive of the Oglala/Lakota Indians since being a young man. Turning to Oliver who had been a true friend ever since they had first met, in fact, he was almost like a father figure, Josiah spoke forth with a "straight tongue."

"Oliver, I was taken captive at age fourteen by a band of Oglala/Lakota Indians who attacked and wiped out my parents and all the other members of my wagon train except my twelve year old sister, while on the Oregon Trail not far from here. The Indians raised me and treated me as one of their own in the years following. In doing so, they taught me many of their ways. Eventually I became a warrior in the band and fought many battles against the white man. When my last adoptive Indian father was killed, I decided it was time to leave the Indian way of life and go forth as a white man. Hence, I am here. Now, I wish to not talk about that chapter in my life anymore because it holds lots of heartache memories not only for me but for many others negatively impacted by the actions of hostile Indians. Can you understand how I feel?"

Oliver rode alongside Josiah for a piece as if processing what he had just heard. Then he turned to Josiah and said, "Josiah, we have been like brothers these last few months. I have no problem with the life you have led. I appreciate you sharing that with me and as far as I am concerned, it is a closed chapter in our lives unless you bring it up once again. For you see, I totally understand. I am from a captured white mother and a Cherokee father and have seen both sides like you. A brother is a brother and now, we must not speak further of the "dead." Now, we have a bear hide to get back to the ranch and get de-fatted and processed before it gets all fly blown." With Oliver's surprising revelation, no mention of either man's earlier life history was directly made ever again.

As it turned out, Josiah only had three horse wrecks on the way back to the ranch headquarters when his horse had enough of the stinking, moving around hide and began 'sun-fishing' to rid himself of his smelly, worrisome load. But eventually the hide was brought back to the ranch, tanned and Thomas Davis, also a skilled worker of leather, made it into two pair of chaps for Josiah and Oliver. Upon receipt of those finished products, Josiah and Oliver wore them proudly in memory of their 'quiet' afternoon riding the range with a grizzly bear as a surprising "companion."

One evening during a Saturday supper hour back at the ranch headquarters, Ma Perkins tinkled her fork on her drinking glass. Sitting around the super table now sat twelve cowboys and the camp cook. Once she had everyone around the table's attention she began. "Gentlemen, we have a problem. The Beachums, Sullies and Grovers have recently complained to me that our herds of cattle on the north end of the ranch are grazing on their lands, eating everything in their gardens and trampling their newly planted orchards and shelter belts. Here is what I propose we do in order to remain good neighbors. I will order two more wagon loads of barbed wire and have them delivered from back east by the train into North Platte. In the meantime, I want all of you to head to the bottoms on the Platte and cut me a mess of fence posts so that we might use them to close off our north pasture. That way, I will have the entire ranch fenced and can be a better neighbor to the surrounding settlers once that is done. When my wire arrives, we will load up our wagons with fence posts and fence off the entire north end of our ranch. My plan is to have Cookie here set up a permanent camp in the middle of the work area and have an east and a west side team start fencing from our existing fences on the east and west side of the ranch. Both teams will work towards and meet in the middle. That way, our entire ranch will be fenced and pastured and then those damn nesters can go to hell. As a reward, I will meet all of you there in the middle with Cookie and have a 'blow-out' for all the hard work you have done. I will make sure there will be plenty of whiskey there for all to drink and you can hoot and holler all you want out there on the prairie without rufflin' any feathers of the good folks back in the Town of North Platte. How does that sound? And if you are really good, I will see to it that there will be fresh Dutch oven pies every evening after a day's work has been done."

There was a happy murmur around the supper table as the hands grinned at the thought of finally having all the fence work done and not having to chase Ma Perkins cattle all over "hell and creation." Then the specter of fresh pies every evening arose and the men all had grins like pigs in slop. Finally super really got interesting. Ma Perkins excused herself from the table as the homemade pies were being served and returned with two quarts of "Grizzly Bear Whiskey" in celebration of ridding the range of a fierce cattle predator, the survival of Josiah and Oliver and the opportunity for the ranch to be fenced in for once and forever. That supper was one that was long remembered.

For the next two weeks, the men with their single-buck cross-cut saws and axes cut and stacked hundreds of fence posts harvested from the North Platte River bottoms. At the end of every day, the fence posts were loaded into wagons and hauled back to the main ranch house. Soon there was a small mountain of fence posts stacked higher than a "cats back in a dog fight." Then the real work began. Wagon load after wagon load of fence posts were transported to the north side of the ranch and following out the flagged areas signifying the ranch's exterior boundaries, row after row of fenced posts were spaced out until the entire north side of the ranch was strewn with the posts. About then the train delivered several wagon loads of the new barbed wire and it too was soon spaced out in rolls waiting for it to be strung. The two crews then started from the east and western sides of the already fenced portions of the ranch and began digging fence post holes as they worked toward each other. And true to Ma Perkins word, Cookie set up his chuck wagon and the men's bed rolls and extra strings of horses in an area central to the work site. It was then that Ma Perkins added the real 'tease' to the hard working men. She offered a twenty dollar gold piece to each man on the team that finished his side of the fence building first! Man, the race was now really on between the two teams and most did not want to quit building fence until it got so dark one could hardly see his hand in front of his face. But the work went on, the holes were dug, posts were set and the wire literally sang as it was being strung. At the end of that month, the work was finally done. Ma Perkins rode the entire northern external boundary of her now completely fenced ranch and pronounced it "fit as a fiddle."

Then being Ma Perkins and proud of 'her boys', she sprung her last surprise on her hard working fence crews. Each man who had worked so hard got a twenty dollar gold piece no matter who finished first and then, she had invited the nearby settlers to a party out on the prairie at the center finish site for an evening of dancing, roast beef over an open spit, homemade pies and biscuits galore and of course, her promised bottles of whiskey! But in that move, she held the ace of spades up her sleeve. By inviting the nearby lonely settlers who were always ready for a party, who would in turn bring their daughters for the dance to be held out on the open Prairie, she knew her whiskey drinking cowboys would behave themselves and not get roaring drunk in front of the people at the party. Especially in front of all those eligible young ladies. She was right on...

"Who said women were the weaker sex," grinned Oliver as he watched the party on the prairie unfold and remain civil until the last nester had packed up and ridden for home. By then the men were so exhausted from all the eating and dancing, all they wanted was to go to bed and Josiah Pike was one of the first to "hit the hay."

Two weeks later after the big 'Party on the prairie', Oliver was riding fence along the north pasture checking in on about 30 steers being finished off for the market. Not seeing any in the big pasture and figuring they were somewhere in an adjacent draw he headed for the gate. When he got to the gate, it was down and from the shod horse tracks on the ground, the steers had been herded out and headed west! In alarm, he took off at a gallop following the tracks and was soon turned back when he discovered his small herd of steers had been mixed in with a larger herd of beeves on the move and were no longer traceable as those belonging to Ma Perkins. That was because those steers so taken had yet to be branded! Turning south, Oliver rode hell bent for the ranch headquarters. Storming into the area around the headquarters on a 'flagging' horse, he drew his pistol and fired one shot into the air to get everyone's attention!

Breaking out from a nearby bucking corral where Josiah had been breaking horses and out from the blacksmith shop where they had been making horse and mule shoes were the Davis brothers. All the rest of the hands were in the process of pushing another herd of cattle to the North Platte railhead for shipment to the packing houses.

Bailing off his horse, Oliver broke for the bunk house shouting, "Let's go boys. Get your gear together and we are riding toward Oglala after a mess of our just rustled steers! Rustlers passing by with their larger herd just opened our north gate and took what they wanted of the boss's stock. Maybe we can't tell our steers from theirs because ours have yet to be branded but we sure as hell can stretch a rope from the nearest cottonwood with every one of those thieving bastards' necks in a noose for what they did."

All four men ran for the bunk house to gather up their bed rolls and particulars for what they figured had to be a long and rough ride and then ran to the corrals to get their riding horses. Saddling up horses for themselves and a fresh mount for Oliver since his was spent in the race for the ranch house, the three men waited in a mounted group as Oliver spoke to Ma Perkins. In that hurried conversation, Ma Perkins advised she would ride for North Platte and get the sheriff and a posse to begin trailing the rustlers. In the meantime, she told Oliver to begin the chase since the trail was still hot and take along whoever he needed to get the job done. And, make sure he had lots of rope in case a 'neck-tie' party was in the offing...With that, she sped off to saddle her riding horse for the ride into the Town of North Platte laying to the east.

Oliver sprinted back to his fresh mount, quickly checked his bedroll to make sure he had his slicker and mounted his new horse. "Josiah, you ride in front with me. I want you to examine the tracks left in the north pasture and tell me what you are seeing. Then we will decide to do that which is best for our success in getting back our stock."

Josiah just nodded and then the four men sped out of the gated area near the headquarters and headed for the north pasture. Only this time, they did not exhaust their horses because those they were after were pushing slow moving beeves. And to push them hard would only run the weight of their rustled herd and that would not do when the buyers were weighing the animals prior to being purchased.

An hour later the four men reached the open gate at the north pasture. When they did, Oliver halted the men a short distance away from where he had discovered the original tracks so he could let Josiah dismount and examine the ground for himself. It was apparent that Oliver had quickly learned during the grizzly bear tracking event who was the best cold tracker on the ranch.

Bending over and examining the ground, Josiah took care to make sure of what he was seeing. After a few moments, Josiah returned to the group of riders sitting on their mounts. "There are seven men riding. Five of the men are riding shod horses and two of the men are riding unshod horses. Probably half breed Indians are riding those unshod horses. Those riding the unshod horses are trailing two heavily loaded pack horses and the group is traveling due west. My guess would be the stock yards and railroad livestock loading docks in Oglala. The tracks are about one day old because the dirt has not tumbled into the hoof prints and the dust spiders have not made their webs in the tracks either," reported a stern faced Josiah.

With that report in mind, Oliver said, "Let's go boys. We have some ground to make up if we want to get those beeves back before they are loaded and end up in the Omaha or the Denver stockyards. They have a good head start on us and if they are going to Oglala, we have a good thirty miles to go so let's ride."

For the rest of that day and into the night under a full moon, the four men rode. Not hard mind you but they did cover the ground in such a manner they didn't wear out their stock. Come dark when the moon was covered with cloud cover and they could no longer easily follow the trail, the men stopped, laid out their bedrolls and staked out their horses so they could feed. Always part of an Indian, Josiah walked on ahead for another mile to see if he could see any light from a fire from those unsuspecting that they were being followed so closely. He had also wanted to go ahead by himself. If he was right and there were two Indian cattle rustlers in the bunch, they would be smart enough to be watching their back trail. And he sure as hell did not want to ride blindly into an ambush. He still was wearing his sacred grouse wing and he knew that would carry him through any battle but the rest of his party had no such symbol of their power to protect them. "Plus, the two Davis brothers were big men and would make easy targets and he sure as hell did not want to have to dig such a big grave out on the prairie in which to bury such big carcasses," he thought with a half in jest smile.

Then there it was! Not another mile distant, Josiah could see a small twinkling light of a campfire at the bottom of a ridge line next to the North Platte River. An hour later, Josiah had crept to within thirty yards of the suspect campfire. And off in the distance in the river bottom, he could hear a herd of cattle bawling! Sure as he had figured, there were seven men gathered around their campfire having supper. Two of the men appeared to be Indians dressed in white man's clothing. But it was obvious the men had been drinking and were having a good time over their new found fortune in the extra thirty ready for sale cattle. Then Josiah froze! Standing there in the back light of the men's campfire stood one David Briggs! The one and same man who had threatened him back when he worked in the Buffalo Bill Wild West Show after Briggs had slammed his horse into the side of Josiah's unexpectedly out of pure damn meanness...The very one who had threatened to stomp Josiah for pointing his rifle at Briggs out of instinct when the affront had happened and then was discovered by Buffalo Bill threatening Josiah and fired on the spot.

That was all he needed to see as he slipped away from the seven cattle rustlers and began moving as fast as he could back to his small band of brothers so they could formulate a battle plan for the four of them to take on the seven of them and somehow get Ma Perkins herd of cattle back.

Daylight the following morning found four sets of narrowed eyes watching seven cattle rustlers fixing their breakfast around a smoky campfire. It was obvious from the size and 'sign' their campfire was leaving, the rustlers had no thought of being tailed by the law or anyone else. About then, the two Indians mounted up and rode their back trail to see if they had been followed during the night. Seeing nothing and satisfied over their wellbeing, they rode back to their camp with that information. Then Briggs could be heard telling the men to head for the river and bring up a small herd of cattle and move them into their makeshift corral by their campsite. This they did then all the men breakfasted, as their small branding fires next to the bawling cattle in the corral heated up several sets of running and branding irons.

After breakfast, the seven men adjourned to the cattle and as two of the men roped and dogged down a steer, another would alter the brand on the side of the animal with a running iron or brand those not branded with their own branding iron. This they did to Ma Perkins stock since they were unbranded. To all other cattle stolen from other ranchers carrying a brand, a quick bit of work with a running iron changed that original brand to one of the rustlers liking. Then the men rubbed fresh cow flop and urine wetted mud from the corral onto the freshly branded area to make it look weathered. With that, the freshly altered animal was moved off into another roped off area and the process was repeated on another beef. As the seven men were engrossed in their 'running-iron' and branding activities, they did not see four determined men in the dense river bottom brush closing in on them from different points of the compass. As it stood, Oliver had seen enough. And being the ranch foreman, had decided the seven rustlers would be given a chance to surrender. Barring that, they would be cut down by rifle fire from the four hidden men once a signal was given if the rustlers did not comply with his command to throw down their weapons. The plan was to have Oliver yell at the seven men, let them know they were surrounded and for them to drop their weapons. If they failed to do so, Oliver would yell "FIRE" and the rustlers were to be cut down where they stood. Oliver just figured men who lived by the sword would die by it as well and that included a rifle bullet and not hanging from a lone oak tree, all the while messin' up a good throwing rope...

As the four men laid there hidden and ready to go, Josiah could not help but notice all the white men were the same men who had joined Briggs in the underground stock holding area at the show in England and were going to join in on 'teaching' Josiah a lesson in manners for standing up to Briggs. It was then that Buffalo Bill had intervened and fired the lot. As a parting shot, Briggs had told Josiah that if their paths ever crossed again, that he, Briggs, would see to it that Josiah went to the 'Happy Hunting Grounds'! Somehow under the present set of circumstances, Josiah did not feel that would be the way things were going to occur that fine day after all the smoke had cleared out and blown away in the ever shifting Prairie winds...

Slowly standing up alongside a large cottonwood tree, Oliver raised his rifle and yelled, "Hey! You there by the corral. Drop your weapons and raise your hands. You are branding rustled cattle and I aim to take all of you back to North Platte and let the mess of you stretch a rope..."

The rustlers' response to Oliver's message was a face full of cottonwood bark and splinters sailing into Oliver's face from a quickly fired shot by one of the rustlers! Then the air was full of explosions as rifle and pistol bullets went every which way but loose. The Indians were the first to fall because they ran right at a kneeling Josiah yelling and screaming their death songs. Being hit in the chest with a heavy lead slug from Josiah's .40-82 Winchester, made for a mess of the two men's life style...Two of the rustlers broke for their tethered horses only to be cleared out from their saddles by the accurate shooting of the Davis brothers! Briggs went for his horse and as it took off running, he only got one foot in a panicked horse's stirrup for about thirty yards and then he was able to swing into the saddle. Then Briggs did what the Indians had done during the Battle of the Rosebud. Instead of riding off sitting upright in the saddle, he laid flat out over his horse's neck and presented almost no target. The two Davis brothers, instead of killing the horse and then Briggs, tried to hit Briggs just like the cavalry had done in the Rosebud Battle. Soon, Briggs was safely out of sight! By then there were so many bullets flying back and forth no one knew who had killed the other three rustlers from the Briggs Gang...But, they were all dead just the same when the smoke had cleared.

Stepping out from their places of concealment, Ma Perkins cow hands quietly stood there drinking in what had just occurred. Men had died. But those that had, were long overdue in the wraps of the Grim Reaper to all of those who were still standing at the edge of the killing field. The only casualty was Oliver. He was still picking bits and pieces of wood chips and splinters from his damaged face from the impact of a close at hand almost killing shot that went into the side of the tree in which he had been using as concealment. But he would live and that was more than one could say for the man from the Briggs Gang who had fired the first shot at Oliver, only to be rewarded with hot lead instead of cold wood splinters for his behavior.

Then looking around, the men noticed that Josiah was nowhere to be found. Shortly after that, they could hear him coming on his horse which had been staked out back on the trail like the devil was on his heels. As he stormed by, Josiah said, "I am going after Briggs. I will be back once I kill that cattle rustling son-of-a-bitch!" With that, Josiah was gone in more flying dirt clods uprooted by his horse.

"Josiah is pretty good at taking care of himself. Besides, I think that Briggs fellow caught a bullet in his foot and he can't get far. Keep your ears peeled for Josiah's shot you brothers. In the meantime, we need to get these cattle rounded up and headed back to our ranch before someone else lays claim to them," said Oliver as he continued watching his friend Josiah riding off after the leader of the rustlers.

For two days Josiah tracked Dave Briggs. Then on the morning of the third, he discovered Briggs's dead horse. The animal had been run so hard, that he had just collapsed and died from an exploded heart from being over exerted. Watching all around him, Josiah began tracking David Briggs as he limped away from his dead horse. Oliver had been right, Briggs had been wounded and was leaving an easy to follow stumbling trail marked with occasional splotches of dark blood. Knowing that cornered animals and humans who were wounded could be deadly, Josiah carefully stalked his enemy on foot. Into the early afternoon Josiah continued stalking Briggs until he spotted the man at a distance, using a limb for a crutch as he slowly walking along the edge of the Platte River. Every now and then he would stop for a drink and then continue pushing on after checking his back trail. Realizing where his direction of travel would take him, Josiah quietly set off to intercept Briggs. An hour later, Briggs, struggling along on his wounded foot, was surprised to see Josiah facing him as he sat on a downed cottonwood log directly in his path.

Once Josiah recognized that he had been spotted, he slid off his log and said to Briggs, "Dave, you are done for. I am here to take you back to North Platte and turn you over to the sheriff. You have a choice. You can go back in the saddle or across it. You make the call."

"What? Is that you Josiah White Buffalo? You will play hell you blue-eyed son-of-a-bitch in taking me in alive," muttered Briggs. The rest of that moment was a blur. Briggs was faster on the draw than Josiah and got off the first shot which hit him along the side, breaking a rib in the process!

Surprised at Briggs's speed in drawing and shooting his pistol, Josiah was spun sideways by the impact of the bullet and slammed back into the downed cottonwood log on which he had been sitting while waiting for Briggs to hobble his way. Quickly recovering from being shot and reaching for his dropped rifle, that was when Briggs got off another shot which grazed Josiah's right hip, blowing his sage grouse wing clear off his side and sending it spinning high into the air and into a nearby brush patch! Realizing his rifle was a 'no-go' because its lever had been caught in the brush when dropped, Josiah drew his pistol and snapped off at shot at Briggs. When he did, Briggs dropped immediately to his knees and rolled forward onto his belly stone cold dead from a head shot! Making sure he was dead, Josiah then staggered over to his horse which was tethered to a small sapling on a sandy flat near the Platte River. Tearing off a piece of the tail of an extra shirt carried in his bedroll, Josiah managed to stem the flow of blood from the wound in his side. Painfully staggering over to another log at the edge of the sandy clearing he sat down as his head spun like the 'blue blazes' from the shock of being hit. After an hour of rest he felt better and the haze of pain had finally left his eyes but his side still burned like all get out. It was then that Josiah realized his grouse wing was nowhere to be seen! He then realized it must have been lost it in the fight with Briggs! Walking slowly back to the body of Briggs, Josiah looked all around in vain for his grouse wing. It was nowhere to be found...By then the pain from his side was clearly getting the better of him and he returned to his sitting log in the sandy clearing and gently sat down.

Sitting there on that log, Josiah all of the sudden realized that he had been to this exact same spot before! Then he noticed a ring of rocks that had sheltered a long time gone campfire. Looking all around the sandy flat, he saw pieces of wood, old steel wagon rims, wagon wheel hubs and other pieces of strap metal that had been part of a covered wagon many years earlier. Then he noticed the signs of old burnt wood scattered all around. Burnt wood from a small wagon train that had camped there along the Oregon Trail and had come to deadly grief. Shaking his head to clear out the remaining cob webs, Josiah noticed the foot hills across the Platte River and then, he got the connection! This was the exact spot where his family's wagon train had been ambushed and everyone killed except for him and his sister Gemma many years earlier!

Then the memories came flooding back. The foothills where he had stalked the huge covey of sage grouse early in the morning. The area where his uncle Lemuel and cousin Jordan had grazed their livestock from the night before. The spot where the wagons had been circled before being attacked by the Oglala/Lakota. Where the wagons had been looted and then burned. Then he saw it! There was a bleached out white skull showing signs of having been split open by a tomahawk. It was in the spot where his uncle Otis had been sitting when he had been in charge of keeping the central fire going and staying awake on watch for any sign of hostile Indians...His split skull and a few rib bones were all that remained partially buried in the sand.

Josiah's head was really spinning so much now with what he was seeing and remembering, that he had to sit back down on his log and collect his thoughts. Several hours later as the sun had long since set, Josiah rose on wobbly legs, staggered back to his horse and painfully unrolled his bed roll. Staking out his horse so he could feed, Josiah laid down on his bedroll and was soon fast asleep. In fact, it turned out to be one of the best sleeps he had in a long time. And it was good to have such a sleep since he had felt so poorly the day before because of his non-life threatening side wound...But by damn, his cracked rib hurt like the blazes every time he made a quick movement toward his wounded side and that included any breaths of air taken.

Chapter Twelve

A CIRCLE OF WAGONS AND A COVEY OF SAGE GROUSE

Waking the next morning to the calls of many sandhill cranes passing overhead, Josiah felt much better. To his way of thinking, the long and deep sleep had been just what he needed. "That good feeling and something to eat since he had not eaten in three days would be nice," he thought! Then off on the prairie side of the river in the dawn's first light, he heard a roar of hundreds wings from a huge flock of sage grouse thundering into the air. Moments later, the huge flock of over 300 grouse whirred noisily overhead and landed on the far side of the shallow river at the edge of the foothills.

"A roasted grouse cooked over an open fire would go great for his breakfast," he thought, as he carefully laid back his bedroll covers in light of his still painfully burning side. Plus, if I can kill a big one, I can replace my lost grouse wing with another and hope my powers transfer into my new wing, he mused hopefully. Reaching carefully over to his side where his rifle laid, he slowly wrapped his fingers around the comforting steel of his rifle and slowly rose to his feet, using it as a crutch in the process. Still a little dizzy from his side wound, he thought, "A .40-82 bullet is a little large in which to kill a grouse but if he could hit one in the head he could have one hell of a breakfast. And right now, his belly was telling him that was a good idea." With that, Josiah jacked a shell into the rifles chamber and walked slowly across the sandy flat as he eyed the landing place of the flock of sage grouse.

Moving slowly through the dense brush alongside the Platte River because of the nagging pain in his side, Josiah waded across the water in a shallow section of the river. Heading slowly up the steep foothill toward the spot where he had last seen the sage grouse land, he gasped for breath over his exertion and sharp pain emanating from his side wound. Closing in on the spot where the grouse were last seen, Josiah slowed even further in order to let his racing heart relax and let the pain in his side subside. Moving slowly toward a thick stand of grass and sage brush, an ideal place for a grouse to hide, Josiah spied the head of a large grouse snap upward at the sign of the approaching human danger. Slowly, ever so slowly, Josiah raised up his rifle and took a careful bead on the grouse's head. The grouse, suspecting something was out of the ordinary standing just a few feet distant, didn't even blink. Its dark eyes just remained focused on the new object to its front looking for any signs of danger. Slowly placing his trigger finger on the trigger, Josiah took in a deep breath, then slowly let it out just as he began squeezing. As he did, he failed to see that the end of his rifle barrel was obstructed! The day before in the shootout with Briggs, Josiah's rifle had caught in the brush and he couldn't quickly use it to return fire. So, he dropped his rifle in the brush patch and then used his handgun to kill Briggs. When he dropped his rifle into the brush patch, Josiah failed to see a dead wooden branch inadvertently jam up into the end of the rifle barrel and firmly lodge...Slowly, slowly, Josiah began pulling the trigger of his rifle so as not to jerk his carefully aimed shot at the grouse's small head...

Suddenly there was a bright flash of light across the back of Josiah's eyes!

Turning away from the still frozen in discovery sage grouse, Josiah looked down below him from where he had just heard a strange mystery noise. There sitting in a small circle were six covered wagons. Smoke lazily curled up from the emigrants' central campfire being tended by his Uncle Otis. Below him and off to one side, he could see his uncle Lemuel and cousin Jordan coming in from their "night hawk" duties returning with the wagon train's horse and oxen herd. Both men waved at Josiah and he waved back. Then Josiah saw his mother piling coals from the central campfire on top of her favorite biscuit making Dutch ovens as she began baking biscuits for her family's breakfast. It was then that Josiah realized just how hungry he was.

Walking back down the steep side hill above the Platte River, Josiah crossed the river in a shallow spot careful to avoid any patches of quicksand and entered the circle of wagons. When he did, he was met by his mother who was holding out her arms welcoming him for a morning's embrace. Just the same as she had done every morning of his life. Gosh it felt good to be back in her arms once again...

Off in the distance along the Platte River, a great horned owl was softly hooting out its plaintive four note call in the remaining early dawn's darkness...A call that in the lore of the Great Sioux Nation sings that a new death was in the wind...

Yesterday is history, tomorrow is a mystery and today is the present. Learn to live in the "present" as did Josiah...

About the Author

Terry Grosz earned his bachelor's degree in 1964 and his master's in Wildlife Management in 1966 from Humboldt State College in California. He was a California State Fish and Game Warden, based first in Eureka and then in Colusa, from 1966 to 1970. He then joined the U.S. Fish and Wildlife Service, and served in California as a U.S. Game Management Agent/Special Agent until 1974. He then was promoted to Senior Resident Agent and placed in charge of the States of North and South Dakota for two years, followed by three years as a Senior Special Agent in Washington D.C., with the Division of Law Enforcement. In 1979 he became the Assistant Special Agent in Charge in Minneapolis, and then was promoted to Special Agent in Charge in 1981 and transferred to Denver, where he remained until his retirement in 1998.

He has earned many awards and honors during his career, including, from the U.S. Fish and Wildlife Service, the Meritorious Service Award in 1996, and Top Ten Award in 1987 as one of the top ten employees in the agency. The Fish and Wildlife Foundation presented him with the Guy Bradley Award in 1989 as the nation's outstanding wildlife officer, and in 1995 he received the Conservation Achievement Award for Law Enforcement from the National Wildlife Federation. Unity College in

Maine awarded him an Honorary Doctorate in Environmental Stewardship in 2002. Humboldt State University awarded Terry their Distinguished Alumni Award in 2008 for his lifetime achievements.

His first book, *Wildlife Wars*, was published in 1999 and won the National Outdoor Book Award for Nature and Environment. He has had 10 wildlife law enforcement true life adventure books published since then: *For Love of Wildness, Defending Our Wildlife Heritage, A Sword For Mother Nature, No Safe Refuge, The Thin Green Line, Genesis of a Duck Cop, Slaughter in the Sacramento Valley, Wildlife on the Edge, Wildlife's Quiet War* and *Wildlife Dies Without Making a Sound, Vol. 1*.

Terry has also had published five historical Mountain Man novels: *Crossed Arrows, Curse of the Spanish Gold, The Sage of Harlan Waugh, The Brothers Dent and The Adventures of Hatchet Jack*. In 2003, Discovery Channel filmed a reality based television program for Animal Planet featuring stories from Terry Grosz's wildlife law enforcement true-life adventure books which was shown nationally. He lives in Colorado with his wife of 52 years, Donna.

Made in the USA
Middletown, DE
18 January 2018